"Kiss me, you idiot."

Cameron laughed. "I'm going to. I just need...a minute."

"For what?" To change his mind? Like hell. Jane was standing there, a caricature of sexual desire. She hadn't confronted her emotional block about sex only to have the proceedings derailed now. She pulled harder on his head and bounced a little on her toes. Maybe this was one instance in which high heels would actually be worth the pain.

The smile disappeared, and for a moment she feared she'd offended him, that he was going to call the whole thing off.

"To pause and take things in. To pause and take *you* in. Because once this starts, Jane..."

"What?" she whispered.

"We're going to set this fucking house on fire."

AND
Only

BRIDESMAIDS BEHAVING BADLY

JENNY HOLIDAY

FOREVER
New York Boston

Copyright © 2018 by Jenny Holiday
Excerpt from *It Takes Two* copyright © 2018 by Jenny Holiday
Cover photography by Claudio Marinesco.
Cover design by Elizabeth Stokes.
Cover copyright © 2018 by Hachette Book Group, Inc.

Forever
Hachette Book Group
1290 Avenue of the Americas, New York, NY 10104
forever-romance.com
twitter.com/foreverromance

First Edition: February 2018

Forever is an imprint of Grand Central Publishing. The Forever name and logo are trademarks of Hachette Book Group, Inc.

The publisher is not responsible for websites (or their content) that are not owned by the publisher.

The Hachette Speakers Bureau provides a wide range of authors for speaking events. To find out more, go to www.hachettespeakersbureau.com or call (866) 376-6591.

ISBNs: 978-1-4555-4240-6 (mass market), 978-1-4555-4238-3 (ebook)

Printed in the United States of America

OPM

10 9 8 7 6 5 4 3 2

For Erika, my first romance friend—and the first person who ever heard me say, "I think I'm going to try to write a romance novel."

Acknowledgments

Zoe York spent a lot of time helping me understand the Canadian Forces, both in terms of logistics and overall culture. She was a great help in making Cam's experience in the reserves (and the way his dismissal would have gone down) ring true. You gotta love a friend who can talk you through a military trial. Any errors, of course, remain my own.

Sarah McDonald, who is younger and cooler than I am, let me take inspiration from her life as a bridesmaid.

My friends Sandra Owens and Emma Barry read early drafts and provided enormously helpful feedback. They also administered pep talks when required, as did my friend Audra North, aka the Dominant Rooster. Sometimes a book takes a village—this one sure did—and I have a pretty amazing village.

My agent, Courtney Miller-Callihan, remains a steadfast advocate, friend, and Skype-walker. Long live Mermica.

My thanks to Caroline Acebo for buying this series. And, finally, to Lexi Smail for inheriting it with such enthusiasm and for really making it sing (and also for being better at counting than I am).

One
AND
Only

Chapter One

*J*ane! I thought you were *never* going to get here!"

"I came as quickly as I could," Jane said, trying to keep the annoyance out of her tone as she allowed herself to be herded into her friend Elise's house. She exchanged resigned smiles with her fellow bridesmaids—the ones who had obviously taken Elise's "Emergency bridesmaids meeting at my house NOW!" text more seriously than Jane had. Gia and Wendy were sprawled on Elise's couch, braiding some kind of dried grass–type thing. Wendy, Jane's best friend, blew her a kiss.

Jane tried to perform her traditional catching of Wendy's kiss—it was their thing, dating back to childhood—but Elise thrust a mug of tea into Jane's hand before it could close over the imaginary kiss. Earlier that summer, Elise had embraced and then discarded a plan to start her wedding reception with some kind of complicated cocktail involving tea, and as a result, Jane feared she and the girls were doomed to a lifetime of Earl Grey. Their beloved bridezilla had thought nothing of special ordering twenty-seven unreturnable boxes of premium English tea leaves. She also apparently thought nothing of forcing her friends to endure the rejected reception beverage again and again. And again.

"Jane's here, so now you can tell us about the big emergency," Gia said. "And whatever it is, I'm sure she'll figure out a solution." She smiled at Jane. "You're so...smart."

Jane had a feeling that *smart* wasn't the word Gia initially meant to use. The girls—well, Gia and Elise, anyway—were always telling Jane to loosen up. But they also relied on her to solve their problems. They liked having it both ways. She was the den mother, but they were forever teasing her about being too rigid. Which was kind of rich, lately, coming from Elise, who had turned into a matrimonial drill sergeant. Jane put up with it because she loved them. Besides, *somebody* had to be the responsible one.

"Well," Jane teased, "this had better be a capital-E emergency because I was in the middle of having my costume for Toronto Comicon fitted when you texted." She opened the calf-length trench coat she'd thrown over her costume at the seamstress's when Elise's text arrived. It was the kind of coat women wore when seducing their boyfriends—or so she assumed, not having personally attempted to seduce anyone since Felix. She should probably just get rid of the coat because there were likely no seductions in her future, either.

"Hello!" Gia exclaimed. "*What* is that?"

"Xena: Warrior Princess," Wendy answered before Jane could.

"I have no idea what that means, but you look hot," Gia said.

Jane did a little twirl. The costume was really coming together. The seamstress had done a kick-ass job with the leather dress, armor, and arm bands, and all Jane needed to do was figure out something for Xena's signature weapon and she'd be set. "It was a cult TV show from the 1990s," she explained. Gia was a bit younger than the rest of them. But who was Jane kidding? The real reason Gia didn't know about Xena was that she was a Cool Girl. As a model—an honest-to-goodness, catwalk-strutting, appearing-in-Calvin-Klein-ads model—she was too busy with her fabulous life to have time to watch syndicated late-night TV. "It's set in a sort of alternative ancient Greece, but it's leavened with other mythologies..." She trailed off because the explanation sounded lame even to her fantasy-novelist, geek-girl ears.

"Xena basically goes around kicking ass, and then she and her sidekick get it on with some lesbian action," Wendy said, summing things up in her characteristically concise way.

"Really?" Gia narrowed her eyes at Jane. "Is there something you're trying to tell us?"

"No!" Jane protested.

"Because you haven't had a boyfriend since Felix," Gia went on. "And you guys broke up, what? Four years ago?"

"Five," Wendy said.

It was true. But what her friends refused to accept was that she was single by choice. She had made a sincere effort, with Felix, whom she'd met halfway through university and stayed with until she was twenty-six, to enter the world of love and relationships that everyone was always insisting was so important. Felix had taught her many things, foremost among them that she was better off alone.

"You know we'll love you no matter what," Gia said. "Who you sleep with doesn't make a whit of difference."

"I'm not gay, Gia! I just admire Xena. She didn't need men to get shit done. We could all—"

A very loud episode of throat clearing from Elise interrupted Jane's speech on the merits of independence, whether you were a pseudo-Greek warrior princess or a modern girl trying to get along in the world.

"Sorry." Jane sometimes forgot that most people did not share her views of love and relationships.

"I'm sure this is all super interesting, you guys?" Elise said. "But we have a serious problem on our hands?" She was talking fast and ending declarative statements with question marks—sure signs she was stressed. Elise always sounded like an auctioneer on uppers when she was upset. "I need to grab my phone because I'm expecting the cake people to call? So sit down and brace yourselves and I'll be right back?"

Jane sank into a chair and warily eyed a basket of spools of those brown string-like ribbon things—the kind that were always showing up tied around Mason jars of layered salads on Pinterest. She wasn't really sure how or why Elise had decided not to outsource this stuff like normal people did when they got married. The whole wedding had become a DIY-fest. "What are we doing with this stuff?" she asked the others.

"No idea," said Wendy, performing a little eye roll. "I'm just doing what I'm told."

Jane grinned. Although she, Wendy, Gia, and Elise were a tightly knit foursome, they also sorted into pairs of best friends: Jane and Wendy had grown up together and had met Elise during freshman orientation at university. They'd picked up Gia when they were seniors and Gia was a freshman—Elise had been her resident assistant—RA—and the pair had become fast friends despite the age difference.

"We are weaving table runners out of raffia ribbon," Gia said. She dropped her strands and reached for her purse. "Slide that tea over here—quick, before she gets back."

"God bless you," Jane said when Gia pulled a flask of whiskey out of her purse and tipped some into Jane's mug. If the "emergency" that had pulled Jane away from her cosplay fitting—not to mention a planned evening of writing—was going to involve table runners, she was going to need something to dull the edges a bit.

Elise reappeared. Jane practiced her nonchalant face as she sipped her "tea" and tried not to cough. She wasn't normally much of a drinker, but desperate times and all that.

"I didn't want to repeat myself, so I've been holding out on Gia and Wendy?" Elise said. "But there's been a...disruption to the wedding plans?"

I love you, but God help me, those are declarative sentences. Sometimes Jane had trouble turning off her inner editor. Job hazard.

"Oh my God, are you leaving Jay?" Wendy asked.

"Why would you say that?" Elise turned to Wendy in bewilderment.

Now, that was a legitimate question, the inner editor said—at least in the sense that it was meant to end with a question mark. The actual content of Wendy's question was kind of insensitive. But Wendy had trouble with change, and Elise pairing off and doing the whole till-death-do-us-part thing? That was some major change for their little friend group. Jane might have had trouble with it, too, except it was plainly obvious to anyone with eyeballs that Elise was head-over-heels, one hundred percent gaga for her fiancé.

"I'm kidding!" Wendy said, a little too vehemently. Elise looked like she might have to call for smelling salts.

"Take a breath," Gia said to Elise, "and tell us what's wrong."

Elise did as instructed, then flopped into a chair. "Jay's brother is coming to the wedding."

"Jay has a brother?" Jane asked. Though she was guilty of maybe not paying one hundred percent attention to every single wedding-related detail—for example, she'd recused herself from the debate over the merits of sage green versus grass green for the ribbons that would adorn the welcome bags left in the guests' hotel rooms—she was pretty sure she had a handle on all the major players.

"His name is Cameron MacKinnon."

That didn't clear things up. "Jay Smith has a brother named Cameron MacKinnon?" she asked. Was that even possible?

"Half brother," Elise said. "You know how Jay's mom is single?" It was true. There had been no "father of the groom" in Elise's carefully drafted program. "Well, she split from Jay's dad when Jay was nine. Then a couple years later, she had a brief relationship with another man. Cameron is the product of that—that's why his last name is MacKinnon and Jay's is Smith."

"But he wasn't always going to come to the wedding?" Gia asked. "Were they estranged?"

"They're not particularly close. There are eleven years between them—Cameron was in first grade when Jay left for school—but they're not estranged," Elise said. "He wasn't going to be able to make it to the wedding because he was supposed to be in Iraq. He was in the army. But now he's...not."

"That sounds ominous," Wendy said.

"Look, here's the thing," Elise said, sitting up straight, her voice suddenly and uncharacteristically commanding. "Cameron is a problem. He's wild. He drives too fast, drinks too much, sleeps around. You name it—if it's sketchy, he's into it."

"And this is *Jay's* brother," Jane said. Because no offense, she liked Jay fine, but Jay was...a tad underwhelming. He was an accountant. No matter what they were doing—football game, barbecue, hiking—he dressed in dark jeans and a polo shirt, like it was casual Friday at the office. To be honest, Jane had never really been sure what Elise saw in him. The girls were always telling *her* to loosen up, but compared to Jay, she was the life of the party.

"Yes," Elise said. "Cameron is Jay's brother, and he must be stopped."

"Dun, dun, dun!" Wendy mock-sang.

"Hey, I can totally switch gears and weave this thing into a noose," Gia said, holding up a lopsided raffia braid.

"I'm not kidding."

Elise's tone made everyone stop laughing and look up. The upspeak was gone, and the bride had become a warrior, eyes narrowed, lips pursed. "He's a high school dropout. He burned down a barn outside Thunder Bay when he was seventeen. He was charged with arson, the whole deal. Jay says his mother still hasn't lived it down. And there's talk he got a girl pregnant in high school."

"What happened?" asked a rapt Gia.

Elise shrugged. "Her family moved out of town, so no one really knows."

"Wow," Wendy said, echoing Jane's thoughts. Jane had initially assumed Elise was being melodramatic about this black-sheep brother—as she was about nearly everything wedding related—but this guy *did* sound like bad news.

"Anyway." Elise brandished an iPad in front of her like it was a weapon. "Cameron MacKinnon is *not* ruining my wedding. And if he's left to his own devices, he will. From what Jay says, he won't be able to help it." She poked at the iPad. "This changes everything. We need to redo the schedule—and the job list."

The words *job list* practically gave Jane hives. Elise had turned into a total bridezilla, but by unspoken agreement, the bridesmaids had been going along with whatever she wanted. It was the path of least resistance. But also, they truly wanted Elise to have the wedding of her dreams. Even if it was painful for everyone else.

But, oh, the *job list*. The job list was like the Hydra, a serpentine monster you could never get on top of. You crossed off a job, and two more sprouted to take its place. Jane had already hand-stenciled three hundred invitations, planned and executed two showers, joined Pinterest as instructed for the express purpose of searching out "homemade bunting," tried on no fewer than twenty-three dresses—all purple—and this Cameron thing aside, it looked like today was going to be spent weaving table runners. And they still had the bachelorette party and the rehearsal dinner to get through, never mind the main event.

It boggled the mind. Elise was an interior designer, so of course she cared how things looked, but even so, Jane was continuously surprised at how much the wedding was preoccupying her friend. She could only hope they would get their funny, creative, sweet friend back after it was all over.

"Cameron is coming to town tomorrow," Elise said. "I don't know why he couldn't just arrive a day ahead of the wedding like the rest of the out-of-town guests, but it is what it is." She let the iPad clatter onto the coffee table. "I don't even know how to add this to the job list, but somehow, we have to babysit Cameron for the next week and a half."

"We?" Wendy echoed.

"Yes. He needs to be supervised at all times until the wedding—until after the post-wedding breakfast, actually. Then he can wreak whatever havoc he wants."

"Hang on," Jane said. "I agree that he sounds like bad news. But let's say, for the sake of argument, he did something horrible and got arrested tomorrow. I don't really see how that would have an impact on your wedding at all, because—"

Elise looked up, either ignoring or legitimately not hearing Jane. "You can't do it, Gia. You're my maid of honor, and I need you at my side at all times."

"Sure thing," Gia said.

Easy for her to say. Gia had purposely not taken any modeling jobs the two weeks before the wedding. She had plenty of time to lounge around braiding dried foliage and looking effortlessly beautiful in sweatpants. Also, there was the part where she was a millionaire.

Elise started scrolling through some kind of calendar app on her iPad. "Now, tomorrow we're supposed to be spray-painting the tea sets gold."

Jane looked around. *Spray-painting the tea sets gold?* Why was no one else confused by that sentence?

"But we'll have to do that in the afternoon," Elise went on, "because—"

"I have to work tomorrow," Wendy said. And when Elise looked up blankly, she added, "Tomorrow is Wednesday."

Jane was about to protest that she had to work tomorrow, too. Book seven of the Clouded Cave series wasn't going to write itself. Just because she didn't have to be in court like Wendy didn't mean her job wasn't important. She had an inbox full of fan mail from readers clamoring for the next book, not to mention a contractual deadline that got closer every day.

Elise continued, seemingly oblivious to her friends' weekday employment obligations. "Tomorrow we also need to do a practice run of boutonniere, corsage, and bouquet making. I finagled a vendor pass to the commercial fruit and flower market, but we need to get there early. So we should do the flowers in the morning and paint the tea sets in the afternoon. We'll meet in Mississauga at five thirty, but someone needs to pick up Cameron and make sure he behaves all day."

"I'll do it," said Jane, mentally calculating that to be at the suburban flower market by five thirty, she'd have to get up at four a.m. Also, there was the part about spending the afternoon spray-painting tea sets. It didn't take a genius to figure out which was the lesser of the two proverbial evils. She could babysit this Cameron dude. She'd treat him like a character in one of her books—figure him out, then make him do her bidding. "Give me the wild man's flight info, and I'll pick him up."

"I thought it would be best if you did it," Elise said, still scrolling and tapping like a maniac. "I mean, your job is so—"

Wait for it.

"Flexible."

But at least she hadn't said anything about—

"And you're so responsible. I feel like this is your kind of task."

Jane stifled a sigh. Everyone always called her responsible, but they made it sound so…boring. She preferred to think of herself as conscientious.

"I really, really appreciate this, Jane," Elise said, finally looking up from her iPad and gracing Jane with a smile so wide and sincere that it almost made her breath catch.

Yes. Right. That was why she was voluntarily submitting to this bridesmaid torture-gig. Her friend Elise was still somewhere inside the bridezilla that was currently manning the controls, and she was so, so happy to be marrying the love of her life. That was the important thing. It made even Jane's heart, which was usually immune to these kinds of sentiments, twist a little. A wedding wasn't in her future, and she was fine with that, but all of this planning made her think of her parents' wedding pictures, the pair of them all decked out in their shaggy 1970s glory. Had they been in love like Elise and Jay, before the accident? Maybe at the start, but probably not for long, given her father's addiction. He was never violent, but he wasn't very...lovable.

But now was not the time for a pity party, so she smiled back at Elise. "No problem."

"You need to meet his plane, take him to Jay's, and make sure he doesn't do anything crazy. Jay will be home as soon as he can after work, and then you can leave for the evening and we'll figure out the rest of the schedule from there."

"Got it."

Elise reached out and squeezed her hand. "Seriously. Making sure Cameron doesn't ruin my wedding is the best present you could give me."

She waved away Elise's thanks. This was going to be a piece of cake. Or at least better than tea set spray-painting duty. After all, how bad could this Cameron MacKinnon guy be?

Chapter Two

*H*ow bad could this wedding be?

Cam kept asking himself that question as the plane taxied endlessly to its gate and he stretched—as much as he could in the tiny seat—to shake off the sleep that had overtaken him.

The flight from Thunder Bay had been short, but he'd conked right out and fallen immediately into dreams of the Middle East. Snippets of dreams, really, everything from both tours all jumbled up: sand and heat and boredom and fear. His instrument panel. Haseeb's face when he'd realized they weren't going to be able to diffuse the bomb. Becky's cries for help.

The trial.

Objectively speaking, Jay's wedding was not going to be as bad as Iraq. Cam knew that. And, he consoled himself, he was in Toronto.

A city. Civilization. Steaks. Ice cream. Hell, *fresh*

vegetables. He smiled to himself as he hoisted his backpack onto his shoulder and shuffled down the aisle.

A drink. Maybe even a joint. He perked up as he ambled down the Jetway. Despite his reputation, he wasn't really into drugs, but after the last couple years, maybe he *could* get into the concept of temporary oblivion.

Television. Trashy American television. Or boring Canadian television, even. Television in English, was the point. Falling asleep with the TV on, warm under a pile of his mom's quilts.

Winter, he thought, as he followed the signs toward baggage claim. Not for five or six months yet, but even just knowing it would come was a relief. And before then, the leaves of fall. Cool nights.

Warm beds.

Women.

It wasn't a bad list. And ticking off the items on it was going to help get him out of the damned country music song he was currently living in. Kicked out of the Canadian Forces and dumped by the girlfriend he'd stupidly remained faithful to for two deployments—the first in Afghanistan and the one he was just coming off of, in Iraq. He was even homeless on account of the fact that the plan had been for him to move in with Christie when he got back to Thunder Bay. All he needed was to get a dog so it could die and make his wretchedness complete.

So much for turning over a new leaf. He'd been trying to remake his life, but apparently a person couldn't escape his destiny.

But whatever. He'd spent his whole childhood wanting to get out of Thunder Bay, so why the hell would he want to move back to that remote shithole of a town now that he had no reason to be at the reserve unit? Christie had done him a favor, actually.

He was totally free.

He closed his eyes and let his mind return to his list as he approached the still-empty baggage carousel. His dream girl...she'd be what? Blond? Yeah. Sleek blond hair. What else? Petite. Hell, if he was going to imagine his ideal hookup, he might as well embrace his inner caveman. He would run his hands all over her—they'd practically span her waist. He started a little as the baggage carousel leaped to life but then closed his eyes again. One more second living in his fantasy: blond hair, blue eyes, a pixie of a girl. Someone with a big, wide smile who would be happy to see him. Exactly...

"Cameron MacKinnon?"

...the opposite of the chubby, mousy woman standing before him.

"Yeah?" Did he know this woman from somewhere? Another Thunder Bay escapee maybe? With her jeans, unadorned white T-shirt, and mud-colored hair scraped back into a ponytail, she sort of had that small-town, unadventurous look he recognized from home. He wouldn't go so far as to call her a hick—her skinny jeans were flattering and looked expensive, but she didn't seem like the big-city type.

"You look *exactly* like I imagined," she said, regarding him with her hands on her hips and smiling with satisfaction, almost as if she had manifested him with her mind.

"And you look nothing like I imagined," he answered.

The smug smile disappeared, and she narrowed her eyes. They were the color of mossy mud. To match the mud hair, he supposed, though really her hair was the color of rusty mud. He laughed, both at her confusion and at himself. He'd gone and conjured a woman, all right, but apparently the universe had decided to give him the opposite version of what he'd ordered.

"I'm Elise's friend," she said. "She sent me to pick you up. My name is Jane."

"Elise?"

"Jay's fiancée?" said the woman he now knew was called Jane. Plain Jane. Muddy Jane.

"Right." He spied his duffel sliding down the chute and jogged over to retrieve it. "So, Jane," he said as she caught up to him, "I hope my brother's marrying up."

"I don't know how to answer that," she said, her nose wrinkling. She had a cute nose. Especially when she scrunched it up like that. It went a little way toward counteracting all that mud.

"It was a joke, Jane." She still didn't look amused. Didn't even crack a smile. Well. His tiny blond dream girl would have laughed. "Let's just say that although Jay presents pretty well these days, he and I both come from what you might call white-trash origins. So I'm pretty sure he can't help but be marrying up."

One—only one—eyebrow slowly lifted. "Are you ready?" she asked.

"Yeah. I've got a car rented." He looked around for signs for the rental companies. "So you didn't actually need to pick me up, Jane." He switched to looking her up and down. The skinny jeans showcased the way her waist nipped way in and then gave way to rounded hips. Pixies aside, there was something to be said for a curvier figure. The proverbial hourglass.

"Jay lives downtown. You don't need a car."

"And yet I've rented one."

"He lives right off the subway," she went on, apparently bent on ignoring him. "It will be impossible to park near his building."

"Look, Jane. I've been driving around the desert in a G Wagon for the past five months. Cruising along a paved road behind the wheel of a good old North American hot rod? I've been dreaming of that." He raised his eyebrows. "Among other things." A pixie, primarily. The kind of woman who would appreciate the kind of car he was imagining.

She sighed like a weary kindergarten teacher, and annoyance flared in his chest. He hadn't asked her to come here, boss him around, and then act all put upon when he was exercising the goddamned freedom he'd been overseas defending.

But he wasn't a bully—he might be a lot of things, but a bully wasn't one of them—so he bit his tongue and turned, setting off for the car rental counters.

He could *feel* her following. And when they reached the edge of the carpeted area outside baggage claim, he could *hear* the clicking of her shoes on the polished concrete floor. He sped up. So did the clicks. *Click-click-click*, like a ticking timer signaling an imminent bomb blast.

He knew what was happening. Jane wasn't here as some kind of innocuous welcome wagon. Jay had sent her because he didn't trust Cam not to fuck up in some way. He expected Cam to embarrass him. And, really, wasn't that fair? From Jay's perspective at least? Jay had no idea that Cam had been three years into Operation: Become an Honorable Person when it had all come crumbling down around him. He was back to being the unreliable loser of a younger brother, but as far as Jay knew, that was what he had always been. At least he didn't have to look into his brother's disappointed eyes after this latest disgrace. If people's expectations of you were already in the gutter, it was hard to disappoint them.

He could probably manage it with Elise, though. Cam hadn't been joking about marrying up. Cam paid attention to his brother's letters—lived for them in fact, though he'd never admit it. So he knew Jay's fiancée was an interior designer. Elise and Muddy Jane were probably peas in a pod: uptight, refined, humorless.

Click-click-click-click-click.

He stopped suddenly, and she crashed into him. Her breasts hit his back, and they were soft and yielding as they met his torso. It was only an instant, but it was enough to remind him—to remind his dick—how much he had missed breasts.

A pixie would not have breasts like that.

He could feel her correct by stepping back, and as he turned, she tripped over her own feet. Instinctively, he grabbed for her, intending only to help her find her footing, but she jerked away from him with enough force that she stumbled even more and landed on her butt a couple feet from him.

He tried not to laugh. He really did.

"Stop laughing."

Oh, she was mad. She had pressed her lips together so hard, they had entirely disappeared. The rusty-mud ponytail had come a little loose, and some wisps of hair framed her face—he could almost imagine them as puffs of red steam. She looked like Yosemite Sam about to have a temper tantrum.

"I don't need a babysitter, Jane," he said, even as he held out a hand to help her up.

"And yet here I am," she said, echoing his earlier refrain about the car as she took his hand—grudgingly, judging by how quickly she dropped it once she was upright.

He looked down at her shoes. She was wearing unremarkable beige flats. How was it possible that such boring shoes could make so much noise? He turned and headed for the rental car counters, counting the seconds until the clicks started up again.

‑‑‑⌒‑‑‑

She should have just gotten up at four a.m. and done the stupid flowers. If she had, she could be spray-painting tea sets gold for some unknown purpose right now. But the point was she would be spray-painting tea sets gold with her best friends. People who would never laugh at her as she lay sprawled on the dirty airport floor. People who appreciated her for who she was, even if who she was was the responsible, reliable one. Yep, if not for her own stupidity, she could be drinking Earl Grey *right now*, maybe getting a little high off paint fumes.

But no. Instead she was preparing to exit the airport parking garage in a royal blue Corvette convertible being driven by a jerk.

"Why is this car so *noisy*?" she shouted as he revved the engine.

"That, Jane, is not *noise*. That is the sound of a 6.2 liter, V-8, supercharged engine. That is the sound of freedom, Jane."

God, the way he kept saying her name. Every sentence he directed at her had an extra "Jane" tacked onto it. It was a joke, *Jane*. You didn't need to pick me up, *Jane*. Normal people didn't do that. It was hard to say why, but it was patronizing somehow. Like he thought he was the big manly man, and she was the simple girl who needed everything explained.

But also . . . she liked his voice. She couldn't help it. The fact that she did made her mad, but there it was. *That is the sound of freedom, Jane.* His voice was low and raspy, and he spoke almost with a southern drawl. Which was impossible because he was from Thunder Bay, Canada, for heaven's sake. It was more that he spoke slowly—like if Matthew McConaughey moved north and lost ninety percent of his accent. He drew out syllables as if he had all the time in the world and was confident that whoever was listening to him did, too. The way he extended the long "a" in *Jane* made her name, which she'd always thought of as fussy and prim, sound almost sensual.

She didn't like that he had that power. That he'd just taken it. Because she surely hadn't given it to him.

He had paired his phone with the car's Bluetooth system, and as they cruised out of the ramp, he pressed a button on the steering wheel and said, "Siri, directions to the closest Keg steakhouse," naming a high-end local chain.

"We are not going to the Keg," she said, trying to twist her ponytail into a bun to prevent her hair from becoming a rat's nest as the wind picked up.

"*I* am going to the Keg. *You* don't have to come." He grabbed a pair of mirrored aviator sunglasses from where they'd been perched on the collar of his T-shirt, slid them on, turned up the volume on the classic rock station he had playing, and gunned it, drowning out any reply she could have made.

She huffed a frustrated sigh he couldn't hear and watched the terminal buildings whip by, followed by the high-rises and hotels surrounding the airport as they got on the high-way and picked up speed. At least he was a competent driver. He was a very good driver, in fact. He drove fast but not recklessly so, and he changed lanes decisively but he always checked his mirrors. Every move he made seemed intentional and well executed.

Well, a little food couldn't hurt. They had several hours to kill until Jay would get home from work anyway, and it would probably be easier to keep an eye on Cameron if he was eating. Inside. In an enclosed space. And he couldn't talk while he was eating, right? Or maybe he could—he seemed like the kind of guy who thought of manners as optional.

Her stomach growled.

∽ᏸ

When the server—who looked amazingly like the pixie of
his airport imaginings—brought their food, she winked at
Cam. "Twenty-ounce rib steak, extra fries," she said, setting
down the enormous plate that held the *meal* of his airport
imaginings. Dreams really did come true. He flashed her a
smile, though he was a little surprised that a server at a place
like this wouldn't have the training to serve the lady at the
table first. She'd tried to take his order before Jane's, too,
which struck him as flat out bad manners.

She plunked Jane's meal down without taking her eyes
from Cam. "Mixed greens with grilled chicken."

Jane murmured her thanks.

"Can I get you anything else?" said the tiny waitress,
who still hadn't made eye contact with Jane.

"I think we're fine, thanks," he said.

"You sure you don't need anything?"

There went Jane's eyebrow. He'd be lying if he said he
hadn't given some thought to the idea of trying to pick up
the waitress. But what were they going to do? Make out by
the Dumpster while Muddy Jane ate her salad? Nah, he'd
wait until tonight. Hit a bar closer to Jay's. *Without* his
babysitter. "Yes, thanks," he said, winking at the waitress.
"But I'll be sure to let you know if any...needs come up."
He was going to pass on the pixie, but that didn't mean he
couldn't enjoy irritating Jane. Though he'd just met her, he
knew, somehow, that she wouldn't approve of his suggestive banter.

The eyebrow went higher. *Bingo.*

"So, Jane," he said, picking up his steak knife and sawing
into the glorious hunk of red meat on his plate as the waitress walked away. "You come to a steakhouse—an iconic

Canadian steakhouse at that—and you order a salad with chicken? What's up with that?"

"I'm trying to lose weight."

He paused with his first bite halfway to his mouth. He hadn't expected her to answer him so easily and honestly. "You don't need to lose weight." When she raised that censuring eyebrow again—he'd never met a person in real life who could raise only one eyebrow—he said, "What? You don't." He meant it. She wasn't thin, no, but everything about her seemed like it was where it was supposed to be, relative to everything else. She looked like she belonged in the kind of body she had.

She considered him for a long time, like she was trying to decide how to respond. "I may have been a little ambitious when I ordered my bridesmaid's dress," she finally said, rolling her eyes as if disgusted with herself, then transferring her attention to her plate and setting to work slicing the chicken breast on her salad into smaller pieces. "Its ability to zip up is going to depend on my caloric intake over the next week and a half."

She reminded him of Christie that way. She had also always been vowing to shed pounds she didn't particularly need to lose. "Why do women do that? Why not get a dress that actually fits?"

"I really, really, wanted to be a size ten. I guess I thought standing in front of three hundred people in a five-hundred-dollar dress would be good incentive." She sighed. "The problem is I really, really like eating."

"So you're an eleven. Whatever."

"Twelve. Sizes go in twos."

"Why?"

"I have no idea."

He shrugged and resumed delivering his first bite of meat

to his mouth. "Oh my God," he groaned. It was almost orgasmic the way goose bumps rose on his arms and his tongue ignited with pleasure. He sawed off another, bigger bite of the gorgeously bloody meat. Nothing was going to be as good as that first bite, but…oh, fuck it *was* as good. Months of mess tent glop—or worse, freeze-dried field rations—had put his taste buds into lockdown. But now. This was a million times better than he had remembered. Maybe the premature end of his army career wasn't going to be *all* bad.

But, no, this was hollow comfort. He would give up steak forever if it meant not having the only thing he was ever good at taken away from him.

He shook his head. He'd never been one to dwell on could-have-beens. What he had now was steak. Damn good steak. He took another bite and sighed.

Jane cleared her throat.

Right. He'd forgotten for a moment that he and steak had an audience for their little reunion. Jane looked like she was trying not to laugh. But at the moment, he didn't care—his meal was too delicious.

He couldn't help wondering if sex was going to be this good, too, once he finally had it again.

Tonight. He'd find out tonight. See? Upside. The army was lost to him, his hopes of becoming an officer dashed, but it was going to be *a lot* easier to get laid back home. He sawed off a piece of steak and plopped it onto Jane's plate. "You have to try this."

"I can't, I—"

"Eat it."

"I don't generally like my steak so rare. When I do eat steak, I—"

"Eat," he commanded, raising his voice a little.

She ate.

He'd give it three seconds. Just like her footsteps at the airport earlier—*click-click-click.*

"Oh my God."

There it was. He smirked as her eyes slipped closed in ecstasy. Her hair was kind of messed up. Her ponytail had suffered some collateral damage in its battle with the convertible. It wasn't a bad look on her, and with her eyes closing on that low moan...well, he was really looking forward to ditching her and getting on with his return-to-civilian-life list.

"I have this mental list going of things I missed while I was deployed, and steak is close to the top of it," he said, sawing off another piece of meat and setting it on her plate.

To his surprise, she didn't object, just cut it into smaller pieces, like she had done with her chicken, and popped one into her mouth, huffing a small sigh as she chewed.

"Atta girl," he said. "Are you sure you don't want some bread?" He shoved the bread basket toward her.

There was a beat of silence. Then she said, "You are a bad man."

He grinned. "Bad is subjective, don't you find?"

"What else is on this list of yours? Driving a really fast dude-car, I assume?"

He grinned. "Guilty as charged."

She looked at him for a long time, then pushed the bread basket away without taking any. "I'm surprised you didn't stay in Thunder Bay and come down next week with your mom for the wedding. I'm pretty sure they have steak and sports cars in Thunder Bay."

"Well, let's just say that the pickings are kind of slim in Thunder Bay as it relates to some of the other items on my list."

He wasn't about to tell her that he *had* been planning to stay in Thunder Bay until the wedding. Right now, in fact, he should have been eating his return-to-Canada steak cuddled up in bed with Christie. But, as he had so recently and jarringly learned, that role was currently occupied by someone else. So he'd turned tail, "surprise, I'm home early" bouquet in hand, and headed back to the airport to book a flight to Toronto for the next day. Then he spent the night in a hotel, without even seeing his mom. He hadn't wanted to face her, to show up on her doorstep jobless *and* girl-friendless. What was he going to do? Move back into his childhood bedroom? No, better to get the hell out of Dodge. Even if it meant he still had to go back to his unit later, once the discharge paperwork arrived, and turn in his kit.

"I would have thought you'd want to spend time with your mother," Jane went on when he didn't answer. "She must have been really worried about you while you were deployed."

"She's not really the worrying type."

She aimed her gaze at him, two mossy-muddy lasers trying to beam into his soul. "I can't imagine any mother not worrying about a son overseas fighting ISIS."

"Technically, Operation Impact is a mission to assist Iraqi security forces," he said, wanting to deflect her from the topic of his mom. He might not have been engaged in hand-to-hand combat with jihadists, but it hadn't exactly been a walk in the park.

"Still," she said again, clearly unmoved by the distinction he'd made and clinging obstinately to her own interpretation of the emotions of a woman she'd never met. "I'm sure your mother worried."

He shrugged, unsure how to say that his mother *had* been the worrying type once, but she had understandably given up on him after the drama of his teen years. He didn't deserve his mother's worry, had squandered it well before he deployed overseas.

Jane turned her attention to her salad, having finished the donated steak. "Well, I'm sure Jay worried about you," she said as she cut her cucumbers into small pieces to match the meat she'd similarly subdivided.

She was sure Jay had worried about him. Not she *knew* Jay had worried about him. She imagined he had. Suspected it. Meaning Jay hadn't said as much.

It was a knife to the gut.

"I was so surprised to find out Jay had a brother," she went on.

And why don't you go ahead and twist that knife, Jane?

But what had he expected? For successful, upstanding Jay to be bragging to his friends about his fuck-up of a little brother?

Half brother, he corrected himself. Jay would probably make that distinction, and God knew the two men had always been different.

"How are you enjoying everything?" Saved by the tiny waitress.

He shot her a grin. "I have to tell you, I'm just back from being deployed in Iraq, and this is the best food I've had in a year. It's a hell of a way to welcome home a soldier." He was being shameless, playing the military card. Would her eyes have widened with that mixture of hero worship and lust if she knew about the circumstances surrounding his departure from the Canadian Forces? He pushed the thought aside. Even though the loss of his career was gutting, he would do it all over again if he had to. There was no way he could stand by and watch Becky be attacked like that. No. Way.

He started to feel that familiar surge of adrenaline that always came when he thought about the attack. He tried to follow the instructions from the shrink they'd made him see after his first deployment and searched for something to anchor himself in the present. A person. A conversation. A habitual behavior. Something that would tip him into a less toxic feedback loop.

"Our steaks *are* known for their incredible flavor," said the waitress. "The taste just explodes on your tongue, doesn't it?"

He cleared his throat. Shameless flirting was probably not what Dr. Salinger had had in mind, but it would do. "I completely agree. I can't imagine anything I'd enjoy having exploding on my tongue more than this steak." He grinned at the waitress and waited a beat before adding, "Well...*almost* anything."

He was watching the server, but he heard Jane's quiet intake of breath. Jay would never say something so rude. But his suggestive talk had worked. The claws of panic were loosening their grasp on him.

The server winked, and the moment she left the table, Jane shot him a disgusted look.

It was just as well. He had a reputation to live down to and a babysitter to ditch.

—⌒⊃

Good Lord. Watching Cameron order dessert from their toy poodle of a waitress was like watching the opening of a porno—a badly scripted porno at that. Their server was already touching his military-style buzz cut. What was next? Would he whip off his shirt so she could admire his tattoos—he had to have tattoos, right?—and feel his biceps?

He was attractive, Jane would admit, if you went for the "I've overdosed on testosterone" type, which obviously their server did. His dark hair was buzzed so short it was impossible to tell what it would look like in a civilian setting, but he had nice eyes. They were a vibrant bluey-green she would have thought were colored contacts except she was certain that Cameron MacKinnon was not the sort of man who wore colored contacts. He was wearing a long-sleeved black T-shirt that stretched tight over his muscled arms. She wondered what the inevitable tattoos would be. Probably some bullshit tribal symbols that he thought meant "brotherhood" but actually meant "motherhood" or something. She shifted in her seat. The idea of using a needle to permanently mark your skin with ink was so…unsettling.

He finally settled on a brownie sundae. A giant brownie practically the size of her head, topped with an obnoxious amount of ice cream, hot fudge, and whipped cream. And a cherry on top. Of course.

"What are you, eleven?" she asked after the server had delivered the dessert and mustered the strength to peel herself away from Mr. Operation Enduring Freedom.

He picked up the cherry and scraped it with his teeth, stopping short of biting it off its stem. He had straight white teeth, which didn't really accord with what Jay had said about his childhood in Thunder Bay. His mom worked hard, but it sounded like there was never enough money for things like school field trips or sports equipment, much less orthodontia. But this guy, with the crazy tropical-sea eyes, strong, square jaw, and blindingly white teeth, looked like he could be in a Listerine commercial. He reminded her of Gia in that way—some people won the genetic lottery.

He set the cherry down on the plate and loaded his spoon with a huge bite of ice cream and whipped cream. "Not eleven. Twenty-seven, actually." He turned the spoon over and stopped short of pressing it down on his tongue. "I just enjoy licking things."

A jolt of anger left Jane breathless as Cameron did just that—let the ice- and whipped-cream-loaded spoon slide slowly against his extended tongue while he stared at her with a completely neutral expression. When he was done with his bite or lick or whatever, he kept that even, level gaze fixed on hers. A good ten seconds of silence passed before she realized with embarrassment that she was just sitting there staring at him like an idiot or like—God forbid—their besotted waitress.

"Keep it in your pants, would you?" she said. No wonder Elise had sent her on this thankless babysitting mission. The man was a genuine menace. She was surprised he hadn't done something *worse* than burn down a barn and get a girl pregnant. Though for all they knew, he had. "Do you kiss your mother with that mouth?"

"I thought we already established that my mother and I are...not close. So, let's see, that would be no."

"Well, I hope you're not planning to talk to the female guests at your brother's wedding that way." She sounded like a teacher giving a lecture in detention. But it was his fault. He was like a child—an ice-cream-eating, dirty-minded literalist. And she was starting to fear that she wouldn't be able to do what Elise had charged her to do: prevent this man from ruining the wedding.

"Probably not," he said. "Probably just you." He tried to hand her the spoon. "Want a bite?"

Chapter Three

Cam knew he was being an ass. It was like landing in Toronto had prompted him to immediately start living down to his reputation. It was a familiar groove to slip back into, and he simply couldn't help himself. Jay didn't know the man he had become, or had been *trying* to become. Nor did his mom. They didn't know that three years of military service had given him some much needed perspective on his lot in life. That he'd drawn a line when he'd signed up for the Lake Superior Scottish Regiment, a reserve regiment of the Canadian Forces headquartered in Thunder Bay. On one side was his old life, on the other, the army. The army and Christie: those were the things that were supposed to have made him into a better man.

At least he hadn't told Jay and Mom about his now-dead plan to go to university so he could become an officer. The discharge aside, what had he been thinking? He wasn't post-secondary material.

Anyway, none of it mattered now. Meeting people's expectations was easier than upending them. He'd spent most of his life doing that, and, perversely, he was good at it.

But, he reminded himself as he pulled the Corvette into a municipal parking garage, Jane didn't have any expectations of him. Or she hadn't until he'd started harassing her at the steakhouse. "So what's your deal?" he asked, jogging around to her side of the car before she could get out and offering her a hand. 'Vettes were notoriously low, and it could be hard to hoist yourself out of them. "How come you're free to babysit me on a Wednesday afternoon?"

She ignored his hand and levered herself out of the car. "I'm not babysitting you."

He raised his eyebrows as he led her to the pay station and stuck his credit card in.

"I'm not really sure why you find it so incredible that your brother and future sister-in-law would send someone to greet you at the airport."

Yeah, nice try. But he let it slide. "Why you, though? You don't have to be at a job of some sort? You're independently wealthy, what?"

She barked an incredulous laugh at that. "I'm about as far from independently wealthy as it's possible to get."

"I don't believe that," he said, eyeing the fancy jeans. "You clean up too well."

"Oh, I do okay now, but my dad died when I was a kid, and my mom didn't really have any skills, so things were...tough for a while."

"You're a self-made woman." He respected that.

"I guess I am." The corners of her mouth turned up a bit. She liked that notion. "But still in touch enough with my roots to notice that you're probably going to pay more to park that thing for a week than you did to rent it." She cocked her head at the machine, which was printing a receipt that was, in fact, for a startlingly high amount of money.

He had plenty of money saved. While on his two tours he'd had no living expenses, so the vast majority of his pay had gone into the bank, and for the year in between them, he'd lived cheaply, socking away all his bartending tips and living in a room above the bar. He'd been saving for tuition. Now that that wasn't the case, he had a comfortable cushion to rely on while he found his feet and figured out what the hell to do next. But he didn't want to admit that Jane had been right about the car, so he pocketed the receipt and said, teasingly, "And how did you make your millions? Let me see. I bet you're...an investment banker. Or maybe a teacher." She was something rigid, he'd bet, something where she got to boss people around and adhere to rules.

"Actually, I'm a young-adult novelist."

"Seriously?" That was the last thing he'd expected her to say. He held the exit door for her, and she preceded him onto a busy downtown sidewalk. "Would I know your books?"

She scoffed. "I doubt it."

That stung, but he wasn't sure why. Maybe she was only saying that he was too old to know her books. But it kind of felt like she was suggesting he was sub-literate. He wasn't a scholar, sure, but he wanted to tell her that his Kindle was pretty much the only thing that had kept him sane—if he could call himself that—on his two tours. But that would make him sound a little too desperate for her approval. So he settled for, "Try me."

"Well, I've been at it since university, so I have a bunch of books out. They're part of a series called the Clouded Cave, and it's turning out to be pretty popular. I'm writing book seven right now." She was picking up speed, both with her feet and with her words, deftly dodging slower-moving pedestrians. "The series is about a girl named Stephanie who's exploring a cave, and it turns out to be a gateway to another world. She takes some friends with her in subsequent books."

"Like *Narnia*," he said. "Actually, like a lot of books. *Alice in Wonderland*."

She was looking at him oddly. "Yes. Portal fiction. There's a reason it endures."

"Portal fiction?"

"Kids cross over into another world through some kind of portal or door—the wardrobe, the looking glass. In mine, it's a cave."

"Right. So why does it endure?"

"These kinds of stories let kids be heroic. They let them practice skills they don't get to use in our ordered, capitalist world—both the characters and, vicariously, the kids reading the books."

What he said was, "Makes sense," because her analysis struck him as spot-on. But what he thought was, "Whoa." He'd known she was smart from the moment he met her, but wow. Also: *This* woman was creating an alternative world in which the rigid strictures of society didn't apply? Apparently, Muddy Jane contained multitudes.

"Here we are," she said, cutting off their little on-the-go literary chat, which was just as well because the idea of her being an author, much less one who wrote about magical portals to other lands, was weirding him out.

She led him through a grand entranceway into a marble lobby and marched up to a concierge desk. "I'm Jane Denning. Jay Smith's fiancée Elise Maxwell was supposed to leave me a key." It didn't escape Cam's notice that the key had been left in Jane's name and not his.

"Yes, here it is, Ms. Denning," said the suit-wearing concierge, who then escorted them to the elevators and hit the call button. When the elevator arrived, he held the door for them and reached inside and hit the button for the eighteenth floor.

Damn. He'd known Jay did all right, but he wasn't prepared for how far a cry this was from their trailer in Thunder Bay. When Jane unlocked the door of unit 1803, he effected an air of casualness as they made their way into the suite. He wanted to walk around and look really hard at everything, to get a sense of the man his brother had become. Because Jay was so much older and had moved to Toronto to go to school when Cam was seven, Cam had always been fascinated by him. As a kid, it had been hero worship, but in later years he'd thought of his brother almost as a character in one of his favorite video games—familiar, compelling, but ultimately from another world.

He took in a fancy kitchen with a breakfast bar that opened on to a living room. But nothing reminded him of his brother. The last time he had visited Jay, when Cam was in high school, his brother's apartment hadn't looked much more mature than a dorm room—huge TV, sofa, gaming system, and not a lot else. But here, the walls were a pale gray-green and the room was full of fluffy furniture and brightly colored art.

He barked a laugh. "This does not look like the brother I used to know."

"It's Elise's influence, probably," Jane said as she went around opening windows. "Jay pretty much lives at her house these days, but she can't see a room without spiffing it up." She yanked open the door to the balcony. "It's hot in here."

"You should try Iraq," he said before he could think better of it.

"Yeah…" She trailed off. "I guess I shouldn't complain."

He hadn't meant to make her feel bad. He'd enjoyed rattling Jane Denning this afternoon, but he wasn't out to make her feel genuinely bad. "Let's see what my brother has to drink," he said, turning and heading for the kitchen. "Beer is definitely on my list." He opened the massive stainless steel fridge. "Ah! Success!" Jay hadn't gotten *too* big for his britches—no fancy microbrews here. He grabbed a couple of Labatts and made his way back to the living room, holding one out for Jane even as he took a pull of his.

"No, thanks."

She was back to looking like the prim detention teacher.

"Suit yourself." He grabbed the remote and flopped onto the fancy sofa. "Do you know any good bars around here?"

"We are not going to a bar."

"No, *we* are not going to a bar. *I* am going to a bar. Later. Alone. For the purposes of (a) getting drunk, and (b) picking up a woman. Maybe two." That last part was a lie, but he was on a roll with riling her, and he couldn't seem to stop.

"I suppose that's also on the list?"

"Hey," he said, "I'm single, young, and back on Canadian soil." He wasn't going to apologize.

She said nothing, simply stood there staring at him. He turned on the TV. When, after he'd flipped channels for a minute or so she still didn't move, merely kept standing there with her silent judgment, he said, "You're dismissed, Jane."

"I beg your pardon?"

"Your babysitting services are no longer needed. You can go back to your cloudless cave."

"I'm not babysitting you," she said.

"So you keep saying."

And eff him if she didn't then turn around, and without a word, walk out of the condo.

⟶ ᏟᏗ

"You just *left* him?"

Jane had to hold the phone away from her ear to buffer Elise's shrieking. It was hard to explain. What could she say? That Cameron was like a little brother who knew how to push all her buttons, but also *not* a little brother because many of those buttons, it turned out, were sexual? She settled for, "He was an ass."

"I *know* he's an ass. That's the whole point."

"How did the tea sets turn out?" Jane asked weakly. It was way too late to ask the real tea-set-related question, which was *what the hell are they for?*

There was a beat of silence. "The tea sets are fine."

"Elise, I'm sorry, I—"

"I gave you one job." Elise's voice had grown small. "I asked you to do this one thing for me."

"The wedding isn't until a week from Saturday, and it's not even in the city. What can Cameron possibly do on a random Wednesday night 125 miles and a week and a half away from your wedding that will have an impact on it?" She wasn't sure why she was arguing, because Elise's basic point was undeniable. Jane had fallen down on the job. But she felt compelled to try to talk some sense into her friend. "He's out by himself and doesn't know anyone who knows you." *Unless he accidentally picks up one of Elise's friends as he crosses items off his stupid list.* Elise and Jay had a lot of friends in the building and in the neighborhood. And what if one of those friends hooked up with him and then they met again at the wedding?

Or what if Cameron hooked up with one of Jay and Elise's *married* friends who was cheating on her husband, and then they met again at the wedding and the husband tried to kick Cameron's ass and there was a massive brawl?

And what if, in the course of said massive brawl, they knocked over some candles and burned the wedding down? After all, Cameron was an arsonist, wasn't he?

Jane would be the first to admit that she had an overactive imagination. It was a job hazard. But crap. She believed in the butterfly effect—a seemingly small action could have huge consequences down the line. And she wasn't convinced that Cameron was capable of "small actions." So, yeah, the more she thought about it, the less she could blame Elise's demands about babysitting Cameron on her bridezilla-itis.

Elise was unmoved by Jane's logic. "Jay's mom called. Jay told her Cameron had arrived safely but had to make bullshit excuses as to why he wasn't answering his phone," Elise said. "She hasn't seen him for five months, and he can't pick up the phone when she calls?"

His poor mother. "She must be so proud of him," Jane said, noting that she'd said the same thing to Cameron. Why did she care so much whether Cameron's mother was proud of him? "You know, being the war hero and all."

"I'm not sure *hero* is the right word," Elise said. "There's something funny about his discharge. He won't talk about it. But no one was expecting him back this early."

"Dishonorable discharge?" Jane had no idea what a person had to do to be dishonorably discharged from the armed forces, but whatever it took, she wouldn't put it past Cameron.

"Apparently we know that phrase from American movies. They call it 'released from service' here. And there are all kinds of degrees of that. But the point is Jay is pretty sure he left under shady circumstances. There was some kind of…proceeding overseas, and all of a sudden he's back and he's not in the army anymore."

Jane thought of Cameron playing the war hero card with the poodle waitress at lunch. What a complete cad.

"Anyway," Elise went on, "the point is, this guy is a wild card and—"

She stopped abruptly, as if censoring herself, but Jane heard what had gone unsaid. *You let him get away.*

"I'll take care of it," Jane said, getting out of bed where she'd been writing on her laptop—her poor, doomed book clearly wasn't going to see any action until this wedding was over—and heading for her closet. She stripped off her pj bottoms and grabbed a drapey silk shirt—one of her "dressy" tees.

"How? What are you going to do?"

"I'm going to find that mofo and have him micro-chipped."

"But how are you going to find him?" Elise wailed. "He could be *anywhere*."

"Don't worry about a thing, sweetie." Jane slipped into a pair of hot pink flats. "I messed up, but I am on it now. On. It."

Time to do a little rewriting of this whole Cameron story. Time to do a little rewriting of this whole Cameron *character*, in fact.

⁓

She found him four blocks from Jay's building. After he wasn't in the Fox and the Fiddle, the Raving Lunatic (though that would have been poetic justice), Bar Benjamin, or Zelda's Big Gay Bar (she *knew* he wouldn't be there, but she was nothing if not systematic, and since she'd decided to go into every bar she passed, she wasn't going to skip it), she started to fear that he had gone downtown to an actual club. She wasn't dressed for that, and she was too old for nightclubs. Hell, she'd been *born* too old for nightclubs. But bar number five, which, ironically, was called Bar Nine, was the jackpot. Or the booby prize, depending on your perspective.

He was sitting at the bar, leaning in toward a woman with long blond hair. Their heads nearly touched, like they were looking at something on the bar.

All right, children, Mary Poppins has arrived. Game on.

Except…She was unaccountably nervous. Clammy-hands, dry-mouth nervous. Which was stupid. She'd never gotten nervous when she'd been a teenager babysitting *actual* children. Maybe she needed a drink first. After her dad's accident, she mostly avoided alcohol, but damned if this wedding wasn't about to drive her to drink for the second time in two days. Though probably whatever she ordered here would be better than Earl Grey with whiskey.

She squeezed herself into a tiny corner table as far from the bar as it was possible to be and hid behind a menu—see, all those years of Nancy Drew came in handy sometimes. It wasn't like Cameron and his prey were paying attention to anything outside their little circle of two, but it was better to be sure. She needed privacy to woman up for her mission. When a waiter arrived, she said, "I need a shot. Something strong but not disgusting. Basically, I don't want my liquor to taste like liquor."

"How about a B-52? It's amaretto, Kahlua, and Cointreau."

"Sold. Bring me a B-52." She looked over to the bar.

The blond was nuzzling Cameron's neck. "Actually, make it two."

─⌒─

The blond was reading Cam's palm. No, *Sherry* was reading his palm. He kept having to reach for her name. It wasn't sticking for some reason. He hadn't had his palm read since he was in junior high and Mrs. Compton, one of their neighbors in the trailer park, bought a book and decided to try to make some cash on the side. He didn't believe in it now, just like he hadn't believed in it then, but he *had* believed in the unlimited stash of Oreos Mrs. Compton let him eat while she practiced on him.

He hadn't tried to pick up a woman since before Christie. Between Alicia, his high school flame, and Christie, the only other girlfriend he'd ever had, there had been a period that Christie had jokingly called his "man-whore phase." She hadn't been wrong, and he was looking forward to a return to form—clearly, he wasn't cut out for relationships.

But he was good at seduction. His current companion was all over him. He was gratified to know that even though he was out of practice, he still had the goods.

"Hmmm." She kept leaning closer to better see the lines on his hand in the dim bar, and it had the effect of lining up her neck with his nose. She was wearing a lot of perfume, and it was really...perfumey perfume.

He wondered if there was any chance he could convince her to shower first. Or, hey, maybe shower *during*. But they'd have to go to her place because he obviously wasn't taking her to Jay's. He almost laughed, thinking about how well that would go over. He'd bolted on the big reunion, leaving Jay's place before five, and had been ignoring

his brother's texts all evening. All of a sudden, as much
as he'd wanted to see Jay, he just...couldn't. He'd kept
thinking about how Jane didn't even know he existed.
About how his brother hadn't bothered to mention him
once to his fiancée's close friend. Not even a single, "Darn,
my brother isn't going to be able to make it back from Iraq
for the wedding."

So, yeah, it would have to be the blonde's place.

Sherry's place.

Someone edged into their space, and as he was about to
tell the interloper to watch it, he heard a familiar voice.

"Cameron!"

"Jane?" *What the hell?*

Her eyes were suspiciously bright.

"Thought you could ditch me, did you?" she trilled in a
voice he recognized as distinctly fake even though he'd only
known her for nine hours. She turned to Sherry, who was
watching them with wide eyes. Sherry snatched her hand
from the bar, where it had been cradling Cam's open palm.
"Cameron," Jane drawled, "aren't you going to introduce
me to your...new friend?"

Goddamn her. But what could he do? He was a jerk
in some ways, but he was a jerk with good manners. His
mother had drilled them into him, and for some reason,
even though he'd disappointed her in every other way, the
manners had stuck. "Jane, this is..." *Shit*. "Sherry!" He remembered just in time. "Sherry, Jane."

"You know what?" Sherry said, flashing him an annoyed
look, "I think I'm going to get going."

He wanted to protest, to exhort her not to leave. But what
would he say? That Jane was nothing to him? That, in fact,
he'd only met her this morning? Such a protest would sound
smarmy even to his own ears. Jane had made sure of it with

her little performance, hadn't she? So he smiled and bade Sherry a wistful good-bye.

Then he wiped the smile off his face and turned to Jane. "What the hell?"

"What the hell what?" she said, plopping onto the stool vacated by Sherry and flagging down the bartender. When the horn-rimmed-glasses-wearing hipster arrived, she said, "I'll have a B-22. I've already had two, and they are *delish*!"

"You mean a B-52?" the bartender countered, settling his elbows on the bar in front of her and leaning in with a rakish smile that seemed to delight Jane. He, all pale and literary-looking, *would* be her type.

She did that nose-scrunching thing of hers, and Cam attempted not to find it cute. "Maybe? The Kahlua thing that is a shot of pure deliciousness?"

"That's the one."

"Hey, if I wanted a double, could I ask for a B-104? Ha!" She threw back her head and laughed at her own lame joke.

But the bartender did, too, the prick.

"Wait." She scrunched again. "Is that math right?"

She was drunk. Or at least well on her way. He recognized the signs from his years behind the bar. "I think you'd better stick to the double-digits," Cam said, not sure if he was talking to her or to the bartender.

She swiveled on her stool. "And what are you? My father? Oh, no, wait. My father is dead."

"You just seem like maybe you should slow down."

"I tell you what. Let's start with a single, and we'll take it from there," said the bartender, assembling the layered shot. "See how the evening unfolds." He winked.

"He's actually right," she said, stage-whispering to the bartender and cocking her head at Cam in a way that was the opposite of subtle. "I'm not usually much of a drinker."

The bartender set the drink in front of her. "On the house."

Cam rolled his eyes. Well, hell, if Jane could cock-block him, she was about to get a taste of her own medicine. He slung an arm around her shoulders. "I'm just looking out for you. Sweetie." He let the last word unspool slowly, drawing out the endearment.

The bartender's megawatt smile dimmed. Jane tried to shrug off Cam's arm, but the drink-slinging poseur was gone. Mission accomplished.

Jane started to turn to him, her mouth open like she was about to let loose a torrent of words, but she stumbled in her seat a little. He tightened his arm around her to steady her and suppressed a grin. "So, not much of a drinker, eh?"

"I drink occasionally," she said, turning thoughtful. Ah, it was so delightfully easy to redirect drunk people—at least a certain kind of non-belligerent drunk person. "I usually only drink with my girlfriends, though, and even then I only have one glass of wine." She grinned. "Or one mug of spiked Earl Grey tea."

"I know you're going to have a hard time believing this," he said, "but first-day-back-from-war aside, I'm usually with you on that." He paused, not sure why he was compelled to say more. But she was drunk, and she was nearly finished with B-52 number three, so she probably wouldn't even remember anything he said. "There was a lot of alcoholism in our neighborhood growing up. It wasn't pretty."

She whipped her head around and met his eyes for an instant before looking away again.

Ding, ding, ding.

Maybe they had something in common, after all. Cam had never met his father, but according to Jay, Angus MacKinnon had been prone to drunken rages, which is why his relationship with their mother had been so short-lived. She had kicked him out when she was still pregnant with Cam, in fact. And he was pretty sure Angus was partly responsible for making Jay so driven, for inspiring him to escape their shitty life. "I drank a lot when I was a teenager and into my early twenties," he told Jane. Hell, there probably wasn't a substance out there that he wouldn't have gleefully ingested in the post-Alicia years.

"But you stopped?" she asked. "You just decided to stop and you...were able to?"

"Pretty much." It was true. Part of his self-overhaul had been to cut way back on the booze, and even though the self-overhaul had failed, he was pretty sure he was going to keep cooling it on the booze. His years behind the bar cutting off mean drunks and consoling weepy drunks had pretty much sealed that deal. "When you see alcoholism in your family and your community...well, I didn't like who I was becoming."

"It's not so much that I'm afraid I'll turn into an alcoholic," she said, but he noticed she hadn't denied that there was alcoholism in her family. "It's more that I'm...not into drawing attention to myself. I like things to be orderly."

"You're a control freak." He wasn't surprised.

"I like to think of life like writing a book," she declared. "You can't just sit down and 'write a book.'" She made air quotes with her fingers. "You have to plan things. Be methodical. Disciplined. If you want things to happen a certain way—if you want people to behave a certain way—it requires specific behavior on your part. You know that saying? For every action there is an equal and opposite reaction? It's true in books, and it's true in life. You have to be careful."

Well. That was quite the worldview. He wondered if Jane

had been born so wound up or if something—or someone—had made her that way.

She waved at the bartender, and Cam sighed. She was now drunk enough that he could not in good conscience leave her alone. She had succeeded in ruining his plans for the evening, and there was nothing he could do about it short of leaving her in the clutches of Hipster Boy Bartender. And that was *not* happening.

She slid her empty shot glass toward the bartender. "May I please have another?"

"*One* more," Cam said, and the bartender, apparently no longer interested in flirting now that he believed Jane was taken, nodded and set to work.

She pouted. "I thought we established that you're not my father."

"No. More like your babysitter. And not doing a very good job of it, either, because that fourth drink is going to put you over the edge." If she really never had more than one drink, she probably had no idea how drunk she was. Those shots might taste like candy, but they were one hundred percent booze.

"Hey! *I'm* supposed to be babysitting *you*!"

"Busted!"

"What?" There was that damned nose scrunch again.

"You've only spent the entire day protesting that you're *not* babysitting me, and—" Oh, shit, she was tipping toward him, as if in slow motion. He hopped off his stool, steadied her, and propped her up—the stools were backless—by leaning her back against his chest. She exhaled a sweet little sigh and burrowed back against him, as if his chest were a fluffy pillow. It put his nose level with her neck, and he gave her a sniff, purely for comparative purposes. There was none of Sherry's heavy, musky scent. Just a clean, bright smell he was pretty sure was Eau du Ivory Soap. It was...surprisingly nice.

He shook himself out of his reverie. "Hey, so we should get you home. Let's get a cab."

She said nothing.

"Jane?" He twisted so he could see her face while still holding her up.

She was asleep.

He sighed. All right. He could always try again tomorrow night. Note to self: find a bar far, far away from Jay's place.

Because come hell or high water, he was getting laid tomorrow night.

Chapter Four

When Jane woke up, she immediately knew two things.

First, she wasn't in her own bed. The mattress beneath her was too soft—soft beds like this one weren't good for your back. Her own mattress had been carefully selected for its spine-supporting properties.

The second thing Jane knew with instantaneous certainty was that she was hung over.

Utterly, totally, embarrassingly hung over.

It had happened once before, during orientation week at university. She'd awakened with a mouth full of cotton. Her head had felt like it was in the middle of a demolition zone. Oh, the shame of it. She might as well have walked around the quad that next day wearing a giant sandwich board that said, "Hi. I lost control. I made a fool of myself. Other people had to take care of me."

Ever since their dad died, her brother Noah had taken care of her. Their mom had checked out, lost in her own grief and barely able to function, and Noah had stepped in to provide for them, both financially and emotionally. She'd tried to make it easy for him. To be good and avoid trouble. What would he have thought of her then?

What would he think of her now?

At least she wasn't in a strange bed. It wasn't hers, but, as she opened her eyes a tiny bit, wincing against the brightness in the room, she recognized the pale green walls and crown moldings as Elise's work. She was in Jay's guest room. She and the girls occasionally crashed here when they were out late downtown.

Well, there was nothing to do but get on with things. The bachelorette party was Saturday and she was going to Comicon Sunday, so that left two days in which to finish her Xena costume and, hopefully, to make some progress on the book before she pretty much had to take a deep breath and let the wedding tsunami sweep her away. But it would depend on what Elise expected on an ongoing basis in terms of babysitting.

God, she was so hot. Why was it so hot in here? She flung the covers off.

Wait.

There was one thing Jane *hadn't* noticed immediately when she woke up.

And that would be the arm slung across her body.

The very male, muscle-bound arm.

She closed her eyes against that arm like it was blinding sunlight. Oh dear God. *Had she slept with Cameron MacKinnon?*

She couldn't remember. Her brain, despite its pain, did a quick catalog of all the times he had been surprisingly chivalrous: offering to help her out of the Corvette, insisting she order first at the steakhouse, steadying her on the bar stool last night. *That* guy wouldn't take advantage of her. But the gentlemanly, almost old-fashioned way he behaved was so at odds with the ludicrous, arrogant things that came out of his mouth. He was a mass of contradictions.

A mass of contradictions she prayed to God she hadn't slept with. The image of Cameron licking the ice cream spoon at the steakhouse popped into her mind. Heck, if she was going to break her self-imposed five-year dry spell, it would be nice to be able to remember something about it. She opened her eyes and tried to crane her neck so she could see him without moving too much and disturbing him. The arm was bare, but was the rest of him?

Yes, yes he was.

And he was wide awake.

He was covered in tattoos. She had known he would be. A sleeve of them ran down one arm—a forest of sorts, trees bleeding into more trees, interspersed with the occasional flower. His chest was covered with an image of an angel in a flowing white gown that was so hauntingly beautiful—it looked like a Renaissance painting—it made her gasp. No co-opted tribal bullshit on this guy.

And muscles. Everywhere muscles. He was a soldier, sure, but still, how was that possible? How did he just walk around with so much contained power as if it were no big deal?

He shot her a lazy grin. God, his jawline—you could cut glass with that jaw.

Maybe she could use it to slit her wrists.

Then that maddening, slow drawl: "Good morning, Jane. Sleep well?"

‿ↄ

It wasn't nice to laugh at people when they were panicking. Cam knew that in his mind. But it was damn near impossible not to laugh in this specific instance. Witnessing Jane regain consciousness and then *really* regain consciousness had been hilarious. He'd been lying there, listening to her breathe, willing his morning wood to go away. That was probably a lost cause, though. She was so soft and pliant—when she was asleep.

He'd been a jerk to agree when she insisted he share the bed. He'd been fully prepared to decamp to Jay's sofa last night, but when she'd grabbed his hand and pulled him down with her, then snuggled up against him and fallen promptly asleep...well, no one was that virtuous. And to his great surprise, when she was asleep, prickly Jane was a snuggler. He wasn't complaining. Well, he *was* in the sense that his plan had been to wake up this morning cuddling with a woman with whom he'd had scorching sex the night before. But still, the human contact was nice. He'd missed it. And sleepy, snuggly Jane—as opposed to awake, talking Jane—was actually kind of pleasant.

But sleepy, snuggly Jane was gone. She sat bolt upright. "Please tell me we didn't..." She was clutching the sheet over her chest, which wasn't necessary because although he'd gotten her out of her jeans and blazer—they'd just seemed way too uncomfortable to sleep in—he hadn't fully undressed her. He wasn't that much of a jerk, and the idea that she might think he was pained him a little. He had even averted his eyes when he was pulling her jeans off.

Her eyes roamed his chest. Right. Women always went crazy for his tattoos. He readied himself to trot out the half-true version of what they meant that he deployed in these sorts of situations, but she didn't ask. She met his gaze again and did that single-eyebrow-lifting thing that was so maddening. "Answer me. Did we sleep together?"

"Depends what you mean by 'sleep,'" he countered, trying to get her to stop looking at him like she was Mary Poppins waiting for him to clean his room.

"Oh my God," she whispered, and she fell back onto the bed. She swallowed hard, the way people do when they're trying not to cry.

"Hey, hey, I'm sorry. I was only teasing," he rushed to assure her. "Nothing happened."

"Really?"

"Jesus Christ, Jane, give me a little credit." What kind of man did she think he was? But of course the answer to that question wasn't very flattering, was it, given what she had seen of him yesterday?

"I'm sorry. I didn't think we had...done anything, but..." She looked around the room, and her eyes landed on her blazer, which he'd draped over a chair in the corner.

"You were pretty drunk," he said, and she massaged her temples and nodded her agreement. "I was going to put you in a cab, but it...didn't seem wise. So I suggested you sleep here. You agreed. But then you..."

"Then I what?"

"I was going to sleep on the couch, but you wouldn't let me. You kind of...tackled me, actually."

She nodded. "Right."

He cocked his head. He had been prepared for more arguing, to have to defend himself a lot more vigorously.

"I can be very adamant when I have my mind set on something," she said. "And I'm sure alcohol only intensifies it. I'm sorry."

Well, knock him over with a feather. "Hey, it's okay." He

pushed the covers off, intending to get up and get dressed, but she shrieked and clasped her hands over her eyes. "I hate to disappoint you, but I'm wearing boxers."

She spread her fingers enough that she could peek through them, and once she'd confirmed that he was, in fact, not naked, she let them fall. Not the usual reaction, to say the least.

"How do you feel?" he asked, walking around to her bedside table, where he'd left a glass of water and a bottle of Advil. "I made you drink as much water as I could last night, but you should probably have some more." He handed her the glass.

She tipped her head back and drank. She was wearing a loose, low-cut, silky T-shirt, and he was a human male who had only recently woken up. Predictable things happened. But, thankfully, she didn't see. He cleared his throat. "Then maybe some coffee when you're done with that?"

She moaned when he said "coffee," which wasn't helping matters south of the equator. In addition to sleepy, snuggly Jane, there was something to be said for this version with the messed-up hair and the low, throaty moan.

He threw on a pair of jeans. He needed to get out of here. "Let's get some food into you, too. I'll see what I can throw together."

"Is Jay home?" she whispered. "Oh my God, is Elise here?" She fumbled for her phone on the nightstand and scrolled through her texts. "Oh, no, the girls are doing more teapots this morning." She sighed in relief.

"Doing more teapots? What does that mean?"

"I have no idea."

When Jane made her way into the kitchen ten minutes later, she felt considerably less like she wanted to die. She'd brushed her hair, swished with some of Jay's mouthwash, and put herself together as best as she could. She was back in control.

"Crap."

Cameron turned from where he was standing over the stove, poised with a spatula in his hand. "Everything okay?"

Had she said that out loud? So much for back in control. "Yeah, everything's fine."

It was just that, confronted with Cameron MacKinnon, with his bare feet poking out of faded jeans and his mass of tattoos only partially concealed by a white tank top, standing at a stove cooking, whatever control she thought she'd gained vanished like a sugar cube melting into a cup of—

"Coffee?"

She shivered as she accepted the mug and a small carton of cream from him. "Can I help?"

"Nah." He gestured to the stools at the breakfast bar that overlooked the kitchen.

He turned back to the stove. God. There was something about the unlikely image of the big manly man padding around the kitchen, totally at ease that . . . did something to her.

"If I had to guess how you take your eggs, I'd say poached," he said as he pivoted to retrieve some toast that had just popped.

"That's exactly right!" she exclaimed.

"Which is why I scrambled them," he said, smirking as he slid a plate in front of her.

She rolled her eyes. But it was good to be reminded that Cameron MacKinnon, despite the solid he'd done her last night, was still, elementally, a jerk.

"Easier," he said. "Way less fussy."

"Wow," she said, her voice intentionally flat. "Eggs as metaphor for personality. How original."

"I do make a pretty mean hollandaise, though," he said, delivering her a couple slices of toast and a dish of butter. "But I only make eggs Benedict for women who actually sleep with me."

The sound of throat clearing came from behind them. Jane whirled.

"Jay!"

On the surface of things, Jay was dressed not unlike his brother. He also wore a white tank, but instead of jeans, it was paired with blue pajama bottoms.

"Jane," he said, making his way to the coffeemaker and pouring himself a cup. "Fancy meeting you here." He took a big gulp of coffee without doctoring it—and Jane knew he normally didn't take his coffee black—before turning to Cameron. "And you. Thanks for waiting for me to get home last night before you took off."

Whoa. Was this the first time Jay had seen his brother since Cameron had been back? She would have assumed they'd had their reunion last night, before Cameron went to the bar.

"Sorry about that," said Cameron, talking to Jay but busying himself refilling the toaster with a new round of bread. "I've been cooped up since I landed back on Canadian soil. I needed to bust out."

Jane was suffused with a growing discomfort. She wasn't used to family conflict. Not since Dad had died. And not really before, either—he had mostly been a happy drunk.

She certainly couldn't imagine this kind of tension between her and her brother Noah.

"And I suppose your phone was conveniently dead last night, so you didn't get my texts," Jay said, moving around the breakfast bar to sit beside Jane. She didn't miss the quick once-over he gave her, even as he kept talking to Cameron in the same deadpan-bordering-on-icy tone. "Or you lost it, maybe."

"I didn't sleep with your brother!" she shouted. She wasn't sure if she was doing it to protect her own reputation or to try to diffuse some of the tension in the room.

Jay turned to her with the barest hint of a smile. "You always were the smart one in Elise's crowd." Then he turned to his brother and said...nothing. Wow. It was probably kind of crappy that Cameron hadn't made contact with his brother yesterday, but, still, where was the "I'm glad you didn't die in Iraq" welcome home man-hug?

Also, where was Doctor Phil when you needed him? Because Jane wasn't good at this shit. She stuffed a piece of buttered toast—how was it possible that even Cameron's *toast* was delicious?—in her mouth in order to avoid having to say anything.

She'd started on her second piece when she realized what she was doing. "Oh, no!" she exclaimed, spraying crumbs.

Both brothers turned to her with looks of concern so identical that they might have been amusing in a different context.

"I'm on a diet," she mumbled, pushing her plate away. T-minus nine days till she had to pay the piper...if the piper was a size ten number in mulberry and not plum (the debate had raged for days) with a fitted bodice and a swingy skirt.

God. She allowed herself a moment of self-disgust. Of course, her plan to not only drop fifteen pounds but to, like, somehow magically acquire Michelle Obama arms so that her own wobbly ones didn't look like bleached sausages at the wedding had come to naught.

"You don't need to diet," Cameron said. She didn't know if his clenched jaw was residual anger at his brother or if it was new anger summoned just for her. But before she could decide, he turned and started rinsing dishes at the sink.

"One thing we actually agree on," Jay said, turning to her. "Is this about the wedding? Is Elise on you about this, because God bless her—you know I adore her—but that is one step too far."

"No, no," she said, waving her hands dismissively. "Elise hasn't said a word." She got up, intending to deliver her dishes to the sink.

"Why *are* you here, Jane?" Jay asked, his brow furrowed as he looked between her and his brother.

"Someone has to rein in the black-sheep brother, right?" Cameron said, his back still to them as he banged around making quite the racket, moving dishes from the sink to the dishwasher. Bitterness radiated from him.

Jane approached with her dishes. "Nope," she said. "I just went to meet Cameron's plane yesterday since you were at work and Elise was busy." Of course that went exactly zero of the way toward explaining why she was in Jay's kitchen the next morning with her messy hair and her wrinkled clothes, but, suddenly, she didn't want Jay knowing that Elise thought his brother needed babysitting. For the first time, she wondered how Cameron had felt yesterday when she, a complete stranger, had picked him up and then refused to leave him alone. "Cameron and I ended up at a bar last night." That was true, if vague. "And I'm afraid I had a bit too much to drink, so Cameron brought me here."

Jay seemed to accept her explanation. He downed the remainder of his coffee and stood. "I need to hit the shower and get out of here. I guess I'll see you both later."

No! Jane wanted to shout! *Do a man-hug! Or shake hands, even!* "It must be so great to have Cameron back from Iraq, huh, Jay?"

Cameron whipped his gaze to her. He was not pleased with her little outburst. But, damn, somebody had to make these two Neanderthals do the right thing. It wasn't her fault that subtlety had never been her strong suit.

Jay cleared his throat. "Uh, yeah, it is." He walked over to Cameron and laid a hand on his shoulder. "I'm sorry things didn't work out in the army, but I'm glad you could make the wedding." He sounded like he was reciting from a script, but at least it was something. Jane held her breath in the silence that followed. It was probably only a few seconds, but it seemed to stretch on forever.

"Thanks, man. It's good to see you," Cameron finally said, and she exhaled.

"So what are you up to today?" she asked Cameron once Jay had headed for the shower.

"Why? You still on duty?"

She had no idea, actually.

Like Cameron, she had been a delinquent texter last night. She had a bunch of them from Elise, but going back in time before the one telling her they were working on the mystery teapots again this morning, they were all of the "WHERE ARE YOU?" and "WHAT ARE YOU DOING?" and "DID CAMERON BURN ANYTHING DOWN?" and "OMG, DID CAMERON KNOCK ANYONE UP?" variety.

"I'm not babysitting you," she said firmly as she scrolled.

"Yes. You've mentioned that a few times." He topped off

her coffee, leaned over, and propped his elbows up on the breakfast bar so they were eye to eye.

"I was just wondering what your plans are for today." She tried to project her voice because she was afraid it was going to come out as weak and wobbly as she felt. The hangover, the virile, tattooed personal chef: it was all a little overwhelming. But she'd overcompensated, and basically yelled the question at him.

He looked like he was trying not to laugh. "My plans are to get laid."

Her eye roll was as involuntary. "Ow."

"What?"

"I rolled my eyes so hard my eyeballs actually hurt."

"Well, you asked. You also cock-blocked me last night, if you recall."

Jane managed to keep her eyeballs reined in, but only just.

And of course that was the moment Jay emerged from the hallway, dressed in his usual weekday uniform of a navy suit.

"Keeping it classy, I see, brother," Jay said.

"I always do," Cameron shot back.

"I gotta get to work." Without another word, or even a glance back, Jay collected his briefcase and phone from a table in the entryway and departed, leaving an awkward silence in his wake.

Okay, WWTBD? What would the bride do? The answer, of course, was that the bride would continue to cock-block the hell out of Cameron. As much as Jane wanted to go home and sleep off her hangover, she needed to do the responsible thing and redirect this dude. Of course, she personally couldn't care less if he slept with half of Toronto, and there were no barns in a city this size that he could burn down, but she was suffused with a general sense of foreboding nevertheless. Butterfly effect and all that.

So she pasted on a smile and said, "Let's go to the CN Tower!" It was the first thing that popped into her head when she thought about what people did when they visited Toronto. But it was also the lamest thing she could have said. The CN Tower was where busloads of tourists from Middle America were disgorged by the hundreds.

"It's actually on my list."

"It is?" Mr. Black Sheep wanted to go to the biggest tourist trap in the city? And here she'd already been scouring her brain for edgier suggestions.

"Yeah, I have this thing where when I'm visiting somewhere, I like to go to the highest point if I can. Take in the view."

She cocked her head. He really was kind of a mystery. "What's the highest point in Thunder Bay?"

"Tower Mountain," he said without hesitation.

"All right," she said, slapping her hands on the marble breakfast bar and sliding off her stool. "I need to get changed." And take about a thousand Advils. And talk Elise off the ledge. She glanced at her watch. She'd been going to suggest they meet there at eleven, which was two hours from now. But was that too long a gap? Could Cameron do any damage in the next two hours? He yawned, interlaced his fingers, and pressed his arms up and over his head, stretching like a cat. A very dangerous, tattooed, man-eating cat.

Woman-eating cat.

"I'll meet you there at ten," she said.

Chapter Five

*W*hen Cam ambled into the lobby of the CN Tower at 10:03, Jane was already there perusing brochures. She had changed into another pair of curve-hugging skinny jeans, and she was wearing a form-fitting black T-shirt and a pair of leopard print flats. The woman certainly had a lot of flats. And T-shirts. Last night, at the bar—and in his bed—she'd been wearing a sort of fancy T-shirt, made out of silk or something, and of course she'd had a blazer over it for the not-in-bed portion of their evening, but it had been a T-shirt nonetheless. He was starting to realize that the jeans-T-shirt-flats combo was her thing. As uniforms went, it wasn't bad. It worked for her.

"This is a total racket," she said, looking up as he approached. "They basically want fifty bucks a head if you want to go to both observation decks."

He took the brochure and peered at it. "Or we could do this EdgeWalk thing, and that package gets you into everything else, too." It was stupidly expensive, but, hell, he had his "tuition" savings burning a hole in his pocket. And life had been a little short on thrills since he'd gotten back from Iraq.

"I knew you were going to want to do that." She put her hands on her hips. "Because I'm starting to understand: You. Are. Insane."

"Not your thing?" he asked, though he already knew the answer.

"Let me count the ways. Numbers one through two hundred and ninety-five are the dollars it would cost me. And then there's the part where you're paying them to dangle you off the freaking CN Tower, Cameron!" She grabbed the brochure back from him and read it aloud, her voice getting higher. "A hands-free walk on a five-foot-wide ledge encircling the top of the Tower's main pod, eleven hundred and sixty eight feet, or a hundred and sixteen stories, above the ground." Then she shook the brochure under his face.

He took it back from her and read on. "Yeah, but also there's the part where 'trained EdgeWalk guides will encourage participants to push their personal limits, allowing them to lean back over Toronto with nothing but air and breathtaking views of Lake Ontario beneath them.'" He was taunting her now, but she was kind of irresistible when she was incredulous.

"What part of 'insane' did you not understand? Do you need synonyms? 'Crazy,' 'deranged,' 'delusional.' Anything ringing a bell here?"

"You don't have to do it with me." He shrugged. "But think how many brownie points this will get you with Elise. You do this, and it's like you're the valedictorian of babysitting."

He'd hooked her. He could tell by the way she tilted her head and squinted her eyes at him. She was searching for a rebuttal, but she didn't have one. "I'm not babysitting you."

He raised his eyebrows. She didn't seem to remember that she'd admitted as much at the bar last night.

"So the whole valedictorian of babysitting thing doesn't apply," she added.

"You were probably the actual valedictorian, anyway," he teased.

"Salutatorian. Wendy was the valedictorian in our high school."

"Wendy?"

"One of Elise's other bridesmaids."

"You and Wendy and Elise went to high school together?" he asked. He was having trouble imagining Jane as a girl. She seemed like the kind of person who had been born thirty years old.

"Nope, just Wendy and me. I've known Wendy since she moved to our neighborhood when we were ten. We picked up Elise—and Gia, the fourth bridesmaid—in university. Gia is four years younger than us, though."

"And how long ago was university?"

"Are you asking how old I am?"

"I might be." He wasn't sure why he cared, except that he couldn't peg her. She was young-looking, with her smooth skin and her cute, if utilitarian, wardrobe. But in other ways, she seemed so world weary, in a way that went beyond her prissiness.

"So just ask me."

"Jane, how old are you?"

"Thirty-one." Four years older than he was. But then his own age felt as un-pin-down-able as hers in some ways. Everyone saw him as the immature boy he'd been for so long. But some of the shit he'd seen made him feel like he was a hundred years old.

She cleared her throat, and he realized he'd gotten lost in his thoughts, so he reached for a joke to cover himself. "Thirty-one is definitely old enough to have your personal limits pushed with nothing but air and the breathtaking view of Lake Ontario beneath you."

"Goddamn you, Cameron MacKinnon."

He grinned. "I dare you. But I bet you won't do it." Suddenly, he really wanted to see Jane hanging off the edge of this impossibly high tower. He wondered if she'd be a screamer.

Whoa. A shiver ran up his spine as that thought brought to mind a totally different image of her screaming.

"And if I take this crazy bet, what do I get?"

"The satisfaction that comes with having your personal limits pushed."

She swatted him.

"The breathtaking views, too, of course."

She swatted him again, harder this time, and he grabbed her hand and held on to it in order to halt her attack.

"How about this?" she asked, not taking her hand back and getting right in his face. "I do this demented EdgeWalk thing with you, and you forgo today's booty call. Or tonight's. Or whenever you were planning it."

He whistled. This woman knew how to bargain. He was, frankly, taken aback. But also kind of impressed. He hoped Elise knew what a first-rate nanny service she was getting.

"Because, really, if you've slept with one random, you've slept with them all," she went on. "But how often do you get to dangle from a one-hundred-and-sixteen-story building with a bestselling young-adult author? I'll post us on my Instagram."

Shit. He was going to agree to her nefarious terms. What was the matter with him?

"Come on," she wheedled. "Tit for tat."

Well, at least he could go down swinging. So he took her arm, steered them toward the ticket windows, and said, "I think you mean tat for no-tit."

—⌒◌

Jane was really scared. Like, really, really scared.

Even the elevator was freaking her out. By the time their guide explained that the ascent would take only fifty-eight seconds, her stomach had already been left behind on ground level. She jerked a little and had to restrain herself from grabbing Cameron's arm.

He must have noticed, because he shot her a concerned look. She summoned a smile she feared looked as fake as it was.

"Let's do this first," he murmured in her ear when the guide announced the stop for the glass floor.

"Yes!" she said a little too vehemently. Because a glass floor was nothing compared to, like, being tethered to the outside of a building more than a thousand feet in the air, right?

Wrong.

"Ack!" She did grab Cameron's arm this time. They were standing at the edge of a glass-paneled floor that showed them the view straight down the hundred and sixteen stories to the street below.

"It's kind of wild, isn't it?" Cameron said mildly, leaning over like he was on an actual ledge. "It's like your brain knows the glass is thick, and it's perfectly safe, but..."

The more he leaned forward, the harder she pulled back

on his arm. He was exactly right. The rational part of her understood there was nothing to fear. There were kids gleefully jumping up and down on neighboring panels, for heaven's sake.

"But sometimes you've gotta open your eyes and jump," he said, breaking out of her grasp and jumping backward so that he landed on one of the glass panels.

She could have kept her hand on his arm, followed him out onto the glass, but she didn't. As their fingers slipped past each other, a twinge of regret pinged around in her chest, but it was swept away as someone on the next panel shrieked in laughter.

Cameron was grinning, too, looking down at his feet.

She turned and walked away, her heart beating as if she *had* walked out on the glass. She busied herself reading an interpretive panel on the wall that informed her that the glass floor could hold forty-one polar bears, or thirty-five moose, or three and a half orcas. So there was basically no way, short of the apocalypse striking, that anyone was falling through that glass. God, what a wimp she was. *Children* were doing this. Her face heated.

For no reason at all, she suddenly remembered a time she tried to have some friends over after school in fourth grade. This was before Wendy had started at Jane's school, back when Jane was...not an outcast really, but struggling to find a place to fit in. Of course, she had fixated, the way kids do, on the pretty, popular girls, thinking that befriending them would make her life so much easier.

So much happier.

Part of her knew, even then, that it was a mistake to invite them over. Having people over was usually too much of a risk, given that she never knew what state her father was going to be in. But she'd talked herself into it. She had told Daddy, coached him, begged him even. Explained the stakes. Promises were made.

But of course she knew the minute she opened the door and he greeted them with a high-pitched "Hi, girls!" that she had been naive to think he could lay off the drinking for even one afternoon. She'd learned her lesson that day: taking risks was usually not worth it.

"Hey."

She inhaled sharply, startled out of her memories. But the shame was still there. She just didn't know if it was the same old packed-down crud or a fresh new layer.

"So I'm thinking maybe we should just hit the observation deck and call it a day?" Cameron said gently, resting a hand on her shoulder.

"What about the EdgeWalk?" she asked.

"I can do it another time. And I'm sure they'll give you your money back. People must change their minds all the time. We can just call off the bet."

What went unspoken was that he recognized her for the chickenshit she was. And that he was being so nice about it was worse somehow than if he'd whipped out his usual jerky banter.

She glanced at her watch. Ten minutes until their assigned start time. She thought of those girls who had never come back to her house but had later been over-the-top with expressions of sympathy when her father died. "Nope, let's do it."

―◌

Cam felt like a dick. Which wasn't all that unusual, really, but this time he hadn't actually done anything wrong. There was no way this could end well. And it felt like his fault.

Which was ridiculous. Yeah, he hadn't initially grasped exactly how much of a scaredy-cat she was, but as soon as he'd realized that the glass floor alone was making her start to come unhinged, he'd tried to pull the plug on the whole thing.

But no. Jane was fronting with false bravado. She was all blustery determination, pasted-on-smiles, and overly loud small talk with their fellow adventurers as everyone lined up to be fitted into their harnesses.

She was also awfully cute in her orange jumpsuit. The same jumpsuit that made the rest of them look like awkward rejects from a *Ghostbusters* casting call somehow hugged her curves just right.

They were all being strapped into harnesses that had cables in the front and the back that fastened to a track in the ceiling that ran the length of the room and then continued on outside. The guides who would make the walk with them were fastened onto a parallel, outer track.

"The platform outside is five feet wide," the main guide said. "That's about as wide as your average sidewalk. Have you ever fallen off a sidewalk?"

That got a mixture of genuine and nervous laughter. Cam eyed Jane. He shouldn't know her well enough to be able to tell, but underneath her breeziness, she was terrified. He understood. He himself was feeling that same zingy anticipation that always preceded a dangerous task on tour. It was human nature. Even though here, unlike in the Middle East, you knew you were perfectly safe, some reptilian part of your mind whose job was self-preservation was screaming, "danger!" It was like the glass floor, but more.

Which was why he was worried. He leaned over to whisper in her ear. "You okay?"

She nodded, too vigorously. He rested his hand on the small of her back.

"Okay, here we go!" shouted the guide as he threw open the doors and the wind, which was something fierce coming off the lake, whipped in. Several among their group started squealing. In fact, pretty much everyone had some kind of audible reaction as they stepped outside.

They were toward the back of the line, and Jane was shaking. He could feel it through her jumpsuit. He consoled himself that even if the worst happened and she went hysterical, or passed out or something, the setup was such that they could tow her back inside using the track and cable system.

Unlike at the glass floor, and unlike nearly everyone else in the group, she was totally silent as she stepped onto the grate that was the floor of the outside platform. He'd thought going behind her made the most sense, so he could steady her if need be, but he saw now that the better choice would have been to go first, so he could watch her face. He was tempted to ask her to turn around so he could see her eyes, but if she was actually okay, in some kind of Zen zone, he didn't want to puncture it.

She was gripping the cable running up the front of her harness with both hands, but so were most of the people ahead of them. Hell, it had been his first impulse, too, as he stepped out. But he reached for her again, and the moment his hand made contact with her back, she let go of her cable with one hand and wrenched his arm around until she was holding his hand with a pretty damned impressive death grip. Now that they were out on the walkway that circled the tower, they were side by side, so he could see her face. Yep, she was scared shitless.

"Isn't it beautiful?" he said, looking out over the lake,

his own heart pounding. "No glass, no walls, just us and the sky." As cliché as it sounded, when you were up high like this, it gave you a kind of perspective on life. Let you rise above all the bullshit. Hence his affinity for towers and observation decks.

Jane was taking deep, shaky breaths, but at least she was breathing. After they shuffled partway around the deck, the guide began walking the participants, one by one, through an exercise where they turned their backs to the view and leaned back, putting their bodies at a sixty-degree angle relative to the tower, making them look a little like they were frozen in place while skydiving.

"Jane!" said the guide, a young outdoorsy dude who had somehow managed to learn everyone's names. "You're up!"

"You don't have to do this," Cam whispered. Indeed, there had been a woman ahead of them who had refused and was currently plastered against the inner wall of the tower hugging herself with her eyes closed. "We'll consider the dare fulfilled." Why he added that, he had no idea. Win or lose, she would never know what—or who—he did after they parted ways.

She shook her head as she turned and followed the guide's instructions to bend her knees and inch backward until her heels came to the edge. When she was crouched in the ready position, she looked up at him and echoed what he'd said to her downstairs.

"Sometimes you have to open your eyes and jump, right?"

And she fell backward and screamed.

God, she was gorgeous. She was laughing even as she screamed, and the super-saturated bright blue of the sky and lake behind her made everything about her pop. Her wide eyes were jades, her hair, much of which had escaped her ponytail and was flapping around in the wind, mahogany fire. How had he ever thought to describe any aspect of her as muddy? She was a goddess, frozen in place as she plummeted to Earth, like the universe had stopped her before she could fall all the way and sully herself by mixing with the mortals below.

"Your turn," the guide said to Cam.

He followed the guy's instructions, turned, and fell. It was his turn to laugh-scream. It was the fear of falling, the relief of not falling, the cold silent sky blanketing the city below them. It was Jane, turning her head to look at him with her mouth hanging open as she hooted and grinned. It was all those sensations swirling as if they were being churned together by the wind that whipped around them.

Unlike most of the others, Jane wasn't holding on to her cable. She had her arms spread wide, like in that stupid Titanic movie. So he mimicked her pose, spreading his arms, too.

Their fingertips brushed. Maybe it was the adrenaline of being out here, but he felt it as a spark, an extra jolt to his already hyper-alert system.

All too soon the guide had them bringing themselves back to standing on the platform.

His hand sought her back again almost of its own accord, though she clearly didn't need the reassurance anymore.

As if to hammer home the point, she looked over her shoulder at him, eyes shining, and said, "That. Was. Awesome."

———ᙅ———

Back in the regular old non-outdoor, non-glass-floored observation deck, Jane felt like a rock star. She couldn't stop exclaiming over the EdgeWalk. Yes, it had been terrifying, but underneath the fear there had also been a whole lot of other stuff. Exhilaration. Wonder at how strange and beautiful the world was from such a radically different vantage point. Then, utter astonishment when she was hit with a revelation that took her breath away: this was how Stephanie, the protagonist of the Clouded Cave series, felt when she first realized the cave was more than a cave.

They were in the Skypod, the tower's highest observation deck. It was higher than the EdgeWalk level, so when they looked down, they could see another group of people inching their way around the outdoor platform. She studied the commemorative photo they'd given her, of the group extended out over the void. It was hard to believe she had really done that. "You were right," she said, still buzzing from their adventure. "Sometimes you *do* have to open your eyes and jump." She'd been thinking about that phrase. Most people would have said *close* your eyes and jump. But not Cameron. He did things with his eyes open.

"I'm sorry, what did you say?" He cocked his head.

He'd been lost in his thoughts—they both had been—so she repeated herself. "Sometimes you have to open your eyes and—"

"No, the first part."

Huh? "What first part?"

"The part where you said, 'You were right.'"

She swatted him, but she couldn't help laughing as she did so. "Once. You were right *once*. Don't let it go to your head."

They were facing the city, looking across and down at the shiny high-rises of downtown Toronto. He really had seemed like he was somewhere else a moment ago, and now he was rubbing the back of his neck, like he was tense. She followed his gaze back out to the skyline. "How long have you been back in Canada?"

He answered without looking at her. "This is day three."

"It must be hard to adjust." When he didn't respond, she added, "I mean, look at this. It's probably like night and day from the landscape you're used to." Then she shook her head. "Well, of course it is. That was a stupid thing to say."

He turned then. "Not stupid. You're right. Coming back is...hard."

She opened her mouth to ask more, but he made a beckoning motion with his arm and said, "Let's check out the other side."

She followed him. "I read that on a clear day, you can see all the way to Niagara Falls from here."

They squinted in the appropriate direction but didn't see anything that looked like it was one of the modern wonders of the world.

"Niagara Falls," he said. "I've never been there. Always wanted to see it."

She sort of assumed that everyone who lived in Ontario had been to Niagara Falls, but of course Thunder Bay, where he'd grown up, was a lot farther away. And since the family had been poor, he probably hadn't gone on trips there as a kid like she had.

"It's really something," she said. "The falls, I mean. The rest of it is cheese ball central."

"What do you mean?"

"Well, the town that's developed around the falls is a total tourist trap. Casinos, tacky souvenirs, carnivals, that sort of thing. They even have an observation tower, but it's like the shrimpy little sibling of this one." She patted the railing. "And I don't think they let you dangle off the side."

"Let's do it."

She blinked. "Excuse me?"

"It's not that far from Toronto, is it? What, maybe an hour and a half?"

"Yessss," she said warily.

"Remember how you just said I was right?"

"Once. You were right about one thing."

"Maybe two?"

"I'm not taking you to Niagara Falls."

"No, *I'm* taking *you* to Niagara Falls," he said, like the decision had already been made. "Tomorrow."

"I can't. I have...stuff to do."

"Beyond babysitting me?"

"I'm not babysitting you," she lied—for the zillionth time.

"What stuff do you have to do?"

"I have my costume for Comicon to finish."

"I have no idea what you're talking about, but I'm sure it can wait one day."

She shook the photo she was clutching. "I have to plaster this all over my author social media accounts." Which would take all of five minutes. But oh! "I have wedding stuff." The universal excuse. She pulled out her phone and opened the calendar app. Crap, she actually *did* have wedding stuff. Calligraphy lessons, to be precise. Lessons Elise had enrolled them in because it would be "fun." Not because the convenient side effect of the lessons would be a gaggle of bridesmaids armed with the skills necessary to produce three hundred hand-lettered place cards.

Ding.

At that very moment, a new calendar invite popped up.

"Papermaking?" she read aloud. What in heaven's name?

Then a text from Elise arrived. She swiped over to it.

Hey squad! I added a papermaking session to the calligraphy class tomorrow. When you see these artisanal place cards we can make, you will DIE. I need you all to bring egg cartons though, and any paper towel or toilet paper rolls you might have. We need fibrous things to get the proper vintage look. And one of you needs to pick up some white felt. Okay? C U soon! Xo

Another text arrived, this one from Gia,

White felt. On it.

Jane looked up. "Pick me up at eight tomorrow morning. I'll text you my address."

Chapter Six

$\mathcal{N}$ormally, Jane was a second-guesser. It wasn't like her to do something as impulsive as a random weekday day trip to Niagara Falls. And if she did decide to do something so out of character, she usually spent the hours following agonizing over it.

That was not happening in this case.

"See?" said Elise, holding up a small square of ragged-edge beige paper so all the girls clustered around the table could see it. "This sample is a little too mushroomy, but that's what the white felt is for. They say that we can get it to look more solidly ecru if we add more white felt. You should see it. It's really something. It's like this big blender you put all this stuff into to make the pulp that will form the paper." She sighed happily and took a sip of her wine. "I was going to use regular recycled cardstock, but I love that this option is even more environmentally friendly."

"But not really," said Wendy, setting her empty pint

glass on the bar table with a *thunk*. "I mean, if you have to *buy* felt for it—"

"Already bought!" Gia chirped, shooting Wendy a quelling look and producing said felt from her handbag. Gia always carried one of those giant, ugly designer bags that cost as much as a small sedan. She placed a square of felt in front of Elise. "Now, I made a little bit of an executive decision here. This is a one hundred percent wool felt from Mongolia." Elise cooed as she ran her hand over it. "I thought that would be a better option than synthetic. I'm friends with one of Karl's drapers, and he hooked me up with a local source."

"Lagerfeld?" Elise asked, even though they all knew that if Gia was referencing a Karl, it could only be Lagerfeld.

Gia nodded.

"OMG, Ladybug, you are the *best*." "Ladybug" was Elise's pet name for Gia, dating back to their university years, and it only came out when Elise was extra emotional. Elise looked around at all of them, getting a little teary, and placed her hand over her heart. "You're *all* the best. Honestly, I love how everyone is coming together around this wedding."

"I'm so sorry I'm going to have to miss the big papermaking and calligraphy session tomorrow," Jane said, coughing to cover the yelp that bubbled up her throat when Wendy stamped on her foot under the table.

"I *know*," Elise said, turning and grabbing Jane's hand. "But that's what I mean. Everyone on this team is really contributing, leveraging her strengths for the common good." She brought her hand back to her heart, but took Jane's along, too. "And you especially, Jane. You have the hardest job of them all. Thank you."

"Oh, he's not that bad," Jane said.

"No, he *is* that bad," Elise said emphatically. "He's hardly spoken to Jay, and you should have seen how he smirked at me when we were introduced this afternoon. But I knew you would be able to manage him. You just...you have such an air of responsibility about you. You're my most levelheaded friend."

"Uh, thanks?" Jane ventured, tugging a little to try to get her hand back.

"Let's do shots!" Elise clapped her hands together, which had the side effect of releasing Jane's hand. "On me! I'll run and get them at the bar. Be right back, squad!"

Jane had trained herself not to wince when Elise referred to them as a "squad," but she still bristled internally. If they weren't careful, Elise would decide it would be "fun" to re-enact Taylor Swift's *Bad Blood* video as part of the wedding festivities. And with Gia in town, they even had their own model.

The moment Elise was out of sight, Jane and her fellow bridesmaids slumped back in their chairs.

"Are you going to finish that?" Gia asked, eyeing Jane's untouched wine. She hadn't been planning to drink but hadn't wanted Elise to get on her case for being a party pooper.

"Be my guest," Jane said, but before Gia could grab the glass, Wendy swooped in, stole it, and chugged it.

Then she slammed it down next to her already-empty beer glass and said, "*Mongolian wool*, Gia?"

"Actually..." Gia leaned forward and gestured for them to come in close. "It's from Dollarama." Then she rummaged around in her fifty-gallon handbag and produced a crinkly plastic bag, presumably holding the rest of the felt, with the chain store's logo on it.

"Oh my God, I freaking love you," said Wendy, throwing

her head back and performing the signature cackle that always made Jane smile.

"Look who I found at the bar!"

They all started a little—they'd been so huddled in on each other that they hadn't noticed Elise's return. Gia shoved the dollar store bag into her purse with such force that she started to slip off her chair. The only thing stopping her was the insertion of a large, masculine arm breaking her fall.

Jane was next to Gia, so her back was to the newcomers, but she didn't need to see them to recognize those tattoos. The idea that she had woken this morning with that arm draped around her made her face heat.

"This must be the famous brother!" said Gia, eyes twinkling up at her rescuer.

Elise, looking less thrilled than she had a moment ago when they were talking artisanal paper, made introductions.

Jay was carrying a tray of tequila shooters and lime wedges, which he proceeded to pass around. Jane was about to decline when he set a different one in front of her.

"Cam said you'd want this instead."

It was a B-52. She glanced at Cameron, who winked at her. Wow, that was…thoughtful. Jane was, frankly, impressed that Cameron was here with his brother. It meant he was keeping to his word about the no hookups thing, honoring the terms of their bet.

He plopped down on Gia's other side and leaned over like he was intending to speak only to Gia, but Jane, since she was paying such close attention, heard what he said. "Well, I don't know about famous." Was it just her or had he turned up that slow, not-quite-southern drawl?

Also: crap! She had been fixated, for some reason, on the idea of him accidentally picking up one of Jay's friends or neighbors and triggering an unexpected chain of fallout that led to disaster.

She hadn't even thought about Gia.

Gia was gorgeous. Jaw-droppingly gorgeous. Jane was used to it—it was like she'd had exposure therapy or something—but when you were meeting Gia for the first time? Well, just hope you weren't simultaneously operating any heavy machinery.

Also, Gia was...how to say it?

A little...slutty.

In the best possible, sex-positive, non-shaming, feminist sense of the word.

But still. If Jane was in a five-years-and-counting dry spell, Gia was more than making up for it. Jane could only hope that Gia's sense of loyalty to Elise—dollar store felt aside, she was taking her maid of honor duties seriously—would mean she would consider Cameron off limits.

Gia scooched her chair closer to Cameron. "So you're just back from Iraq?"

Apparently not.

"I am indeed," he answered.

"And what's up next, Cam?" asked Jay, who, like Jane, must have been listening in on the conversation. "I don't think you ever said."

On the surface of things, it was a benign question. Jay's eyebrows were slightly raised, as if he'd merely asked about how his brother's day had been. Aside from those elevated eyebrows, Jay was his characteristic cool and unflappable self. Still, though, there was an unmistakable undercurrent of...something there.

"Not sure yet," Cameron said. A muscle in his jaw twitched.

"And how's Christie?" Jay asked, so immediately on the

heels of Cameron's answer that it brought to mind a lawyer badgering an opposing witness in court.

"Who's Christie?" Elise asked.

"Christie is Cameron's girlfriend," Jay said, not taking his eyes off his brother.

What? Hadn't Cameron proclaimed himself "single, young, and back on Canadian soil" just yesterday?

"Christie is my *ex*-girlfriend," Cameron answered, staring back at Jay.

Jane found herself strangely relieved. But only because she was glad Cameron wouldn't be cheating on his girlfriend when he finally got around to checking "hook up with some randoms" off his return-to-civilian-life list.

She was also *very* curious about this Christie person.

"And how long did you wait after you got back to downgrade her status?" Jay asked.

Elise opened her mouth like she was going to say something. But then she closed it. Jane didn't blame her. It was hard to know how, or whether, to intervene in this brotherly "discussion." But she did kind of want it to go on, if only so she could learn what kind of woman Cameron had been with.

But Cameron wasn't having it. He stood and said, "I'll see you tomorrow, Jane." Then he walked away, leaving everyone else staring at the spot where he used to be.

Elise sat back down with Jane and the other girls and stage-whispered, "See? He *is* that bad."

⎯⎯ᴄ⎯

"What the hell is your problem?" Jay asked as he returned to the condo a couple hours later.

Cam was watching TV. Well, okay, he was half-watching TV while reading reviews on Amazon of Jane's Cloudless Cave books, but whatever. "I might ask the same of you, dear brother."

"When did you dump Christie?"

It never occurred to his brother that perhaps Cam was the dumpee. But Cam wasn't about to correct him. "I'm not sure that's any of your business." Because it really wasn't.

"You stay with her while you're overseas and then dump her the minute you're back?"

Yeah, that was about enough of this conversation. If Jay hadn't gotten that message when Cam left the bar earlier, he would just have to keep delivering it. He stood, mock-saluted his brother, and headed for the hallway.

"Have you called Mom yet?" Jay called after him.

Cam sighed and turned around. "Mom doesn't want to hear from me. I'll see her soon enough."

"Are you kidding me? She's been texting me incessantly, asking about you."

That gave Cameron pause. When he was deployed, his mother had sent him cards on Christmas and his birthday, but that was the extent of it. Not that he blamed her. His fuck-ups had caused her disappointment after disappointment. *He* had caused her disappointment after disappointment. Because he was pretty much indistinguishable from his fuck-ups at this point.

He started to turn back toward the hallway when Jay said, "You forgot your phone." He strode over to where Cam had been sitting and picked up the phone—and of course saw the pile of papers underneath it that Cam had been perusing earlier. Aww, *shit*. He tilted his head to the ceiling. He so didn't want to have this conversation right now.

"Are these...financial aid forms?" Jay started pawing through the pile of what was indeed info on financial aid at a couple local universities. Cam had been looking into attending Lakehead University in Thunder Bay after his last deployment—which of course hadn't been scheduled to end as early as it had. You couldn't become an officer in the Canadian Forces without a university degree. He hadn't told anyone about his plan.

When his military career came crashing to a premature halt, he'd assumed that was the end of that. But today, after hanging off the CN Tower with Jane, and hearing her echo back his "Sometimes you have to open your eyes and jump" advice, he'd had a moment of bravado and thought, *what the hell? Why not do it anyway?* Since Thunder Bay was no longer home, he had gathered info from the three universities in Toronto. Just to look. Just out of curiosity.

Of course, he had been deluded. Besides the tuition problem—yes, he had money saved, but the cost of living in Toronto was astronomical compared to what it would have been sharing an apartment in Thunder Bay. Anyway, what had he thought? That he could show up on a regular campus, a big twenty-seven-year-old punk with a GED, and fit in with the freshman class who all had dreams and aspirations bigger than his? He'd been thinking he'd study history, but he already knew the most important lesson, didn't he?

History always repeats itself.

Jay finished ruffling through the papers and lifted a surprised gaze to Cam. "Are you thinking of…going to university?" The incredulity in his tone told Cam everything he needed to know.

"No," he said. "No, I am not." He turned and headed for the guest room. Time for bed. Alone. Thanks to Jane. He stripped and climbed in, catching a whiff of her lingering scent as he pulled the covers over himself. He hadn't noticed her wearing any overt scent before. In fact, hadn't he been thinking that first day at the bar that she smelled like Ivory soap? But somehow, now there was this other smell, and he recognized it as hers. It was...bubble gum? No. He turned his face to the pillow she'd slept on and inhaled deeply. Watermelon?

Whatever the fuck it was, it tented his boxers. Which wasn't saying much because pretty much everything tented his boxers these days. That was what five months of celibacy followed by sudden immersion in civilian life did. In the field, he tamped that shit down. Of course, there were women around. His best buddy over the past two deployments had been a woman. And Rebecca Mannerly had been, objectively, an attractive woman. But those types of feelings and the brotherhood—for lack of a better word—didn't mix. For him anyway.

He'd known that Becky took a lot of shit from a lot of guys, including their commanding officer. Captain Biggs had been on her for months before that night. Nothing you could ever really put your finger on, but he'd needle her in ways he wouldn't any of the guys. Which wasn't a surprise, really, because Biggs was a grade-A dick. Cam's CO on his first tour had been a stand-up, honorable guy. He'd been the reason Cam started entertaining the idea of university as a path to becoming an officer. But Biggs? He fulfilled every stereotype of the hyper-masculine soldier who picked on those he perceived as weaker and got off on the power he held. Cam and Becky were part of a group of reservists who'd been called up to fill some gaps in Biggs's reg force team, and as such they were used to being ribbed about their second-class status. But Biggs's behavior went way beyond that.

He could still feel his fist connecting with that asshole's jaw. He wanted to regret his actions that day. He did regret them, in the sense that they'd destroyed his career. He *definitely* regretted that after he'd landed the punch that had dislodged Biggs and summoned the others, he didn't stop.

Cam followed his own code of honor. One that dictated that you put your dick on ice when actively deployed. One that dictated that you protect someone—man or woman—when they're being hurt. Ironic that it had turned out to be his downfall.

The flip side of that code of honor, of that long period of celibacy combined with stress, meant that when he came back, he was ready to go. It was like someone turned on the TV with the volume at full blast in what had been an utterly silent house. And, after his first deployment, Christie had been happy to see him. Or so he'd thought. She'd been happy to fall into bed with him anyway.

He wasn't sure what the hell had happened to him this time. He should have been able to get laid ten times over by now. The tiny waitress. Sherry of the too much perfume. That Gia girl in the bar earlier. And those were without him even *trying*.

But no. Instead of ticking that item—the most important one—off his return-to-civilian-life list, he was in bed alone with his hand in his pants and a head full of watermelon.

Chapter Seven

*W*hen Jane got into Cameron's car, it took her all of five minutes to ask, "So what did you do last night after you left the bar?"

I stuck my nose in your pillow and jerked off to this weird watermelon smell that reminded me of you.

But of course he couldn't say that. So he settled for, "I presume that what you're actually asking me is, 'Did you sleep with any randoms last night?'" The way she called potential hookups "randoms" was pretty funny.

"I am not!" she protested. She shifted her gaze out the window. "I probably shouldn't be so hard on you. I didn't know you'd just gotten out of a long-term relationship. I think sleeping with randoms is probably pretty normal when you're on the rebound?"

The way she'd phrased it as a question suggested she didn't have firsthand knowledge of post-relationship slutty phases. Damn if he wasn't happy about that. He didn't like the idea of Jane sleeping around. It took a while to get to know Jane. To *appreciate* her. He didn't trust "randoms," to use her term, to do a decent job of it. He didn't mean it in a sexist, double-standard sort of way—it wasn't like he thought Jane needed to remain "pure" or anything. But she deserved someone better than your average bar-trolling, right-swiping Neanderthal. Someone with his shit together who could be all in.

She still wasn't looking at him, but there was alertness about her that suggested she was waiting for him to speak.

"Well, I have no idea about 'normal,' but my ex and I had been together for three years. I'm not really looking for anything serious right now." *Or ever again.* "So I admit I was kind of looking forward to a little wild oat sowing once I got to town. *But*," he added before she could say anything, "I also enjoy betting—even though you kicked my ass with that CN Tower one."

"Damn right I did."

He grinned, checking over his shoulder before merging onto the highway that would take them to Niagara Falls. "So all that's to say, Ms. Denning, that thanks to you, my virtue remains intact."

She finally looked at him, laughter in her eyes.

"I'm a man of my word," he added, though he wasn't sure why. It just seemed important, at that moment, that she know that.

"I know," she said quietly.

He sighed, a big, content exhale that took with it some of the tension of the past few days—hell, of the past few *years*. It was another gorgeous day. Sure, he wasn't doing very well with his return-to-civilian-life list—hell, steak, beer, and TV were pretty much the only items he'd managed to tick off. He pissed off his brother just by being alive. And he had no fucking clue what he was going to do with the rest of his life. But for one minute, none of it mattered. He was in a sweet car with a pretty amazing girl, and there was nothing but blue skies ahead of them.

"Okay, I did some research," Jane said, dumping a stack of paper out of her purse.

He chuckled. "Of course you did."

Ignoring him, she said, "There's a lot to do in Niagara Falls, so I figured we'd want to maximize our time there. So I printed out some stuff to help us decide."

"We could grab a hotel room if we feel like we've not done all we want to do by the end of today."

The withering glance she shot him followed by the raising of one eyebrow told him what she thought of that idea. And, uncharacteristically, he hadn't even meant it like that.

"How do you do that?" he asked, reminding himself that "I was watching my passenger raise one eyebrow" wasn't going to get him out of a ticket when he got pulled over for erratic driving.

The eyebrow plummeted, joining its twin in a furrow. "Do what?"

"Raise only one eyebrow at a time."

The eyebrow shot back up, and he laughed. "And it's always the left one."

And there came the furrow. It was like watching her eyebrow bungee jump.

"It is?"

Eyes on the road. "Yes, so what do you do when you're not writing portal fiction or babysitting me?" he asked.

"Not much, actually," she said. "I'm kind of boring."

He noticed she hadn't fallen back on her usual protest

that she wasn't babysitting him. "What about this costume ball thing?"

"Not a ball! Comicon."

"Huh?"

"It's a convention for people who like comics and sci-fi and stuff. And people dress up like their favorite characters." She laughed. "It's a nerd convention, basically."

"And who do you dress up as?"

"Do you remember the show *Xena: Warrior Princess*? Probably not—you're probably too young. And/or too cool."

"Hell, yes, I know that show. I used to watch it in syndication." He'd loved the mixture of goofiness with, as dumb as it sounded, Xena's quest to atone for her past sins. There was something about the noble warrior that had always appealed to him. Of course, there was also the part where his thirteen-year-old self had sexually imprinted on Xena. Not really, but he did appreciate how well Lucy Lawless could rock a leather corset.

Jane's jaw fell open. She was surprised he knew the show.

"Hey," he protested. "Xena and Gabrielle run around scantily clad and kick ass. What's not to like?"

She laughed. "Yeah, well, Comicon is this weekend. I'm going Sunday, which totally conflicts with the wedding, but Elise knows I've been planning this since last year. I went as Gabrielle last year, which is the obvious move for me because my hair has a red tinge, but Xena is my brass ring, and I've been working on the costume for months, so Elise doesn't dare say anything." She grinned like she was particularly pleased with herself. "So barring total wedding apocalypse, I will be transforming into Xena this coming weekend. I'm all ready to go except for the chakram." She eyed him. "You know what a chakram is?"

It felt like some sort of test. "It's that circular weapon thingy, right?" She beamed. Hell, that might have been the only test he'd ever passed on his first go. "This all sounds great." It really did. Goofy, and definitely nerdy, but great. "But I don't see what the scheduling problem is. The wedding isn't until the weekend after this coming one, so it doesn't conflict, does it?"

"For mere mortals? No. But a bridesmaid is not a mere mortal. Alas. A bridesmaid must bend space and time so as to make herself continuously available at the whim of her friend the bride. I have *duties* this coming weekend."

Right. Because why else was she here if not because she was doing her bridesmaid duty, looking after the wild-card brother who couldn't be trusted?

"Well," he said, glancing at the pile of papers in her lap, "I'm up for something totally low-brow first." He'd had enough of playing tourist in his brother's refined life. Swanky condos and interior designer fiancées and ten-dollar pints of beer were wearing on him. Apparently you could take Jay out of the trailer park, but not so much Cam.

"Oh, that should be easy," she said, reading from one of her printouts. "Dinosaur mini-golf, wax museum, or, oh! If you're not into dinosaurs, there's *wizard* mini-golf! Also, Ripley's Believe It Or Not, Nightmares Fear Factory, some kind of indoor roller—"

"Nightmares Fear Factory."

She whipped her head around to look at him. "I'm not going into a haunted house, particularly not one named Nightmares Fear Factory."

"Why not?"

"Because I have an overactive imagination. Haunted houses scare the crap out of me. Horror movies, too—all that stuff."

Wow. He had expected her to give a speech about how stupid and juvenile haunted houses were, not to admit that she was just plain afraid. "Even though you know it's all fake?"

"Does that really make a difference in the moment?" she asked.

"Well, I worked on a haunted hayride when I was in high school. So I think the illusion is ruined for me."

"Really?" She seemed out-of-proportion delighted by his seasonal teenage job. "What did you do?"

"Well, I started in the support crew—mixing up vats of cooked spaghetti and red food coloring for example."

"What?"

"Yeah, you have no idea what goes on behind the scenes to make the experience seem authentic."

"Kind of like being a bridesmaid."

He barked a laugh. "Yeah, well, I worked my way up over the years. My last year there I was Freddy Krueger, complete with the long fingernail-knives."

"Oooh! I'm impressed. And then what? You graduated high school and that was the end of your haunted hayride career?"

"Nope," Cam said. "Never graduated. Just moved on." He had to force himself to let up on the gas pedal. They were going too fast, even for him. "Got my high school equivalency later, though," he added, seized with the desire that she not think him any dumber than necessary. He cleared his throat. "Anyway, I can't believe you'd do EdgeWalk one day and then let a dinky little tourist trap haunted house get the best of you. Come on. I have a professional interest."

"No way. No. Way."

"I dare you. Let's make another bet."

"Hmm." He glanced over. She had her head tilted and

one finger pressed against a cheek in an exaggerated "I'm thinking" posture. "What do I get if I do it?"

"I'll buy you dinner."

She pretended to think about it for a few more seconds. "No. Well, yes, you can buy me dinner, but you know what I really want."

"What are you? A professional cock-blocker?" he said, laughing, knowing he was going to agree.

"Not usually!" she said. "But I'm deriving a strange sort of enjoyment from it in your particular case."

The fucked-up thing was that he sort of was, too. He glanced at her again, then forced his eyes back to the road. But the image of her stayed with him, burned into his retinas. She'd worn her hair down today. She looked different without the ponytail. Softer. And her eyes had been twinkling. He liked that he could make her eyes do that.

So he stuck his hand over the center console for her to shake and said, "You got yourself a deal. You do the haunted house, and I stay pure another twenty-four hours."

An hour later, they were lined up outside Nightmares Fear Factory, which Jane, who had studied the attraction's Wikipedia page while he found parking, informed Cameron was the oldest continuously operating haunted house in North America.

"This is a former coffin factory, too," she said, reading on her phone as they approached the entrance. "Its owner was supposedly killed when a stack of coffins fell on him. Now *that* is a nice touch." It appealed to the storyteller in her.

A sullen teenage employee explained the rules to them.

You could shout "nightmares" if you were panicking and needed out, and "something" would come get you. But from then on, your name would be forever entered on the house's "chicken list," which he reported was one hundred and thirty thousand names long and counting.

"I want you to know that I have absolutely no problem with my name going on that list," she told Cameron. "They need a better deterrent than that." She was joking to cover her fear. But actually the chicken list *was* kind of a deterrent. Normally, she wouldn't care about appearing on it, but for some reason she wanted to show Cameron that she wasn't afraid of silly things. For heaven's sake, the man had been a soldier in a combat zone, and she couldn't face a little fake gore?

"But what if you bail and once you're gone, I strike up a conversation with a nice young lady?" Cameron said. It should have been a gross threat, but he was smiling as he said it. He was trying to make her feel better by making her laugh.

"I bet you've never picked up a girl in a haunted house before," she said, using the banter to distract herself. But suddenly, she was thinking of some girl shrieking and grabbing Cameron's hand for "comfort."

"Well, there was this barn portion of the haunted hayride, and it was really, really dark in that barn..."

Hmm. Elise said Cameron had burned down a barn in his youth...There was also the rumor that he'd gotten a girl pregnant. She really wanted to know about that one. She could see how young Cameron, if he was as handsome and wild as the current incarnation, would be a total heartbreaker.

A low, ghostly moan came from the speakers that pumped "ambience" onto the sidewalk, and Jane winced.

She tried to think of a teenaged Cameron mixing red food coloring into spaghetti. It was all fake, she reminded herself. Fake, fake, fake.

"You ready?" he asked.

She gulped, but... what the hell. "Ready."

They stepped into the house and were plunged into total darkness.

Her heart rate quadrupled, and she grabbed for his hand. She tried to tell herself that nothing had even happened yet.

Follow the red dots of light. That's what the kid out front had said. The faster they did that, the faster they'd be done. She searched the floor, and when she located them, she gave Cameron a shove.

"We really don't have to do this," he whispered.

"Go!" she said, and shoved harder.

—☙

It wasn't actually so bad once she got the hang of it.

And by "got the hang of it," Jane meant, "figured out that if she plastered herself to Cameron's back and closed her eyes, she could move through the haunted house without actually having to see anything."

She could deal with the sounds, it turned out. They were mostly people screaming, chain saws, eerie moans, that kind of thing. They were scary sounds, yes, but without the accompanying visuals, she could more easily classify them as generic haunted house noises.

"Go faster," she kept whispering to Cameron. To his credit, he was obeying her. He had dropped the teasing and wasn't trying to force her to experience any of it.

So she was getting into kind of a... well, not a groove, but they were moving forward, and her coping mechanisms were working. She was even starting to feel kind of smug that she'd managed to game the whole system. Suck it, Nightmares Fear Factory.

There was also the part where being plastered to Cameron wasn't the worst thing in the world. Surprisingly. His back was solid underneath her, hard where she was soft, and his muscles bunched and shifted as he moved.

Then they started touching her, and that was the end of her little swoony moment.

It was a hand on her back first. A light touch—there and then gone. But she screamed and hugged Cameron even as she tried to shake the hand off. She had been holding on to the back of his T-shirt, gripping handfuls of the fabric and resting her forehead on his back to hide her eyes as they shuffled forward, but now she wrapped her arms around him like she was riding behind him on a motorcycle.

"It's not real," he said as he continued to press onward. "None of it is real."

She nodded against the muscles of his back, unable to speak.

"Do you want to say the password and get out of here?"

"No!" She feared what saying the password would bring. The kid outside had said, "something" would come for them. Would that "something" separate them? Because she would rather be here with Cameron, where she didn't have to open her eyes, than on her own for even a minute.

But then something latched on to her leg. Something low, on the ground. And it *grabbed*. Took hold and pulled so hard that she lost her grip on Cameron as he continued to move forward. She stumbled, trying to catch up to him, but she couldn't get her leg free.

"Jane!" Cameron called, but then there was something else, right up against her face, whispering low and gruff in her ear, "Jaannnnneee." Whatever it was ran a finger down the back of her neck.

She was beyond screaming. She started to cry.

But then there was Cameron. The thing that had been terrorizing her had been touching her lightly, after that initial sharp grab anyway, running a finger almost imperceptibly along her skin. But now Cameron's hands were on her, and his touch was the opposite of light. A strong hand grasped hers and pulled her toward him, away from the thing behind her. He pulled her tight to his chest and wrapped his arms around her. She tried to think about the many colors of his tattooed arm, shielding her from the darkness.

"Are you okay?" he asked, his tone urgent, almost like he was scared, too.

"No," she tried to whisper, but nothing came out. She was ready to shout the password, to do whatever it took to get out, but she couldn't seem to make her voice work. She shook her head violently back and forth against his chest.

"I've got you," he said, and he scooped her into his arms. She spared a passing thought for what a baby she was, and also for how heavy she must be, but then he started to move, and all she could do was bury her head against his chest and try to stop crying.

⟋

Well, shit. That had been a mistake. Cam had thought it would be like the CN Tower. Jane would be spooked, but then she'd conquer her fear and surprise herself by having fun.

But instead of the exhilarated, grinning goddess in the sky that she'd been yesterday, what he had now was an embarrassed, shaking, mortal human woman.

He also hadn't considered the consequences for *him*. He'd been thinking of the whole haunted house thing in the context of his old job in Thunder Bay. He *hadn't* been thinking about what it would feel like when someone hiding in the dark tried to snatch Jane away from him.

His heart still beating out of control, he set her on her feet once they were out, and she blinked against the light. She had tear tracks on her cheeks—thin paths where her makeup had been washed away—and her mascara was smudged.

It was like a knife to the heart. "Oh, sweetheart," he said. "I'm sorry."

"*I'm* sorry," she said, rolling her eyes at herself. "That was...a lot worse than I thought it was going to be."

"So I'm guessing you don't want the souvenir photo?" he asked, hoping some humor would calm them both. There had been a covert picture taken of every group at a certain spot in the house, and they were being projected on a screen as people left. Most of the images were actually pretty funny. Everyone was terrified, but seeing their expressions outside of the context of the house was amusing. Most people were laughing at theirs, and some were stepping up to buy copies.

"Whoa!" she exclaimed when their picture came up. "You're not scared at all."

He followed her gaze to the image. He was staring straight ahead, almost like he was looking at the camera, though he hadn't known it was there. She was wrong, though. He had been scared, but he'd hidden it well. He was holding her in his arms, and she was snuggled against his chest. The only part of her head that was visible was the curtain of auburn hair that hung down to her shoulders. He had one hand pressed against the back of her head. He had been encouraging her with the gesture to hide her face from the horrors, to use his chest as a shield. His other arm was hooked beneath her bent knees, and his hand rested on her outer thigh, fingers splayed wide as if they wanted to cover as much of her as possible.

It was strange to look at himself from the outside, to see himself standing tall and unmoved, using his body to safeguard Jane even though he'd been as freaked out as everyone else.

He looked . . . strong.

Steady. Dependable.

Not at all like the kind of person who had screwed up his life, leaving broken hearts, unmet expectations, and juvenile criminal records in his wake.

"Would you like to purchase this, miss?" said a girl working behind the counter. She held out a print of the image that had been projected on the wall.

"No!" Jane smiled. It was good to see her smile, to know there wasn't any lasting damage. "I don't think I need to be in possession of permanent photographic evidence of my epic cowardice." She heaved a sigh and looked up at him. "Can we go to the falls next? I think I need a dose of the wonders of nature. It'll be an antidote to all this."

"Sure thing. I'm going to hit the restroom first. Why don't you get out of here, and I'll meet you outside in a couple minutes?"

She nodded and headed for the exit.

And once she was out of sight, he bought the damn picture.

Chapter Eight

God, she was an idiot. By the time Cameron reappeared outside in the summer sun, Jane had already cycled through sheepishness, embarrassment, and had moved on to self-disgust. The fake stone façade of the haunted house was so obviously not real. And the building was attached to a bar and grill advertising beer specials. There was a family with two toddlers sitting on the patio, for heaven's sake.

"I'm sorry," she said again when he reached her side. It felt lame to apologize, but it felt lamer not to.

"Hey, don't worry about it," he said, blinding her with that ultra-white smile. "I'm the one who's sorry. We shouldn't have done that."

"I mean, you've probably seen real horrors," she said, feeling the absurd need to embroider her apology.

He merely shrugged. But he didn't deny it.

"You must think I'm such a chicken," she went on.

"Nah. That was pretty scary."

"Worse than the haunted hayride?"

He laughed. "*Way* worse than the haunted hayride."

"And, God, I didn't even *see* any of it. But the loud noises that you can't identify, the fear that people are after you." She shuddered. He was looking at her with a funny expression she couldn't decode. Was he...sad? She thought back to her previous, offhand comment about him having seen real horrors. Oh God. She'd been so focused on her own fear. But was it possible that he'd been affected by the haunted house, too? "Are you...okay?" she ventured. "Because what I just said? Loud noises and people after you? Now that I think about it, I could've been describing a war zone."

He gave her a small smile, but it seemed like a resigned one. "I didn't really think. It usually doesn't work like that. At least not for me."

"What doesn't work like that? War zones?"

"PTSD."

Holy crap. She forced herself to keep her tone even as she asked, "You have post-traumatic stress disorder?"

He shrugged. "So they say."

Jane opened her mouth, then shut it. Because what did you say? *I'm sorry you witnessed things so awful they gave you PTSD? Thank you for serving?* She wanted to say both those things. She *meant* both those things. But she feared they would only come out sounding like platitudes, and Cameron was not the kind of man who tolerated platitudes.

"Dangling off the CN Tower was fun," he said, clearly trying to change the subject, "but not so much Nightmares Fear Factory, huh? Who knew?" He shrugged. "But that's how it goes. You take a risk; it doesn't always work out."

Jane realized with a start that she pretty much never took risks. Not anymore, anyway.

She didn't have time to ponder this revelation, because

Cameron held out an arm, like they were preparing to walk down the aisle at a wedding. "Come on, Xena, we've got a big-ass waterfall to see."

—❧—

"This is more my speed," Jane said as they donned translucent yellow rain slickers and lined up for Journey Behind the Falls. Normally, she'd be afraid she would look like an idiot in the getup—like a plus-size rubber duckie. But she found herself not caring, possibly because only an hour ago she'd been crying in Cameron's arms, so comparatively speaking, a little plastic raincoat-induced humiliation was nothing.

They'd walked down to the falls from the haunted house. It had been probably fifteen years since Jane had been to Niagara, and she'd forgotten how stunning the main attraction was. Cameron must have shared her awe because he'd maneuvered them through the crowds to a spot right against the railing and stared silently at the roaring water for a long time. Longer than he realized, she suspected.

Why was it such a surprise to find out that Cameron had PTSD? It must be fairly common among military people. It was just that she thought of him as invincible. He stalked through houses of horror and hung off buildings without batting an eyelash. He was the consummate daredevil, but with a protective streak. She shivered.

Now that she was out of the haunted house, she could think back to the experience separate from the fear that had been attached to it in the moment. The way he'd scooped her up like it was nothing. Feeling those strong arms around her. Seeing them, later, in the picture. She'd laughed off the notion of buying the picture, but a part of her had wanted it.

It was stupid really, but when was the last time someone had taken care of her like that?

Never.

That was the horrible truth. Her parents had meant well, but her father's addiction had been all-consuming for both him and Mom. Her brother had stepped in after their father died. He had, for all intents and purposes, become her parent. The only reason she was where she was in life was because of her brother, and she loved him like crazy for it.

But when was the last time someone had taken care of her without being *obliged* to?

It wasn't lost on her that she'd used the word *invincible* earlier, in her mind, in reference to Cameron. She used to think of him as cocky. What was the difference between cocky and invincible? The writer in her pondered the question. Maybe invincibility was only justified cockiness.

They boarded an elevator that would take them down through the bedrock behind the falls. Yesterday, she'd been dangling off the highest building in Canada. Now she was headed down behind one of the largest waterfalls in the world. What had happened to her? Cameron held the door for her to enter before him. It seemed impossible that only three days ago, she hadn't known him.

And why did he look so good in his poncho? It wasn't fair. If she was a plus-size rubber duckie, he, with those brilliant blue-green eyes, was a movie star. A movie star in an ugly rain poncho, but still. There was no rational reason to be attracted to Cameron MacKinnon, but the more time she spent with him, the stronger his pull was.

The elevator disgorged them into a series of tunnels and lookouts they were free to explore. The first lookout was a little to the side of the falls, about halfway up. It was crowded, but as he had at ground level, Cameron made a beeline for a spot on the railing, where they would have an unobstructed view. It was misty this close to the falls, and the pavement beneath them was wet, so he took her hand. He'd used the hand from the tattooed arm, and she looked down at the swirling, mostly green foliage that came all the way down to his wrist. His hand engulfed hers, and it was warm, despite the cool, wet air swirling around them.

When they reached the edge, he propped his elbows on the rail, but he didn't drop her hand. It had the effect of tucking her close to his side. He stared at the falls with the same intense concentration as before. The water was louder here, more forceful, and it demanded one's attention.

After a few minutes, he said, "My shrink used to make me do this meditation exercise. I was supposed to visualize a waterfall. It was supposed to wash away pent-up...shit."

It had seemed initially like he was going to say something more specific than "shit," but she didn't press him, asking instead, "Did it work?"

"Nope." He dipped his head at the falls. "But, hell, I'm thinking now that maybe I was imagining the wrong kind of waterfall. I was thinking more Snow-White-cavorts-in-the-woods-and-stumbles-across-a-gentle-woodland-waterfall kind of scenario."

"But this isn't that," Jane said, nodding her understanding even though he wasn't looking at her. "This is pure, unstoppable power." It was easy to get distracted by the hordes of tourists, by the cheesy haunted houses and other schlock in town, but truly, the raw force of the falls was something to behold.

It was his turn to nod. "Exactly."

"Maybe you haven't been doing it long enough?" Probably nothing she could say would be helpful, but she found herself wanting to try. "You've only been back, what? A week?"

His attention was back on the falls. "Nah, the, ah...PTSD is from my first tour—from Afghanistan. So I've been doing this visualization shit for almost two years now."

"Oh. I see." She didn't miss that he had trouble even saying "PTSD."

"I don't have it so bad, really. Not as bad as some guys. No nightmares or flashbacks."

"So what...happens?"

"I have trouble when I'm in settings that remind me of the...incident."

She wanted more than anything to ask about "the incident," but she was counting herself lucky that he was saying as much as he was. She had a feeling he didn't do that, and he hardly knew her.

"But usually the landscapes have to be the same," he went on. "Wide open spaces, sunshine—something that mimics the desert. So I didn't even think. I mean, that was a dark, enclosed space. I was fine until..." He swiveled his head to look at her. "Until something snatched you away from me."

She started to apologize but stopped, knowing that he'd wave it away, say it wasn't her fault. He'd be right, technically. But she felt terrible anyway.

He shook his head. "Anyway, I thought I was over it. I haven't really had a triggering event for the better part of a year, even on my second tour."

"Well, that's...good I guess?"

"Of course, they say that some of the other symptoms are difficulty maintaining relationships, reckless behavior, and numbness." He huffed a bitter laugh. "I told them, hell, that's not PTSD; that's just me."

She squeezed his hand. He must have forgotten he was still holding it, because he looked down as if he were startled. But then a slow smile blossomed on his face, as if the surprise were a pleasant one.

"I gotta say, Jane, as babysitters go, you're not half bad."

"I'm not babysitting you!" she said, even though she knew he didn't believe her. The strange thing was, for the first time, *she* did. Sure, she was here because Elise had deemed supervising Cameron necessary, but she was having . . . well, *fun* was too insufficient a word.

Something had started loosening in her chest since she'd met Cameron. It was as if there was an icebreaker in there, churning up big solid masses she hadn't even realized were there. And, God, it was so much easier to breathe once there wasn't an iceberg in your chest anymore.

But there was no way to put that into words, so she tugged on the hand that still held hers and said, "Come on. There's lots more to see."

They dropped hands as they made their way into the network of tunnels that ran behind the falls. There was no danger of falling and so no reason to keep up the contact. It made Jane realize that she hadn't held hands with anyone since Felix. It wasn't something she missed. Or it hadn't been until now.

She busied herself reading the signs on the walls of the tunnel. There were a lot of them, but she hated going past interpretive signs without stopping. She liked to know what was happening, and she didn't care if it made her a nerd.

Cameron would hover nearby, listening to her read sections, and then he'd wander off, poking down another tunnel or into another lookout nook. But he always circled back to her.

Until, all of a sudden, he didn't. She looked up from a plaque about some of the thrill seekers who'd gone over the falls in barrels or other assorted containers, to find herself surrounded by people. A huge group of them, in fact, and they were all speaking Japanese. She let herself be swept along with them, keeping her eyes peeled for Cameron.

Ah! There he was! The tunnels were interrupted from time to time by cutaways that opened onto the back of the falls. The crowd shuffled along the tunnels and then jostled to try to squeeze into the small nooks where there were views to be had.

Cameron hadn't put up his hood. She supposed he didn't have enough hair to worry about it getting wet. So his almost-black hair stood out among the crowd of yellow-hooded tourists. Once again, he was leaning on the railing and staring at the rushing water. There must have been water flowing in what had been the frozen sea of her chest, too, because all of a sudden she was suffused with emotion toward him. It felt like . . . respect? She considered what she knew about Cameron from Elise's warnings: he was reckless, impulsive, dangerous. Then she thought about what she knew about him from direct experience: he was reckless, impulsive, dangerous.

Well, yes, but that wasn't *all* he was. She remembered him holding car doors for her, taking her hand on the slippery pavement. Not abandoning her when she was drunk at Bar Nine and she'd ruined his evening. Knowing who Xena: Warrior Princess was. Carrying her through the haunted house. Staring at the waterfall as if his life depended on it.

And, most of all, she thought of that tattooed arm. Slung over her body as she slept at Jay's.

The crowd changed direction, moving on to the next thing, and, jarred from her reverie, Jane had to plant her feet not to be swept along with them.

"Cameron!" she called, laughing because she was like a salmon swimming against the current.

He turned, though she was amazed he'd heard her over

the rushing of the water and the chattering of the selfie-taking tourists. Once he realized what was happening, he laughed, too, and tried to make his way to her, but he was as stymied as she was.

She waved as she was carried away by the receding tide of tourists. He flashed that Listerine grin at her and followed as best he could, but the distance between them was maintained, kept consistent by the wall of bodies between them. She had a feeling that he could part the crowd if he really wanted to, but it was like he was a giant surrounded by peasants that he good-naturedly tolerated. He was content for them to float along, though she knew somehow that he wouldn't let her out of his sight.

As they shuffled along in slow motion, keeping eye contact, it occurred to her that what was happening was actually kind of sexy. If you went for that sort of thing. Which she normally didn't, but...the way he just calmly kept his eyes on her. He was laughing, but he was also insistent. He wasn't going to let her go. They couldn't reach each other, but it was like they were connected by an invisible thread he wasn't going to allow to snap.

They had drifted to the next cutout in the tunnels, and it was on his side. He turned, and, seeing that there was another lookout that would afford them a view of the falls, he beckoned. His face changed—the smile disappeared. But it wasn't as if he was angry, more like the giant had decided to stop tolerating the mortals.

He was bracketed by the opening, almost like he was standing inside a picture frame, except the background, instead of being a flat, generic blue or a fake library, was a living, breathing curtain of falling water. The water he was supposed to imagine had the power to wash away his fears.

The water that could wash away hers?

There was a question she'd been asking herself a lot in recent weeks: What would the bride do? She asked herself a more relevant one now: What would Xena do?

He was backing up into the nook, into the picture frame, seemingly into the waterfall itself. Was there such a thing as a male siren? Because suddenly, she started pushing back against the crowd. It was very unlike her, to shove and elbow people out of the way. She didn't even say "excuse me," allowed no Canadian "sorrys" to pass her lips.

The closer she got to the waterfall—the closer she got to Cameron—the more deafening the rush of water became.

It made it easier to block things out: the crowd, her pounding heart.

Her fear.

It made it easier to do what she wanted, which was to walk up and kiss him.

―⸰―

Despite his reputation, Cam hadn't kissed anyone for five months. And he hadn't kissed anyone but Christie for years. His last kiss had been as he set out for his most recent tour, when she kissed him good-bye at the airport in Thunder Bay.

And of course, since he'd been in Toronto, Jane had frustrated all his attempts to get lucky.

Jane. Jane who had walked right up to him after this extraordinary day, grabbed his head, pulled it down, and pressed her lips against his.

Probably he would have had the sense to stop her if it hadn't been for the ear-splitting rushing of the falls. Realistically, they were several yards from it, but it felt like it was right behind them, like they were inside it even, suspended in a world where the normal rules and consequences didn't apply.

He hadn't been kidding before when he'd said that his mental picture of "waterfall" had not done justice to this particular example. It comforted him somehow. The knowledge that no matter what stupid shit all the petty humans on this Earth got up to, these falls were impervious to it. It was strangely soothing. People could betray each other, disappoint each other, assault each other, even kill each other, and this water would keep rushing over this cliff. None of it mattered.

And if none of it mattered, he could say, "Fuck doing the right thing," and kiss Jane back.

And holy shit. Maybe he was out of practice, but he was pretty sure that Jane was planting on him what was, objectively, the best kiss he had ever had.

The kiss was just like her: strong but a little tentative. Was it wrong that he found that slight hesitancy attractive? It was like she had to overcome her own doubts first, and for some reason, that made his dick as hard as the rocks these tunnels were carved into. Like she was choosing him despite her better judgment. She was full of contradictions, this one. Scared and brave—look at the last two days. Compelling and maddening.

Sexy and sweet: that was Jane. That was this kiss.

And her lips. Oh God, her lips. It was like he'd been crawling through the desert dying of thirst, staring at a waterfall but unable to touch it, and then there was Jane, bearing water. Bearing absolution it felt like even, which was ridiculous.

She'd been holding his cheeks, and when she let go, he had a flash of panic that she was going to pull away. He wasn't ready for this to be done yet—he hadn't drunk his fill—so he wrapped his arms around her and pulled her against him.

She sighed into his mouth, and her body relaxed. It was like she was giving herself over to his care, and it drove him wild. They had been kissing with slightly open mouths. He'd been letting her tongue make tentative incursions into his mouth. But it was no longer enough. He wanted more. He *needed* more, so he angled her head back and plunged his tongue into her mouth, relishing the whimper the maneuver summoned from her. Normally, in a situation like this, he would try not to be too overt about his hard-on. He certainly wouldn't be enough of a jerk to rub it against the lady in question. But hot damn, he couldn't help it. He *wanted* her to feel it. Wanted her to know what she was doing to him. So he pressed their bodies together even harder. He would stop the moment she asked, but until then, he was lost in her.

Her whimpers became moans, and he wanted to pump his fists in victory to celebrate having cracked the reserve of composed, demure Jane. To have made those sounds come from his goddamned babysitter—it was making him crazy.

He became aware only gradually of a tapping on his shoulder, a tapping that wasn't coming from Jane. He tried to shrug it off, but it grew more insistent. With a groan, he broke the kiss, dragging his lips from hers, gratified that she hugged him tighter as he did so. She didn't want it to be over any more than he did.

It was a family of tourists. "You're blocking the view," the father said.

"Also, there are children here," said the mother, frowning at them.

Jane took a step back and clamped a hand over her mouth. "Oh my gosh, I'm so sorry!"

Right. That was his cue. He had to get her out of here before embarrassment took over. *He* could embarrass Jane, but he'd be damned if anyone else did.

Chapter Nine

*H*e bought her dinner. She tried to protest. "I didn't make it through the haunted house."

"Yes, you did," he said.

"Because you *carried* me."

He shrugged. "You're not on that stupid chicken list, are you?" Though he wasn't sure why he was arguing. What was the point of a bet if you started actively campaigning against your own position? "Anyway, it's done."

And it was. He'd slipped the waitress his credit card when she delivered their dessert.

Jane lifted her hands in a gesture of surrender. "Well, thank you," she said. "This has been surprisingly good for a tourist trap."

It had been. They'd found a mom-and-pop Italian joint, complete with red gingham tablecloths and Chianti-bottle candles, and had consumed vast quantities of pasta and veal Parmesan. It turned out that confronting demons—whether of the fake-blood-and-strobe-lights variety or of the more insidious psychological sort—worked up quite the appetite.

And, man, he loved watching Jane eat. That first day, at the steakhouse, she'd said that she "really, really enjoyed eating." And she had. He remembered how she had moaned when she'd taken a bite of his steak. Tonight, unlike then, she hadn't been cautious about her intake. There was none of that cutting everything up into smaller-than-bite-size pieces. No shoving the bread basket away like it was made of fire. She hadn't been squeamish over the idea of veal like so many women were—they'd ordered pasta and veal parm and shared both. She'd acted like each dish their server brought was the greatest thing she'd ever laid eyes on, even going so far as to clap her hands in glee when their molten chocolate cake arrived. It was almost like she'd forgotten about—

"Oh my God!" Her fork clattered to the table. "I forgot about my dress." She let her head fall forward so it was cradled in her hands and wailed, "Noooooo!"

Cam dropped his own fork, which drew her attention. He didn't know if he was annoyed at her, or at Elise, or at, like, the patriarchy (and that would be a first). He only knew he *was* annoyed. They'd been having a perfectly nice time— dare he say even a great time?—and now they had to stop and have this conversation again.

Well, best to get on with it. "Jane, who the hell cares about the dress? You're going to wear it for one day. One day in which presumably everyone will be looking at Elise and my brother." Though that might not be true. If Jane was in what he'd come to think of as "goddess mode," a term he'd come up with after her spin outside the CN Tower but had seen displayed again as she'd stalked toward him and kissed him at the falls, how could anyone *not* stare at her?

He wasn't really sure how he'd gone from thinking of her as plain, muddy Jane to a goddess, but he didn't feel like analyzing it.

"Yes, but, *Cameron*," she said, emphasizing his name in a way that made his dick twinge—"let's assume for one minute that I don't care that I'm going to look like a ruffly, purple hippo. I still have to actually *fit into* the dress. It has to physically *zip up*."

"You are not going to look like a hippo." There went that eyebrow and, with it, his annoyance at having to have this conversation. It was replaced by outright anger—though he still wasn't sure at whom, or what, it was directed. "Jane, you are as sexy as they come, so shut the hell up."

She had her mouth pre-opened to lob her next argument at him, but she clamped it shut as her eyes widened. He tried not to laugh. He probably shouldn't have said it like that, but it was true.

And it sure as hell shut her up because she stopped arguing about the bill. Didn't say much of anything, really, as they walked back to the car. The silence continued as they navigated to the highway and settled in for the drive home.

But it wasn't an uncomfortable silence, which was a little surprising because they hadn't said one word about their kiss behind the falls. Not that there was anything to say. They'd had a moment. A hot moment, but moments were by definition fleeting. The fact that she didn't want to "talk about it," as most girls would, was actually awesome. And she'd already heard his "I'm not looking for a relationship right now speech" in the car ride on the way up, so it wasn't like she hadn't known the score when she'd kissed him.

So companionable silence was more than fine by him. It

gave him time to appreciate that, despite his haunted house freak-out, he'd had a really good day. That was...a novelty.

Then she started yawning.

Then *he* started yawning.

Then they started laughing.

"I'm sorry!" she said, covering her mouth and trying to stifle another yawn. "They're contagious."

"No problem," he said—or tried to. It came out all garbled as another one hit him. "I should have taken the top down. That would have kept us awake."

"I'm not sure it would make a difference in my case. Getting the shit scared out of you, then stuffing yourself with carbs: it makes a girl sleepy."

He noticed she didn't mention "making out like the world was about to end."

Which was fine, he reminded himself, because hadn't he just been thinking about how he was glad she didn't want to talk about that? He cleared his throat. "Feel free to nap."

She shook her head through another yawn. "I will not abandon you," she declared with a vehemence that was awfully cute as she opened her eyes comically wide. "You should stop and get yourself some coffee."

"I will if I need to." He didn't tell her that thinking about their kiss was having a...wakeful effect on him—or at least on certain parts of him.

She cracked her window. "Do you mind? I think it will help keep me awake."

"Not at all," he said, appreciating the cool air as she let loose yet another enormous yawn. He smiled. He was pretty sure nothing was keeping Jane awake, despite her noble intentions.

As predicted, it wasn't five minutes before she was fast asleep, her head lolling back and against the passenger-side window, which drew his attention to her long, graceful neck. He'd never thought of necks as particularly sexy before, but apparently there was a first time for everything.

Alicia used to fall asleep in his car sometimes, too, back in Thunder Bay. When he'd turned sixteen and gotten his license and scraped together enough to buy a beat-up Chevy, the freedom had been intoxicating. They would hit McDonald's and then drive and drive through the night, talking about everything, until they'd pull over behind Our Lady of Charity school, which abutted a big park, and lose themselves in each other. Later, on their way home, Alicia would fall asleep.

To his mind, sleeping in the presence of someone who was awake was to make yourself vulnerable. And to do it when the other person was driving, shepherding your unconscious body through space at high speeds, struck him as the ultimate act of trust. When Alicia fell asleep in his car, he always had to remind himself to watch the road and not her. It had been so intoxicating, the idea that she was his. That someone had chosen to give herself to him, the loser kid from the trailer park who was perpetually on the verge of flunking out of school.

Of course she hadn't really. Or at least not exclusively to him. What an idiot he had been. He'd thought it was true love. And when she'd announced she was pregnant, after he'd gotten over the initial panic, he'd dropped out of school, tripled his shifts at the hardware store, and bought her a shitty cubic zirconia engagement ring, promising to exchange it for a real diamond later when they were in a better financial position.

When he thought about what happened next, the familiar shame rose in his chest. It never went away. *It's not yours,* she'd said, tears streaking down her face. *I wish it was.*

The stupid thing was, he'd kind of loved that baby anyway. Which was impossible because not only was it not a baby yet but a mere mass of cells, it apparently wasn't even *his* mass of cells. He could see now that she'd done him a favor by not taking him up on his offer to claim the baby regardless of its parentage. That by letting her parents hustle her out of town, he'd dodged a bullet.

But all that logic didn't matter, not really, because the shame and heartbreak that had come rushing in to fill the void after Alicia left had turned him into a fucking idiot bent on living down to the expectations everyone had of him. What kind of guy knocks up his sixteen-year-old girlfriend and doesn't do the right thing by her? He was simultaneously so heartbroken and so angry at himself for trusting her in the first place that he hadn't even bothered correcting the record when the rumors started swirling. Even if they weren't right about that particular situation, they were right in general, weren't they? So he'd resisted his mother's attempts to get him to go back to high school, moved out of her trailer and into his own, and became the person everyone thought he was.

He sighed, dragging himself out of the past. Despite the sour memories, when he thought back to Alicia sleeping in his car, it made him happy. It was the best part of those nights.

Christie, on the other hand, had been a night owl, so there had been no sleeping in cars for her.

And anyway, he was pretty sure Christie hadn't trusted him. He had been faithful to her on both tours, but again, his reputation had not worked in his favor. And he *had* been using her, in a way. Her and the army. Their whirlwind romance had begun a month before his first deployment. When he'd asked her to write to him, he hadn't been totally honest with her. He hadn't told her that she was going to help save him. That there was the old Cam and the new Cam and that he, having finally decided to man the fuck up and make something of his life, was in transition between them. He had drawn a line in the sand. On one side of it was the delinquent high school dropout. On the other was a man with an honorable job and—he hoped—a steady girlfriend.

Neither of which, it turned out, he'd been able to hold on to. You couldn't escape your destiny, apparently. No matter how hard he'd tried to get away from Old Cam, that bastard just kept coming back.

Jane must have sensed the shift in the car's rhythm as he pulled off the highway, because she opened her eyes and stretched. Then she really woke up and sat up straight, only to find herself restrained by her seat belt. "Oh my God, I did fall asleep. I'm sorry."

He laughed. It reminded him of when she ate something and only belatedly remembered her campaign to lose weight. In some ways, Jane seemed to be at war with herself, subsuming her real desires beneath a set of behaviors she prescribed for herself. The juxtaposition was amusing.

"No worries." He pulled up in front of her house. She lived in a neighborhood that was mostly home to three-story Victorians, but her house was a tiny one-story cottage with a peaked gable. It looked like the runt of the litter. It was cute and tidy and homey—the opposite of Jay's imposing luxury high-rise. A wall of exhaustion hit him at the prospect of going back to his brother's downtown. It was only eleven. He might have to kill some time to make sure he didn't cross paths with Jay. Cam wasn't sure he had it in him tonight to deal with his brother.

"God, you must be so tired," Jane said.

Oh shit. He hadn't even realized that he'd let his head fall

forward onto the top of the steering wheel. He sat up straight
and shook it, as if he could shake some sense into himself.
"I'm okay. It's not that late."

"No," said Jane, tilting her head. It was too dark to see
her eyes properly, but he could imagine them narrowing as
she contemplated him. "I mean, you must be, like, exis-
tentially tired. You've been at war, for heaven's sake. And
now you're thrust back into this family wedding where the
bride—and God bless her, I adore her—is becoming a little
unhinged and, well..." She trailed off.

Probably he should say something, assure her that he
was fine. But the sudden display of what seemed like genuine sympathy—sympathy that wasn't tinged with pity—
had robbed him of his ability to speak.

She shook her head and unbuckled her seat belt. "I don't
know what I'm talking about. Ignore me."

"Yes," he said, finding his voice, because suddenly he
didn't want her to get out of the car. Not yet. "I hadn't really
thought of it like that, but you're right. I'm pretty fucking
wrecked. Like, elementally. And I just..." He trailed off. It
was one thing to agree with her, another to turn her into his
shrink.

"You just what?" she prodded.

His head found its way back to the steering wheel. He
simply could not keep it upright anymore. "I don't want to
go home and deal with my brother. I probably owe him an
apology. But it's all so goddamned exhausting."

"Then don't go home. I have a guest bed in my office.
You can crash here."

His head popped back up. He was turning into a fucking
marionette. Which was an uncomfortable thought, because
if he was the puppet, who was pulling the strings here?
But that question faded in favor of a more astonishing one:

Was she propositioning him? Because that was generally what was going on when you spent a day with someone that included a wicked make-out session and delivered them home only to be invited in. But she'd said, "guest bed." And Jane wasn't like everyone else. Maybe she truly was worried about his existential exhaustion. She was a good enough person that he wouldn't discount the possibility. Unsure how to respond, he fell back on his usual methods. "I know what's going on here," he said, teasing, but kind of not. "This works in your favor doesn't it? If I'm underfoot, it helps with the babysitting mission."

"I'm not babysitting you," she said, and he mouthed the words along with her, which made her purse her lips in annoyance. But then she cracked a smile and said, "Suit yourself," and got out of the car.

He got out of the car, too.

—☙

"You don't need to remake the bed," Cameron said as Jane threw back the covers on the daybed in her office.

She tossed the cushions that sofa-fied the bed by day onto the floor, and said, "Yes, I do. I nap here a lot when I'm working."

"So? You don't have cooties, do you?"

Ignoring him, she stripped the sheets. Not furnishing a guest with fresh linens offended her sense of order. Jane was surprised that Cameron had taken her up on her invitation to stay. She was surprised at *herself*, too, for offering. It was just that she felt...sorry for him wasn't really the right phrase. Cameron was not the sort of man who invited pity.

She'd always been good at putting herself in other people's shoes. It was what she did professionally, of course, imagining how any given character would react emotionally to certain scenarios. But she'd been good at it when she was younger, too. It was how she'd always known how stressed out her brother was, as he attempted to maintain his good grades while working nearly full-time to keep them afloat. She'd been able to mold herself into the smallest, least objectionable person she could be in order not to add to his burdens.

"I do not have 'cooties,'" she said, belatedly answering Cameron's question while making air quotes with her fingers. "I do, however, have standards. Hang on; I'll be right back."

It took her maybe fifteen seconds, tops, to walk the two steps to the hallway linen closet and locate a set of matching sheets and pillowcases. And, okay, maybe another fifteen to stand there and catch her breath. Her house was small. The rooms in it were small. And Cameron was...not small. He was tall and muscular, and beyond that, he took up a lot of psychic space. She was starting to second-guess herself. Empathy was one thing, but her bed was just on the other side of the wall from the guest bed in the office. Now that she'd tasted his lips, felt his hands roaming over her body, how was she ever going to fall asleep knowing he was mere feet away from her?

She took a deep breath. She could hardly rescind the invitation. Nothing for it now but to push through.

She had only been gone those thirty seconds, but when she pushed back into the office, she saw that it had been thirty seconds too long. Because it had taken Cameron no time at all to open the top drawer of the small filing cabinet she kept next to her bed. She used the bottom drawer for actual files and the top drawer for—

"A fine collection of vibrators you've got here, Jane," he drawled, the McConaughey coming on strong.

Her skin heated, but she refused to be embarrassed. Well, she *was* embarrassed, but she refused to cop to it. There was nothing wrong with having a "fine collection" of vibrators. It was a heck of a lot less problematic than having a collection of messy ex-boyfriends. And she didn't have a current boyfriend around to take issue with them, so she was holding her head high. Even if it was steaming from how hot her cheeks were.

As she busied herself putting the fitted sheet on the bed, she pondered whether she should take the vibrators out of the room with her when she left. But then would he think she would be...using them that evening? No, better to play it cool. She unfurled the top sheet with a flick of her wrist.

This was the problem with spontaneity. Normally when she had guests over, she cleared out the "fine collection." But when you invited your friend's fiancé's brother to spend the night on a whim after a discombobulating day in which you made out with your friend's fiancé's brother, it was possible for your Hitachi Magic Wand, your Love Egg, and your Jessica Rabbit to slip your mind.

Whatever. She was not embarrassed, right? "There's nothing wrong with vibrators," she said, wincing at the defensiveness that had crept into her tone. "Anyway," she said, trying again, "I would hardly call three 'a collection.'" Nope, still defensive. *Ugh*.

"Hey," he said quietly. "No judgment here."

Shock prompted her to jerk her gaze to his. She was sure he had been playing her, that when she found his blue-green eyes, they would be full of mockery. When she met his gaze, though, she was surprised to find it free of any ridicule. Instead there was just...heat?

She must have been looking at him funny, because he showed her his palms and said, "What?" His turn to be defensive. She tamped down a smile at the turned tables. "What's not to love about a vibrator?" he added.

She shrugged and turned her attention to the pillowcases. "I had a boyfriend once who had a massive problem with them." She'd always kind of assumed that most men would share Felix's feelings on the matter. And she could kind of see it. It was hard for a mortal man to compete with Jessica's "unique oscillating motion."

He took the second pillowcase from her and started stuffing a pillow in it. "Well, he sounds like a fucking idiot."

She did smile then, and she didn't try to hide this one from him. "He was actually a big brainiac. Premed major when I met him. Now he's a surgeon."

"Really? Because to my mind, being threatened by something you can use to give your girl screaming orgasms doesn't sound like a very smart move."

"He was a member of Mensa," she said, laughing, both because it was funny but also because she was thrown off kilter by the rush of arousal that his declaration had summoned. There was something about Cameron talking so matter-of-factly about giving a woman "screaming orgasms" that made her nether regions want to volunteer as tribute. And the way he'd said, "your girl." Not "your girlfriend." They should have been synonyms but somehow were not. And it was easy—too easy—to imagine him replacing the pronoun and saying, "*my* girl." She squeezed her thighs together in an attempt to lock down the party that was starting between them.

"Oh, I see," said Cameron, shaking out the duvet she handed him. "I'm getting a picture of this dude. Premed. Mensa. Threatened by a piece of pink silicone shaped like a bunny rabbit. He was clearly overcompensating for a huge insecurity complex."

She laughed again. "You know, I think you might be right." She hadn't thought of it like that, but Felix was always making a point to explain things to her that didn't need explaining, and he'd been really into proving his "stamina" in the bedroom, which for him meant pounding away at her for what felt like hours. When she'd finally worked up her courage to suggest they introduce a vibrator, he had lost his mind. Told her a real woman didn't need battery-powered assistance. "Anyway," she said, "I find vibrators very... efficient."

"I do not disagree. Though there is something to be said for human touch, too, don't you think?" Cameron asked, finishing the bed by smoothing the duvet over it. It was so strange to be standing here doing something so mundane as making a bed together while they were having this conversation. Talking about anything remotely sex related with Felix, outside of when they were actually having sex, had not been possible. And, sure, she talked about sex with the girls, but that usually just involved her having to defend her practice of preferring her "fine collection" to the "real thing." Though, in their defense, they didn't mean that in the way Felix had. They were always on her case about her stance against dating (Elise) and her stance against casual sex (Gia), but they weren't mean about it. Wendy mostly left her alone, because one of Wendy's many amazing best friend qualities was that she was profoundly nonjudgmental. And possibly also because she knew Jane well enough to know that even though she'd never admit it, Felix had thrown her for a total loop. God, when she thought of that night, their last together, where she'd finally gotten her courage up to suggest they move in together, and he'd shot her right down... well, the shame was as fresh as ever— both over the stinging rejection and over her own blindness.

How had she spent six years with someone who didn't satisfy her sexually *and* didn't want to move toward anything more permanent than "dating"? Where had her self-respect been?

"I don't know that there *is* that much to be said for the human touch," she said, answering Cameron's earlier question. But maybe she should have just agreed with him rather than answering it honestly, because now she was going to have to give him the same speech she always gave the girls. Or at least an abbreviated version. "I don't really believe in the idea of 'the one,' you know? The notion that there's one and only one perfect match for each person? I don't think that's true for me. I haven't had a boyfriend for a really long time, and I haven't missed it."

"Well, if Mr. Bunny Hater was your last one, I don't blame you. But you don't have to be in a relationship with someone in order to, uh, avail yourself of human touch."

She would have thought maybe he was propositioning her. The Cameron she'd met a couple days ago would have been. But the slight hesitancy in his speech and the total absence of any leering or eyebrow wagging suggested he wasn't. So she decided to go with it. She was actually finding this conversation kind of...stimulating. "Yeah, well, I considered trying Tinder, but really, why would I?"

He shrugged, encouraging her to answer her own question.

"Because vibrators don't give you sexually transmitted infections or pregnancy scares. They don't ax-murder you. You don't have to cuddle with them. They don't treat you like a sex doll." *When you go out on a limb, they don't break your heart.*

"Hmm," he said. "You don't want to be treated like a sex doll, but you *also* don't want to cuddle."

It did sound a little contradictory, but she didn't care. "It's a fine line."

"What about marriage, kids, the white picket fence?"

"Nope, nope, and nope." And that was it. She held up a hand to signal the end of the conversation. Because the only thing left to say was, *I already ruined one family,* and those words would never be uttered aloud to another soul. Not even Wendy. Because it was impossible for anyone, except maybe her brother, to understand. And she was never going to be more of a burden to him than she already had been by dumping *that* confession on him.

That had been the one great thing about Felix—he hadn't wanted kids. Maybe that's why she'd stuck around for so long. With him, she'd been able to imagine a future that included a life partner, but one who wasn't going to pressure her to procreate.

"One more question," Cameron said.

She shook her head. She was done with this little stroll down memory lane.

He asked anyway. "Why are these in here and not in your bedroom?"

She laughed. And here she'd been expecting him to insist she was making a big mistake, that women weren't fulfilled without love and family. That she just had to keep searching until she found "the one." It was an insidious cultural norm and she expected it at every turn. To have Cameron *not* go down that road was refreshing.

So she answered him honestly. "They are not in my bedroom because I tend to use them more in here." That would have been a sufficient answer, but she decided to throw him for a loop by adding more of the truth. "I find that when I'm writing for long stretches, they're, uh..." But, crap, her bravado faltered, and she trailed off.

"You get yourself off in this bed," he said, grinning. "That's what you meant when you said you 'napped' in here a lot."

Her face was heating again, but she clung to her "no shame" stance. "It's good for productivity, I find."

He was nodding, eyebrows raised, but still there was no mocking in his gaze. "I can totally see that."

She waited, because surely there was more. Cameron MacKinnon couldn't let this whole conversation pass without making some kind of suggestive remark, could he? This was the guy who'd ordered an ice cream sundae the other day specifically so he could use it to make lewd gestures.

But she was met with silence. "Well, okay then. If you're all set, I'm going to go to bed. Tomorrow's the bachelorette party, so tomorrow morning is my last chance to figure out something for that danged chakram I'll need for Comicon on Sunday." When he smiled, she added, "A warrior princess's work is never done."

She had the strangest impulse to blow him a kiss, but she stifled it.

Chapter Ten

*B*y the time Jane got up the next morning, Cameron had made his bed, helped himself to a shower with the towel she'd left for him, and made breakfast. He'd even thought about looking up a recipe for hollandaise sauce on his phone. He'd been lying before when he'd fed her that line about only making eggs Benedict for his lovers. Cam could make passable versions of lots of basic dishes. He'd had to learn, as a kid, because his mom often worked nights at the diner. But his repertoire wasn't very extensive.

He'd thought better of hollandaise, though. Not only did it sound like an easy recipe to mess up, it was better not to go there, having declared that there was a certain level of intimacy associated with the dish.

So scrambled eggs it was again. But he didn't think she'd mind because he had also made her a—

"Oh my God, is that a chakram?" she shrieked.

The juxtaposition between her sleep-rumpled hair and pajamas and the fact that she was literally jumping up and down in front of his work-in-progress was pretty amusing. "Yeah. I saw a flattened box in your recycling, so I decided to give it a shot." He moved to stand by her side at the tiny kitchen table. "I made the basic shape out of cardboard using my pocketknife." She *ooohhed* like he had informed her he'd conducted open-heart surgery with his pocketknife. "So I think all you need to do is get some spray paint." He showed her the image on his phone he'd been using as a guide. "Silver on the outside here," he said, pointing to the corresponding part on the cardboard, "and gold here."

She'd gone completely silent. She stood there mutely, blinking at his creation. All of a sudden, he felt like a total fool. She'd probably just been being polite before. What had he been thinking? Was he a five-year-old at the craft table? She probably had some much more elaborate creation in mind. Something classier than spray-painted cardboard. "I, uh, saw that there were a few different versions of her chakram when I looked online," he said, because, hell, why not add to his idiocy by *talking about it*? But he couldn't seem to stop. "Of course, I don't know the difference between them like you do, so maybe I made the wrong one. I thought this yin-yang-style one looked cool, but—" *God. Stop.* He forced himself to shut his mouth.

She turned to him, her eyes shiny with—were those tears? "Oh, hey," he said as one escaped from the corner of her eye. "Don't cry. You can tell me it's shit. I've been through basic training, sweetheart." Not to mention a summary trial. "I've got thick skin."

She shook her head, and the motion dislodged another tear on the same side. "It's perfect," she whispered.

Whoa. That was not the reaction he'd been expecting, and he lost his breath for a moment. Warmth suffused his chest, and he reached out to brush away the two tears. He used his thumb to get them, and he'd been going to pull away when she grabbed his hand and brought it to her lips, kissing the back of it like she was the duke and he was the maiden in a fairy tale or something.

"Thank you," she said. It was almost like no one had ever done anything nice for her before.

He cleared his throat, in search of his voice. "Damn, if that's what I get for a little cardboard craft project, you need to raise your standards." He busied himself setting out the eggs that he'd been keeping warm in the oven. "I hope you don't mind I whipped together some breakfast."

"Are you kidding?" she said, clearing away the newspapers he'd laid under his little DIY-fest. He noticed she very carefully moved the chakram to the top of the refrigerator, which was pretty much the only surface in the tiny kitchen that was empty. "I'm sorry I slept so late. You should have woken me."

"I have to say, I didn't take you for a lie-about," he said, pouring her a cup of coffee and gesturing for her to sit.

She grinned. "I hate getting up in the mornings. Last night's exhaustion aside, I'm usually up late working."

An image flashed into his mind of her hunched over her computer in the dark. More of a movie, really, than a still image, because then she got up and laid down on the very bed he'd slept in last night, and—

"And I have to say, I didn't take you for an early bird."

He tamped down the spike of desire the dirty movie in his mind had summoned and loaded her plate with eggs and two pieces of toast. "In the army, there's no sleeping in," he said.

"I suppose not." He slid the plate over to her and she moaned, which didn't help on the whole desire-tamping front. "The only thing I think I love more than eating is eating without having to cook."

Damn, and right now, there was nothing he loved more than feeding Jane Denning.

"So, Cameron," she said through a mouthful of eggs. "I feel that you and I have achieved a sort of détente. Would you agree?"

"I guess so," he said, wary because it seemed like he was being set up for something. Were they going to have to talk about yesterday's ill-advised kiss now?

"So tell me about the bachelor party."

"The bachelor party?" he echoed.

"It's tonight." She cocked her head. "I assume you're going?"

Shit. He didn't know. It would be weird for the brother of the groom not to go to the bachelor party, he assumed, but not only had he not received an invitation, he hadn't even known it was happening. But then, he hadn't really been around, had he?

Jane leaned forward on her chair like she was going to whisper a secret to him, though they were, of course, alone.

"I need to know if there's going to be a stripper."

"I'm sorry, what?"

"Stripper," she said, enunciating the word like he wasn't a native English speaker. "I don't care what the answer is, but I need to know. Elise keeps talking about crashing the boys' party, but she is not going to be cool with a stripper, and it's infinitely better that if there is one, she not know about it. So do me a favor and tell me now and I'll be able to keep her away if need be."

"I honestly don't know," he said.

"Can you text me an update?" she asked.

"I guess so?" Shit. That shouldn't have come out as tentative as it had, like he was asking rather than answering a question. "Yes," he said more firmly. "I'll try to find out what's going on and let you know." *Of course* he was going to Jay's bachelor party, for God's sake. Despite their recent clashes, they were *brothers*.

Maybe it was time he started acting like one.

"So you quit the army?" Jane asked suddenly, waving away his offer of more eggs.

He blinked, taking a moment to adjust to the new topic. "More like the army quit me," he finally answered, hoping she wouldn't press matters.

"What's next?"

Damned if he knew. *I was going to go to university* would make him sound like a lunatic. He was so clearly not university material that anyone with any sense would laugh in his face. And Jane was nothing if not sensible. But, his tour having ended several months earlier than planned, he had no fucking clue what was supposed to come next. "Honestly, I was planning to take a couple months to readjust to civilian life and go from there." That sounded passable. He had savings. It wasn't an unreasonable plan.

"And by 'readjust to civilian life,' you mean 'sleep with the female half of it.'"

He would have thought she was teasing, on account of the aforementioned détente and all, but her tone was hard to read. When he didn't answer fast enough, she said, "And where are you going to live? Jay's condo?"

Another question he couldn't answer.

That was probably his cue to leave. He pushed back from the table and took his dishes to the counter. She didn't have a dishwasher, so he ran some water into the sink.

"Look, I'm sorry," she said. "That came out all naggy. I just think you have so much..."

"So much what?" he snapped. She winced, and he immediately felt bad, but he needed to know how she'd been planning to finish that sentence. "Were you going to say 'potential'?" When she didn't answer, he added, "That seems to be the word. *Cam, you have so much potential.*" He was trying not to be a bully, but he couldn't quite keep the sneering tone from his voice. "That's what Jay always said."

"I had a great time yesterday." Her voice had gone all quiet, like she was afraid of how he would respond. "You seemed...different."

"Different from what?" he pressed. And why were they suddenly having this heavy conversation about his future?

She looked at him without speaking, but there was something in her eyes. Affection, maybe? A fondness that hadn't been there before? Well, shit. It was better that she knew the truth about him before she started getting ideas. He wasn't the kind of man she could go on day trips with, flirt with, and then rely on to be there, cheerfully making breakfast and solving her cosplay problems the next morning. The last twenty-four hours had been an aberration. If she was getting ideas, she needed to stop.

"When I said the army quit me, I meant I was dismissed from service. I was charged under the military's code of service discipline, tried, and..." He held out his hands. "Here I am."

Her eyes widened. She had probably only heard of stuff like that on TV. It hadn't been dramatic like that, his trial. Mostly because although Becky had testified on his behalf, he had quite clearly committed the offense he'd been charged with. He didn't even blame them—you couldn't just contravene the code of service and walk away. He *did* blame them, though, for the fact that Biggs's trial had resulted only in a demotion to lieutenant while his had resulted in dismissal. But what had he expected? Biggs was a reg force officer, and he'd been a reservist.

"What happened?" Jane asked.

"I broke the code of service: Striking or Offering Violence to a Superior Officer. Offense number 103.17." He still remembered the number. Could even recite the relevant section from memory. God knew he'd spent enough hours staring at it, trying to think of some way to salvage his career. To explain that yes, he'd done what they charged, but it had been in service of preventing a larger crime. But the military rightly didn't deal in shades of gray.

Her eyes got even wider and she repeated her question. "What happened?"

"Exactly what it sounds like. I attacked my superior officer. Two guys had to pull me off him."

"But you must have had a reason. It can't just be—"

"My point," he said, raising his voice to talk over her, "is that you were wrong about me. I don't have potential. Never did. All the shit people say about me is true."

She stood there blinking at him. Good. He had finally shut her up. He reminded himself that he was doing this because he *liked* her. Maybe she truly believed her own story about not wanting a boyfriend. But just in case she had read too much into that kiss, he needed her to know that he was never going to be the man for the job. If she ever changed her mind about moving beyond her "fine collection" of vibrators, she deserved better than him.

"I'll try to find out about the bachelor party," he said as he turned to show himself out. "And if I don't see you tonight, good luck at Comicon."

―◌―

"At least we're not in Vegas or at a spa in the middle of the woods or something," Wendy grumbled to Jane later that afternoon as they made their way up the elevator of Wendy's building laden with bags of decorations for Elise's bachelorette party. Gia was taking the bride to lunch, and then the four of them were going to a not-in-the-middle-of-the-woods salon. After that, the rest of the revelers would arrive at Wendy's for gag gifts and drinks before heading out on the town.

"Amen to that," Jane agreed. Elise had floated the idea of a "destination" bachelorette party, but it had only taken a little gentle manipulation to talk her down from that idea, mostly because Elise was intent on crashing the bachelor party and Jay could not be talked into moving his out of his favorite local pub, much less out of the city. "I don't really get why she's so keen on this 'invade the boys' thing. Doesn't that kind of defeat the purpose of a bachelorette?"

"God knows," Wendy said. "She probably saw it in a movie. She's got some visual in her head that we now have to bust our asses to recreate."

"She probably saw it on Pinterest," Jane said. "You know, all those 'Invading Your Husband-to-Be's Bachelor Party in Style' boards?"

Wendy barked a laugh, which perked Jane up immensely after her weird morning with Cameron. Wendy, a take-no-prisoners defense lawyer, was usually all business, but she had a loud, infectious laugh that, if you knew her, was all the more remarkable for how incongruent it was.

"If this was anyone besides one of you girls," Jane said, "I would have put my foot down long ago."

Wendy unlocked her door and held it for Jane. "Agreed. If it was anyone else, I'd be staging an intervention, sitting the bridezilla down, and reminding her that the point of all this isn't the wedding but, like, the marriage itself. But in this particular case, it's clear that despite the fact that Elise is off her rocker, the marriage itself is going to be just fiiiine."

"What are you talking about?" Jane asked.

Wendy dropped the box she'd been carrying on a counter and sank onto one of the stools at her kitchen island. "Have you seen the way he looks at her?"

"What do you mean? Jay?"

"Uh, yes. Hello? It's like he's eye-fucking her all the time. And it's been that way since they met. It never, like, wears off." She sighed.

"We're talking about *Jay* here? Accountant Jay?"

"What planet are you on? Yes. Didn't Gia tell you about walking in on them a couple days ago?"

"No!" God. What had she been missing by skipping all the flower arranging and calligraphy-ing? "Tell me!"

Wendy let loose a low whistle. "I can't. It will make me blush too much. You'll have to wait for Gia." Jane was about to protest that nothing made Wendy blush when her friend sighed again and said, "Let's just say that even though she's uptight about what shade of ivory or bone or whatever her shoes are, Elise is being extremely well fucked." She grinned. "Those two are going to have a very happy marriage."

Wendy generally had a potty mouth, and she called things like she saw them, but...wow. It was Jane's turn to blush, and not only because of what Wendy had said. For some reason, the image of Cameron lounging on her guest bed and talking about giving "screaming orgasms" to "his girl" had popped into her mind. She took a deep breath to calm her runaway pulse.

"So what about this Cameron dude?"

"What about him?" Jane countered, taking her time unpacking the bags so as to avoid looking at Wendy. She and Wendy had been inseparable since fifth grade, so it was totally weird that she hadn't told Wendy about anything that had gone down with Cameron. It was also totally weird that she didn't want to.

"Whoa. Defensive much?"

"I am not!" Jane turned around. Face your accuser and all that.

Wendy raised her eyebrows skeptically. That was another problem with the whole joined-at-the-hip thing: it also came with ESP. Jane made a split-second decision. "I do kind of have a confession." It wasn't an untrue confession. It wasn't a totally comprehensive confession, either, but whatever.

Wendy clapped once, hard, as if in triumph. "Spill it."

Jane lowered her voice to a whisper. "I'm kind of using him to get out of my bridesmaid duties." Wendy narrowed her eyes—the hardened lawyer could smell the lie of omission, no doubt—so Jane kept talking. "As far as I can tell, being a bridesmaid is kind of like being a lobster slowly boiled in a pot. It all sort of creeps up on you, and suddenly you're shoving white felt into a blender." There. Hopefully that would be enough to put her bloodhound of a BFF off the scent.

Wendy let loose another one of her signature cackles and rolled off the bed. "You're not wrong there. Come on. We have to cover this condo in plastic dicks because that is, apparently, how our bullshit society says you are supposed to celebrate the impending end of singlehood. And you're not getting out of this one."

~ᴄ

Jay says no stripper.

Cam's text arrived while Jane was perched in a pedicure chair, an hour into the "getting ready" part of the festivities. Never mind that "getting ready" for Jane generally meant deciding which flats to wear and slapping her hair into a ponytail, and she could be counted on to do that in all of ten seconds. If "getting ready" for the bachelorette party was this elaborate a process, she hated to think what the primping before the actual wedding would entail.

But I can't guarantee that because there are a couple dudes here who keep trying to change his mind.

Jane hated to be "that person" who texted while getting a pedicure—could you get any more entitled?—but she sat back and replied.

Where are you guys? What's the plan?

We're at Jay's playing video games. Then off to Finnegan's Wake. As far as I can tell, the plan seems to be: drink.

Oh, man, I envy you. I am getting toenails that no one is ever going to see painted. Then I'm going for pre-pre-drinks. Then actual pre-drinks at Wendy's. Then dinner. Then we're crashing some kind of gay club. Because that's what

*everyone at a gay club wants: a bunch of drunk
straight girls invading. And I've ALREADY spent
an hour decorating Wendy's place with fake
penises. And piping frosting onto cupcakes to
look like penises. Etcetera, etcetera.*

YOU are complaining about fake penises?

She laughed out loud, drawing Gia's attention.

"What are you doing?" Gia lunged for the phone. Jane
tried to keep it out of her reach, but her pedicurist was in
the middle of applying the glittery emerald-green polish
Jane had chosen, so she couldn't really move. She tried not
to whimper as Gia captured her prize.

"Oh my God, is this Jay's brother you're texting with?"

Jane wanted to die. She wanted the Earth to open up and
swallow her, pedicure throne and all. She could only comfort
herself that Wendy and Elise were getting their fingers done
across the salon and therefore hadn't heard Gia's outburst.

"I, ah, asked him to let us know if there was going to be a
stripper," she offered feebly, knowing there was no way Gia
would accept that explanation.

"Yeah," she said, scrolling on Jane's phone. "And you
covered that waaaay back here. You know, before the part
where you start talking about penises." She tapped the
phone a couple times. "I'm going to answer him."

"No!" Jane's shriek was so loud that it did draw Wendy
and Elise's attention from across the salon, as well as that of
most of the other customers. "Sorry!" she chirped, waving
at everyone. Then she hissed at Gia, "If you don't give me
back that phone, so help me…"

Gia handed the phone back silently, all the mirth gone
from her face. "Oh, sweetie."

"What?" Jane had no idea what was going on, but she didn't like the way Gia was looking at her.

"You like him."

"I don't like him."

"You do." She heaved a huge sigh. Then she perked up. "Well, we know you're not gay, Xena!"

"What's wrong with liking Cameron?" Jane protested, but then quickly added, "Theoretically, I mean. Because I don't."

"He's trouble, that one."

"Says Elise. But he's actually kind of..."

"Kind of what?" When Jane didn't answer, Gia said, "My concern is not what Elise says. You can tell by interacting with him for five seconds that he's trouble."

Jane supposed Gia was right. She was the world-weary, jet-setting model, after all. She had tons of horror stories of being harassed on the job, and just as many of, uh, enjoying herself in her travels. She knew stuff, was the point. Certainly more than Jane, whose last relationship with something not made out of silicone had ended five years ago.

"Which doesn't mean he doesn't have his uses," Gia said, cocking her head and tapping a finger against her pursed lips as she regarded Jane. "He *is* gorgeous."

"Yeah, if you're into the whole testosterone overdose thing," Jane said.

"And really, who isn't?" Gia said with a grin. "At least temporarily." But then her face grew grave. "Seriously, though, Jane, have some fun if you want, but don't get your heart broken."

"Whoa. Why would you think I'm going to get my heart broken?"

"What were you going to say before? You said, 'he's

actually kind of...' And then you didn't finish. You were going to say he has qualities that no one else sees, right? That under all that womanizing and bluster, he's actually a misunderstood teddy bear?"

Jane didn't answer, but she feared her face betrayed her, because Gia shook her head, looking at her like she was an innocent child who didn't know the ways of the world. "You know that Maya Angelou quote?" she asked. "It goes something like, when people tell you who they are, believe them."

Jane's first impulse was to correct her, because the quote was actually "When people *show* you who they are, believe them." And *showing* was something quite apart from telling. And that was the thing about Cameron: what he told her about himself was different from what he showed her. But then she thought better of it, because probably that was too fine a distinction. Cameron had stood before her and said, "All the shit people say about me is true." He'd calmly informed her that he physically attacked his commanding officer, for heaven's sake.

"Gia," she said, her voice catching, which pretty much confirmed that she *was* an innocent child who didn't know the ways of the world. She could feel herself flush with embarrassment.

"Aww, sweetie." Gia laid a hand on her forearm, which was weird because although she was their resident extrovert and party girl, Gia was usually the least demonstrative of their group.

"You won't tell anyone?"

"What? That you like fake penises?"

"No. About...this whole conversation."

Gia mimed zipping her lip and throwing away the key. Then she mimed crossing her heart, and Jane's own was suddenly full of affection for her friend. Gia was a lot of things, but foremost among them was loyal.

Jane slumped in her chair, a bit off kilter as a result of the uncharacteristically frank exchange with Gia and preemptively exhausted when she considered the night ahead.

"But by all means," Gia said, the forearm pat turning into an aggressive poke. "Do the dude. Break the Felix spell already!"

"There is no Felix spell!" Jane protested, laughing at the exaggerated skeptical face Gia made.

But the truth was, she was starting to fear there *was* a Felix spell. And she wanted to break it. *Crap.* She wanted to break it with Cameron.

Chapter Eleven

Cam felt like a double agent, texting Jane updates as the bachelor party wore on. Most of them consisted of variations on "Still no strippers," but he kept sending them anyway, mostly because she always replied with pithy, amusing reports on what she was up to.

He could see why she was such a successful writer. She managed to retain a kind of critical distance from her surroundings that allowed her to comment on them objectively. It's like she was at the party but not *at* the party. Which was pretty much how Jane operated all the time, he realized. Which, in turn, was actually kind of sad. She was a bit of an outsider, a position he identified with, but it was no way to live all the time.

Maybe that's why she'd been so gorgeous and exhilarated at the CN Tower and at the falls—she'd been utterly immersed, so fully present that she wasn't able to stand outside the experience in order to comment on it. Maybe that's what the "goddess mode" phrase that had popped into his head to describe her in those scenarios had meant.

The thing was, he liked her both ways. He liked the goddess; he liked the wry commentator. But he needed to shut that shit down because whoever she was, she deserved better than him.

She'd even sent him a picture of her painted toes along with a frowny face emoticon. "You're the only person who's ever going to see these besides the girls," she'd texted. When he'd asked why, she'd replied, "The wedding shoes are close-toed, as are all of my own. Elise would never allow green for the ceremony, anyway, so they're gonna be short-lived."

If you'd asked him, he would have said, objectively, that bright green was not a sexy color for toenails. It should have brought to mind fungus. Gangrene.

It turned out he had been wrong. Which was why he kept going back and looking at the damned picture.

"Whose foot is that?"

Cam fumbled the phone. He hadn't realized that Jay had slid into the big semicircular booth that was otherwise empty. Though the beer was still flowing, the party had diffused as the night wore on. Some of the guys were playing darts, and a couple were daring each other to try to pick up women. Small groups formed and reformed. Everyone was making Cam feel welcome—Jay's friends were good guys—but he was enjoying a bit of a breather. Well, he was enjoying Jane's toes, truth be told.

"Come on," Jay said, trying to grab the phone. "Who is that?"

"Cut it out!" Cam laughed as he rolled away farther down the booth, the maneuver reminding him of when they used to play-wrestle when he was a kid and Jay was home from university on visits. Jay would swarm him and then teach him how to escape his holds.

"Ah, the patented Jay Smith rollaway!" his brother said. "I've taught you well, young Jedi."

Maybe it was the shooters Jay's friends kept bringing around, but Cam hadn't felt this at ease with his brother since…well, since those days when he was little. "You did," he agreed. "You taught me a lot of good stuff."

Jay looked startled for a moment. "Was that Christie?" he asked, handing the phone back without snooping into it any further. "Are you guys back together?"

He shook his head. "Nah." He waited for the forthcoming lecture, but it didn't come. Hell, he would blame it on the booze later, but damned if he wasn't going to tell the truth. Well, not about the green toes. One thing at a time.

"Christie dumped me, actually."

Jay's eyes widened. Yeah, that was so not the role Jay had cast his brother in. "Oh, man, I didn't realize. I'm sorry."

Cameron shrugged. "It was for the best, probably."

"When did this all go down?"

"Well, I was…back unexpectedly early, as you know. So I went to her place to surprise her."

"Wasn't it your place, too? You guys were going to move in together."

Cam nodded. He'd given up his apartment before the last deployment, which was what most reservists did before a tour, but he hadn't bothered worrying about post-tour accommodations because they'd decided he'd move in with Christie when he got back.

"What happened?"

The humiliation was still fresh. He'd been imagining one of those emotional "soldier surprises loved one" reunions like you saw on YouTube. "Well, she wasn't expecting me just then. Neither was her…friend." God. He couldn't even say it.

But Jay must have understood because he said, "Jesus Christ. I'm sorry." Then his eyes narrowed and he added, "You know what? Fuck her."

Cam barked a startled laugh. His brother was pretty straitlaced. He didn't swear much. "Well, I can't, see. That role is already taken." It was Jay's turn to laugh, and it was gratifying. Cam couldn't think when was the last time he'd made his big brother laugh. "I honestly think it was for the best, though."

Because, really, it had set him straight. He'd gotten comfortable enough with Christie that he'd been starting to write off Alicia as an aberration. But the universe had bitch-slapped him back to reality. What do they say? Fool me once, shame on you; fool me twice, shame on me. So, yeah, lesson learned: no more relationships for him.

"Did you love Christie?" Jay asked.

Whoa. How had they gotten from laughing to this heavy shit so quickly? Cam's normal MO would be to make a joke at this point. He opened his mouth to do just that but then closed it. Maybe if he said nothing, his brother would back off. But no, Jay wasn't letting him off the hook, was gazing at him evenly with those bright aqua eyes that were the only trait the brothers shared. Well, shit. He'd started this whole truth thing, hadn't he? "I thought I did. I wanted to." He made a strangled noise of frustration. It was hard to explain, both because he was having trouble finding the words but also because he didn't do shit like share his feelings. "I was trying to grow the fuck up. To commit to something. To someone. To her."

Jay nodded. "It's an admirable impulse, but I don't

think you can *decide* to love someone, no matter how good your intentions. It's more... oh, forget it. Who am I? Dr. Phil?"

"Nah, you're the Jedi Master, remember?" Cam knocked his shoulder against Jay's. "So go ahead, dispense your wisdom, Oh Wise One." He was kidding, but he really did want to hear what his brother had to say.

"I don't really have any wisdom. It's just that it probably wasn't fair to either you or Christie to try to force things. I mean, I'm sorry it ended like it did, and cheating on your deployed boyfriend is pretty much the worst thing I can imagine a person doing, so I still think she's a grade-A asshole..." Cam smiled as Jay trailed off and steepled his fingers, which was something he did when he was thinking hard. "You can be open to love, I guess, but I don't even think that really matters. I think love is more something that happens to you. Hits you. A 'ready or not' kind of thing." He smirked. "So there's your Dr. Phil sound bite."

"Is that what happened to you?"

Jay's thoughtful expression was replaced by a sheepish grin. "Yeah."

Cam slapped him on the back. "Well, that's awesome."

"I know Elise has gone a little bit crazy with this wedding. You're not seeing her in her best light..."

"Don't worry about it, man." Elise wasn't seeing Cam in his, either. The problem was he feared he'd lost the version of himself that Jay could be proud to introduce to his wife-to-be. Like when he flew home from his trial to find some other dude in what was supposed to be his home, he had become untethered from the man he was becoming. And it didn't feel like something you got a second chance at, certainly not after having failed as spectacularly as he had—on both the home and career fronts.

A commotion drew his attention to the far end of the bar, which was just as well, because he was getting maudlin. "Well, speak of the devil."

Jay looked up. Cam wouldn't have thought it possible, but his brother grinned and groaned at the same time. "Hey, don't call my lovely bride the devil."

He hadn't been. He'd been thinking of another devil. One with green toenails.

"Whoa. My lovely, extremely drunk bride." Jay stood up. "Excuse me."

The pub where they'd spent the evening had definitely been humming, but it was a chill sort of hum as beer flowed and groups of friends—Jay's party included—enjoyed their evening. The arrival of Elise's posse turned everything up to eleven. There must have been fifteen of them, their pink cheeks and flushed eyes heralding their inebriation. They were dressed up, most of them in skirts and heels. Elise was wearing a sparkly silver skirt, a tight T-shirt that said, "Pop the bubbly, I'm getting a hubby," and a veil.

Gia made a beeline for him. She was wearing a skirt, too, a tight black one, and her pink T-shirt said, "I Do Crew." He picked out another woman in the same shirt, one he remembered from drinks the other night—that would be Wendy.

"Who'ya looking for?" Gia asked, plopping down next to him.

"I'm just taking in the sight of all you lovely ladies."

Gia rolled her eyes, picked up his beer, and took a long swig. He liked Gia. She had balls.

She slammed the beer down. "Listen, you asshole. I don't know what kind of whammy you're putting on Jane, but—"

"Whoa. I'm not putting any 'whammy' on Jane."

"Oh, shut up. I know you."

"Uh, you actually don't."

She waved her hand dismissively. "I know your type."

"And what type is that?" he asked, not bothering to try to keep the annoyance out of his voice.

"The player type." She leaned in and looked him right in the eye. "Now listen. Jane could use some fun. I'm all for that." She poked him in the chest. "But you manage her expectations, you hear me?"

"I'm not really sure what expectations you—"

"Oh, shut up, Cameron. The bottom line is this: you hurt Jane, and not only do you have me to answer to, you'll have Elise and Wendy all up in your face. We're a goddamned sisterhood, so don't fuck with us." She picked up his beer and chugged the rest of it. "Understood?"

"Understood," he said. Because it was. He could bluster and pretend he didn't know what she was talking about, but she saw through him. From the sounds of things, Jane's last boyfriend had been a dick. It was understandable that her friends wanted to prevent her from repeating the same mistake. He and Gia were totally on the same page there. He and Jane had had the one crazy kiss, but it stopped there.

Without a word, Gia slid out of the booth. He watched her return to a cluster of women, and as if to illustrate her earlier point, she slung her arms around two of them— Wendy and Jane, clad in matching "I Do Crew" T-shirts. Wendy continued the skirt theme, but not his Jane. Nope, she had on her usual jeans—dark, dressy ones, and a pair of pink flats that matched the shirt. She would say that the shirt was too small for her. He would say that the shirt fit just right. Damn. Gia was a model. She was beautiful, objectively. She was also about six feet tall and built like a beanpole. Jane, on the other hand...you could grab on to Jane.

"Cameron!"

His dirty thoughts were interrupted by the fourth member of Gia's self-proclaimed sisterhood and his future sister-in-law. Elise slid right up next to him and kissed him on the cheek. "Jay says I have to be nicer to you."

Jay, sliding in on her other side, said "Lise, give it a rest."

"What?" She batted her eyes with faux innocence. "You know I always do what you say, Jay."

Whoa. That last bit was delivered in a sultry tone that made Cam flick his gaze to his brother. If Cam wasn't mistaken, there was a bit of heat in them as he looked at his bride-to-be. Well, damn. Apparently his mild-mannered accountant brother had a bit of the bad boy in him, too.

His other conclusion: everyone in the world was getting laid except him. Because it wasn't only the sparks flying between the bridal couple as Jay leaned over and whispered something into Elise's ear that made her suck in a sharp breath, it was the scene around him. The bachelorettes had dispersed themselves among the bachelors, and the air was charged. He started to slide out of the booth, figuring a trip to the bar to replenish the drink that Gia had stolen would be an excuse to give the lovebirds a little privacy. He'd only just made it to his feet when he heard a quiet voice from behind.

"I want you to make me eggs Benedict tomorrow."

He jumped about a foot even though the voice was low-pitched so only he could hear it. How had she managed to sneak up on him? He'd barely had his eyes off her since she arrived. And, more importantly: *holy fuck*, was she propositioning him?

"Jane," he said, trying to buy some time to get his

bearings—and possibly also to get his dick to calm down. He looked at her feet, which was dumb because he already knew her toes were going to be covered by her shoes. "How are you?"

"I am hungry. For eggs Benedict. In the morning."

Jesus Christ, she *was* propositioning him. "What happened to pregnancy scares? Ax murderers? What happened to efficiency?"

"Cameron, I've just come from a gay club. It was full of hot, shirtless men writhing against each other. The girls have been talking about sex all evening. I'm starting to think you might be onto something with that whole human touch theory of yours."

"Aha!" He couldn't help gloating. "You're horny." And so was he. She was right; there were pheromones in the air tonight, and that shit was contagious.

"You are correct."

"You're also drunk." And thank God for it. He needed an out, an excuse to do the honorable thing. "I don't do drunk hookups."

She tilted her head at him. "Why not?"

"Because there's this little thing called consent? Give me a little credit, Jane."

She smiled, a slow, knowing Cheshire cat sort of smile, and lifted a glass that appeared to be full of cola. "I am stone-cold sober, my friend. Which is another reason this party is wearing on me."

His dick twitched. "Yeah, you don't realize how stupid drunk people are until you're the only sober one in a group of them."

She hitched her head toward the exit. "So let's get out of here."

He sighed. "I can't."

"You're turning me down."

He winced, and though she hadn't phrased it as a question, he nodded, trying to think how to say some variation on "it's not you, it's me," and not sound like an asshole. "It's not a good idea, Jane. I can't be the kind of guy you—"

"It's just sex, Cameron. That's all."

Her declaration gave him pause. Was it possible that he and Jane really could enjoy a fallout-free hookup? Because, *damn*, he could get into that idea. But no. He thought of Gia all up in his face a little while ago. It was too slippery a slope.

"Are you, who have been talking about nothing but getting laid since you got to town, trying to tell me that I'm not allowed to have meaningless sex?" Jane went on.

"That's not what I'm saying..." *I'm saying I like you too much to have sex with you. I'm saying you deserve someone better. I'm saying I'm not sure it would* be *just sex, and it's not just* your *reaction I'm worried about.*

He wished she would interrupt him again, but she did not. She simply stared at him with that single damned eyebrow raised. He started again. "Of course you can have meaningless sex. I just don't..."

"You don't want to," she said, and the hurt that flared momentarily in her eyes might as well have been an inferno engulfing him.

"No!" God, could he dig a bigger hole for himself here? He was trying to protect her from him, but was it possible he was hurting her more by turning her down?

The answer to this late-breaking question was irrelevant though, because the hurt disappeared from her eyes, replaced by steel, as she said, "That's okay. I'll find someone who does."

And eff him if she didn't then turn on her heel and march up to a group of guys at the bar. And they weren't even bachelor party guys. No, they were, to use her term, "randoms."

⸻

Ten minutes later, Cam was accosted again, this time by two of Jay's groomsmen, a fellow accountant named Kent, and Andy, who was Elise's brother.

"She's cute, eh?" said Kent, a quiet guy who hadn't made much of an impression on Cam.

"Who?"

"Jane," he said, nodding to where Jane was clinking her glass against the beer bottle of some pretty, overgrown frat boy type. "You know, the one you've been staring at?"

Andy snickered.

"I haven't been staring at her," Cameron said, staring at her. *Shit*. She leaned in to let Captain America whisper something in her ear, and then she threw her head back with laughter that seemed irritatingly genuine.

"I'm just checking because I've been thinking of asking her out," Kent went on. "Wanted to make sure that you guys weren't...you know."

Cam shook his head as Jane put her hand on the Ralph Lauren model's forearm. For someone who claimed to not date *and* not hook up, she was pretty good at flirting. He had to make a conscious effort to unlock his jaw to say, "Jane doesn't date."

"What do you mean, she doesn't date? She's single, isn't she?" It was true, but even if it wasn't, this unassuming Kent dude was not the guy for her.

"Yeah, but she's not in the market for a guy," Cam said.

Except tonight, apparently, she was. Kent, however, did not need to know that.

"I have to say, I'm afraid he's right," Andy said to Kent, nodding in Jane's direction. "I've known Jane since she and Elise were freshmen in university. She's had one boyfriend in all that time. She doesn't seem interested."

Cam refrained, but only just, from turning to Kent and saying *neener, neener, neener*.

"So what is that, then?" Kent asked, nodding as Jane went on her tiptoes to say something into the prepster's ear that made him drop his drink like a hot potato, grab her hand, and start towing her out of the pub.

"That is…"

…not happening.

Cam was up, propelled across the room by pure unadulterated jealousy that was as shocking as it was strong. He had never been jealous before, not even when he'd walked in on Christie with his replacement, not really. He'd been angry, yes, but more at the loss of the life he'd thought he was coming back to. And even that had rapidly been replaced by resignation.

But right now he could murder both Kent the Accountant and Captain America without blinking. And he'd do it, too, before either of them touched Jane.

Goddammit. If Jane was bound and determined to pick up a guy tonight, he was the least problematic one here. Which was ironic as hell, because the whole point of rejecting her had been to protect her from him. But despite his many faults, Cam appreciated Jane—her quirks, her insecurities, her humor. He knew how to make her loosen up.

He would regret this later, but not as much as he would regret watching her leave with one of the other assholes here.

When he came up behind Jane and Captain America, the dickhead had his hand on her lower back as he propelled her toward the door. Cam reached out and took hold of the guy's cuff between his thumb and forefinger and lifted his arm away from Jane like it was a bag of stinky garbage. He was wearing a long-sleeved pinstriped button-down, for fuck's sake. Even if she was only in it for a hookup, this banker-wanker was not the right guy for the job.

"Excuse me?" The dude turned with a kind of amused superiority that drove home Cam's point.

"Time to go, Janie," he said, placing his hand firmly against her lower back, aiming for exactly the spot where Captain America's hand had been. She raised her eyebrows and opened her mouth. Before she could issue the protest he knew was coming, he closed his mouth over hers, a quick kiss, but a deep, decisive one. One that made his point to her admirer. To her, too. Then he pulled away and said, "Your eggs Benedict awaits."

Chapter Twelve

*J*ane might have changed her mind in the taxi if Cameron hadn't rested his hand on her thigh as soon as he gave the driver her address. She was sober—she hadn't been lying about that—but once they got outside, away from the weird fairy-tale-hopped-up-on-sex hormones that had been the bachelorette-meets-bachelor party, she started to wonder if someone had roofied her Diet Coke.

Because what in Xena's name was she doing? She was not a reckless risk-taker. Never in her life had she picked up a guy at a bar. That alone would have been enough, but did she stop there? No, she did not. Forever an overachiever, she had picked up one guy, then left with another.

One who had, not twenty minutes previously, rejected her. If she had any pride, any self-respect to speak of, she would have left with Brian. Bryce? Dang, what was his name? Whatever. Heck, she would have left by herself.

If she had any sense at all, she'd put a stop to this now.

But that hand.

The way it had sought out her back at the bar, with a calm air of possession, like it belonged there.

The way it sat on her thigh now, heavy and solid, spreading heat up her leg and to her center. They were almost at her house, and they hadn't spoken yet. But they didn't need to. That hand communicated volumes.

He'd been right, before. She *was* horny. And it was his fault. He'd planted the idea of this "human touch" nonsense, and she hadn't been able to get it out of her mind. Maybe he—and Gia, and everyone—was right. Maybe she and Felix simply hadn't been compatible. Yeah, she'd felt his rejection as a major burn, but maybe she'd been letting it have too much power over her. She was older now. She knew what she wanted and what she didn't. She was capable of compartmentalizing.

Well, maybe. Regardless, it's what she *wasn't* capable of that was ruling the evening. And she wasn't capable of shaking that hand off her thigh. She needed that hand.

She needed it all over her.

The taxi pulled up to her house, and she heaved a shaky sigh, feeling like she was one big exposed nerve masquerading as a bridesmaid. Felix had always been frustrated with her because it took her so long to come, if she did at all, but tonight she felt like a box of gunpowder that might explode if Cameron looked at her the wrong way. Or the right way. Or at all.

"You can send me home," Cameron said, low into her ear, crowding her from behind as she unlocked her front door.

She shook her head, too embarrassed to say anything out loud, to claim her desire for him.

"I can't be your boyfriend."

"Oh my God, no!" she answered, suddenly finding her words, then laughing at his mock-offended face as she flipped on the entryway light. "Sorry! It's just that...I told you I don't want one of those." Baby steps—she had only just talked herself into the idea of casual sex.

She kicked off her shoes and—"Oh my God, what are you *doing*?" He had dropped to his knees.

"I'm looking at these toes that have been tormenting me all night." He ran a hand from her ankle down over the top of her foot, and she shivered. "One photo of them, and I've been thinking about them nonstop. These are some powerful toes."

"Hmmm. You might even say they have brought men to their knees," she said, biting back a grin. Damn, she was bad at flirting. But she was rewarded anyway when he barked a laugh, and smoothed a line on the top of her foot where her shoe had dug into her flesh.

"This looks painful."

"Nah," she said, wondering if he was planning to stay there on the floor, at her feet. "That's nothing. Have you ever tried high heels?"

"Can't say that I have."

"Well, don't. They're torture devices. I am morally opposed to them."

He looked up at her, and she was startled to find that she'd placed her hand on his head, without even realizing it. His buzz cut was growing in a little, and the fuzz of his hair was surprisingly soft. They stared at each other, and for a moment, fear flared in her belly. The idea that anything could happen. That she'd brought him here planning to invite him into her body. What had she been thinking? It was...too much.

But then he moved his head a little so her hand slid down to his cheek. His breath hitched and his eyes closed as he leaned into her hand, as if he wanted to rest a weary head on her palm.

Was he afraid, too?

He opened his eyes, and she could see that the answer was no. But there was something there, some emotion beyond what she would have expected, that she couldn't quite identify.

He must have seen the question in her eyes, because he whispered, "It's been a long time."

"Since you've been back, you still haven't..."

"No. Well, that's true, but beyond that, it's been...since before I last deployed."

Wow. *Wow.* She had kind of imagined him sleeping his way through Iraq, though that was probably stupid since she'd just found out he'd had a girlfriend during the deployment. And even though it had only been a day since their trip to Niagara, when he'd assured her he hadn't reneged on their various bets, they hadn't made another one to cover the time since then. There had been nothing stopping him from spending all day today working on his stupid "list." Knowing that he hadn't caused a surge of emotion. Guilt for having thought so poorly of him that she'd even entertained the notion. But also pride, as if he'd somehow been faithful to *her*, which was ridiculous.

Lust. There was also lust.

And it was stronger than the fear.

So she used her hand to gently tug upward on his chin, communicating her wish that he rise.

He did. She took his hand and led him toward her bedroom, but at the last minute he surprised her by stopping at the threshold of the office. "The good stuff's in here," he rasped, pulling her inside and then against him.

She buried her face in his chest, embarrassed in a way she hadn't been when they were discussing her vibrators before. That had been a theoretical discussion, and this was...not theoretical. "We don't need those," she whispered, but she very much feared that she did.

She felt rather than saw his shrug, since she was still hiding her face. "Maybe we don't need them; maybe we do." His warm palms came to rest on her cheeks, and he gently tipped her head up to force her to look at him. "Regardless, we might *want* them. Either way, a man likes to be prepared."

It was the perfect thing to say. The kindest, sexiest, most astonishing thing, and those few sentences somehow tipped a giant weight off her shoulders. Men were the ones who were supposed to have performance anxiety, but she'd been tied up in knots. The idea that he didn't have a particular vision in his head of how their encounter would unfold, that there was no script, was strangely liberating. Insanely sexy.

She lifted herself up onto her tiptoes, intending to kiss him, but he didn't seem to be getting the message. He still had his hands on the sides of her face, so she put hers on his in a mirror-image gesture and tried to tug his head down. But he resisted, stared at her with a small smile.

"Kiss me, you idiot," she said.

He laughed. "I'm going to. I just need...a minute."

"For what?" To change his mind? Like hell. She was standing there, panties wet and nipples almost painfully tight, a caricature of sexual desire. She hadn't confronted her big emotional block about casual sex only to have the proceedings derailed now. She pulled harder on his head and bounced a little on her toes. Maybe this was one instance in which high heels would actually be worth the pain.

The smile disappeared, and for a moment she feared

she'd offended him, that he was going to call the whole thing off. "To pause and take things in. To pause and take *you* in. Because once this starts, Jane..."

"What?" she whispered.

"We're going to set this fucking house on fire."

He didn't wait for her to respond, just lowered his head—*finally!*—and oh, if she thought she'd been turned on before, she hadn't realized. If she'd thought their kiss at the falls had been hot, she'd had no idea.

His tongue plunged into her mouth, but it might as well have been between her legs, because the shot of desire through her core was almost painful. She hissed against his mouth, and he started to pull away, but that wasn't happening. So she slid her hands, which still rested on his cheeks, around his neck and hitched herself up on his body, wrapping her legs around his waist, and oh, her aim had been accidentally perfect. It was his turn to hiss as the very center of her slammed against his erection.

He didn't miss a beat, though. His hands came around to cup her bottom, and he took two steps until her back was against the wall and pressed his hips against hers even as he returned to working her mouth with his. She arched her back, seeking more pressure, and he knew what she was after, because he ground into her, making tight circles with his hips, never letting up in the way a thrusting motion would have.

And then..."Oh God!" she bit out, because she had forgotten that he had hands and that she had breasts. She had forgotten, or maybe she'd never really known, how good hands could feel on breasts.

His hands slid up under her T-shirt, deftly undid the clasp at the back of her bra, then came around front and plucked her nipples, summoning a cry of pleasure from her.

She wanted to arch away from and into his touch at the same time, so intense was the sensation. But it was gone as quickly as it began as he ripped his mouth from hers and spread his palms, pressing and kneading, cupping, as if he were trying to get as big a handful of her as possible.

Dear God, she was going to come right here with his hand up her shirt. That seemed, suddenly, not okay, so she lowered her feet to the ground and shoved him away. Or tried to—he grunted, resisting, renewing his assault on her until she managed to say, "I need to get my clothes off."

She almost regretted her words, because that was all it took. He sprang away from her, and the loss of sensation made her breasts ache, and her vagina... it actually hurt. He whipped off his shirt, and oh God, those tattoos. The idea that she could openly look at them, that she could touch them. Put her mouth on them. He bent over to remove one leg from his pants but paused to look up at her.

"Naked," he rasped. "I need you naked."

She stared at him, stunned. His pupils were dilated so there was only a slim ring of blue around them. His breath was ragged, and she could see the thrumming of his pulse in his neck. He wanted her, and he wasn't trying to hide it. She moaned, and he wasn't even touching her.

"Please," he added.

She was always going to obey; she had just been caught momentarily in him, helpless in the tractor beam that was his obvious desire. But the combination of the gruff command followed by the polite entreaty was like a fast-forward switch. She pulled her shirt and already-undone bra off together. She gave a passing thought that she should have started with her jeans because now he was going to see her muffin top, but it was forgotten when he closed his eyes, let his head fall back, and ground out, "Awww, fuuuck."

The surge of triumph in her chest told her that it was a good "Awww, fuuuck." So she unzipped her jeans. The sound in the otherwise silent room had him opening his eyes. They latched on to her hands as she pushed her jeans over her hips. His jaw hung open, and feeling drunk with power and as saturated with desire as he appeared to be, she decided to name what she wanted in a way she never had with Felix. "Yes. Fuck. That's correct." His eyes whipped up to hers, practically sparking. So, to be clear, she added, "That's what I want. For you to fuck me."

"Oh, sweetheart, that's exactly what I'm going to do." She wasn't done taking her jeans off, but he grabbed her and walked her backward to the daybed until the backs of her legs hit it and she sat down. "What should I fuck you with first? My hands or my tongue?" He yanked on the bottoms of her jeans and then slid his hands back up her bare legs. He was coming for her panties, next, she could tell.

"No." She shook her head, both to illustrate her "no," but also at herself, because it wasn't that she didn't want those things, for him to fuck her with his fingers and tongue. She just didn't want them as much as she wanted something else. "I want you to fuck me with your cock," she breathed, and he stopped in the middle of sliding her panties down her legs.

"I don't have a condom," he rasped. He worked her panties the rest of the way off. "These are so wet," he growled.

"What do you mean you don't have a condom?"

He repeated his earlier move of sliding his hands up her legs, but this time there was nothing to stop him, no barrier or fabric, and when he got to the V of her thighs, he pressed one hand against each and said, "Open for me." She did, unthinkingly.

"What do you mean you don't have a condom?" she said again. It was like they were having two different conversations.

He stroked a hand gently across her outer folds. "Oh, shit, baby, you're so wet."

"Cameron!" she panted, to try to force him to listen to her but also because even that light, exploratory touch had her arching her hips up off the bed.

"Yes," he said, taking his hand away now that he was finally listening to her. She wanted to curse herself for making him stop. She wanted to grab his hand and press it back against her body. He stuck out his tongue and licked a quick line straight up from her belly button, between her breasts, and through the notch of her collarbone. It was the single most erotic thing that had ever happened to her. So far. She had a feeling the record might be broken a few times if things continued on like they were. He ended his journey by covering her body with his own, bracing himself on his forearms so she wasn't bearing all his weight. "It was a bachelor party," he said when they were nose to nose. "I thought I was going to be hanging out with a bunch of guys all night."

"But..." she trailed off, aware that she sounded like a whiny child. "I want to have sex." She had tried to replace the "whiny" with "sultry," but it wasn't really working.

"We're going to," he said. "We *are*."

Then he reversed directions and started heading back down her body, but he stopped at her chest this time and took an aching nipple into his mouth. She cried out from the relief of it, of having his mouth on her. That relief was short-lived, though, because having that part of her soothed only threw into stark relief how much she ached for him between her legs, how empty she felt.

He knew, though, somehow, because as soon as the

thought arose, his fingers were there, pressing into her. That was the thing about Cameron. He was aggressive, but responsive. He was utterly in control of their encounter, but he played her so expertly that she wanted to surrender forever.

"How can you be this wet?" he demanded. She lifted her head, suddenly embarrassed. She was about to stammer an apology when he added, "Fuck, I could come just from touching your sweet pussy."

Then he was gone, and she cried out at the loss of sensation, but before she could get her bearings, he was back with one of her vibrators.

"We *really* don't need that," she whispered, but he ignored her, switching it on. He'd grabbed the Love Egg, and it looked so small, dwarfed by his big hands.

Ignoring her protest, he rolled her onto her side and pulled her flush against him, her back to his chest. He kept one arm around her torso, securing her to him, and pressed open-mouthed kisses on the side of her neck. Then he used his other hand to press the vibrating egg against her clit—but only for a second.

"Ahh!" she shouted. The moment her pelvis, of its own accord, bucked after the retreating egg, the arm that had been slung casually around her tightened like a vise, pulling her back against the solid muscle of his body. Then he pressed his hand—his whole palm—over her, almost as if he was soothing an ache, which in a way, he was. She was surrounded by him. His cock pressed into the crease of her bottom, and his arms a vise securing her to him, his hand covering the front of her sex.

"See? It doesn't have to be either-or," he said before tugging on her earlobe with his teeth. And before she could respond, the egg was back, but again, only for a heartbeat.

Again she struggled, though she wasn't sure why. He was going to do what he was going to do. It didn't matter what she wanted. Well, that wasn't right. It was more that he knew what she wanted, before she did even. He knew about things she hadn't imagined yet.

A few more rounds of teasing with the egg, and she was almost weeping. She was an exposed nerve. It was like he was dismantling her with his touch. She'd given up trying to chase the egg and had gone limp in his arms.

When he realized as much, the arm that had been bound over her chest slid down and he parted her folds. The next time he brought the egg to her clit, he plunged a finger inside her, then a second. His cock pulsed behind her.

"Oh my God!" she moaned. He left the egg on a little longer this time. It was too much. She didn't want it to be over. "Stop!" she said.

He stopped everything, all at once, immediately. Not only did he stop touching her, he pulled his body, which had been plastered to her back, away.

"Gaahhh!" she nearly yelled, grabbing the egg-free hand and shoving it between her legs. When it was back where it belonged, she clarified, "Stop with the egg. I only want you."

"You want to come all over my hand?" he practically growled.

She nodded frantically, writhing against him, hating that the end was so close but unable to stop bucking, to stop running to meet the wave that was barreling down on her.

And then she was coming.

"Jesus fucking Christ, Jane," Cameron ground out as she kept coming.

The aftershocks were still rumbling through her when he said, "Next time, I want to feel you come on my face."

As the orgasm receded, it made way for self-consciousness. And for the awareness that she had basically sat there while he did such wicked, incredible things to her, heedless of his own pleasure. His penis was still tucked behind her bottom, and it was still hard as steel.

Next time, I want to feel you come on my face.

Next time.

Jane had always viewed fellatio as a necessary chore attached to couple-hood. When she was with Felix, she used to try to space it out. She even had a little internal schedule that he didn't know about. She'd basically make an effort in that regard every four or five times. She didn't *hate* it, but... well, to be honest, it was one more reason to prefer vibrators.

But holy crap, right now? She needed it. She needed to make him feel as good as she did. Heck, she needed to make him feel one-tenth as good as she did. And it wasn't an "it's polite to return the favor" kind of need. She *wanted* it, to come back to his use of the words *want* and *need*. What had happened between them had conflated the two concepts, blown apart the dividing lines between them. She didn't even care that she probably wasn't that good at it. Her mouth was watering. So she wiggled out of his embrace, turned over so she was facing him, and said, "I want to feel you come on *my* face *this* time."

—⟋⟍

Holy, holy, *holy* fuck.

After Jane let loose that astonishingly dirty statement, she wasted no time. It wasn't five more seconds before her mouth was on him. And there was no warm-up, no teasingly light kisses. She opened her mouth and took him in as deeply as she could.

"Oh Christ!" he shouted.

He was flat on his back on the daybed, and she was strad-dling his shins and bent over his dick, her hair a curtain of flame that was fucking gorgeous, but also blocking his view. "Wait. I want to see you if you're going to do that. I *need* to see you."

He sat up, intending to scoot back so he was sitting against the back of the daybed and would have a better prospect, but she slid off it entirely, kneeling on the floor and tugging his legs to get him to come sit on the edge.

"Jane, " he started, but he wasn't sure what he was trying to say. Maybe that she didn't have to kneel, but Jesus, to see her like that. She was a perfect hourglass, her waist nipping in between gorgeous full hips and those criminally addictive breasts. And now that her hair was hanging loose around her shoulders, he could see her face. She smiled a little and ran her hands up the tops of his thighs. He feared perhaps this repositioning might mean a loss of momentum, that now she *would* backtrack and start with the teasing foreplay. Not that there was anything wrong with that. He would take Jane's mouth on his cock in any configuration she liked. He just— "Oh my God!"

She took him all the way in, as she had before, and began moving her mouth up and down his shaft, but from this van-tage point he could see *everything*. Her cheeks hollowing as she sucked. Her perfect breasts bouncing as she estab-lished a rhythm. Her big green-brown eyes looking up at him. It made him realize with a jolt that Christie had always closed her eyes when she was blowing him. But this. This was so much hotter. This was—*oh, shit*. The pressure had been building all over, in his back, his balls, everywhere. But he'd thought he could hold back, prolong the pleasure. He'd always been pretty good at controlling himself, in the bedroom if not elsewhere. But she was undoing him, tearing him apart.

"Jane, Jane," he gasped, trying to gently push her away. She pulled up but didn't move back, kept hold of his thighs with her hands.

And he came for the first time in five months with another person.

"Holy fuck."

⁓

They fell asleep with the light on, a tangle of sweaty limbs on the too-small daybed. When Jane woke up and glanced at the clock she kept on her desk, it was three a.m. She ached all over, her breath was atrocious, and she was pretty sure she had come in her hair.

But she didn't care. She shifted a little because one of her legs, which had been draped over Cameron, had fallen asleep. She felt like she weighed a thousand pounds, but for once, in a good way. She was heavy with satiation. Well-used.

She almost had her leg free when an arm came out of nowhere and clamped down on it. "Where do you think you're going?" Her head was tucked under his chin, and she was curled up against his chest, so she felt the words rumbling inside him as he spoke them.

"My leg is asleep," she said, her voice muffled by his body.

"Mmm." He stretched in place, then sat up and scooted to the end of the bed and began massaging her leg.

"Oh, you don't have to…oh!" It felt so good, the pins and needles being worked out by deep, long strokes of his strong hands. So she swallowed her protest and shifted into a sitting position at the other end of the bed, facing him. She had the vague notion that maybe she should cover herself. Or at least suck in her stomach.

She and Felix had never really lounged around naked. She didn't have a lot of experience with non-sex nudity. But she was still suffused with that languid heaviness. It was too delicious to let go of, and it kept her pinned in place.

"These toes," he said, having worked his way down to her ankle. "I thought about them all night." He lifted her foot and, to her utter astonishment, bent over and bit her big toe.

"Oww!" she squealed, though it hadn't really hurt, had just been a little nip.

He kissed the same spot and began rubbing her foot.

"Do you have a foot fetish?" she teased.

"Not previously." He wagged his eyebrows.

It did something to her. She was suffused with a sense of gratitude and appreciation. He had been so much like what she expected, and yet not. There had been the confidence, the mastery, his utter control of her body's response, but also the tenderness. The foot rub, for heaven's sake. "Thank you," she whispered.

"What?" He looked up, genuinely confused. Then he grinned and shrugged. "Hey, post-orgasm foot rubs— standard operating procedure."

"No," she said, wanting to reward his tenderness with honesty. "I've never...had sex like that before."

"Ha!" he said, giving the arch of her foot an extra-hard squeeze that nearly made her eyes roll back into her head. "So you admit that I was right."

"About all this doing-it-with-an-actual-human business? Well..." She pretended to think about it. "I didn't hate it."

He made a mock-outraged face and nipped another toe.

"It's funny," she said, thinking back on the sexual component of her relationship with Felix. "The vibrators became such an issue with my last boyfriend. I tried to introduce them because things were...not really working for me. But he hated them so much that I backed off. Used them privately. I guess I built up this either-or thing in my head. But..." Her face heated thinking back to the way Cameron had tormented her with the vibrator, bringing her closer to the edge, then backing off. And also because here she was again, casually chatting about sex. She didn't *do* that. But she also didn't want to stop. It felt like she was getting a real perspective on things—on her past, on what she wanted out of life.

"Well, as discussed, your ex sounds like a real winner."

"It was like he was mad that I didn't just fake it," Jane said. "I never thought about it in those terms, but I think that would have made things easier between us."

"Easier, maybe," Cameron scoffed. "But I personally would rather cut off my dick than know someone I was sleeping with was faking it on the regular."

"Right?" She laughed. His directness was so refreshing. It had rubbed her the wrong way when they first met, but she was coming around to seeing things his way. There was something liberating about saying what you wanted with no obfuscation. About "opening your eyes and jumping," to quote him from the CN Tower.

"I'm glad you came to your senses and dumped him. Vibrators are *clearly* better than he was."

"I didn't dump him, actually." She had no idea why she was saying this. The rational thing to do would be to just let him assume that she'd been smarter and more confident than had actually been the case. But she had literally bared herself to him just now, and she couldn't seem to stop doing it.

Cameron screwed up his face, trying to make sense of the situation. "So he was a lousy lay, you suggested an avenue for improvement, and then he dumped you? What the hell?"

Jane giggled—his indignation was gratifying. "No. He dumped me a couple years later when I suggested we move in together. Well, that's not exactly right." She deserved *some* credit here. "I *did* kind of dump him at that point, I guess, but it was only because his reaction to the idea of cohabitation suggested that I was basically nothing more to him than a convenient habit."

"What?"

Oh, boy. Cameron wasn't just indignant, he was *pissed*. His nostrils were flaring and everything. Was it wrong that she liked that? It was one thing for her friends to express outrage about what had gone down with Felix, but for some reason, Cameron's anger was different.

"Yeah," she said, warming to her tale of humiliation. "We'd been together six years at that point. We were both twenty-six. Neither of us had a ton of money—I was determined to make a go of it with the writing, but things hadn't really taken off yet—so it just seemed like the natural next step as well as a financially practical one. It was his birthday, so I took him out to dinner and did this little proposal-type thing. I got us these stupid little matching heart key chains. You know, like we could use them for the keys to our new place?" She scoffed. To think that she'd ever been so naive.

"And he said no." Cameron was clearly working to control his voice.

"To be fair, he tried not to be mean about it, but yeah.

He said he was happy having a girlfriend and didn't really see that changing. And it wasn't like I was pushing for marriage or kids," she added. "I just thought...well, I don't know what I thought." It seemed like another lifetime ago.

"But then you dumped him."

"Not right that moment. I was too...mortified. Trying not to cry and all that."

Was she mistaken, or had Cameron just *growled*?

She looked at him, giving him a moment to speak if he wanted to, but when he didn't say anything, she continued. "I talked to Wendy that night, and she said, 'You're not happy with him, and you haven't been for a long time. So why are you still doing this?' And it dawned on me that she was right. I hadn't even told her about the vibrator stuff—it was too humiliating. But I started thinking 'I never get off with this guy and he doesn't really want to be with me in any meaningful way. What am I doing?' It took my heart a little longer to get the message. We met when we were twenty, so in some ways, we grew up together. It was hard to let go. But, yeah, I listened to my brain and not my heart and broke things off the next day."

"And where is this motherfucker now?" Cameron spoke quietly but there was barely controlled rage in his tone.

Jane shivered but tried to cover it up with humor. "Why? So you can go beat him up?"

"Seriously. What's he doing now? You said he was a surgeon?"

"Let's not talk about this anymore." She appreciated his outrage more than he knew, but now that she'd told him her sob story, she felt light. Happy. She wanted to stay that way, to prolong this extraordinary night. "I think we've given Felix enough airtime, don't you?" Her stomach rumbled audibly, and she laughed. "I'm starving. Should we make sandwiches? Are you hungry?"

He kept her pinned with his intense, borderline-angry gaze for a long moment, but just when it had started to become awkward, he dropped her foot and licked his lips. "I *am* hungry."

She started to get up, but his hands clamped down on her thighs, one on each, at the widest part of them. Then, very slowly, he lowered his head until his mouth was inches from her mound.

"Open your legs," he said.

And she did.

Chapter Thirteen

"Cameron."

There was a voice penetrating Cam's consciousness.

And someone tapping his shoulder.

His first impulse was to pull a pillow over his head and ignore it, because he was so exhausted. He actually thought for a minute that he was back in Iraq, being roused at who knew what ungodly hour for who knew what drill or exercise.

"Don't wake up all the way. Stay asleep," said the voice, and it all came flooding back.

He reached for her. They'd moved to the queen-size bed in her bedroom after round two last night—after he'd eaten her out and she'd jacked him off in her office. But the bed beside him was empty, the sheets cool.

Christ, what a night. Who knew Muddy Jane had it in

her? He smiled. Finally, he'd ticked the number one item off his return-to-civilian-life list. And he was going to need a new name for her. Wicked Jane, maybe?

"Sleep in," said the voice. She was nearby. She must be in the bathroom now. He was only too happy to comply, so he scooted over to make room for her when she came back. They would need their strength for later.

Please let there be a later.

Probably they'd have to have the "I'm not your boyfriend" conversation again, to assuage his guilt, but maybe not even. His mind roamed back over the conversations he'd had with Jane, last night and earlier, about her vibrators and her waste-of-space ex. It seemed entirely possible that she was using him as an experiment. He let his eyes slip closed. Sleep was so close. He wanted to wait until she was back in his arms, but it was taking all his strength not to succumb.

"Hey." The voice was louder now. He turned toward it.

She was standing next to the bed, towering over him.

No, correction: Xena: Warrior Princess, was towering over him.

His breath hitched. His dick hitched. Everything hitched. Because she was stunning. The knee-high boots—flat, he noted with amusement; she'd picked the right character to cosplay—the leather skirt, the armor, the black wig, the arm bands. All of it. Maybe the name he was looking for was Warrior Jane.

"I happen to know that Jay's condo is going to be transformed into a dance studio today," she whispered. "Elise decided to make Jay and all of the wedding party she could manage to get a hold of—the ones who weren't previously committed to Comicon, mind you—to practice some kind of choreographed recessional she's become obsessed with.

So I suggest you hide out here today. I'm leaving a spare house key on the kitchen table. If you go, lock up and then shove it through the mail slot. But stick around as long as you like. If you're still here when I'm back, maybe we can grab dinner."

He tried to answer, but he was still struck dumb by the sight of her.

Also, he had no fucking idea what to say. He wanted to have dinner with Jane tonight. Like, *seriously* wanted it. The prospect of watching Jane eat food was now all he was going to think about for the rest of the day. But was that a good idea? He could hardly condemn Felix for leading her on and then turn around and do exactly the same thing.

She wasn't waiting for an answer, though. She tipped the cardboard weapon she was holding so he could better see it in the low light. It was the one he'd made for her, and she'd painted it. "I did what you said with the chakram, and it's perfect. Thank you."

Then Xena saluted him and spun on her heel, leaving him alone with a boner the approximate size and hardness of the acropolis.

⁓

He stayed.

There were plenty of ways he could have filled the day without going back to Jay's. He could have taken his over-priced rental car for a spin. He could have called his god-damned mother. Hell, he could have signed up for a campus tour at one of the universities in town. Not that he'd remotely made any decisions in that regard, but it couldn't hurt to check things out.

Instead, he went to the grocery store and got the ingredients for eggs Benedict.

Also condoms.

He told himself that he needed to give Jane some credit for knowing what she wanted. It was entirely possible that he could make Jane eggs Benedict for dinner and then sex her up some more without her getting all starry-eyed and imagining them in a cozy domestic happily-ever-after scenario.

Cam might not be boyfriend material, but now that Jane had decided she liked having sex with humans, *someone* was going to get tapped for the job, right? All he had to do was think about that douche bag she'd been hitting on at the bar last night to decide that he was the best candidate. He cared about her pleasure. He cared about *her*. So what was the harm in giving her a few more screaming orgasms while they passed the time until the wedding? And, hell, maybe he'd find some more buildings for them to dangle off of while he was at it. Anything to induce "goddess mode."

He would just have to keep his own emotional shit on lockdown. He could do that. If the army had taught him one thing, it was discipline.

It turned out that hollandaise sauce was really damn hard. Fussy. Easy to ruin.

Which he did twice while he practiced. He ended up locating a diner nearby that did all-day breakfast and had decided that taking her out for eggs Benedict would be close enough.

He spent the rest of the day fixing shit in her house. It started when her smoke alarm went off. He initially thought his hollandaise disaster might have been the cause, but upon further inspection, he realized that he was actually hearing the alert that signaled dead batteries.

So before heading out to buy new ones, he took an inventory of the other alarms in her house, and sure enough, their "low battery" lights were all blinking.

While he was at the hardware store, he thought he might as well pick up some caulk and redo her bathtub—he'd noticed it desperately needed it.

And the hinges on all her doors were squeaky, so he grabbed some oil, too.

So began his home repair spree. Once he started, he just kept going. He'd moved on to pruning back an overgrown hedge in her front yard when she appeared, still in her costume. She was pink-cheeked and smiling and... gorgeous.

The warrior princess was in full-on goddess mode.

"How was it?"

"It was *amazing*. I went to a bunch of awesome panels. I spent a small fortune on some rare early *Wonder Woman* comics." She produced said comics from a bag she was carrying, and did an adorable little unveiling gesture that reminded him of Vanna White. She sighed happily. "The best part was I got to see my comics nerd acquaintances who I pretty much only see at conferences."

Damn, she was positively glowing. It was easy to see what the day had meant to her. He only wished he could have been a fly on the wall, because clearly, she'd spent the entire day in goddess mode.

"Hey," she said, belatedly taking in the sight of her tidied yard. "What are you doing?"

He was suddenly embarrassed. She had been so delighted with the stupid chakram he'd made her that he'd only been thinking of other ways to make her life easier. He'd had time to pass anyway, and it had been nice to putter around and attack problems that were actually solvable. But suddenly, all the home repairs and garden improvements seemed very boyfriend-like. He was glad, in retrospect, that the hollandaise had been a bust.

"Hey."

This "hey" came from someone else. It was Wendy, coming up the sidewalk and, thankfully, saving him from having to account for his ill-considered home improvement frenzy.

Jane squealed in delight and blew her friend a kiss as she approached, which Wendy mimed plucking out of the air and pressing to her heart. "What are you doing here?"

Wendy's eyes darted between Jane and him, then narrowed. "You weren't answering my texts, so I thought I'd be all impulsive and just pop by, see how Comicon went."

"Yeah," Jane said. "My phone ran out of juice. I was trying to record so much of the conference that it died."

Wendy held up a white box. "I bought pastries."

Jane grinned. "Come in—both of you."

"I should go," Cam said. This was good. Wendy's appearance had given him the perfect opportunity to retreat. To recalibrate. He should have just gotten up and left this morning. But okay, no harm done. Probably. He just needed to step back and play it cool. Cooler than becoming her own personal manservant, anyway. Maybe there was a way he and Jane could continue to get it on, but it would have to be because *she* initiated it with a full understanding of the circumstances—not because he was going all in with the domestic shit. So from now on, he was taking his cues from her.

"Oh, okay," Jane said.

He was a bit disappointed that she didn't try to object. That she didn't seem even a little bit sad to say good-bye.

Which was a problem.

He cleared his throat. "All right, then. I'll see you two soon, I'm sure." He thought about telling Jane that she shouldn't use her bathtub until the next day on account of the still-drying caulk, but Wendy was looking at him strangely, so he decided to save it for a text.

Xena waved at him, then went inside to eat pastries with Wendy instead of eggs Benedict with him.

It was for the best.

⁓ ⌒ᵔ

"What was Cameron doing here?" Wendy asked as she sat at Jane's table and opened the bakery box.

"He was doing some yard work for me."

That was true. Apparently.

She had no idea *why* it was true, but he had clearly beaten her tiny slice of overgrown paradise into submission—something she'd been meaning to get around to for ages.

"Cameron likes to be useful," she tried to explain, the thought striking her as absolutely true the moment she put it to words. "He likes to—"

"Let's play a game," Wendy interrupted. "Let's see how long we can go without talking about the wedding."

"Oh, okay," Jane said. "I—"

"Or its obnoxious guests."

"All right," Jane said, forcing herself not to give into her impulse to defend Cameron. It wasn't like she was dating him. Her reputation and his weren't intertwined.

She stuck her phone in the charger-stereo she had set up on a kitchen counter and futzed with it for a minute, scanning through playlists to give herself a second to adjust to the loss of Cameron. He'd left so . . . suddenly.

"Where's your next trip gonna be?" Jane asked, reaching

for a topic Wendy would warm to. Her friend was a devoted traveler, often jetting off to exotic places on short notice. Jane admired that. She didn't have the independent spirit Wendy did.

"That's why I'm here." She dumped a bunch of brochures out of her purse. "I think we need a recovery trip."

"A recovery trip?" Jane echoed.

"From the wedding, which I am heretofore officially calling 'the w-word.' It'll be just you and me. Somewhere far away. Somewhere with no job list."

Jane grinned and joined her friend at the table. That sounded awesome. "Sign me up."

Wendy picked up Jane's phone and silenced it as she shot Jane a look of disgust. She and Wendy had wildly divergent taste in music.

"Hey! Josh Groban is a genius."

"So," said Wendy, ignoring Jane's defense of her beloved baritone. "I know you don't really do adventure-type stuff, so I was thinking your basic beach resort—"

"I do adventure," Jane protested.

Wendy looked up from the pile of pastries and papers, confused. "Not in real life."

"What?"

"You do adventure in your books, and at your conventions, but not in reality." She held up a hand to stop Jane's further protest. "That came out wrong. I only meant that you're cautious. *Smart*." Jane opened her mouth, and another hand came up. "Look, it's not an insult. It's why we met, right? We're the overly serious outsiders. The Lost Girls."

Jane couldn't help but smile at that. Jane and Wendy had become close, as kids, because both their dads had died. They called themselves the Lost Girls. Everyone knew the

Wendy character from the Peter Pan books, but most people didn't realize that, in one of the Disney films, Wendy had gone on to have a daughter named Jane, who had her own adventures with Peter. Jane and Wendy read the books and watched the movies with the single-minded devotion that only pre-teen girls are capable of, lionizing the stories' qualities of adventurousness and fearlessness. In fact, it was a few tween Peter Pan–themed Halloweens that had ignited Jane's interest in cosplay.

"The Dead Dads Club," Jane said with a sad smile, referencing another phrase they'd come up with to describe their relationship back in the day.

"Right," said Wendy with her characteristic lack of sentimentality. "Your dead dad made you cautious. Mine made me all carpe diem-ey."

It was sort of true, though it stung to hear it stated so baldly. After the car accident that killed Jane's father—after the car accident that she could have prevented—Jane had made a conscious decision never to rock the boat, to make life as easy as possible for her mom and brother by getting good grades, being helpful, and never getting into trouble. She hadn't thought that necessarily translated into a cautious life devoid of adventure, but maybe Wendy had a point.

Of course, Wendy didn't know that in the last three days Jane had hung off the CN Tower, gone through a haunted house, made out by a waterfall, and had meaningless sex—all with the "obnoxious wedding guest" whose name they weren't supposed to mention.

And she wasn't *going* to know about it, either. It felt weird, not telling Wendy something, but since her thing with Cameron wasn't an actual relationship, why set herself up for the interrogation that would follow if she confessed?

"Okay, so beach. When?" She went back to her phone and opened the calendar app.

"The week of June twentieth," Wendy said.

"I can't," Jane said, smiling at the entry in her calendar. "My brother is coming that weekend." God, she missed him. He'd raised her, basically, because after their dad died their mom had been pretty much useless. And all that boat-not-rocking she'd done in her youth had made the siblings extra close. He was like her father, her brother, and her non-Wendy best friend all rolled into one.

"Your brother is coming later this month?" Wendy said, looking slightly alarmed.

Jane cocked her head, trying to figure out what that was about. "Yeah. He's winding up a trial, so he booked off some time to come see Mom and me. So can we do the beach trip the next week?"

"No," Wendy said quickly. "I can only go away that week."

"Well, you're going to have to count me out, then. I haven't seen Noah since Christmas. I'm planning to work on him some more to try to get him to move home."

Her brother was a prosecutor in New York and was always saying that he needed to stay there because the Big Apple was "the pinnacle of both law and urban life," whatever that meant. He definitely did okay. Jane knew because he kept trying to send her money. She'd taken to e-mailing him her royalty statements to prove that she was fine, financially. "There's got to be prosecution jobs in Toronto, though, no?" Jane said, thinking out loud. "How different can it be? His degrees are from the U.S., but there must be some way to qualify to practice here."

"You should leave him alone," Wendy said. "Let him do his New York thing. He's obviously happy there."

"I knew you were both going to become lawyers," Jane

said, reaching for a pastry. "You're so similar in some ways. It's too bad you'll miss him if you're away while he's here."

"Yeah," Wendy said. "Bummer."

"Damn!" Jane dropped her croissant. "I can't eat this." She spread her hands and looked at the ceiling as if maybe there was a deity up there she could appeal to for the quick loss of ten pounds. "I'm never going to fit into my—"

"Don't say it!" Wendy shouted. "Throw the pastries in the trash for all I care, but no w-word talk!"

Jane grinned. For some reason she thought of Cameron saying, "Jane, you are as sexy as they come, so shut the hell up."

She ate the croissant.

Chapter Fourteen

*C*am texted Jane the next morning. They were moving to the rural wedding site on Wednesday, so he had two empty days ahead of him. He had done everything on his list except smoke a joint, and, really, he'd added that item because he could. Pot wasn't really his style. At least as an adult—he'd smoked enough of it as a kid to last a lifetime.

He couldn't stop thinking about repeating certain items on his list, though.

One in particular.

But still, as hot as Saturday night had been, as enthusiastic as Jane had been as she'd come apart in his hands—and under his mouth—he had decided that texting her a straight-up booty call was a bad idea. He'd freaked himself out with his weird, post-coital home repair session yesterday, and he was sticking to his stance that if anything more was going to happen, she should initiate it.

In other words, if there was going to be any booty-calling, she should be the caller and he should be the call-ee.

But that didn't mean he couldn't give her the opportunity to make the call.

So he texted to invite her to Canada's Wonderland. Because for some reason the image of Jane on a roller coaster had lodged itself in his mind. He didn't want her to be scared like she'd been in the haunted house, but another exhilarating experience in the vein of the CN Tower would be just the thing to...set the mood. So he'd done a bit of research and come up with the idea of the amusement park that was a little ways outside the city. They would go on the gentler rides, and she'd shriek and clutch at him, but also laugh. Her russet hair would fan out behind her, and when the ride was over she would be pink-cheeked and tussled.

Just thinking about it was making his dick hard.

Canada's Wonderland, like, the amusement park?

Her return text made him laugh. He could just see her scrunching her nose in confusion.

Yes. I've got roller coasters on the brain.

After he pressed send, he started composing another text because he knew she was going to take some convincing.

I know you probably think you're not the roller coaster type, but...

What could he say to convince her that she was more adventurous than she realized? He needed to see her in goddess mode again, but he could hardly say that. It turned out he didn't have to say anything.

I am. I am the roller coaster type. What time are you picking me up?

When Cam pulled up in front of her house an hour later, Jane was already outside. She speed-walked down the path to meet him where he was parking on the street. She was wearing white jeans, and this time her T-shirt was a flowing, silky bright yellow. Instead of flats, she wore cute little tennis shoes covered with tiny yellow daisies. She was like a fucking ray of sunshine.

Man, she was really busting her ass to get to him. He couldn't help grinning. He wanted to kiss her but checked the impulse. She was in charge here. Still, it stroked his ego to see her rushing to reach him. Kind of stroked something else, too.

"Just remember, I'm sorry," she said, making an apologetic face.

"Sorry for what?"

His question was answered by the appearance of Wendy, Gia, and Elise, who came spilling out of Jane's little house like clowns out of one of those mini cars. They were all talking a mile a minute, too, about roller coasters, whether anyone would brave the water rides, and the importance of sunscreen.

"I don't want anyone getting tan lines for the wedding," Elise said. "Or—God help me—a sunburn."

Jane did the single eyebrow raise and shot him a knowing look. But then she added, "I'm also sorry about—"

"We can't take your muscle car, Cameron. It'll be too tight in the backseat," Elise said. "We'll take my SUV." She tossed him the keys. "But you can drive." She clapped her hands excitedly. "Yay! Spontaneous amusement park trip!" Then she turned to Wendy. "See? I told you taking the whole week off work would be worth it."

And so he found himself navigating a giant-ass Ford Explorer through the narrow streets of Jane's urban neighborhood with four grown women in the back arguing about something that sounded like "twall," but he suspected was spelled differently.

Unlike most group car rides, no one had called shotgun. They'd all slid into the two rows of backseats like he was their chauffeur, chattering a mile a minute about whether the black and white "twall" dishes Elise had registered for were a mistake and should she have gone with the more classic blue and white?

Well, they were all chattering except Jane, who was seated on the opposite side of the car in the row behind him. He had a perfect view of her in the rearview mirror.

And she was looking right at him. He pressed his lips together in an attempt not to grin. She raised her eyebrows in amusement, and a kind of tender affection flooded his chest. This must be what parents felt like in a car full of hyper kids, like they were in on a secret together, each other's lifelines. While he could see how long-term doses of the bridezilla might grow tiresome, he liked Elise and the others. Elise had spunk, and he could imagine, if that spunk was directed at something other than her upcoming nuptials, that she was a lot of fun. And as much as he and his brother had grown apart, he could still see Elise complementing Jay.

So, it wasn't the day trip of his dreams, but, hey, he'd take it.

"Cameron!" Elise called from the far backseat.

"At your service, ma'am," he said, playing up his chauffeur role.

"This is really nice of you to drive us to Wonderland. Are you really the bad boy everyone says?"

"Depends how you define bad," he teased, refraining from pointing out that it wasn't so much that he was "driving them" as they had crashed his planned party of two.

"How many tattoos do you have?" Elise asked.

"Well, really only three, if you count the sleeve as one," he answered.

"That's a little disappointing, actually," said Elise. "I imagined you covered with them."

"Well, they're really big, so he kind of is," Jane said. He whipped his eyes to hers, shocked that she'd told her friends about their encounter. But then the panic that appeared in her eyes as she clamped her mouth shut suggested that she actually hadn't.

"So you've seen his tattoos," Gia said.

"No," said Jane. "I mean, yes, but..."

"She arrived at Jay's one morning when I was walking around in my pj bottoms," he said, rushing to cover for her for reasons he couldn't fathom, given that he'd spent the first few days of his acquaintance with Jane bent on hassling her. "You know, when she was doing her assigned babysitting duty, Elise."

"I'm sure I don't know what you're talking about," Elise said. But then she added, "Jay said you have a criminal record."

"I did," he said, watching Jane in the mirror. They hadn't talked about his past. "I was a juvenile, though, so it was expunged when I turned eighteen."

"What did you do?" Wendy asked.

"I burned down a barn," he said.

"On purpose?"

"Does it matter?"

"It matters a lot."

"Wendy's a defense lawyer," Jane said. "It's like you're waving catnip in front of her."

"It wasn't on purpose," he said. "I knocked over a candle when I was, ah, otherwise engaged."

"What were you charged with?" Wendy asked.

"Arson."

"433 Arson—disregard for human life, or 434 arson—damage to property?"

"Huh?"

"She's quoting the criminal code," Jane said.

"I think the property one," he said. "But I don't really know. It was a long time ago."

"Well, your lawyer should have gotten it down to at least 436 arson by negligence, if not just disorderly conduct."

"Didn't have a lawyer, really, just some legal aid guy I met in the hallway five minutes before my court date."

He couldn't see Wendy, but a scoffing noise came from her general direction, and Gia said, "Down girl. Concentrate on your own stable of criminals."

"Who I'm hanging out to dry this week while I ride roller coasters and...stuff," Wendy said. Cam could see Elise's eyes narrow, and he suspected a bridal death glare was the cause of Wendy's aborted complaint.

"So!" Jane chirped. "I had a look at the Wikipedia entry for Canada's Wonderland."

He shook his head and grinned. Of course she had. But he was all for her blatant attempt to direct the conversation away from the mistakes of his youth. He waited for her to pull some printouts from her purse.

And, *bingo*. She rustled through her papers for a moment, then said, "Yeah, so there are sixteen roller coasters at this place, and a twenty-acre waterpark."

"Did everyone bring bathing suits?" he asked. He'd instructed Jane to do so when they were texting.

A chorus of affirmative answers broke out behind him.

"But no tan lines, guys," Elise ordered. "No. Tan. Lines."

—☙

"I'm really, really sorry," Jane said the moment she could get Cameron alone. They'd just entered the park, and the other girls had gone to the bathroom *en masse*. "There was this group text after we made our arrangements. Elise wanted to do something 'fun.'" She made air quotes with her fingers. "I was trying to get out of whatever she had planned, but somehow it ended up being…this." She wasn't even sure how it had happened, really, but somehow, she'd lost control of the conversation and all of a sudden they were on her doorstep and Elise was lecturing them about sunscreen.

"Don't worry about it," he said.

Jane flashed him a relieved smile as the bridal party returned. She was glad he didn't mind the company, but also glad things weren't going to be weird between them. They hadn't communicated since he'd left her house yesterday— left her house and yard in tip-top shape—so she wasn't really sure where they stood. She had been hoping to see him again. Well, truly, she'd been hoping to *bone* him again. Ha! Look at her, the queen of casual sex! So things being "not weird" between them was a promising sign. She might actually get her wish.

Eventually.

It was going to be a long day.

"All right," she said, perusing the map and trying to figure out the most logical way to tackle things. "What do you say we do rides in the morning, then lunch, and then we can spend the afternoon at this Splash Works thing?"

"Whatever you say," Elise said at the same time that Gia said, "You're the boss."

"Okay." She looked around to orient herself relative to the map she was holding. "Why don't we walk to the far northeastern corner, and then we can work our way back. That will maximize—hey!"

Cameron had grabbed the map from her hands. "Or we could go on that thing because it's right here." He pointed at a yellow and blue monstrosity with huge plunges and sharp angles.

She read the tall yellow lettering at the entrance to the coaster. "Leviathan." The word was surrounded by some kind of dragony sea monster–type creature with enormous teeth.

"I'm in!" Gia said. "Will you hold my stuff, Jane?"

Wendy, who wasn't an overt thrill seeker the way Gia was but was nevertheless quite the adventurer in her quiet, determined way, silently handed Jane her backpack.

"Whoa," Jane said, lifting her hands over her head so she couldn't accept any of the bags and sunglasses being shoved at her. "If we need someone to hold stuff, we're going to have to go in shifts, and I'm going to be on the first one." Heck, better to get it over with.

She was confronted with three dropped jaws and one wide grin.

"What is she doing?" Elise was speaking to Wendy—and looking at Wendy like she was Jane's mom instead of her best friend. Wendy shrugged.

Elise sniffed. "Well, I'm not going on that thing. Normally I would, but I don't want…"

Jane was glad that Elise's hesitation drew everyone's attention away from her.

"I don't want anything to happen to me before the wedding." She smiled sheepishly. "I know that's irrational. I've been kind of insane lately, you guys."

"Hey, don't worry about it," Gia said, giving her a squeeze. "Your wedding is going to be amazing."

"It's going to be the most beautiful wedding in the history of weddings!" Wendy said, slinging an arm around Elise's shoulder from the other side, as if she hadn't been calling the forthcoming nuptials the "w-word" a day ago.

"It's going to blow the lid off Pinterest," Jane chimed in. There were no sides of Elise left to hug, but she blew a kiss, which of course Wendy had to "catch" with a wink.

"Hey!" said Elise with mock outrage. "That was mine!" But then her eyes filled with tears. "I love you guys so much."

"Aww! Group hug!" Gia yelled as she let go of Elise enough to make room for Jane to slide into the pack.

Jane was suffused with emotion. The wedding had everyone on edge, but at the core of things was her crew of girls, and that would never change. She was so lucky. Her friends, her brother: people didn't get better than them.

She felt someone watching her and lifted her eyes from the hug.

Cameron.

Right.

"Should we get this show on the road?" he said, and she shivered.

She really was scared of the ride she was about to get on. But one of the things she'd learned from Cameron in the past few days was you could be scared of a thing and still do that thing.

—ᨆ—

Jane was scared of the coaster. Cam could tell by the determined way she marched to the end of the lineup. Wendy and Gia chatted and exclaimed as the ride made crazy loops above them, but Jane remained silent, staring straight ahead as they inched their way toward the head of the line.

As they moved closer, it became apparent that there were four seats to a row on the coaster. Jane walked onto the platform first, still concentrating on her target and seemingly oblivious to everything else.

But he must have been wrong about that, because when he hung back, gesturing out of politeness for Gia and Wendy to precede him up the steps, she whipped her head around, her eyes darting all over until she found his gaze. She hung back then, which initially caused a traffic jam because Gia and Wendy came to a stop behind her. She waved them ahead of her, avoiding their eyes. It was hard not to arrive at the conclusion that she wanted him to sit next to her. It was also hard to disguise the stupid, proud grin that idea generated.

"Want to wait for your boyfriend?" one of the teenagers working the ride said. "That's so sweet."

"He's not my boyfriend," Jane said, just as Cam was about to issue the same correction. It was good to know they were on the same page in case she wanted to get busy later. *Please let her want to get busy later.* He even had condoms this time.

They settled themselves into the coaster. Jane was silent,

her lips pressed into a thin, determined line. She was turning inward, like she had as they'd begun shuffling out onto the deck outside the CN Tower. He wanted to take her hand. His own were itching to touch her somewhere, anywhere, and not only because she needed soothing. But he didn't want to get her into trouble with her friends, whom he gathered were already on her case about matters of dating and relationships.

As the coaster made its way slowly up the first hill, its ominous clacking had his own heart beating fast, and Wendy and Gia on the other side began squealing.

Jane, still staring straight ahead, grabbed his hand, took as much of his arm as she could grab, in fact, into her lap. He grinned and squeezed tight.

As the car approached the top, Jane shut her eyes. After what seemed like ages teetering there, it tipped. People started screaming. He only had eyes for Jane. He watched her like a hawk. She squeezed her eyes tighter and twisted her face into a harsh grimace.

Just when he was starting to fear he had miscalculated, that maybe roller coasters *hadn't* been a good idea, her eyes popped open, and so did her mouth. She turned to him as much as she could, given the restraining apparatus, and whooped. Her eyes danced, her grin was as wide as the sky, and her hair was a curtain of fire.

There she was in all her glory: his goddess.

It was almost as good as watching her come.

Almost.

───⌒○

"Are you sure you want to go on *this one*, though?" Cameron asked when, one hour and three rides later, Jane pointed to a ride called Wonder Mountain's Guardian. He would gladly follow Jane around the park all day and strap himself into any contraption she liked to be flung around defying gravity in any way that suited her. But this particular ride didn't seem like a good match. "It's dark," he said, reading about it in the brochure they'd been given on their way into the park. "They give you 3D glasses, and you shoot at creepy-crawlies."

"That's fine," Jane said.

"*Jane*." He grabbed her arm. "It's a *haunted* roller coaster."

"No problem," she said again, shaking off his hand and following her friends into the line. He wasn't going to be able to bodily carry her out of this one, but, hey, she was free to make her own mistakes.

As they prepared to board the coaster, she did that same thing where she maneuvered so she was sitting next to him. She probably thought she was being subtle, but Gia was onto them. Every time Jane did it, Gia raised her eyebrows at him, and this time was no different, except she added an "I'm watching you" gesture by moving her index and middle fingers back and forth between her eyes and him.

He shrugged and sat where Jane wanted him to. Each car had four seats—two facing front and two facing back. Jane had arranged things so Gia and Wendy were facing front. She seemed unconcerned as the ride began to move, which wasn't altogether surprising. With each subsequent ride they had gone on after the Leviathan, she'd appeared less nervous out of the gate. He wanted to offer his hand, but he didn't think she needed it. Or wanted it, frankly, because she was pretty much ignoring him.

As the coaster ascended the first hill, her face remained impassive. This wasn't as steep a coaster, but still. It was like she had been desensitized. As they made the first dip, which was combined with a turn, he gave up looking at her and focused on what was ahead of them, which seemed to be a tunnel. That was probably the dark part.

"What the hell?"

He recoiled instinctively against the sensation of someone coming after him, but calmed when he realized that all that had happened was that Jane had grabbed his 3D glasses off his face. He was about to protest, to say that the glasses were the whole point of the ride—you couldn't see the stuff you were supposed to shoot at without them—when they plunged into darkness.

And that's when he realized that the point of the ride was *actually* to make out with the clever girl sitting next to you.

Jane grabbed his head and brought it down to hers. Their mouths missed each other in the dark—his lips ended up on the bridge of her nose, and she giggled. It was perfect: not only was it dark, but Gia and Wendy were back to back with them so Jane's fellow bridesmaids would never see what they were doing. Her fingers came to his mouth, as if she were trying to feel her way to him. He sucked one into his mouth and bit down gently on it. She leaned up as far as she could, he leaned down, and this time, their aim was better.

He didn't waste any time. The ride was going to be mere minutes long, and who knew how long they would be in the dark portion of it? He'd been tamping down his desire for Jane all day, hoping that tonight they'd be able to maneuver some privacy and she would initiate something. The notion that she couldn't wait that long opened the floodgates on all that restrained lust. So he grabbed the sides of her head to make sure she didn't move, plunged his tongue into her mouth, and feasted. He licked deep into her mouth, and when her pulse immediately kicked up as a result he felt it as a surge of possessive triumph in his chest. She kissed him back, her tongue battling his in an aggressive, almost-confrontational way that made his dick go hard as iron.

The car rotated 180 degrees, and he tightened his hold on her head as her hands came up to his forearms as if he were the only thing tethering her to the coaster. It was like they were spinning in the center of it all, the quiet but mighty energy source that was powering the whole ride and, hell, maybe even the whole world. He wanted to lose himself in her forever, but he needed to protect her, too, which meant keeping his senses divided. The sounds of laughter and good-natured screaming made up the soundtrack for their silent, furtive kiss. He deepened it, tilting her head back to improve the angle, even as he remained attuned to what was going on around them.

When he could sense they were coming out of the tunnel, he lifted his hands from her face like she'd burned him. His break from her mouth was less clean. He tried to stop the kiss, but she hummed her displeasure, and he almost gave in. Almost said, *fuck it, turn on the goddamned spotlights*. But he couldn't do that. He wasn't her boyfriend, as she'd told the kid operating the first ride. It would be better for her if this...thing between them stayed in the dark where it belonged.

He started to pull away again. She kept trying to resist, to cling to him. His ego loved it. His dick loved it. But he was stronger than his dick and his ego. He was stronger than her. So he pushed her away for her own good.

Pushed her away for her own good. Now there was a metaphor for his entire entanglement with Jane.

The car emerged from the tunnel, its inhabitants, including Gia and Wendy behind them, exclaiming and laughing and generally making a ruckus. Well, most of its inhabitants. The one next to him remained silent and still. Blinking and shell-shocked, she might have been able to convince an onlooker that she was overwhelmed from having battled schools of killer fish on a haunted roller coaster, but he knew the truth.

So did she. She turned to him with stunned eyes and a swollen, red mouth rounded into an *O* of shock.

He winked.

Chapter Fifteen

*I*f Jane had been harboring any doubts about her... thing with Cameron, the haunted roller coaster had chased them all away.

Of course, she still had no idea what that "thing" actually was. He'd been up-front about his lack of interest in a relationship, and she was down with that. The fact that they *didn't* have a relationship was probably the only thing that had made her shed her inhibitions so thoroughly two nights ago as he'd made his point about the awesomeness of human-assisted orgasm. She was pretty sure that, paradoxically, if she thought Cameron might want to date her, she would be a lot more inhibited.

She just hadn't been sure that he would be interested in a repeat performance. He seemed like he might be a "one and done" kind of guy. Had there been an implicit agreement that what had happened between them had been a one-time thing? Would she seem like a slut if she suggested they do it again? Or, worse, would she seem like she was pushing him into a relationship?

She had been tormenting herself with these questions, but then, somehow, once he appeared in the flesh, those questions faded.

Well, that wasn't quite right. They didn't go away. It was more that they got drowned out. They didn't stand a chance against the overwhelming, all-consuming nature of her attraction to him.

How was it possible for a mortal man to be so stupidly hot? It wasn't fair. But there he was, winking at her in the rearview mirror with those should-be-illegal aqua eyes, or putting his big, tattooed arm around her as she shrieked in exhilarated terror on the rides.

He made her palms damp. He made *other places* damp. Just by standing there, being alive.

So although when she stopped and thought about it rationally for two seconds, she was still worried about all those questions that had been dogging her—*Is he going to think I'm a slut? Is he going to think I have designs on him? Does he even want me again?*—her body didn't let her think about them for too long before it took over. Shoved her intellect aside with an inarticulate "Let's paaarrrrty!"

He grabbed her arm as she moved away from a concessions stand inside the waterpark where they'd decided to spend the second half of their day, startling her and almost making her drop the limp iceberg lettuce monstrosity she was carrying. The girls had opted for hot dogs and were clustered around the condiment stand, loading them up.

He leaned down to whisper in her ear. Or—*okay!*— actually, to *bite* her earlobe.

So, yeah, clearly, she'd been overthinking things. She was pretty sure they would be getting it on again in the near future, which made her very, very happy.

It had been going on since the haunted roller coaster, this sexed-up game of cat-and-mouse. It was as if, by kissing him in the dark, she'd given him permission or, more accurately, unleashed the beast. After that ride, he grabbed her every chance he got. There had been a quick kiss at the very top of the Ferris wheel—he must have rationalized that even though the girls were in adjacent cars, there was no way they could see them when they were at the apex of the ride. Then there had been an epic ass groping as they stood in line for the Windseeker.

And it wasn't just him. She was dishing it out herself. She had discovered the most effective way to torment him was to accidentally brush against him with her breasts. Like now, for instance. "I forgot a napkin," she said, moving by him as she headed back to the snack bar. "Oh, excuse me," she said, widening her eyes and looking up at him as she passed. And if she let her gaze drop, for a second, to his crotch to check if she'd had any impact (she had), could anyone really blame her? He was too easy to rile. When she looked back up at his face, he was scowling.

As they conferred about where to set up, Elise said, "Oh, let's get one of those," and pointed to a cabana.

"I think you have to rent them," Jane said, having remembered reading something about that in her Wikipedia research.

Elise tilted her head, looking puzzled. "I'm surprised you didn't do that, Jane. You're usually so...organized."

The hint of disappointment in Elise's voice annoyed Jane. "Well, remember, I didn't know you were coming until this morning." Honestly, Elise expected to crash a party *and* have all her needs foreseen?

"Your wish is my command," Cameron said, surreptitiously patting Jane's butt before spinning on his heel and taking off. It had been the lightest of touches, but Jane swore she ached as if he'd spanked her.

"Let's go change," Gia suggested. "We can leave our food here." She spread out a towel and set down her drink and hot dog, and everyone else did the same.

Jane girded herself as she followed her friends into the changing room. Though she and Cameron were trying to be subtle with their groping, what were the chances that the girls hadn't noticed the sparks flying between them?

Thankfully, they hadn't. Or, more likely, there was no time for anyone to get on her case because Elise pulled out the industrial-size bottle of 100 SPF sunscreen she'd been dabbing on their noses all morning and started slathering it on Wendy's back.

"Asian skin doesn't burn!" Wendy protested, twisting away from the bridezilla.

"I'm pretty sure that's a myth you are selectively invoking, but even if you don't burn visually, your skin can still be severely damaged by the sun," Elise lectured, wrestling Wendy into submission.

"And, what? Invisible skin damage doesn't go with your color scheme?" Wendy said.

"I'm going to pretend I didn't hear that," Elise said, flipping the bottle to Jane and giving her a stern look.

When everyone had been slathered to Elise's satisfaction, they trooped back out to find Cameron waiting for them.

And, oh God, he was shirtless.

Of course he was shirtless. Did she expect him to hit

the water donning Mormon modesty-wear or something? And she had seen him naked already, so what was the big deal?

The big deal was the bright sun glinting off his tattoos.

The big deal was the muscles in his chest and back, rippling as he arranged a towel on a lounge chair.

The big deal was the way he lifted his head when he sensed them approaching and looked directly at her, his gaze bypassing everyone else, even the model in the string bikini.

Gia whistled, low enough that he couldn't hear. Probably. But he had to have heard Wendy's "Wow."

"Sorry, Elise," he said, oblivious to all the ogling. "The cabanas are all booked. You'll have to slum it with the plebes."

Elise huffed a little sigh of frustration. Jane couldn't help thinking it was directed at her, but that was ridiculous. Yeah, she was the den mother of the group, but she couldn't read minds.

"Let's eat, and then we can hit the slides. We'll hardly be here anyway," said Wendy, glaring at Elise. Jane patted Wendy's arm. Though she appreciated the attempt at peacemaking, there was no need to antagonize the bride unnecessarily. She had faith that when this was all over, they'd get their sweet, funny friend back.

Everyone spread out their towels. For once Jane wasn't trying to manipulate things so she could be next to Cameron. In need of a breather, she purposely took the chair farthest from him.

"Nice tats, Cameron," Gia said, pulling a magazine out of her bag. "What's the story with them?"

He shrugged. "No story."

"I know I crashed the party, Jane," said Elise, forcing Jane to stop eavesdropping. "I just thought you would have, like, booked a cabana this morning when we all decided we'd do the rides this morning and the waterpark this afternoon. You're usually so good at organizing that kind of stuff."

Wow. Elise wasn't going to let this go, was she? Jane struggled to think what to say. She wasn't keen on the idea of apologizing for not booking a cabana she didn't know existed for a group outing she didn't know was happening.

"Yeah, Jane," said Wendy in a teasing, singsong voice. "You really fell down on the job there." Jane shot her a grateful smile for trying to break up the tension.

"Yeah!" Gia exclaimed, taking up the mantle. "You're supposed to be the responsible friend!" She infused her voice with joking, artificial drama. "It's like we don't even know who you are anymore!" She darted a glance at Cameron, then back at Jane. "What have you been doing that's more important than anticipating our every need?"

Crap, and here she thought she'd pulled one over on her friends.

"Okay, you guys are right. I'm being a bitch." Elise rolled over and looked at Jane. "I'm sorry, hon. You didn't deserve that."

"No problem," said Jane as her phone dinged, signaling an incoming text. She seized on it as an excuse to move past the uncomfortable moment.

They might not know who you are anymore, but I do. I know who you are—and what you've been doing.

Her stomach dropped. It was Cameron, apparently texting from four lounge chairs over. She risked a glance at him. He appeared to be perusing the map they'd been carrying around all day but probably had his phone tucked inside it. Another one arrived before she could even begin to think how to reply.

You are a very bad girl masquerading as a good girl.

Her face heated instantly, blazed with such intensity that she feared Elise would start accusing her of being sun-burned. Her fingers shook as she typed a reply.

Oh? And what have I been doing?

You have been driving me to distraction all day, you little tease.

She glanced at the girls. Wendy and Gia were eating their hot dogs, and Elise, having finished hers, was absorbed in her own phone.

So she went back to...holy crap, was she *sexting* with Cameron? Well, why the hell not?

Sorry/notsorry

And now you're going to spend the rest of the day parading around in that fucking incredible pinup swimsuit that has my dick hard as a rock. You're killing me, Janie.

She bit the insides of her cheeks to prevent herself from grinning like an idiot as she looked down at her body and tried to see it through his eyes. She was rather pleased with the bathing suit. She'd bought it last winter when she and her mom and brother had gone to Florida. It was a bikini, but, on the surface of things, a modest one. The bottom was high waisted and the top a halter style. She'd thought when she bought it that the cut flattered her curves and that the white background and hot pink polka dots were fun and retro. It *did* make her feel like a pinup girl from the 1940s or 1950s, back when her body type would have been more idealized.

Sorry/notsorry?

She typed the same response as before, hoping the repetition would come off as coy and sexy, but probably she was going to have to get better at this sexting thing. She was a writer, for heaven's sake. She tried again.

What can I do to help?

She cocked her head at her phone. That probably didn't come off as sexily as she'd meant it. She couldn't quite get the hang of this. But, hey, she was going to cut herself some slack because last time she'd had a person to sext with had been the flip phone era. And Felix would *not* have been into sexting anyway.

It didn't seem to matter, though, because her mediocre effort earned her a response that made her have to stifle a gasp.

Nothing. Nothing will help except getting inside you.

Oh my God! Her body was in full-out mutiny. She shifted in her chair, turning away from everyone because she was afraid they would somehow see the rush of moisture between her legs that his dirty words had summoned.

Later?

Crap. She really, *really* needed to get better at this. But again, it didn't seem to matter.

Yes. For now I'll have to settle for riding down one of these damned slides with you. You'll go in front and when you feel my cock against your sweet ass, you'll know exactly what you're doing to me.

She whimpered. It was out before she realized.

Wendy turned to her. "Are you okay?"

"Yes!" Whoa. That had come out too vehemently. She cleared her throat and tried again. "Yes, fine." She dropped her phone into her bag. "I'm getting really hot." As soon as it was out, she realized that wasn't the right way to phrase things. She let her gaze flick to Cameron, who was still absorbed in his map. "I'm going to hit the water," she added, standing and looking around. She needed a moment before Cameron made good on his pledge. "I'm going to pop into the pool for minute." She didn't wait to see if anyone was following, just strode toward the wave pool that was mostly filled with kids.

"Come back soon to reapply sunscreen!" Elise called after her.

Usually, Jane was a toe-dipper. Her normal process for immersing herself in a body of water was to draw it out so much that she annoyed even herself: a toe, an ankle, a shin, a knee. Then she'd finally stand around on her tiptoes squealing and letting the tips of her fingers skim the surface.

But not this time. This time, she walked right in. And kept walking until she was up to her boobs. Then she bent her knees and submerged her head.

Because it was cold and silent beneath the surface. She didn't have to worry about how she was conducting herself underwater. There was no sexting underwater. No responsibilities. Underwater, no one was watching her.

⎯⎯⎯☙

Cam watched her the whole time. Given that his goal was to get rid of his raging boner so he could actually, like, get up and walk around, the decision to do so had been self-defeating. But he couldn't make himself stop. *Could. Not. Drag. His. Eyeballs. Away. From. Her. Pink. Polka-dotted. Ass.* To begin with, that retro bikini thing was kiiillling him. It wasn't overly revealing—Gia, for example, was showing much more skin—but there was something insanely hot about Jane's suit. The playful confidence of those pink dots, the sexy expanse of bare back with the big bow at her neck. The heaviness of her breasts, weighing down the fabric that was cradling them. The way her hips and ass splayed way out from her trim waist. Those curves were the perfect resting spots for his hands. His fingers flexed of their own accord, wanting to press her hips down, to hold her immobile while he made her moan.

"Cameron? Hello?"

He jumped a little, turning toward Elise's voice but keeping his eyes on Jane's head as it disappeared into the water as she submerged herself. "Yes?"

"So Jay told me he asked you to be an usher?"

"What? Right. Yes." After their apparent truce at the bachelor party, Jay had indeed asked Cameron to play the role of usher. "You're my brother," he had said. "You should be in my wedding party." He'd gone on to explain that if he bumped one of the actual groomsmen, Elise would lose her mind, so usher was the best he could do. Cam had accepted with a studied casualness, but in truth, he'd been touched. "Oh, no."

"No?" Elise's voice was tinged with confusion.

"No. I mean, yes." Shit. He'd been responding to the sight of a drenched Jane making her way out of the pool, coming toward them with water running off every part of her body. Forget making good on the lewd threat he'd issued via text. He was never going to be able to get off this damned chair. He needed to think about taxes. Or maybe his recent trial.

"I wanted to talk a little bit about the wedding if you don't mind," Elise said. "About your specific duties."

Bingo. That would be perfect. He shifted so Jane was out of his field of vision. "Hit me. I'm all ears."

⁓

"Does anyone want to go on the Body Blaster with me?" Jane asked, trying to will Cameron to say yes and everyone else to say no. She'd cooled off enough from her little freak-out that she was ready to take him up on his promise-slash-threat.

Either that or she was crazy. Because it was only two o'clock and the girls were talking about going out to dinner after they were done at the park, so it was going to be hours before...stuff could really happen. She had, however, selected the slide that seemed best suited for Cam's, uh, stated purpose. It was a good thing her suit was already wet.

"I will!" Gia jumped up, adjusting the tiny white triangles that barely covered her boobs. Jane sighed. It was hard not to hate Gia sometimes. Even though she knew with one part of her brain that Gia's body was the result of genetics, and that it happened to coincide with the body ideal of the day, another part of her brain was hella envious.

"I will, too." Cameron unfolded his long limbs from his chair and took off his mirrored shades, and the envious part of her brain flew the white flag of surrender. Because the phrase "he only had eyes for her" applied. It was like the size two supermodel wasn't even there, and how often did *that* happen? Jane smiled to herself and allowed a little extra sashay in her step as she turned and led the way. Sadly, though, even though Gia wasn't, apparently, going to steal Cameron's attention, her presence was going to end up tanking their plan. Sneaking kisses was one thing, going down a water slide cozied up against the bad-boy brother of the groom quite another.

When they got to the top, though, it was moot, because the park's regulations didn't allow two riders to slide together. The guy manning the top was leaving a good ten seconds between riders. Which made sense, assuming most people didn't want to dry hump their way down. Or wet hump.

She was more disappointed than she should have been.

There were two slides to choose from, and Jane went to one.

"After you," Cameron said to Gia, which prompted Gia to move to the other one.

Which in turn left Cameron in line behind Jane. As the attendant nodded at Jane and Gia that it was time to go, Gia took off, but Cameron held Jane back with a hand on her arm. Then he leaned over and whispered in her ear, "Use your imagination."

It wasn't, on the surface of things, an untoward thing to say.

But it made her gasp all the same. *Use your imagination.*

And when the attendant gestured again for her to go—she was holding up the line—she plunged into the cold water and did just that.

Chapter Sixteen

They made it into the elevator at Jay's building before they launched themselves at each other.

The evening had been interminable. It had basically been a repeat of the afternoon, forcing Cam to watch Jane shriek with delight while partaking in the thrills offered by the amusement park. Except the afternoon version of Jane had been wet and wearing a bikini.

And then there was the sexting.

They had established a rhythm by which they would hit a few waterslides and then rest for a while on their lounge chairs, the girls enduring re-application after re-application of sunscreen. (Ushers, apparently, were allowed tans.)

The adorable thing was that Jane wasn't actually that good at sexting. She would start things with a vaguely suggestive topic like:

Do you have condoms in your possession today?

And he'd write back:

I do.

He figured out pretty quickly that she didn't want him to leave it at that. She wanted him to escalate things, even if she couldn't quite make herself respond in kind. She kept prodding, asking flirty-but-benign questions until he hit her with something like:

I got a jumbo box actually, because I'm going to fuck you so many times before this wedding that you're not going to be able to walk down the aisle properly.

And then she would blush hard enough to send Elise into a panic.

Then she would get into the pool, come out drenched, announce her intention to hit one of the water slides, and the whole damn cycle would start again.

And then there'd been dinner, a never-ending meal at some kind of bullshit "small plates" place. They must have ordered thirty tiny plates of poached quail's eggs, thimble-size chicken pot pies, and other assorted hipster bullshit, yet Cam left the restaurant as hungry as he'd arrived.

Then they'd dropped the girls off one by one, ending with Elise, because they'd made the trip in her car. Jay had been at her house, which had meant they'd had to go inside for a drink and lots of discussion about who among the relatives was going to be ushered into the wedding ceremony in what order. Then, finally, *finally*, he and Jane had hit the road, intending to take the subway to Jane's house, where his car was parked. It was endless, logistical torture.

But then, when they hit their transfer point, where they were meant to change trains, Jane said, "Do you think Jay will spend the night at Elise's? When we were at her place it sort of seemed like he might be staying over."

"No doubt," Cam had answered, gesturing for her to precede him up an escalator. "This is one of their last nights together before the wedding. Elise has this thing—"

"The sex palate cleanser," Jane interrupted, turning toward him as she stood on the step above him.

Cam laughed. "Yes! She says they can't have sex a certain number of days before the wedding."

"Believe me, I know all about it. I just thought it would have kicked in already—I thought it was a weeklong 'cleanse.'"

Cam shrugged. "They apparently had a discussion about it." And a very forceful discussion it had been. He'd overheard them bickering in Elise's kitchen on his way to the bathroom. Cam had a feeling his sexting with Jane was nothing compared to what went on behind closed doors with his brother and Elise, but he chose not to think too much about that. "The terms have been renegotiated, and the sex palette cleanser now officially kicks in when we move to the wedding site."

They stepped off the escalator at the top. "So that means..." Jane paused under a set of signs. One directed them to another subway line, the one they needed to take to get to Jane's house. The other directed them to the street above them.

The street that was a two-minute walk from Jay's condo. The condo that Jay was not in.

"Let's go," he said.

He had to admire her restraint. She knew exactly what he was talking about. Hell, it had been her idea. But she walked calmly as she led them up the stairs to street level. Sailed serenely down the crowded street as if they had all the time in the world. Murmured a polite "thank you" when he held the door to Jay's building for her. Nodded at the concierge as if she were a bored aristocrat.

And then, the instant the elevator doors shut behind them, that restraint shattered and she catapulted herself at him.

Damn. Their day had been one long, ball-busting bout of the most maddening teasing he'd ever experienced, and now it was finally, finally time.

He caught her with a groan and put his hands all over her. Mouths and hips slammed together as they fought to grab handfuls of each other. When the elevator dinged and the doors opened to the eighteenth floor, he staggered out, backward, relishing the momentary cry of displeasure from her that lasted until she realized what he was doing—that he was, in fact, dragging her along with him in an attempt to get them inside Jay's place.

"This isn't going to be some long-drawn-out thing the first time," he said against her mouth as they fumbled their way down the corridor. "It can't be. I have to get inside you now." He felt bad about it, but there was nothing to be done because the day behind them, and the woman in front of him, had taken him to the very edge. He was a teenaged boy, ready to blow at any moment. No, actually, correction: he was a goddamned saint, a master of the *Kama Sutra*, given that he hadn't already lost control half a dozen times today.

"Yes," she said, panting as he pulled away long enough to stick his key into the lock. She took the opportunity to unbutton his fly and shove a hand into his pants. He grabbed her ass as he pushed the door open, then spun her around and pressed her back against it. She was grinning from ear to ear, trying not to laugh.

"What?" he asked, reaching up under her T-shirt to unclasp her bra.

"The *first* time?" she asked.

"That's right," he said, groaning as his hands made contact with the bare flesh of her breasts. He allowed himself one caress before going straight for her nipples, rubbing each between a thumb and forefinger. She gasped and arched against the door. He hadn't been kidding when he'd said this was going to be fast, but he was still going to do his damnedest to make sure she kept pace with him. "After fast there's going to be slow. Or fast again. Or whatever you want." He paused in his assault long enough to slide her shirt over her head. "Take off your pants."

She obeyed, and he had to close his eyes as he reached into his pocket to grab the condom he'd optimistically stashed there this morning. He needed a moment to collect himself because there was "fast," and there was "over before it started."

"Hurry up," she urged, grabbing the condom and tearing it open. He shoved his pants down. They only made it as far as his knees before she rolled the condom onto his shaft.

"I can't even believe how much I want you inside me," she whispered, wonder in her voice.

He'd been going to take his clothes off, too. Surely there was time for that, he'd thought. But he had been wrong. So he did what he had to do, which was to swipe two fingers over her opening to confirm what he suspected. "Oh God, how can you be this wet for me?"

"How can you be this hard for me?" she countered in an

almost confrontational tone that somehow made him even harder, which should have been impossible.

The image of her standing there, naked against the door while he was fully clothed with his pants around his knees, was suddenly too much. He took himself in hand and positioned his cock outside her entrance. She moaned and rocked her hips, grabbing at his chest like she was trying to climb up him, inside him. So he pressed his palms flat against the door behind her and slammed the rest of the way inside her, relishing the sharp, satisfied exhalation that resulted.

Then he did it again and again, harder each time, driving her higher and higher up on her tiptoes. And each time he was rewarded with a louder response from Jane.

He hadn't been lying when he'd said this was going to be quick. He lasted only a few more strokes, but it was okay because by the time he exploded in ecstasy, she was screaming and her pussy was shuddering around him, squeezing out every drop of pleasure from him. His arms, still braced on the wall on either side of her head, shook and his heart felt like it was going to jackhammer out of his chest.

She was panting, too, as she slumped against him like a rag doll.

"Sorry," he said. She had come, and rather spectacularly, too, but he still felt compelled to apologize for how brief their encounter had been.

A vague scoffing noise emerged from where her head was tucked into the crook of his arm.

Still. He continued to feel the need to throw out an excuse or two. "I guess that's what happens when you meet a pretty girl after five months of celibacy." Though he was pretty sure that wasn't what was going on here. He and Christie had enjoyed themselves plenty when he'd returned from his first deployment, but he'd never had a sexual encounter that had been quite so...intense.

Her head popped up, which was good because after a day tromping around in the heat, he couldn't smell very good. Her expression was hard to read. It looked like she was contemplating some big problem, trying to solve a riddle, which was impressive because his own brain was still firmly lodged in his pants.

"What's next?" she said, still with that strange expression on her face.

"I'm thinking shower," he said, watching her like a hawk to gauge her reaction. He couldn't articulate why, but it felt like a lot hinged on his answer. "Shower, then slow."

"Slow?" She sent that single eyebrow up, and he let himself relax a little. It felt like he'd passed a kind of invisible test.

"Yeah." He leaned in, way in, wanting to recapture the sexually charged aura that had surrounded them all day. He put his nose right against her neck and inhaled the mixture of sunscreen and her. "Nice and slow," he drawled. "Like we've got all night."

Which they did.

It was a damn good feeling.

"My brother has shampoo and stuff," Cam said a few minutes later as he shed his clothes in the bathroom and watched the still-naked Jane unload some miniature toiletries from her bag. "And Elise has some girly junk here, too."

"I know, but I like my stuff," she said, unwrapping the tiniest bar of soap he'd ever seen. "I brought a toiletries bag to the park because I wasn't sure if we would be showering there. So since I have it, I might as well use it."

"All right," said Cameron, taking the soap and a travel

bottle filled with shampoo from her. He lifted the soap to his nose and sniffed. Yep. Ivory. As he'd suspected that first night at the bar when he'd noticed how good she smelled relative to that chick whose name totally escaped him now. He flipped open the lid of the small bottle. "Watermelon," he said with satisfaction. He'd called that correctly, too.

She shrugged as she tested the temperature of the water. "Elise's stuff is much nicer than mine," Jane said. "But I don't care. You like what you like, right?"

He held both the bar of soap and the bottle of shampoo up to his nose at the same time and took a good long inhale. His senses filled with Jane. "I like it, too," he said.

He liked it a lot.

—⟢—

After the water ran cold and Jane had another orgasm—there was something to be said for "slow"—she started to think she might have a problem.

It was just an inkling, a little unformed thought niggling at the corners of her mind, hinting that something wasn't sitting quite right.

It was easy enough to shove out of her consciousness, though, once she was seated at the breakfast bar in Jay's kitchen watching a shirtless Cameron make them grilled cheese sandwiches. "That hipster dinner was too small," he proclaimed, and she had to agree.

She stared at his tattoos. It was so cliché, but they were the hottest thing ever, and when he was otherwise engaged like this, moving silently around the kitchen, she was free to observe them. She couldn't imagine letting someone drag a needle across your skin in order to permanently mark it, and in that sense, they still sort of freaked her out. But she was starting to understand the power of being made to sit with your own discomfort. Roller coasters, tattoos...wild, animalistic sex. It was all rather exhilarating.

"Will you tell me about your tattoos?" she asked. She'd heard him say earlier to Gia that there was no story behind his ink, but she hadn't believed him. He froze in place, his back to her, as he stood over the pan the sandwiches were cooking in. "You don't have to," she added quickly. He clearly didn't like talking about the tattoos, so why had she thought she'd be the exception?

"Okay," he said, flipping a sandwich but not turning around.

She waited a beat for him to start talking, and when it became clear he wasn't going to, she said, "The one on your back is Flanders Fields, right?" The field of poppies was an iconic symbol of Canada's war dead, something any citizen would recognize as such, and was probably a pretty logical tattoo for a soldier to have. She figured it was the safest one to inquire about.

"Yes," he said after a beat. "The crosses at the top are for dead buddies."

"What were their names?" she asked, feeling like Cameron was the kind of guy who'd rather she skip the platitudes.

"Eric and Haseeb. They were our IED guys."

"IED?"

"Improvised explosive device. They were the bomb squad."

"Oh God."

"That's what the PTSD is from," he said, his voice matter-of-fact, devoid of inflection. "We all watched them get blown up. We...couldn't save them. Or the boy who was the bomber. He was so young."

"Oh my God," she breathed, feeling like a stupid broken

record, but she realized with a thud that next to the crosses was a small crescent and star, the symbol of Islam. He'd immortalized his fallen comrades *and* the boy who'd killed them.

"I mean, who does that to a child?" he spat, his voice suddenly angry. "Uses a child as a weapon like that?"

There were a million more questions swirling around in her throat, but she swallowed them in favor of asking, "And the angel?"

He was still standing at the stove, so the tattoo in question, which was on his chest, wasn't visible, but she could see it in her mind. It was an angel, all sleek and muscular and masculine—kind of like him. But its head hung, semi-obscured behind one of its mammoth wings, while the other extended to its full, fearsome wingspan. The image was huge—it covered most of his chest. It was hard to explain why exactly, but there was an aura of sadness about it.

"You don't have to tell me," she said when he remained silent and still. "It's none of my business."

"I was a bad kid," he said, seeming to come to life as he used a spatula to move the sandwiches from the frying pan to a plate. But he didn't do any more than that. Just kept standing there facing away from her.

To hear him call himself "bad," so clinically and with such detachment, made her shiver.

"We lived in this trailer park, and everyone hated me. They were scared of me."

"I'm sure your bark was worse than your bite," she said, hating the way he was talking about himself, wanting to somehow make it un-true with her words, though that was impossible.

He finally turned, and he flashed her a small, defeated smile. "Maybe. Maybe not. Either way, I became what they saw. The trailer park was called Deer Haven, which was stupid because there were no deer anywhere and the place was *not* a haven." She smiled. The way he could inject humor into what was clearly a painful subject made her heart twist. "They started calling me the Devil of Deer Haven."

"Well, that's a little melodramatic."

He shrugged. It was strange to be talking to him from so far away. She was still on the stool at the breakfast bar, and he was leaning against the counter next to the stove, which was as far away from her in the kitchen as it was possible to be. "It suited me, for the most part. I was a loner by that point. I didn't need people bothering me."

"So you're the devil with an angel tattoo?"

"There was this woman named Mrs. Compton who lived in the park. She was exactly what you picture when someone says the term 'trailer trash.' Looked much older than her years, bad dye job, constantly talking about conspiracies and supernatural shit, usually had a wine cooler in hand. But she liked me. She was the only one who did. She had this crackpot idea one summer that she was going to start reading palms and doing tarot cards. So she had all these library books out, and she'd practice on me. She'd give me Oreos. I'd eat with one hand and let her examine the other against the charts in her books. She was always telling me that I was a fallen angel."

"Oh," Jane breathed, understanding dawning. Of course. The tattoo was a fallen angel. The tattoo was *him*.

"She'd go on and on about it. I wasn't the devil like everyone said, she'd insist. I'd just fallen out of heaven." He rolled his eyes. "I didn't see much difference. Wasn't Lucifer himself a fallen angel?"

"No." She wasn't much of a theologian, but she knew

comics and science fiction, which were littered with otherworldly beings. "I think there's a subtle difference."

He looked up at her, and she was startled anew by his brilliant turquoise eyes. "And what is that difference?"

"If you're a fallen angel, I think it implies that you might get back in. To heaven, I mean."

He nodded once, a sharp, decisive nod, like she'd given the correct answer on a test.

Then he picked up the plate of sandwiches, crossed the kitchen, and set it down on the breakfast bar. "Eat up," he said, back to his usual gruff self. "You're going to need your strength for what I'm going to do to you later."

There was still something tapping at the edges of her consciousness, a pre-formed thought that wanted to be examined, but she couldn't quite grab it. Didn't really want to, truth be told. Instead, she let the innuendo wash over her, warm her, and then chased that warmth away with an involuntary shiver of anticipation. "I can't eat that," she said, though the perfectly golden toast with a line of cheese oozing out the sides made her want to cry. "T-minus four days now; it's after midnight."

"Eat," he commanded, sliding the plate directly under her.

"Goddamn you," she said, picking up half a sandwich.

"Now it's your turn," he said, coming around and sitting down next to her at the bar.

"My turn for what?" she asked even as she groaned through a heavenly bite of buttery, sharp cheddar.

"If we're playing midnight confessions, you're up."

She laughed. "Okay, hit me." She was an open book. He'd seen her vibrators. He'd had his face between her legs, for heaven's sake. She couldn't think of anything she wouldn't feel okay about confessing. Cameron was cool that way—he could be kind of jerky when he chose to, but now that she knew him, she could safely say he was utterly trustworthy. She really could tell him anything.

"You hardly ever drink. What's up with that?"

Except that.

She exhaled and leaned forward, resting her elbows on the counter and her head in her hands.

"It's okay," he said quickly. "You don't have to answer." It wasn't lost on her that she'd used the exact same words on him earlier, when he'd reacted to her asking him about his tattoos. She was pretty sure that he had never told anyone the true meaning behind that angel tattoo. He had trusted her. Could she do the same?

Warmth flooded her chest. Of course she could. Hadn't she just been thinking how trustworthy he was? She took a deep breath. "My dad was an alcoholic."

He nodded. "That's rough."

She shook her head, not because she disagreed, but because that wasn't the hard part.

"I used to kind of cover for him," she started, trying to think how to put everything in context. "I was the youngest—my brother is four years older. And my mom was deep in denial. He hated disappointing her, but it was like he couldn't…"

"Couldn't not drink?" Cameron finished gently.

She nodded, hating that a lump had formed in her throat. "So I kind of took it upon myself to try to…minimize the evidence. Like, I'd put him to bed in the guest room. Or if he was out late, I'd try to stay up and meet him at the door with a snack to make sure he didn't make too much noise banging around in the kitchen. Or…" God, it was so humiliating, though she wasn't sure why. Her mature, rational mind knew that none of it was her fault. "When he got sick,

I'd clean it up." She swallowed hard. "Somehow, it was important to me that my mom not know how bad things really were. But of course, as an adult I can see that she had to have known."

"Oh, sweetheart," he said, laying a hand on her forearm. She could feel his gaze, but she didn't turn her head. Since they were sitting side by side, she could get away with not looking at him, so she kept staring straight ahead. It was the only way she could do this.

"How old were you when this was going on?" he asked quietly.

She shrugged. She couldn't remember a time when it hadn't. "Five, maybe, when it started? Six?" she ventured. "I don't really remember. It was just always a thing I did, until..."

He squeezed her forearm tighter, and she appreciated that he didn't prod her to continue. In fact, paradoxically, it was his patience that made her want to keep going. Now that she'd started, she wanted to unburden herself fully.

"So anyway, I was a big reader. The library was my happy place, you know?"

He raised his eyebrows. "You don't say?"

She chuckled, loving the gentle teasing. "When I was eleven, I found this shelf of books in the kids' nonfiction section about being the child of an alcoholic. There was this stuff in one of them about how often kids of alcoholics are forced to parent their parents. It was like a lightbulb went off—that was exactly what I was doing. So then I went and got grown-up books on the subject. There was this one targeted at spouses of alcoholics. It had a chapter about protecting your children from your spouse. Not physically— my dad was never violent. But, like, stuff about how it wasn't fair to expect the child to step into the parental role, and how it could actually create lasting psychological damage, blah, blah. Anyway, I got mad." Her skin felt hot and prickly just thinking about it, a mixture of residual anger and shame over what that anger had spawned. "Cameron, I got *so mad*."

She paused. Was she really going to continue? She kind of felt, stupidly, like telling this story to another person would make it more real. And making it more real might make it more painful. And she wasn't sure she could deal with that. But then the hand that had been resting on her forearm slid down and grabbed her hand.

His hand was so big. So warm.

She took a shaky breath. "I didn't dare bring those books into the house. I read them in the library, put them back on the shelf, and I went home. I was *seething*. I mean, I'm sure puberty had something to do with it, but mostly I was just *done*. Like, a switch had flipped inside me. When I got home, he was drunk, which wasn't unusual. I was the only one there. My brother was a top student, and his schedule was loaded with extracurriculars." Extracurriculars that he had to quit, later, so he could work to support them. Jane would never forget that. "My mom wasn't home. He was out of booze. That used to happen a lot, and it would tick me off. Like, didn't he know by now how much he needed? Why couldn't he plan ahead? Normally, I'd talk him out of driving to get more. I'd make him a sandwich and tell him I needed help with my homework. I never did, but that always seemed to trigger something in him. Like, he was fine with being a drunk, but some part of him didn't want to be a shitty parent. So sometimes food and math homework would be enough to sort of land the plane, and he'd go pass out. But sometimes it wouldn't work, and he would be determined. Those times, I used to feel like the best thing I could do was call him a cab. I'd stall him and do it on the sly, so that when it arrived it was easier for him to accept without damaging his pride—like, oh, this cab is here, might as well take it."

"You had to grow up too soon," Cameron said.

She wanted to say that it was fine. That it was probably nothing compared to what lots of kids go through. That her *brother* was the one who'd had to grow up too soon. But more than that, she wanted to keep going with the story. Now that she'd started, now that she had this big, warm, safe hand to hold on to, she needed to get it all out, to voice the words that she'd never said to another human being. "But that day, I decided not to do anything. I came home, took stock of the situation, and…told him I was done. I didn't yell or anything, just basically recited everything I'd learned from my reading. I told him he had ruined my childhood. He was shocked. *I* was shocked. He tried to apologize, but I'd freaked myself out so much with the confrontation that I shook off his entreaties and went to hide in my room."

She appreciated that Cameron didn't say anything. He simply sat there next to her, listening without judgment. She held on to his hand like he was a life raft and let the next sentence rush out of her mouth before she could swallow it back. "I heard him leave. I heard him close the front door and start the car. I did nothing. He drove off and crashed into a giant tree and died."

"Oh, sweetheart."

She could tell there was more coming, and she didn't want it. She turned to him for the first time since she'd started her sad tale, and, yes, there was sympathy in his eyes. Pity even. Not acceptable. So she tugged her hand from his grasp and held it up to him, palm open. "Don't try to tell me it's not my fault. If I had done my usual caretaking thing, my dad would still be alive today."

To his credit, Cameron didn't say what she expected, which was some variation on "it's not your fault." Or "he was the addict." He merely nodded, not like he was agreeing with her necessarily, but like he was hearing her and wasn't going to contradict her.

So she took a deep breath and confessed the rest. "The worst part is that my big decision to stop enabling him was selfish. I wasn't doing it because I wanted him to get better, to stop drinking. It was entirely self-interested. I simply didn't want to deal with him anymore."

She took a shaky breath. It was out. It was kind of anticlimactic, but it was still a huge relief. She had considered confessing, but to whom? It would have destroyed her mother. Her brother was too busy keeping them together. And later, with some distance from the situation, she'd thought about telling the girls. But they would have tried to talk her out of feeling the way she felt, and the way she felt was *part of her*. It had shaped everything that had come afterward.

But as relieved as she felt to have told someone, now she needed a way to figure out how to get things back to normal with Cameron. Because she didn't want to talk anymore. Later, she'd have to examine what it meant that she'd told her deepest secret. Later.

"You haven't asked about the sleeve," Cameron said.

"Huh?" What was he talking about?

He laid his tattooed arm on the counter between them. "You asked about the others, but not the sleeve."

Jane's breath caught a little. God bless him; he was giving her exactly what she had been silently wishing for—a return to normalcy. He knew somehow, and he was turning the conversation back to him, trying to draw her pain onto him.

She smiled, overwhelmed with emotion because at that moment, it felt like the nicest thing anyone had ever done for her. It took a few seconds for her to find her voice. "Right, so, Cameron, what's the deal with the sleeve?"

He rotated his arm back and forth, showing off the swirling mixture of trees and flowers and stylized waves and stars. "It doesn't mean anything." He grinned. "It's just generalized badassery." Then he shoved the rest of his grilled cheese into his mouth.

"I don't know," she said, picking up her own abandoned sandwich even as she took the cue he was so generously handing her. "I don't know how badass *flowers* are. You should have gotten a Terminator arm or, like, naked ladies and AK-47s."

He put his hands on his hips in mock outrage. "Are you impugning my manhood?"

She shook her head. "Oh, no. I would never do that. I've *seen* your manhood."

He swatted her butt playfully. "Yeah, well, finish your sandwich, because you're about to do more than see it."

Chapter Seventeen

*S*ome guys had a thing about sleeping with a woman after sex. If it was just a hookup, they wanted out as soon as the main event was over. Cam never saw the big deal. After sex, he was tired. And if he was in a warm bed with a soft woman, the path of least resistance was to stay there. So he had done his share of sleepovers, in the era between Alicia and Christie. Guys were always like, "But, dude, you gotta manage her expectations. You gotta get out of there."

Cam's take was that he was *going* to get out of there—the next morning. You could communicate a lot with the way you left a situation, so what did it matter if you left in the middle of the night or waited until the sun came up? Women weren't stupid—at least not any stupider than men—and when you left before breakfast, issuing a vague "I'll text you," everyone knew what it meant.

So, yeah, he was fine with the sleepover in theory. This

particular sleepover, though, was giving him some trouble. Namely, he wasn't actually sleeping. Usually he fell into a sated sleep after sex. The military shrink he'd seen after his first deployment had been forever asking him about nightmares, trouble sleeping, racing thoughts at night. No, no, and no. He'd always figured he was lucky that way. He was definitely fucked up from watching his brothers blown to bits, but it didn't invade his daily life too much. It manifested itself only in particular surroundings—usually in wide-open spaces where he felt like the enemy could come from anywhere.

But tonight. Jane. With her gentle questioning, it was like she had opened a box that had been hidden deep inside his chest, one he had gotten so used to it had become like furniture, something to be walked around but not, fundamentally, of any concern. Mostly, he avoided talking about his tattoos. Or, when people pushed him, he gave some kind of bullshit answer. It was easy. People expected him to have tattoos. He was that kind of guy. They *didn't* expect him to have a big emotional story behind them.

God. The idea that Mrs. Compton had planted all those years ago. That he was more than what he'd done. That maybe his fucked-up-ness could be temporary. That he could get back into heaven. He hadn't done anything with it then. Had continued doing his thing—working just enough to not get fired, sleeping around, partying.

But then Jay had come back for a visit, a few years after Alicia's family had left town and Cam had quit school, and suggested Cam consider the military. Cam hadn't done anything with the advice just then—except reject it—but underneath Cam's defensive dismissals that day, the idea lurked. The image of himself in another place, somewhere halfway around the world where nobody knew him. Where they might be able to teach him how to do something important. He owed Jay a lot. It had taken balls to come home and initiate "the chat." Cam had been so angry then, so utterly unable to see beyond his own misery. "What are you waiting for?" Jay had asked, his tone not angry but also not kind. "Are you waiting for your father to come back?" When Cam had scoffed—perhaps a little too hard—at that, he'd followed with, "Are you waiting to die? Because that's about all I can see that's going on here."

No, Cam had said, and he'd meant it. He wasn't suicidal. But Jay's words had staying power. They rattled around inside him over the next few years. They made him wonder about the difference between being actively suicidal and just sitting around taking up space, passing the time until death arrived.

What *was* he waiting for?

On his twenty-second birthday, while blowing out the candle on a cupcake his mom had brought over to his trailer—his trailer that had been such a falling-down disaster that it had embarrassed even him—the answer had come into his brain fully formed, and it had shocked the hell out of him. He wasn't waiting to die; he was waiting for everyone to give up. His mom and Jay, specifically. Because they were the only ones who hadn't. They were the only ones left who loved him—hell, who tolerated him at all. Even Mrs. Compton had died by then, and her kids had come over and cleaned out her trailer and sold it.

Once Jay and Mom stopped tolerating him—as he knew in his heart they would one day—he would be alone. So he was practicing. Or trying to encourage them to get on with it, like pulling off a Band-Aid quickly rather than drawing it out.

But what if Mrs. Compton, and later, Jay, had been right? What if he could reverse direction? Stop the free fall?

And so it had begun. His Hail Mary pass. And for a while, it seemed like it was working. Basic training kicked his ass, but he stuck it out. His first tour had been a success. Yes, it came with PTSD as a door prize, but he'd actually been good at being a soldier. Not that he had any particular skills, but he flattered himself that he was strong and loyal. A good grunt.

And Christie. The unlikely girl he'd met a little before that first deployment. She'd written to him. He came to depend on those letters, to live for them. He loved being a soldier, but he also loved fantasizing about being normal. At home. *What if I wrote her back?* He thought to himself, amazed, after her first letter arrived, even though he had been the one who'd suggested they correspond. And then when he did and the second one came, he thought, *what if I wrote her back again?*

The army and Christie saved him. The army made his body and mind strong, and the deployment gave him space. A do-over.

A life where he could get back into heaven, or at least some reasonable facsimile of it.

But no. He'd done nothing but fall again, and landed squarely on his ass, embarrassed as hell that he'd ever been so naive as to think he could escape his destiny.

So, yeah, with all this shit from the past taking up residence in his brain, it had been a mostly sleepless night, and he was pissed. Not at Jane, though he did sort of feel like her questioning had been the impetus for his insomnia, but at himself. He'd had his balls thoroughly milked—several times. He had a warm, soft, *naked* woman who did not want to become his girlfriend curled up next to him in a comfy bed.

So what was wrong with him? He should have been sleeping the sleep of the dead.

The blaring of Jane's phone on the nightstand cut short his existential crisis. She had insisted on setting it for the ass crack of dawn in case Jay came home before going to work.

She reached out, patting the edge of the bed as if searching around for an alarm clock that wasn't there. When she didn't find it, the pats became faster, more insistent, even a little frantic. A rush of tenderness toward her had him tightening his arms around her, reassuring her. "Shhh. We're at Jay's, remember?" She had been dead asleep—as any reasonable person would be, given that they'd gone at it until two in the morning.

"What?" She lifted her head from where it had been resting on his chest, squinted her eyes like she was looking into the blinding sun, and did her nose-scrunching thing. Her befuddlement was awfully cute. His dick took notice, pulsing a little as she opened her eyes all the way. "Oh," she said. "*Oh.*"

Watching her remember where she was—and what she'd done—was funny. The befuddlement was replaced by a wash of pink. She was delicious—the perfect antidote to all his maudlin thoughts.

Where should he start? Letting a lazy hand slide between her legs, he planted a kiss on her forehead.

She reared back, not from surprise this time, though. It was more like she was…trying to get away from him? That couldn't be right, not after the stuff they'd done last night. Maybe she was truly embarrassed. There was no call for that. He'd show her how not-embarrassed she should be. He moved back just enough to make room to burrow under the covers. His mouth started to water at the mere idea of her.

"I...ah, can't," she said, hopping off the bed and pulling the top sheet around her like a robe.

He narrowed his eyes. What was going on? Why was she hiding herself from him?

"I've got to get home," she said, spinning around the room, probably looking for her clothes. "Last day of work before we hit the road for Prince Edward County."

He wanted to tell her to drop the sheet, that he'd seen it all already. *Tasted* it all. But she seemed genuinely agitated.

"I think your clothes are still by the front door," he said gently. When she nodded and started to turn, he added, "Although, remember, I can do fast. I can have you out of here in twenty minutes, ten if it comes to that." He shook his head. Listen to him: he was bragging now about how fast he could be? Damn. She had him all turned around. But he couldn't help it. He'd pretty much do anything to get his hands on Jane again.

Also, he just really didn't want her to leave yet. He was about to suggest that they at least have a quick cuddle, but stopped himself in time, because *a quick cuddle*? What the *hell*?

She shook her head. "I can't...sleep with you."

Uh, what? Did she mean she couldn't sleep with him right now? Or in general? Because the way she'd said it was weird. As if they hadn't *already* slept together a bunch of times. He blinked, trying to think how to ask her to clarify without making himself look desperate. After a few awkward moments elapsed, she turned and opened the door, the sheet still wrapped around her. He hopped out of bed—what else could he do?—and said, "I'll get your clothes for you."

"Thanks," she said, changing direction and heading down the hallway toward the bathroom. "If you can just shove them through the bathroom door, that would be great."

Shove them through the bathroom door? What the hell? Something had happened, though he couldn't say what. Well, that wasn't true: he knew exactly what had happened. Jane had changed her mind about him.

He'd always known she was smart.

⟶∽⟵

Panic.

Jane was not a panicker. All her life, she had made decisions about what she wanted to do, how she was going to be, and she had done and been those things. She'd never experienced any of the symptoms she'd read about as associated with panic attacks.

But that must have been what had happened to her earlier this morning, she decided, as she sat on the streetcar, on her way to meet the girls for a "last night in the city" drink.

Last night, with Cameron, a niggling sense that something was wrong had kept dogging her. It was like trying to remember a dream after you woke up, even as it was sliding from your grasp. But in this case, waking up had brought clarity. Absolute, utter clarity.

She was falling for Cameron. She'd woken up in his bed—in his *arms*—and she'd known it with utter certainty.

Somewhere along the way, in a matter of mere days, the shit-talking, arrogant, testosterone-overdosed, bad-boy soldier had gotten under her skin. Look at her: she was riding roller coasters, dangling off buildings, and having sex with a human like it was no big deal. Hell, she wasn't just having sex, she was *sexting*, which, somehow was a bigger deal than the actual deed.

But all of that was okay. Well, she could have made it okay.

But then she told him everything. What. The. Hell? Objectively, she could understand the circumstances that had led to her impulsive gut-spilling. He'd been surprisingly forthright about the stories behind his tattoos. He'd made her feel safe, not only with his own confession, but with his conduct all week. He'd made her feel wanted. Like she was a person worth having around, and listening to.

But she couldn't let herself go there. Couldn't get used to waking up in his arms. Couldn't crave it...crave *him*.

Because the other amazing thing about Cameron? He had never lied to her. He made it clear he wasn't looking for a relationship. Heck, so had she. Because she *wasn't*. He had a return-to-civilian-life list, and she was merely an item on it.

"Hey, sweets!" As Jane disembarked the streetcar, there was Gia, strolling down the street. Damn. Jane had been aiming to get to the bar before everyone else. She'd been restless in her house, going a bit cuckoo, in fact, and had resigned herself to the fact that no writing was going to get done until after the wedding. Well, until after Cam was gone, if she was being honest with herself—and being honest with herself was absolutely what she was doing now, as painful as it was.

So she'd left her house early, thinking maybe a change of scenery—and a few Diet Cokes' worth of caffeine to compensate for her late night—would do her some good.

Gia had obviously come armed with a similar plan because she looped her arm through Jane's and said, "I thought I'd sneak in early and get a buzz on before Elise—God bless her—gets here."

Jane smiled. She had to admit that one unforeseen benefit

of the wedding was that she was spending more time with Gia, who was usually somewhere else in the world working. The four girls had been tight since university. But because the rest of them had only overlapped with Gia there for one year, Gia was like the plus-one that came with Elise to their friendship group. She and Jane hadn't ever had an independent relationship, and Jane had to admit that she'd always been a little intimidated by the model's beauty and jet-setting life.

So she let herself be led to the bar, where she ordered her Diet Coke.

"How come you hardly ever drink?" Gia asked after their drinks arrived.

"Because my dad was an alcoholic."

What the hell? How had she let that slip *again*? She didn't talk about that. Wendy knew, but only in general terms. It certainly wasn't something she talked about with people she'd met later in life. Elise didn't know, either.

"Ah." Gia nodded. "I see."

Jane was a little surprised at how mild Gia's reaction was. She was sipping her vodka soda like what Jane had told her wasn't a big deal.

"He died driving drunk," Jane added, watching Gia out of the corner of her eye to see what a little more truth would do to her friend's reaction.

"I'm sorry," said Gia simply. "I'd known he died in a car accident, but not that it was related to drunk driving."

"Yeah," Jane said, her stupid heart pounding like she was back on one of the roller coasters at Canada's Wonderland instead of telling a close friend about something that had happened twenty years ago.

"There's a lot of drinking in the fashion world," Gia said. "Too much, a lot of the time, I think. When you have to stay a size zero or two, you sometimes have to pick and choose what you consume. A lot of models choose to drink their calories."

Wow. Jane had always imagined Gia's life like one of the magazine spreads she posed in. "So there's not, like, hot guys feeding you bonbons all the time?"

Gia scoffed. "Try creepy middle-aged art directors feeding you chocolate-flavored laxatives."

"And here I am stressed about trying to fit into my dress this week." Jane hated to think what it would be like to live with that shadow over her head all the time.

"It's not a good way to live," Gia said. "I'm lucky that gaining weight hasn't been a problem for me." She paused. "At least historically."

Jane wondered if there was something more beneath that statement, but she didn't know how to ask. Gia pre-empted her anyway, lifting her drink in a wry toast and shaking her head. "Gah. Let's talk about something else."

"Okay!" Jane said. That had been enough of True Confessions for her, anyway.

"Let's talk about sex," said Gia.

"What?" Jane laughed to cover her wariness. Could Gia tell? Was she some kind of sex bloodhound?

"I haven't had any for a long time, and I would like to."

"Ah." She was safe. "Define 'a long time.'"

Gia gazed at the ceiling as if she were doing math. "Uh, maybe five weeks?"

Jane laughed. "Well, what about someone from the wedding party?" *But not Cameron. Because he's mine. Even though I don't want him. Or I don't* want *to want him, anyway.*

"Nah. No offense to Jay, but his friends are kind of…"

"Boring?"

Gia shrugged, but her eyes twinkled.

"You think five weeks is a dry spell," Jane said, "but I hear that, and I'm like, whoa, your heart is getting a workout!"

"My heart has nothing to do with it."

"Really?" said Jane, suddenly curious how Gia pulled it off.

"Really," Gia said decisively.

"How do you do it?"

"What? Be a slut?" Gia laughed.

"No!" Jane cried. "I only mean, how do you separate sex from love?"

"It's easy. I don't do love. So no separation required."

"But how? How does that work? You just decide?"

"It's nothing so calculating. I just...don't fall in love." Jane was about to object again, because that didn't make sense, but Gia must have anticipated her because she turned in her stool and said, "Look. The way I see it, some people are made to fall in love. Most people, probably. Or they have the capacity anyway. Me? Not so much. Maybe I don't have the gene for love or something. It's like we all have different ways of being. I come from skinny stock, and I have light brown eyes. I also can't fall in love."

"I see," Jane said, but she didn't.

"To be honest, I always thought maybe you and I were alike that way," Gia said, cocking her head as she looked at Jane. "I mean, assuming all this Xena stuff isn't sublimation and you're not actually a closet case." She winked.

Jane grinned. "Nope. Not a closet case." She chose not to address the rest of what Gia had said. A week ago she would have agreed with Gia's characterization of her as immune to love. She'd had the odd crush as a girl, and with Felix there had been...a kind of love. Until there wasn't. And after that...nothing. For five years.

Now? She wasn't sure. But she did know enough to know that she needed to back away from Cameron before she got burned. That no good could come of testing the waters with a guy who not only didn't want to swim but had, in fact, chained himself to dry land.

"So you're love-proof and calorie-proof," Jane teased, hoping to get them on to more comfortable topics.

Gia smiled. "It would appear so."

"Ahhhh! Team Elise is here already!"

Jane and Gia looked over their shoulders to see Elise waving at them from near the door. Gia started humming the wedding march but morphed it into the theme from *Jaws* as Elise approached the bar. Jane stifled a laugh.

"Okay, you guys," Elise said, sliding onto a stool on the other side of Gia. "I should wait till Wendy gets here to tell you this, but I'm about to burst from how good this idea is!"

"Well by all means, let's have it," Gia said. "Wendy snoozes; Wendy loses."

"Okay, so you know how the site is large?"

Jane nodded warily. The wedding was being held at a "farm," which as far as she could tell was code for "expensive fancy rural event center." They had visited a year ago when Elise was trying to decide on venues, and there hadn't been an animal or a crop in sight on the "farm."

"So I got this cute idea from Pinterest last night of making way-finding signs?"

"Way-finding signs?" Gia echoed, her voice full of skepticism that Jane shared.

"Yeah, you know, like cute signs pointing people to the reception, the ceremony, the bar, and so on. The only thing is should we do cute little chalkboards or should we get, like, pieces of wood and do some cute lettering on them?"

"As long as it's cute, I don't think it matters," Jane said, relishing the fact that her comment caused Gia to press her lips together like she was trying not to laugh.

"Oh!" said Elise, throwing her hands heavenward like they were at a revival. "We can do the same kinds of signs on the bathrooms!"

"Won't the bathrooms already have signs?" Gia asked. "I feel like bathrooms in public spaces are generally labeled."

"But, Gia," Jane said, "they're not going to match. They're not going to be cute."

Elise pointed a finger at Jane. "Exactly."

Chapter Eighteen

*C*am was fine until they got there.

Well, fine in relative terms. He had been, after all, trapped in the 'Vette with Groomsman Kent, he of "Isn't Jane cute?" fame, for two and a half hours on the drive to the wedding site.

Kent was nice. He was an accountant at Jay's firm. So he was probably pretty well off. He was blandly handsome—with his jeans, Polo shirt, and wavy, short brown hair, he was like a Ken doll come to life. Ken Doll Kent.

And he clearly had a crush on Jane.

Which, to be fair, was totally understandable.

He wasn't gross about it, at least. There were no crude remarks, no sexist jokes. He was a gentleman. Respectful. Which was a hell of a lot more than Cameron could say about himself when he'd first met Jane.

And Kent wanted to talk about Jane, and nothing but Jane, the whole drive. He thought he was being subtle, in the way that people under Cupid's spell always were, seizing on any opportunity to bring the conversation back to their target.

"I think it's so cool that she writes books, don't you? I mean, do you know anyone else who writes books? It's kind of a big deal."

Cam made a vague grunting noise.

"Have you read any of her books?" Kent asked.

"Nope."

"You should. They're good. Really clever."

"Aren't they for kids?" But Cam asked himself why he hadn't. He'd read *about* her books online. They were well reviewed. Everyone seemed to like them. And he was an avid reader—or he'd become one, anyway, in the Middle East.

"I guess technically. But they're like the *Hunger Games* books. It doesn't really matter that they're classified as young adult. She draws you right into the world she creates."

She draws you right into the world she creates.

Cam grunted again and stepped on the accelerator, enjoying the *vroom* of the engine.

"I noticed that you guys left together from the bachelor party," Kent said with studied nonchalance. "That was just you trying to get her away from that guy who was hitting on her, right? What happened after you left?"

What happened after we left is that she took me home, and I fucked her.

But of course he didn't say that, merely grunted something noncommittal. His gentlemanly streak might have been late blooming when it came to Jane, but he didn't kiss and tell. Oh, how he wished he could say that, though—that and more. *You've read her books; I've been inside her body. I know what her pussy tastes like.* Ha. That would have derailed Kent the Ken Doll Accountant once and for all.

But it wasn't like he had any meaningful claim to her. In the twenty-four hours since Jane had left him at Jay's, she had made it clear that they were done. Not overtly, but in the coolly polite way she'd responded to his texts. Gone was the abashed sexting. He would text, and she would reply, sometimes hours later, with short notes about how busy she was with wedding stuff.

He'd gotten the message.

It was for the best.

It was also unexpectedly disappointing.

Somehow, Jane Denning had wormed her way into his heart. The only way he could make sense of it was to conclude that he, erroneously assuming that he didn't have any heart left to speak of, had foolishly left it unguarded.

But regardless of the fact that his little fling with Jane was done, Kent the Ken Doll Accountant was *not* what she needed. She needed someone who appreciated Goddess Mode. No, someone who would *cultivate* Goddess Mode, who would treat it like a goddamned imperative.

As they turned onto the dirt road that would take them to the farm, Cameron sighed. Resigned himself to spending the next four days being treated with friendly indifference by Jane and ~~fucking~~ frolicking in nature with Kent-Ken and the rest of the wedding party.

He just hadn't realized exactly what the "nature" part was going to be like.

It should not have been a problem. And at first, it wasn't. There was a B&B on site, and the wedding party was staying there while the guests would be bused in from neighboring inns on Saturday for the ceremony. As Cam and Kent drove into the parking area, a woman emerged from the administration building. "Welcome to Fournier Farm! I'm Lacy, one of the event coordinators here." The chipper blonde looked like she had stepped out of a brochure for a dental office. "You're the first ones here!" She clapped her hands like it was an accomplishment worthy of an award rather than a logical consequence of Cam's lead foot. "Oh, but look, here's everyone else!" Lacy walked toward other cars, which were pulling in and parking. "Where's my bride?"

Much squealing ensued as Lacy and Elise found each other. Everyone watched them shriek-talk until it was decided that the whole gang should immediately go out to inspect the lavender fields to decide specifically where they should have the ceremony.

He watched Wendy and Gia look at each other and shrug. Jane appeared to be struggling under the weight of…a bunch of small chalkboards? He moved to help her, but she twisted away from him. "I'll actually leave these in my trunk for now." He tried again to take some of them from her, but she trilled, "I'm fine!" in a voice he easily recognized as false.

Screw that. She might not want to screw *him* anymore, but she didn't have to be purposefully difficult.

"Will you let me help you?" he snapped as he pushed past her, opened the back of her hatchback for her, and guided her—the pile of chalkboards semi-obscured her sight—to the trunk.

Everything was fine, he told himself. Fine-ish. He wasn't particularly looking forward to inspecting lavender fields. Or to any of this so-called bucolic "escape," especially given that he apparently was going to spend exactly zero percent of it in Jane's bed, but it was fine. Fine-ish.

Until it wasn't.

Lavender fields were nothing like the desert. It was apples and oranges. Lavender fields and the desert. It shouldn't have mattered.

And yet.

He'd become pretty adept at avoiding wide-open spaces since the PTSD hit after his first deployment. Christie's apartment was in the urban part of Thunder Bay, such as it was. He'd been fine there. Fine-ish. But he'd learned pretty quickly that as soon as he got out of the city limits, the panic would hit and he'd be left sweating and shaking. So he learned to stay safe, which meant limiting himself to places with a certain density of buildings and concrete and people.

And anyway, it had gotten much better. He'd thought.

Regardless, as they trudged away from the main buildings, across a series of gardens and a meadow that bordered the herb fields, it started happening. It didn't matter that the air was ripe with the scent of lavender instead of the sulfurous smell of gunpowder. It didn't matter that the sun was shining on purple fields as far as the eye could see instead of sand as far as the eye could see. It didn't matter that it was a pleasantly warm seventy-five-degree day in freaking Canada and not a balls-melting one hundred ten with ISIS fighters and IEDs hiding all around them.

His stupid body didn't know the difference, even if his brain did. His heart was jackhammering out of his chest, his lungs were constricting, and he was sweating so much he might as well have been back in the unrelenting desert heat. *Fuck*.

He tried to tune into what was happening. What was *actually* happening, which was that the mundane details of a wedding were being discussed. Elise's mouth was moving, and he struggled to make out what she was saying through the roaring in his ears. Something about not wanting the guests to be blinded by the afternoon sun and should they have made sun hats for everyone?

He was safe, he tried to tell himself. Everyone was safe. He was home in Canada.

But it wasn't working. He was starting to see gray spots in front of his eyes. He had to get out of there before he made an utter fool of himself.

But where to go? He started to stumble back down the trail they'd followed to get to the fields. He didn't have a room yet. There was nowhere he could escape.

His car. The Corvette.

Having a destination calmed him a little. Not enough to stop the panic in its tracks, but enough to allow him to propel himself forward in space.

He didn't even bother getting in the driver's side. The passenger side was closer, and as much as he wished he could rev the engine and fly out of here, he was in no condition to drive. So he hurled himself inside, doubled over, rested his head on the dashboard, and settled in to wait out the storm.

⟿

"Cameron is being kind of weird, don't you think?" Wendy said as she and Jane put their feet up in Jane's room later that night after dinner was done and the evening's duties discharged.

"Really? I hadn't noticed," Jane said, lying through her teeth.

"Yeah, I get that he's kind of antisocial by nature, but he

keeps bailing on everything," said Wendy with a sigh. "The lucky dog."

It was true. Jane *had* noticed, because she apparently noticed everything about Cameron now. In fact, she had attained the "if they were in junior high she would have his class schedule memorized and would be 'accidentally' running into him outside chem lab" level of noticed.

But to be fair, it wasn't like he was being subtle about it. When they'd come back from the fields, he'd been sitting in his car. It kind of reminded her of a kid in time-out, near but separate from the action, except he'd put himself there.

Later, they'd opted for a picnic dinner near a stream that ran through the property, but he hadn't come with them. And though he, along with the other groomsmen and ushers, had been asked to walk around the property helping the bridesmaids put up the stupid way-finding signs, he had spent about five minutes actually doing his job before slipping away.

He was quite clearly avoiding something. And she wasn't stupid. She knew what that "something" was.

It didn't matter, though. This was what she'd wanted, right, when she'd awkwardly extricated herself from Jay's condo after their spectacular sex-fest two nights ago? She hadn't handled that well, but he'd obviously interpreted her weird, sudden coldness correctly. She was actually uber-relieved that she hadn't had to talk to him today. She had a lame little "we had some fun, but since it's never going to last, best to quit while we're ahead" speech worked up, but she was happy not to need to make it. He was getting the message.

She just hadn't expected that in getting the message, he would have retreated so utterly, so much that he couldn't even stand to look at her.

And it was hard to see him, harder than she'd expected. She wanted him still, so badly. The hardest part was that she could probably have him if she wanted. She could say the word, and he'd be back in her bed. But, stupidly, maddeningly, casual sex with Cameron wasn't enough anymore.

So it was better that he was hiding.

"Well, it's probably for the best," said Wendy. "Because aren't you still supposed to be babysitting him?"

"I don't know," Jane said, huffing a laugh because the idea of being forced to spend time with Cameron, that she had been so averse to him initially, was so absurd now.

"Well, if he's going to sulk in the corner by himself the whole time, how much damage can he do?" Wendy went on. "Less work for you."

"Hmm," said Jane.

"Three more days, and you never have to see Cameron MacKinnon again."

"Yes," she said. "Great."

Because that was what she wanted.

Right?

Chapter Nineteen

THURSDAY—TWO DAYS BEFORE THE WEDDING

$\mathcal{D}$o you think it's okay if they're sort of on-purpose ugly?" Elise asked, tilting her head as she contemplated the straw hat she was holding on her lap as she wove strands of lavender through its loose weave.

"It was the best I could do out here in the boondocks," said Gia, who was standing behind Elise and miming strangling her.

Jane stifled a laugh.

"I think it's great!" Wendy chirped. "Sun hats for the guests! So thoughtful! And if they look a little handmade, well, they go with all the Mason jars everywhere, right?"

"Because we could take the other route and have a big bucket of dollar store sunglasses for everyone," Elise said. "Maybe that's what we should have done. Because then the guys could wear them, too. I don't really see any men wearing the lavender straw hats."

Jane sighed. Elise had decided yesterday, during their

lavender field inspection, that they needed to offer the guests some sun protection. So she'd sent Gia to the nearest town, and the maid of honor had come back with fifty cheap straw hats she'd scored at some kind of craft wholesaler she'd tracked down. And now everyone was trying to poke lavender strands through them.

"I'm concerned that people might not get that these hats are ironic," Elise said.

"Oh, but think how cute they'll be in the photo booth!" said Gia, clapping her hands with false enthusiasm. "You already have all those funny props for that, so these will fit right in. We can take them over there right after the ceremony."

"You're right," said Elise, brightening. "We'll use the hats for the photo booth, and we'll get sunglasses for everyone for the ceremony. Like, cute, funny ones. An assortment they can choose from when they go to sit down."

Still behind Elise, Gia closed her eyes and turned her head heavenward as if appealing for divine patience.

"Maybe..." said Wendy, drawing everyone's attention. "Maybe you can get, like, a really, really big Mason jar, and you can put the sunglasses in that."

Gia burst out laughing but covered it with a cough. Jane bit down hard on the insides of her cheeks. Elise furrowed her brow, confused. Then she patted Wendy's hand and said, "Great idea, sweetie," in a way that conveyed that the idea was, in fact, the opposite of great.

"Okay, can one of you run back to town and see if you can find a dollar store or a Walmart or something and clean them out of sunglasses?"

"On it!" Gia chirped. "Let me grab some quick lunch inside, and then I'll head out." As she turned to go, a group of the guys appeared from the direction of the fields, where they'd been sent by Elise earlier to harvest lavender for the hats. Cameron was not among them.

Kent was, though.

Jane braced herself as Kent set a basket of lavender at her feet. What was wrong with her? Who didn't want a nice, reliable guy to set a basket of fragrant herbs at her feet?

"You need some help, Jane?"

"Nope, I'm fine!" she said. "I think Elise has changed her mind about the hats anyway."

Undeterred, he plopped down beside her under the tree. He looked so incongruous, with his khaki shorts and his short-sleeved plaid button-down shirt. She herself was wearing yoga pants and a tank top, having very much taken to heart Elise's instruction that they could dress casually in the days they would spend at the site before the wedding. What did Kent see in her? Compared to him, she was a slob.

But he definitely saw something, because he was manipulating the strands of lavender, tying one end to the other, almost like he was making...oh, no.

"I made you a crown."

"Oh...wow." She pasted a smile on her face and ordered herself to stay still while he coroneted her.

"Oh, that is *cute*..." Elise trailed off in the way she did when she was getting thoughtful, which Jane knew could only spell doom.

Great. Now she was going to have to hand-weave several hundred lavender crowns in the next two days *and* fend off Kent.

Kent who was kind of...fixing her hair? What was happening? He had finished placing the crown, but he was sort of tucking loose strands of her hair behind her ears now, which was really—

Then there was the sound of someone clearing his throat.

Not even that, really, more of an indistinct growly sound.
She knew that growl.

"Ah, Cameron, my man," said Kent, who had, at least,
stopped touching her hair. "We wondered what had happened to you."

Cameron looked awful. Like he was hung over, maybe?
It was possible. She had gone to bed early, so she had no
idea what the guys had gotten up to last night. His eyes were
bloodshot and ringed with dark circles, and he was sweating
something awful.

And goddamn him, even in this diminished state, he lit
her up like a sky full of fireworks. It wasn't fair.

He blinked rapidly several times and heaved a big, shaky
inhale. Was he going to barf right here? His eyes darted toward the B&B. She followed his gaze. All the other guys were
clustered around the entrance, talking to Gia, who apparently
hadn't left for Operation: A Thousand Sunglasses yet.

Then Cameron's eyes darted around in all the other directions, like he was trying to plot an escape, which, as
evidenced by the fact that he spun on his heel without a
word and made for the wooded area opposite the lavender
fields, he clearly was.

"What the hell is his problem?" said Elise. Wendy's observation from last night, that Cameron was being weirdly
antisocial, even for him, had become common currency.
Jane had tried to avoid the conversations about him, because, frankly, it hurt like hell that she was the reason he
was being so violently antisocial. What did it say about
her that he couldn't even compartmentalize enough to make
small talk in her presence for five minutes?

"You know what? I've had enough of him," said Elise.
"I'm going after him, and I'm going to find out what is up
his butt. He can't be allowed to ruin my wedding."

"I'll go," said Jane, hopping up as Kent attempted to place a lavender bracelet on her wrist. Elise could *not* find out that she'd slept with Cameron, that she was the reason he was being so impossible. And anyway, he *did* need a talking to, and keeping Cameron in line was what she'd signed up for, right? She smiled wanly at Elise, saying, "After all, he's my job."

⌒

The ground was cool against his cheek. The ground was hard beneath his body. As his lungs heaved, they expanded with each inhale against the ground he was hugging like he was taking cover in an enemy attack.

The ground is cool. The ground is hard.

These were real, physical facts. Find something to anchor yourself to the present, the shrink had said. He'd been headed for the stream that ran through these woods. It was hardly the waterfall that had been prescribed, but the gently rushing water had calmed him last night, and it had reminded him a little of Niagara Falls. Of standing next to the rushing falls while Jane kissed him.

Too bad she wasn't here now. He had a feeling a kiss would work pretty well as an anchor. It was hard to freak the fuck out when you had a lush, curvy woman pressing herself against you, when you had Jane, with her snappy comebacks and her gentle questions, deigning to press her lips against yours. When you had—

"Cameron?"

That voice. Though it was soft, it was a lance, cutting immediately through the panic, arresting it in its tracks. It was a quick, blessed injection of air when he'd been drowning. Enough air, enough energy, that he could roll over so he was on his back, to check if it was really her and not the product of his fucked-up mind. Because wouldn't that be the cruelest thing? Being haunted by the shit he had seen was something he could accept. It made a certain sort of macabre sense. But if the universe decided to start sending him visions of Jane that turned out to be mirages? He wasn't sure he could survive that.

He reached out a shaking hand to brush her ankle, to check that she was real.

She didn't say anything, just towered over him with the sun backlighting her lavender-adorned hair so that it became a curtain of flame, letting him clutch her ankle like some kind of animal. Goddess Mode: Woodland Edition.

She lowered herself to the dirt next to him, and said, "What's wrong?"

He wanted to tell her not to sit there. It was the perfect fucking metaphor for them. He was literally wallowing in the dirt, battling the demons that plagued him, and she was lowering herself to sit next to him, concern written all over her beautiful, open face. She was wearing stretchy, light gray pants that hugged her gorgeous curves and a tank top with tiny straps, leaving her arms and much of her chest bare. If she sat here with him, she was going to get dirty.

If she sat here with him, she was going to get hurt.

He wanted to tell her all that. To save her.

But he couldn't talk. No words would come. He could breathe again, now that she was here, but speech wasn't attainable yet. It was impossible to force the sentiments his mind was shouting through his closed throat.

So she sat, damning herself.

Because he grabbed her. Once more than her ankle was within his grasp, he scrambled to a seated position and reached for her.

She wrapped her arms around him, and the minute they closed around him, he started shaking like a fucking baby bird tipped out of its nest. His whole body was racked with shudders, in fact. She held him, stroked the back of his head while he quaked.

But he was still breathing. He could still breathe.

And he could feel.

She was kneeling across from him and, as they sat facing each other and she held him, only their upper bodies touched. It wasn't enough, suddenly. He needed to feel more of her. His body had finally tuned into something besides its own panic, its own sense of imminent danger, and it was such a goddamned fucking relief.

He let his hands slide down her back and settle on the globes of her ass. He squeezed, and she whimpered a little.

"Get over here," he rasped, his heart rejoicing that he'd managed to produce words to accurately represent the thoughts inside his head. "Please."

She obeyed, scrambling to straddle his lap, settling herself so snugly against his growing arousal that he gasped. He'd only meant that he needed to touch more of her, for more of her body to be in contact with more of his, but now that she was here, he wasn't giving up an inch. He kept his hands on her ass and thrust his hips up, shamelessly grinding his cock against her. He could feel her heat through the thin fabric of her pants.

"Oh," she moaned. "Cameron."

"Yes," he said, not precisely sure what he was agreeing to, maybe just the sound of her speaking his name in pleasure. God, he had missed her. It had only been two days since they'd woken up together at Jay's, but it was like a lifetime had elapsed, entire battles waged, since he'd had his hands on her, where they belonged.

He slid his hands up inside her tank top. She was wearing some kind of stretchy sports bra, so he kept sliding them up under that, too, grabbing handfuls of flesh and squeezing, kneading.

"Oh my God," she said, letting her head fall back, which exposed her throat to him.

He licked it, and she yelped, lifted herself off him a little despite his protests, and started trying to shove her pants down. "I need you," she pleaded, and the sound of it nearly made him come in his pants. "I need you inside me right now."

"We don't have any condoms," he said against her neck as he nuzzled it. The noise of protest she made was nearly his undoing. "Don't worry, baby, I can still make you feel good."

"Please," she said, "please."

He took over where she'd left off, moving her pants down enough that he could get his hand in there.

"Oh, fuck, you're so wet." Just like last time. Just like every time. Her responsiveness made him crazy.

"I need you," she said again, whimpering.

"I know. Shhh." He breached her with a finger, arranging his hand so his thumb was free to press against her clit. Normally, he would have liked to take more time to tease her, but she was so ready. And though they were in the woods, they weren't very far from the main buildings.

Making a hooking motion with the index finger inside her, he searched for the telltale spot. None of her vibrators had had a g-spot stimulator, and he wanted to fucking rock her world. His finger brushed over something different from its surroundings, something slightly spongy. There it was. Watching her like a hawk, he pressed down gently, experimentally.

Her eyes flew open, and she shattered in his arms.

He wanted to pump his fists in victory. Because he'd made her feel good, but also because it had felt like something only he could do for her. Which was ridiculous, objectively not true. But all the same, he held stubbornly to the notion.

It took her a few minutes to come down, for her panting to return to normal. He held her, as she'd done for him earlier, waiting for her to solidify, to come back to herself.

When she did, she was embarrassed. Her cheeks pinked, and she had trouble meeting his eyes. He pressed a finger under her chin and tilted it up. "Thank you," he said.

"Thank you?" she echoed, incredulous. "I haven't done anything yet." She glanced meaningfully down at the bulge in his jeans.

"I'm fine," he said, and, miraculously, he was. He was back, fully in his body, fully in the present. It was he who should be thanking her. She had brought him back. And as much as he would love for her to return the favor, anyone could stumble by and discover them. It was time to get her—literally—out of the dirt. So he tried to gently dislodge her from his lap, but she held tight.

"Oh, come on," she said. "You can't be that selfless. Tell me what you want."

She was still wearing the lavender crown. So instead he reached over, grabbed it, threw it on the ground, and said, "What I want is for you not to hook up with Kent."

She surprised him by laughing. The musical sound washed over him like a benediction. Then she tilted her head, narrowed her eyes, and said, "What happened here?"

He looked around exaggeratedly, trying to make her laugh. "I finger-fucked you in the woods?"

She shook her head like that was the wrong answer. "It's

the PTSD, isn't it? You were having some kind of flashback when I first got here."

Shame washed over him. He didn't want her to know how weak he was, how much he'd needed her just then. But how could he hide it? He'd been shivering in her arms. And after what she'd done for him, he owed her the truth.

"This is about what happened with Eric and Haseeb, isn't it?" she said gently.

He shook his head. "No. This is about what happened with Becky."

                          —✑

"It wasn't the same at all," Cameron said, pressing his hands into his temples. "So I don't know why it's all happening again."

He was clearly frustrated with himself, angry even. Jane wanted to take him in her arms and tell him everything was going to be okay, but she couldn't. Whatever else had or still would happen between Cameron and her, they didn't lie to each other. "Tell me," she said, scrambling off his lap and pulling up her pants, which, in almost any other circumstance she would have found comical. "What happened that wasn't the same? Who is Becky?"

"Master Corporal Rebecca Mannerly. Becky was my best friend in Iraq...I guess."

She raised an eyebrow. "You guess?"

That drew the smile she'd been going for. "Well, you know. I'm not very likable."

She shrugged. Maybe that was true for other people, but *she* liked him. As evidenced by the spectacular orgasm he'd just given her. Which was a problem. But now was not the time to argue the point or to embark on an analysis of what the hell kind of whammy Cameron MacKinnon had put on her. So she waited.

The silence between them stretched on. He lifted the hem of his shirt to wipe some sweat from his face and took a deep breath.

"It's hard being a woman in the military."

"I can imagine," she said.

"Guys can be jerks, you know?"

"You think?" She was teasing him—she hoped not too much. She wanted him to keep talking, and she suspected the best way to do that was to treat him like she always did. If she was overly solicitous, or if she did what she really wanted to, which was, astonishingly and against her better judgment, to wrestle him to the ground and wrap her lips around his dick, he would clam up.

"Yeah, so Becky was one of us." He absently picked blades of grass as he spoke. "Any of the guys would have taken a bullet for her, I think. Well, most of them would have. But she also *wasn't* really one of us, you know? She put up with so much shit. Like, every day. I sort of...made friends with her."

"You stuck up for her, is what you mean." Cameron shrugged, but Jane could imagine it very well. The lone woman in a group of male soldiers. It couldn't have been easy. And despite the bad-boy image that Cam projected, and seemed to believe in so fervently himself, he had a definite white knight thing going on.

"Our captain was a real dick. And it makes such a difference in terms of the culture of the unit. My first tour, my captain was a real stand-up guy. He was why I went back for a second tour. It sounds cliché, but he was a role model. He's part of why I thought I might..." He broke off, shaking his head. A corner of his lip curled up, as if he were about to sneer at some unseen enemy she was pretty sure was himself.

"Thought you might what?" she asked gently.

The sneer arrived full force. "I was looking into going to university. You can't be an officer without a degree."

"I think that's great," she said. She meant it. It made sense. He was smart. And equally as important, he was kind. He would be a great leader.

"A moment of temporary insanity," he said dismissively. "Anyway, that part is beside the point. This captain of ours—Biggs was his name—was a grade-A prick. A real power tripper, you know? One of those guys who got off on being in charge. He was always barking out ridiculous orders just for the sake of it, making us run laps at noon in the sun because he felt like it, that sort of thing."

"Sounds like a real charmer."

"Yeah, well, so at some point he started hitting on Becky."

She could picture it. Unfortunately she, like probably all women alive, knew the type. "Gross."

"It was his latest little exercise in dominance, you know? She wasn't interested, but he kept pushing."

"Oh!" Jane exclaimed as the pieces fell together in her mind. "The trial." Oh God, Cameron had gotten himself kicked out of the army over this.

Cameron started throwing the grass that he'd pulled up into the stream. "I thought it was low-level stuff. She and I talked about it sometimes. She said she could handle it. She was used to it, unfortunately. I kept telling her to document it all and encouraged her to go up the chain of command, but she always refused. She didn't want to be a shit-disturber or a test case or any of that. She begged me not to make a big deal of it. She just wanted to put her head down and be a soldier. That was the ironic thing: she was the best soldier in the bunch. I sometimes wonder if that's why Biggs picked on her."

"Like he was threatened, you mean?"

"He shouldn't have been. Becky and I were only non-commissioned members—that's army-speak for grunts—but yeah. I guess I can sort of see why. She was going places. But shouldn't that have reflected well on him, as her commanding officer?"

"So what happened?" Jane asked, even though she was afraid she knew the answer.

He turned to look at her, his eyes glittering with rage. "What happened is that I walked into her tent and found him attacking her, and I lost my mind."

"And you were charged and tried," Jane said, her stomach swirling.

"Pretty much. I'm lucky I wasn't court-martialed, I guess."

"But there were some really big extenuating circumstances!" she protested. It didn't seem fair that he had to throw everything away—and not only his career, but the whole university thing, too.

"Irrelevant. I was quite clearly in violation of the code of service. And Biggs was tried separately."

"What happened to him?"

"He was demoted to lieutenant."

"So you can attack a woman and get a slap on the wrist, but you defend the same woman and they kick you out?"

He sighed. "It's complicated. I was a reservist, and just a driver. I was a lot more expendable than a career officer in the regular force. Also..."

He made a frustrated noise and looked up at the sky. There was clearly more to the story.

"Also what?" she prompted.

He kept his head tilted back and spoke on an exhale, as

if he were trying to exorcise the sentiments he was voicing. "Also I didn't stop."

"What do you mean, you didn't stop?"

"I got him off her, but then . . . I kept hitting him. I broke his jaw. It was like all the months of accumulated bullshit she'd taken from him—that we'd all taken from him—ignited inside me somehow." He scrubbed his hand against his own stubbly jaw. "There were witnesses—our scuffle drew the attention of some others in our unit—which is probably the only reason Biggs faced any consequences at all."

"But also the reason you got kicked out," she said with a sigh.

He finally righted his head and his eyes found hers. "I deserved to get kicked out. I don't regret what I did, but I should have stopped when I'd diffused the situation. I lost control. You can't have the army full of guys who can't control themselves."

"Unlike Biggs," she retorted. She didn't know why she was arguing with him. It wasn't like it was going to change anything. But it all seemed so unfair.

He shrugged. "Anyway, my sob story is not the point; it's just the context. The point is, that incident was nothing compared to the last one—the one I told you about from my first tour, when the suicide bomber hit. The head shrinkers did their voodoo on me after that tour, and eventually, I was mostly fine. Yeah, the thing with Becky on this latest tour got my adrenaline going for a while there, but it was nothing like the previous incident. So what the hell is my problem now?" He gestured angrily at himself. "I'm at a wedding at a fucking lavender farm, and I'm totally losing my shit?"

"I'm no expert, but I'd say that the thing with Becky and Biggs *was* as traumatic as the suicide bombing. It may not have been as horrific in the moment, but it had huge personal consequences for you. It ruined your career."

"*I* ruined my career," he corrected.

She chose to ignore that claim. It wasn't true, but she didn't want to argue with him. "Anyway, I don't think it works like that," she said. "I mean, I'm not a doctor, but it's probably not a linear thing, where a certain input leads to a certain output, you know? There's probably some kind of complicated soup of memories and experiences in your head, and maybe this latest thing magnified your first experience, and then being out here kind of ignited the whole thing."

He sighed and slung an arm around her, his whole body deflating. But it didn't seem like a sad, defeated deflating, more like relief you get after the cessation of effort. "How did you get so wise, Jane Denning?"

She performed a comically exaggerated shrug, wanting more than anything to see him smile. "I read a lot of long-form magazine articles?"

It worked. He laughed out loud and pulled her tighter to him in a sideways half hug.

"What can I do to help?" she asked.

"Be with me. Stay with me," he said. "Remind me that I'm here, not there."

Be with me. Stay with me.

She wanted to ask him what he meant, exactly, by that, but now was not the time.

She could do what he asked, though, as long as she took care to protect her heart. It would be hard to spend time with him, but she would have to be a monster to turn him away. "Hey! I have an idea!" She jumped to her feet and tugged him to stand beside her. "If we hurry, we might get back before Gia leaves, and we can take over her assignment!"

"And why would we want to do that?"

"Because then we can drive to the nearest town and buy a boatload of sunglasses. Can you imagine? Three hundred pairs of crappy sunglasses in the back of your Corvette? I bet that won't remind you of the Middle East!"

He grabbed her hand and squeezed it.

"Then maybe we can figure out what the highest point in Prince Edward County is. There's got to be some glorified hill around here somewhere."

He smiled—and didn't let go of her hand as they walked back.

⁓

Cameron shoved the plate of French fries toward Jane.

She shoved it back. "You don't seem to understand what I'm saying. My. Dress. Is. Not. Going. To. Zip. Up."

Undaunted, he passed it back to her. "You don't seem to understand what *I'm* saying. You. Are. Hot. Exactly. The. Way. You. Are." The pile of iceberg lettuce and carrot shavings that passed for a "salad" in the small-town diner they were in made him angry in principle. She had to have worked up an appetite, because in addition to hitting two Walmarts and three dollar stores, they had trekked up a hill in nearby Picton, from which they'd had a great view of Lake Ontario.

She cracked a smile. "I appreciate that. I really do. But listen to me. You can pin a dress that's too big and make it look halfway decent. But you can't do anything for a dress that's too small. I'm not making a big antifeminist statement here. I mean, I've learned my lesson: I should have ordered the twelve. But if my dress doesn't zip up on Saturday, not only is Elise's head going to start spinning around a la *the Exorcist*, but I'm going to be humiliated."

He pulled the fries back to his side of the booth, feeling the sharp sting of humiliation as if it were happening to him. God, he was an ass. He'd just wanted to please her. To do anything to make her happy. To lay the world at her feet, basically, even though it would never be sufficient to thank her for what she'd done for him today. So he settled for, "I'm sorry," hoping she would hear the sincerity in his voice.

"It's okay," she said, halfheartedly spearing a piece of limp lettuce. "You can take me out for the biggest, greasiest plate of fries on Sunday." Then she looked up, her eyes wide and borderline panicked. "I mean, not really. You'll be on your way...somewhere, I'm sure. After the wedding, I mean."

He hated how quickly she corrected herself, rushing to assure him that she had no expectations of him. But she had always been smart, his Jane. She knew the score.

He could fall for her. He *had* fallen for her, if he was being honest with himself. But damned if he was going to let *her* fall for *him*.

But he could certainly stick around long enough to buy her some post-wedding fries, so he said, "Sunday morning. Fries. It's a date."

Chapter Twenty

It's a date.

As she skipped up the stairs to her room after the sunglasses mission, the phrase ricocheted around in her head. She hadn't had a date since Felix. And they never would have gone to a diner for fries. He was more of a sushi-and-the-symphony type.

Not that it was a real date. And she and Cameron had hung out a lot already, without the "date" label.

So why was she so giddy over the idea?

Ducking into her room to stash her purse, she stopped to check herself in the mirror. She was grinning like an idiot. She looked...pretty. Her cheeks were rosy, and she might even say there was a twinkle in her eye. What was next? Was she going to burst into song as birds and woodland creatures helped her do her chores?

Trying to rein in her out-of-proportion enthusiasm, she ran down the stairs and out the door to one of the meeting rooms—the farm hosted corporate events, too—that she'd commandeered for the hat project. She'd left Cameron after showing him how to thread lavender into the hats, promising to be back momentarily. Bedecking the hats was no longer on the job list, since Elise had moved on to sunglasses, but Jane had the feeling that giving Cameron something mindless to do indoors would be good for him. She wasn't sure what the actual solution to his PTSD was. He needed a doctor for that, but first he needed to get through the rest of the week. And she planned to help him do exactly that.

Because she had a date on Sunday, and, against her better judgment, she was counting the minutes.

─❦─

"What are you guys doing?" Elise popped her head into the room. Cam looked at Jane because he wasn't actually sure how to describe what they were doing. Something with lavender and hats.

"Oh, we were kind of at loose ends, so I thought maybe we'd finish the hats anyway. Even if you only want them for the photo booth." Jane smiled brightly at Elise in a way that seemed a touch false to Cam.

"That's a great idea!" Elise exclaimed. "I was looking for both you guys because we're all going to take a hike. Apparently if you cut through the fields, you can connect up with a provincial park that has some great trails."

"Oh, I don't think I should do that," said Jane, sniffing a little. "My allergies have really been acting up. It's part of why I moved this project inside."

"You have allergies?"

"I guess so!" Jane said—a little too enthusiastically.

"Maybe they're dormant in the big city!" She coughed. "Anyway, didn't Lacy say you could lay the place cards anytime? Why don't we do that after we finish these hats?"

"Well, there's a very specific order, as you know," Elise said, looking uncertain.

"I do know!" Jane chirped. "You have a map, don't you? Give it to me, and I'll set out the cards. Then you can inspect and see how it feels in the actual space. It might be good to live with it for a bit, see if you want to change anything up."

"Jane, you are a genius," Elise said, smiling. "Do you think you could also take the photo booth props down? They're in boxes in my room."

"You got it. Place cards and photo booth props. Check and check."

Elise blew Jane a kiss, then turned her attention to Cam. "You want to join us on the hike, future brother-in-law?"

He glanced at Jane. He knew what she was doing, coming up with all these excuses to stay inside. She was still babysitting him. But this time for an entirely different reason. And this time, as much as he hated to admit it, he needed it. "You know, I think I'll keep Jane company. And, hey, it turns out I'm actually pretty good at this." He held out a hat for her inspection, and Elise smiled, buying their lie.

"All right then! You kids be good! Ta-ta for now!"

He let a few moments of silence elapse after Elise left before saying, quietly, "Thank you."

Jane looked up and graced him with a smile. "No problem." Then she let another beat go before adding, "But you should probably, I don't know, see someone about this?" She winked at him. "Because God knows, you can't avoid lavender fields the rest of your life. You never know when you're going to be going about your day and suddenly find yourself stumbling into a rogue lavender field."

Something in his heart twisted. How did she do that? Toe the line between concern and humor so perfectly? If anyone else had made the suggestion, he would have become defensive. But she made him see that she was right without wrapping her concern up in a cloak of judgment.

"How many people have you slept with?" she asked suddenly, and the question made him bark a laugh. Here he was, getting all emotional about how sensitive and wise she was, and she hit him with that?

"Why?" he said, eyeing her warily.

"I just want to know."

"I don't know. Lots." He wished he could give her a number—a respectable one.

"How many girlfriends have you had?" she asked as she concentrated on a hat. The question didn't seem to be loaded. She had delivered it in an unremarkable, conversational tone. "Like, where it's been more than just casual."

"Two," he said, relieved that for once he could give her a straightforward, true answer.

She looked up. "And you got one of them pregnant in high school?"

Whoa. Apparently his reputation preceded him. He'd never denied it. To do so had always seemed cruel. It would have exposed Alicia unnecessarily. The town didn't need to be talking about her sleeping around, which is exactly what they would have done if they found out the baby wasn't Cam's. Everyone had already made up their minds about him anyway—he was the Devil of Deer Haven. They already thought he'd burned down that barn on purpose, and he was constantly up against his reputation for being a delinquent, so why not add one more item to his bad-boy résumé? It protected Alicia, and it cost him nothing. But for once, for the first time in his life, in fact, he was considering telling the truth on the matter. Because for the first time in his life, he cared what someone thought about him. He cared a lot.

"No. She got pregnant, but I had nothing to do with it." He huffed a bitter laugh. It still stung, truth be told. "Or so she said."

Jane's jaw and the hat she was working on both dropped. "Cameron MacKinnon, you come with these warning labels, you know? Burned down a barn. Got a girl pregnant. And you're saying neither of them is true?" Her voice had risen, and she was almost yelling at him.

"I did burn down a barn."

"By accident!"

He shrugged. "Well, they might as well be true. It's a letter of the law, spirit of the law sort of thing."

She shoved him. Hard.

"Ow!" He winced and grinned simultaneously. She had some hidden strength there, his Janie.

"So what happened to the girl?"

"Alicia," he said, feeling, for some reason, that it was important that "the girl" have a name.

"What happened to Alicia?" she asked, picking up on his cue and rephrasing her question.

"I don't know. She moved. Her parents wanted her to get rid of it. She wanted to keep it. I'm not sure what she decided, but the whole family moved, and they cut all ties."

Jane was nodding like she was listening to a familiar tale, though he'd never spoken about that time to anyone. "And you let everyone in your family and your town think you were the ne'er-do-well father."

"I tried to get her to marry me. The…actual father wasn't stepping up, apparently."

"Of course you did." She was still doing that knowing-nodding thing.

"What does that mean?"

She stood. "I think we've made enough hats, don't you? Let's move on to photo booth props and place cards."

He was a little confused about what had just happened. How did things get so heavy so quickly after they'd been flirtatiously talking about how many people he'd slept with? He'd been intending to ask what her number was. He knew about the shithead ex that had sparked her recent dry spell and inspired her devotion to her vibrators, but now that she brought it up, he found himself intensely curious about the rest.

He wanted to know about other boyfriends, too, if there were any.

He wanted to know all kinds of shit about her.

That wasn't good.

So he stood, too. "Lead the way."

⎯⎯ ⌒⎯⎯

"Okay, so I guess the stuff must be in these boxes," Jane said a few minutes later as they stood contemplating the pair of sealed boxes stacked in a corner in Elise's room. She moved to pick one up.

"Let me get them," said Cam, gently moving her away. He hefted them up, and Jane let loose a big sigh. "What's wrong?"

"Honestly? I'm sick of this wedding. Being a bridesmaid is like being an indentured servant."

"You should join them on the hike." He didn't want her to leave him, but he couldn't hold her hostage. "Take me downstairs and show me what to do, and then you can catch up to them. I'll be fine." He hoped.

"Nope, trust me, it's better here. Elise is in DEFCON one

right now. I just meant, like, how can an event that costs this much money not come with *actual* servants?"

He laughed. "I know you're not much of a drinker, but Jay gave all us guys flasks of vodka when we got here. Said Elise told him he had to give gifts to the wedding party. So he got us these classy silver flasks with our initials engraved on them. I don't think she knows they're full."

"Ha! I like Jay more and more. Give me those boxes, you get the vodka, and I'll meet you in the reception room."

He twisted away from her—she wasn't going to carry all this shit. "Nope. I'll take these down. You stop in my room and grab the flask. I think it's in the top dresser drawer—room nine on the third floor." He shuffled the boxes to one side, dug in his pocket for the key, and then flipped it to her.

"Okay!" She flashed him a smile so warm and guileless, it made his heart wrench. "See you soon."

—♋︎—

Jane was consumed with one thought as she switched on the light in Cameron's room: she wanted to have sex with him again.

Would that be so wrong?

It had been a rather astounding day. If Jane had felt, earlier in her room, like Cinderella singing while she did her chores with some Wild Kingdom helpers, she sort of felt like Cinderella getting ready for the ball right now. She still couldn't stop thinking about her stupid French fry date with Cameron. Good, honorable Cameron who bore so much more than he had to.

She eyed his unmade bed. The B&B was luxurious, but it was still an old house converted into an inn. The rooms were small. Cameron's bed was a twin. She had a double in her room.

Technically, their little romp in the woods earlier had been a mistake. She had been swept away in the moment, first with the impulse to comfort him, then with a wild lust that was impossible to constrain. Either way, though, more sex hadn't been in the plan. She had decided, after that bone-shattering night at Jay's condo, that she couldn't sleep with Cameron anymore, because she was too close to giving away her heart to someone who would only break it.

It was so hard to keep holding the line, though. Now that she knew his history, she knew his reputation was not what it seemed. And he was so impossibly magnetic. Even just sitting there next to him in that conference room, working on the stupid hats, she'd had to hold herself back from crawling on top of him yet again.

She opened the top drawer of his dresser, surprised to find it full of stuff. He didn't strike her as the type to bother unpacking. But then, he'd surprised her over and over again, hadn't he, no more so than today.

She shifted through socks and boxers. There was a tie he must be planning to wear to the wedding. She pulled it out to examine it under the lamp on the dresser. It was a gorgeous red, gray, and black plaid. It made her wonder about his surname, MacKinnon. About his father. There was so much about him she didn't know.

She put the tie back and continued her search. Her fingers came to rest on a piece of paper. She started to move it aside. It was actually a . . . photograph? It was none of her business, but she couldn't resist. Would it be a picture of one of his fallen army brothers? Of Becky? Or—a flare of irrational jealousy ignited in her chest—would it be the high school girlfriend who betrayed him?

It was none of those things.

It was her.

Well, it was *them*. She sucked in a sharp breath. It was the shot from Nightmares Fear Factory, the one where he was carrying her, shielding her face from the terrors. She'd seen it only momentarily, projected on a screen on their way out of the haunted house. At the time, she'd been embarrassed, had thought the message the image conveyed was fear. She had been ashamed to see herself so weak.

But now, she looked at it with different eyes. Cameron's high school girlfriend. His fellow soldier Becky. It wasn't only that he hadn't done the things that everyone accused him of; it was more than that. They had each been opportunities for chivalry—unseen, unacknowledged, unrewarded chivalry, chivalry for its own sake.

So when she looked at the picture through that lens, looked at it as a whole, instead of focusing on only herself, she saw it differently. Instead of fear and humiliation, she saw protection and bravery. Caring. He had seen her when she was at her weakest, and he'd helped her. Just as she had done with him earlier today.

She let the picture flutter back into the drawer.

Screw it. She needed those strong arms around her again. She'd worry about any consequences for her heart later. Right now, she was going to take a big slug of this vodka, and then she was going to proposition Cameron.

Emboldened, she got out her phone and typed a text.

⸻

I'm in your room, and I need some help.

Cam took the stairs of the B&B two at a time. She was fine, he told himself. *It's nothing.* He'd been repeating that phrase like a mantra, in fact, since her text arrived and he tore out of the reception hall, nearly knocking the door off its hinges.

It's nothing.

He didn't like the vagueness of her note. If it was nothing, why had she summoned him? Why hadn't she come back to him as planned? Or been more specific with her text, if, say, she couldn't find the flask?

He couldn't imagine what kind of harm could have befallen her in the few minutes since they'd parted ways. But that was the problem: he couldn't imagine.

So all he could do was give in and let his growing unease propel him up to the third floor, prompt him to practically break down the door, all the while repeating to himself: *It's nothing.*

Which it was, if by "nothing," he meant Jane Denning naked in his bed.

She sat up, alarmed, as he panted, his back pressed against the inside of the door. "What's the matter?"

The sheet that had been covering her fell, exposing her full, heavy breasts with their perfect, pink rosebud tips. Her hair was disheveled and her color high. She looked like she'd *already* been fucked. His dick rose, as if in protest, staking its claim.

"Nothing," he groaned, and for the moment, it was the truth. That was the incredible thing about Jane. His life was full of problems. But somehow, through some strange alchemy he didn't understand, all that shit just disappeared when she was around. Earlier, when she'd come to him in the woods, when she'd come *for* him in the woods, he would have said that she brought him back to himself. Because that's what it had felt like. He'd been in the throes of panic, being carried further and further from reality, and she had brought him back to himself. But now he felt the opposite: she was taking him *away* from himself, from the jobless, lonely, disgraced soldier with no plan. She was a respite, an escape. An oasis.

And what else was a man dying of thirst supposed to do when he saw an oasis shimmering in the distance?

The scene snapped into focus, like putting on night vision goggles in what had been pitch-black. He turned around and locked the door, part of him protesting for the brief moment he had to break eye contact with her to do so. Then, after reestablishing it, after claiming her with a look, he broke it once more, this time to pull off his T-shirt.

When his eyes found hers again, she smiled, slowly, triumphantly. Like she had made this all happen. Like even though he was beginning to stalk toward her, she was the hunter and he the prey.

Maybe so.

He could live with that.

When he reached the edge of the bed, which put her at eye level with his waist, he slowly unbuttoned his jeans.

Her eyes glittered as she watched him. God, just the sight of her watching him made him painfully hard. When he'd freed himself and stood before her with his dick at attention, she licked her lips.

Slowly—he forced himself to move slowly because he wanted to torture her more than he wanted to soothe his own ache—he walked over to a dresser on the other side of the room on which he'd placed his toiletries bag. Thank God he had condoms in there. Carefully, shaking with the effort of moving slowly, he ripped one packet off the row.

Turning, he tossed it the few feet to the bed, where it landed on her lap.

She started to open it.

He shook his head and said, "Later." He was gonna stick with this slow thing, even if it killed him.

—◦—

The maddening thing about Cameron was that you could never get him to do what you wanted him to do. Well, that wasn't precisely fair. In a broad sense, he was actually really good at what she wanted, which was, she supposed, to be seduced. To be racked with pleasure.

But he rarely did it *precisely* the way she wanted.

Like right now, for instance, when she wanted him to come over, put on the damn condom, and slide into her already, he was just standing there staring at her, pupils dilated and a sly smile spreading across his face.

"Come here," she said. She had been covered to the waist with his bed sheet, so she kicked free of it, hoping the full monty might serve to move him along.

He licked his lips. "Oh, I'm going to, Jane. I'm going to."

He still wasn't moving, so she spread her legs for him. Let them fall open as he stood there, to give him an eyeful. It might have been the boldest thing she'd ever done, and it made her hot. Hotter.

He groaned, and moisture rushed between her legs. "Then what are you waiting for?" she whispered.

"I'm just…" His voice broke, and she looked up, startled, from where she'd been admiring his chest. He cleared his throat. "I'm taking you in."

What did that mean? Suddenly suffused with self-consciousness, she started to close her legs.

"No," he said sharply. Then he gentled his voice. "Please keep them open."

Taking a shuddery breath, she complied.

He closed his eyes for a moment and bowed his head. When he looked back up, he smiled, but he still didn't move.

God, she was dying for him to touch her. She opened her legs wider and drew her fingers over her clit, hoping to draw his attention there, to inspire him.

"You are so impossibly gorgeous," he said, setting his knees on the bed on either side of her as she laid back on it, but still not touching her.

She reached for the condom again. She was going to scream if he didn't take her right now.

"Not yet," he said, laying one finger on her stomach, above her belly button, and slowly drawing it up her body, coming to rest in her cleavage.

She sucked in a breath, arching her back to try to get more pressure from him. He didn't comply. In fact, he let his hand float up so that it was no longer touching her, making her cry out her frustration.

"Goddamn you," she whispered.

"I'm pretty sure that's already taken care of," he said, and she would have argued the point, but he let the finger float back down and settle on a nipple, teasing it with the lightest of touches. She twisted her torso, chasing after him as he removed his hand once more. Her breasts ached. Her vagina ached. Every part of her needed him.

"Oh!" she said aloud, then laughed at herself as his eyebrows lifted inquisitively. She'd been lying here like she was half dead, but didn't she have hands? Ha! She could *make* him do what she wanted. Triumph-spiked lust surged through her, and she went straight for his dick with both hands.

He hissed as she made contact, but before she could really get a grip, he grabbed her hands and pushed them away. Kept pushing them until her arms were above her head on the bed. Keeping one hand pressed down firmly on her wrists to keep her immobilized, he said, "Patience, baby, patience. Don't I always give you what you need?"

The words alone were almost enough to send her over the edge.

He didn't wait for a response. Keeping one hand on her wrists, he let the other trail slowly down her body, stroking the side of her face, her neck, sliding over her breast and stopping to tease her nipple. But as soon as she'd resigned herself to enduring that particular brand of sweet torture for a while, he was on the move again, his hand trailing down over her soft belly and into the hot moisture of her opening.

"Oh God," she moaned, because he knew. He always knew. He knew that by denying her, by not giving her what she thought she wanted, he was actually giving her what she needed.

She bucked wildly, chasing his hand, even though she knew it was futile. As expected, he removed it.

He'd been kneeling over her this whole time while he worked her over, but now he lowered his body enough that he could whisper in her ear. "Was that what you needed?"

She nodded violently. But no, that wasn't right. She needed his cock. So she switched to shaking her head equally adamantly.

He stopped her with a kiss. Oh, his lips! She'd forgotten about them. Her world had shrunk to the size of the fingertips he had been using to conduct his masterful assault. But now his lips were on hers, hard and demanding—but only for a moment.

She cried out again. Damn him! A vague rustling sound was replaced by his lips at her ear. And by, thank God, his cock at her entrance. "Is this what you need, then?" he rasped.

"Yes!" she said. "Yes!"

He slid into her, and she was finally full. The relief as her body stretched to accommodate him made her gasp.

"Oh, fuck," he ground out, and he stopped moving entirely, frozen in space for a very long moment while he contorted his face like he was bearing an impossibly heavy weight.

Then he lost control.

And she loved it. Her triumph was back because she'd finally managed to tip him from his measured, controlled approach into...this.

He was slamming into her, over and over, harder and harder. His hands pressed her hips into the bed, rendering her immobile while he pistoned into her.

Her hands were still lying on the bed above her head, so she grabbed hold of the rails of the headboard, keening as she held on for the storm that was barreling down on her. She gave a vague thought of trying to hold it back, to prolong the pleasure, but it was too much. It demanded her submission.

With a scream, she came. Harder and dirtier and longer than she had imagined possible.

"Jane!" Cameron cried, and with a final few pumps, he slumped onto her. She wrapped her arms and legs around him, and let the truth wash over her.

She loved him.

She wasn't "falling for him," which was how she'd phrased it in her mind when she'd been warning herself off him, when she'd fled his bed the other morning. No, that sentiment was weak, limp. It angered her with its inadequacy.

She *loved* him. Wildly, fiercely, with everything in her.

She loved everything about him. His entire past. Everything that had brought him to her.

And as if that revelation wasn't enough, suddenly, from nowhere, something Wendy had said to her recently popped into her head. She squirmed out from under Cameron and sat back against the headboard, relishing his cranky grunt as he tried to prevent her from leaving his arms.

"I need to ask you a question," she said.

He must have heard the seriousness in her tone, because he sat up, too, and arranged himself across from her, cross-legged.

"Wendy said this thing to me a week or so ago. She said that I'm only adventurous through my books, or in my cosplay personas. Like, I think she was commenting on the fact that I'm pretty risk-averse. Do you think that's true?"

"I think that might have been true historically." Cameron's brow furrowed and he spoke slowly, like he was struggling to articulate his thoughts. "You took some really big risks and got burned pretty badly, and I think maybe you overcorrected for a while there."

"What risks? I've had a totally sheltered life. I haven't seen..." She gestured at him. "Nearly the stuff you've seen."

"I'm talking about emotional risks."

Yes. Yes. That was right. That's what Wendy had meant. "You mean like I took an emotional risk when I confronted my dad?"

"Yeah. And when you asked Felix to move in. Both times, you got majorly slapped down."

"Huh." He was right. It was so obvious now. Why had

she never seen this before? "And then I became the ultimate good girl. Which, to be fair, I mostly did because I had to. My brother busted his ass keeping us afloat, and he didn't need any trouble from me. But then it kind of...became real?" She didn't know how to describe it. "Like a self-fulfilling prophecy. And now I'm the responsible one. Levelheaded, reliable Jane."

Cameron nodded. "I get that. But look at you lately. Dangling off the CN Tower, making out on roller coasters." He waggled his eyebrows. "Having wild sex with your babysitting charge. So I think everything you're saying might have been true at one point, but not anymore. You broke yourself free."

She tilted her head. There was one common denominator in those examples he'd given. "I think *you* broke me free."

"No. You broke *yourself* free." His tone was fierce, insistent. "I'm glad I could be along for the ride, but *you* did it. You, Jane, are pretty badass."

She laughed because she was delighted. But also because it was true. She *was* pretty badass.

She reached a hand out and ran it lightly over Cameron's angel tattoo.

He shivered, and she made a plan to take her biggest risk yet.

Chapter Twenty-One

FRIDAY—ONE DAY BEFORE THE WEDDING

*C*am woke up on Friday morning with one thought in his head: today was the day he'd have to see his mother.

God, he had missed her.

That thought was quickly followed by a second one: Jane had really fucked him over.

Because it was her fault that he was lying here getting all emotional about missing his mommy. And this after he'd trotted out the whole pathetic story of Alicia, which he had never told a single soul. What the fuck?

He didn't do this. He didn't wallow in the past or throw himself pity parties. He owned his mistakes, and their consequences, and got on with things. Normally.

But the last couple of days had been such a roller coaster—the particular metaphor that arrived in his head did not go unnoticed—of emotion. It was all Jane's doing. She had...put the whammy on him, to use Gia's wording.

It was like she was...made for him.

Cam fancied himself decent in bed. He'd learned pretty early on that if the woman he was entertaining enjoyed herself, it made things better for him, too. So he had become good at reading tiny signs, at delayed gratification. But it was ultimately selfish.

But the way he could play Jane like a violin? Holy shit. It was almost scary. The attraction between them was out of this world. He'd never experienced anything like it, so searing, so out of control. He couldn't *control* himself—that was precisely the problem. Take yesterday afternoon. He had embarked on a mission to tease her into orgasm, to drive her crazy by meting out his touch. He'd wanted to blow her mind, to make her feel so good that she let go of everything and became his goddess.

But he'd lost it. He'd utterly and totally lost it. He'd been completely wild, would have done anything, made any sacrifice, at that moment, to not have to let go of her.

He sighed and rolled over, sore from yesterday's exertions. He wasn't blaming her. None of it was her fault. In fact, he owed her a huge debt. Sure, he was sitting here having a little Kumbaya-emo moment, but it was better than the alternative, which was shivering at the bottom of a PTSD freak-out. She'd saved him from that.

Because she knew. She somehow knew what to do. Drive into town! Make some hats! Even after they'd gotten out of bed yesterday and the rest of the wedding party had come back from their hike, she'd subtly manipulated things so they stayed inside. She had volunteered him to drive to town to pick up pizzas.

She took care of him.

Christie had never done that.

Christie had been fond of him in her way. While he was around, she enjoyed him. But he could see now that she hadn't looked after him. Certainly hadn't ever kept his needs front of mind.

Had *anyone* ever done that for him? Alicia, he supposed, in the immature way of young love, at least in the beginning. But not ultimately. Not in any real way.

Which brought him back to...his mother.

She had put his needs first. Had truly cared for him. At least as long as he'd let her. He'd always been a challenging kid, but those years after Alicia, he'd done nothing but push her away. *Shove* her away, violently and with all his strength, making sure with his actions that she'd have to give up on him.

And things had never been the same. They had a cordial but distant, and ultimately not very meaningful, relationship. Which had suited him fine because *he didn't do the emo shit*.

There was a knock on his door.

He sat up, panicking. It had to be Jane.

He wasn't sure he could deal with Jane, not the same morning he had to see Mom.

Because it wasn't just the spectacular sex that had him marveling over how well matched he and Jane were.

It was everything else. The way she acted like a fucking grilled cheese sandwich he'd made for her was a lobster dinner. The way her cheeks flushed with excitement when she was playing Xena. The way she ruthlessly faced her fears.

He was in love with Jane.

It was a huge fucking problem.

As glorious as it had been to watch her have a psychological breakthrough yesterday afternoon in bed, it was also his worst nightmare—because it meant it was time for him to step away.

Jane had shut herself down as the logical response to the hands she'd been dealt—namely men who hadn't deserved her love. Now that she was coming out of her shell, she would give her heart to someone else.

That someone could not be him, as much as he might wish otherwise. She had deserved better than Felix, but she also deserved better than him—better than a rough, ex-army, ex-criminal with no prospects.

The knocking continued. He had been trying to become an honorable man. So here was his chance to do the right thing.

He took a deep breath and swung open the door.

It was Jay.

"Hey," his brother said with a guarded smile. "Mom texted. She's close. She'll be here in fifteen."

Cam was stupidly relieved to be able to postpone his reckoning with Jane. He'd gotten himself so twisted into knots, convinced it was Jane at his door. But why did he assume that there even had to *be* a big reckoning? Here he was imagining that he'd need to explicitly tell her they couldn't have a relationship, but when had she ever asked for one? He was no catch—he'd just been thinking as much—and Jane was smart.

"Ha!" He laughed at himself.

Jay's brow knit in confusion. "Thought you might want to...shower or something."

"Yeah." He nodded. "Thanks, man. I'll be down soon."

～⌒

"Oh my God, I'm so nervous!" Elise said.

"Why?" Wendy asked. "You've met Jay's mom before."

"I know, but only a couple times, and don't forget, this is my *wedding*."

"I'm pretty sure no one has forgotten that," Gia said, winking at Jane.

The girls were sitting on a bench outside the main building.

And they were not doing anything.

They were not doing anything!

It was such a weird feeling. Jane's hands felt like they needed to, like, weave something, or randomly do some calligraphy. She settled for tapping them manically on her legs.

"Why are *you* so nervous?" Elise asked, her attention drawn by the tapping.

"I'm not nervous." Jane stilled her hands. She was getting good at lying. Which should probably concern her, but she consoled herself that she had a greater purpose in mind.

"Good morning."

They all turned at the sound of Jay's voice. Cameron was with him, which shouldn't have been a surprise since it was his mother they were waiting for. But still. He was looking right at her, but quickly looked away, as did she. The tips of her ears burned. God, it was like they were in junior high.

In her search for something to look at that wasn't Cameron, Jane's eyes landed on Gia. Well. That wasn't helping. Gia's eyebrows were sky-high, and she was looking questioningly at Jane.

A gray sedan pulled into the parking lot, providing a welcome distraction.

Jay walked to greet it. Cameron hung back.

A short, slim woman in a jean skirt and black T-shirt disembarked the car. Jay immediately enveloped her in a hug. Mrs. Smith managed to look like both her sons. She had Cameron's strong jaw and Jay's thick, dirty-blond hair, though hers was streaked with white.

Elise started to step forward, too, but Mrs. Smith's eyes slipped right past her, past everyone, like she was looking for someone in particular.

Which of course she was.

When her gaze landed on Cameron, she stopped still, like a statue, both hands pressed against her heart.

"Hi, Mom," he said, walking toward her. His voice sounded a little off, though probably not enough that anyone besides Jane noticed. It wasn't an overt waver, just a slight change in pitch.

"My boy," she said, choking on the words as she started to cry. "My sweet boy."

He bent over to hug her, and after a couple beats, stood up, picking her up off the ground entirely and holding her tight to him. His mom's eyes were squeezed shut, and Jane could see the tension in her arm muscles, she held him so tight.

Elise sniffed, drawing Jane's attention to the lump in her own throat. She turned and grabbed her friend's hand.

Just when the moment became almost painful, started to feel like they were intruding on something too private, Cameron set his mother down. She moved to Elise next, and Jane was vaguely aware of the two women kissing and hugging. But mostly she watched Cameron. He had walked to the edge of the parking lot, and there he remained, looking out at the road as if he were standing at the edge of a lake or contemplating a vista. She wished she could see his face, but his back had been turned to them through the entire reunion.

"This is my friend Jane," said Elise, drawing Jane's attention from Cameron.

Mrs. Smith smiled and offered her hand, which Jane took. It was strange, to be holding Cameron's mother's hand, the hand that had no doubt held his so many times. *I'm in love with your son!* She wanted to burst out with the truth that was rattling around in her chest, to confess as if Cameron's mother had benedictory abilities, as if she knew the secret to winning her son's heart.

But Jane was pretty sure no one knew that secret.

Yet.

But she was going to give it a go—she was going to open her eyes and jump.

—❧—

The day had passed quickly and without incident. His mom had been pretty much glued to his side, which was...nice. Cam wasn't sure what he'd been expecting. Maybe more of the generic sentiment she'd expressed in the cards she'd sent him. Maybe more of the "tough love" she had dished out before he'd joined the army.

Instead he had...his mom. From the moment he'd picked up her bag and shown her to her room, she'd stuck to him. Monopolized him even.

"This place reminds me of that series of books I used to read to you," she'd said as they sat down to lunch with Jay and Elise. "Do you remember? *Mystery Inn?*"

"Yes!" He hadn't until that very moment, but once she'd said it, it had all come back. "The inn where every guest came with some kind of mystery!" He laughed from pure delight, and when was the last time that had happened—without Jane being involved anyway?

"You used to beg me not to stop, not to turn the light out," she said. "Then you'd acquiesce, but I would catch you later under your covers with a flashlight."

He'd forgotten that, too. It was funny: when he looked back at childhood, he generally saw all the misery. The crimes, the betrayals. The fallen angel stuff. But, to be fair, that had all come later. There had, in fact, been some good times when he was younger. "I, uh, got back into reading in Iraq," he said, feeling like he was confessing something a hell of a lot more important than that he'd developed a Stephen King habit while in the desert.

"Did you?" she said, squeezing his hand under the table. "I'm so glad. When did you have time to read? At night?"

"Uh, yeah, mostly." His mom was probably curious about his experience in Iraq, but she wasn't the type to ask him about it outright. She didn't push. He appreciated that more than she knew.

The rest of the day went much the same. It seemed that Elise was out of tasks to assign, so mostly they all just hung out. He even gave in to his mom's insistence that he take a walk with her and Jay. He had been expecting everything to go to shit once they cleared the main area of the property, for the familiar fingers of panic to start clawing at him. He was on edge, waiting for disaster—disaster that never came.

It turned out that having his mom around made him calm. Kind of like Jane.

Except not, actually.

Not at all like Jane.

"Did you have a good walk?" Jane asked as they tromped back to the B&B. Ostensibly, she was talking to all of them, but he knew her question was for him. He knew what she meant: Did you freak out? Normally, that brand of hovering concern would have irritated him, but somehow, from Jane, it was fine. So he looked right at her and told her the truth. "We did."

"Great!" She flashed him a small smile. "The day went fast, didn't it? I'll see you at dinner. I have to go change."

He did, too, so he said good-bye to his mom and followed Jane up the stairs. Should he say something? Clearly, they didn't need to have a heart-to-heart about her expectations, but they *had* slept together yesterday, and it seemed like, regardless of everything else, that called for a little friendly chitchat?

God. This day. This week. All this emotional shit was exhausting, but he could do chitchat. He picked up the pace, because she was getting away from him. Her room was on the second floor. He reached her at the landing and put a hand on her shoulder to stop her from heading off down the corridor.

She turned and looked at him over her shoulder, a question in her eyes. His heart twisted. In that instant, he saw her as a girl. Well, that wasn't right. More like he saw her all ages at once. The girl who believed she'd killed her father. The woman who still managed to make herself so vulnerable, who embraced experiences. The goddess.

How could she be all those things at once? How had what happened to the girl not prevented the emergence of the woman, much less the goddess?

"What do you want, Cameron?" She grinned and gestured at her body. "Because I gotta go try to improve on this ugly duckling look, and that's gonna take a while." She was wearing the same stretchy athletic pants from the other day, and a ratty Toronto Maple Leafs T-shirt. Her hair was in a ponytail, and her face was bare, not a stitch of makeup visible.

"You're already a swan," he said, because it was the truth. She was beautiful.

The smile she graced him with took his breath away.

She skipped off down the hall.

So much for chitchat.

Chapter Twenty-Two

*Y*ou. Look. Amazing."

Jane did a little twirl in front of the mirror in Gia's room. She liked what she saw. She had taken a gamble on the dark red lace dress. She had almost put it back on the rack when she bought it a couple weeks ago. It was a form-fitting sheath—not her usual MO. Well, her usual modus operandi was jeans and a T-shirt, so that wasn't saying much. Maybe her subconscious had known she was going to turn into a risk-taking daredevil.

And because the dress hadn't been ordered a year ago, it fit perfectly. Normally, she had to be careful with red because of her auburn hair, but the deep almost-burgundy shade worked, somehow.

"Thanks," she said. "And thanks for doing my makeup." She had thrown herself on Gia's mercy, knowing she wanted to take things up a notch—or several. Her high-fashion friend had not disappointed, painting smoky cat eyes and a classic, deep red lip that matched the dress onto Jane's otherwise-understated face. She'd used a heavier hand than Jane would have, but that had been the point.

"Are you sure I can't convince you to borrow a pair of heels?" Gia said, dangling a pair of nude strappy ones that were, objectively, beautiful.

"Nope," said Jane. She had plans, and they didn't involve heels. "I have to wear heels tomorrow"—she hadn't been able to talk Elise into granting her an exemption—"so I'm sticking with my flats for tonight." She balanced on one foot and lifted the other off the floor so she could better admire a sparkly black shoe. "I got *fancy* flats for the occasion, though."

"You know what I love about you, Jane?" said Gia.

Jane turned, startled, and lost her balance a little.

Gia laughed as she steadied Jane. "You are always so authentically yourself. Never change."

"Um, thanks?" Jane said, embarrassed and a little bewildered by the sentiment, but warmed by it all the same.

"I mean it. If anyone ever...doesn't appreciate you, that's their problem."

She narrowed her eyes. "What do you mean?"

"Nothing!" Gia smiled and offered Jane her arm like she was an old-fashioned gentleman. "You ready?"

Jane was, indeed, ready. As ready as she was ever going to be, anyway. She swallowed hard and discreetly wiped a sweaty palm on her dress, nodded, and took Gia's arm.

Game. On.

—⌒—

Despite her nerves, the rehearsal was actually kind of fun. Maybe because Elise hadn't made them produce it down to every last detail. There were no Mason jars in sight, no assigned seating, and no calligraphy anywhere.

They'd eaten dinner first, in a private dining room in the B&B. Between the wedding party, Cam's mom, Elise's parents, the DJ, and the minister, they numbered sixteen, so they'd been seated at two tables. Jane had given a moment's thought to trying to manipulate things so she could sit near Cameron—it had been her first impulse—but she reasoned that that would only make her more nervous for what was to come.

That didn't mean she wasn't hyper aware of him. She had lost her breath when he and Jay appeared, a couple minutes after everyone else had gathered. Thankfully, everyone's attention had been on the beaming groom, so no one noticed Jane's jaw drop. Damn. She could easily imagine Cam in his army gear. But it turned out he could rock a suit pretty well, too. It was a slim-cut, dark gray suit, and since they'd walked across from the B&B, he was still wearing his aviator sunglasses. And there was the plaid tie she had seen in his dresser drawer. He looked like a badass CEO. Emphasis on the badass—somehow, even though she couldn't see his tattoos, the idea that that full sleeve was there, under all that fancy clothing... She cleared her throat. Then he took off his sunglasses, and once the mirrored shades were gone, it became apparent that he was looking at her, too. Well. She had to take a long drink of the ice water on the table in front of her.

So, yeah, if she didn't want to spontaneously combust before she'd said her piece, it was better to stay away from him for now, and try to enjoy herself as much as possible.

And she *had* enjoyed herself. She'd been seated next to Elise's brother Andy, who was her groomsman partner. Jane had come to know Andy well over the years. He was almost like a second big brother, and she cheerfully submitted to his teasing. The food had been delicious—local trout and vegetables at the peak of freshness—and the warm feeling of being among friends soothed her frayed nerves. It was touching, really, how all these people had come together to make this wedding happen. Some more than others, she thought with a private laugh, because certainly not everyone here had stuffed felt into blenders for the cause, but still, the room was filled with such goodwill. And love. The room was suffused with love.

Hopefully it was catching.

After everyone was done with dessert, the minister ran them through a rehearsal of the actual ceremony, instructing the guys to move some chairs to mock up an aisle of sorts meant to mimic the one that would be set up outside the next day. Jane lined up next to Andy, who looked handsome and happy in his suit. Elise had instructed everyone to wear cocktail party attire to the rehearsal, and the guys had not disappointed. "Looking good, Jane," said Andy, winking at her as they linked arms, preparing to process up the makeshift aisle. Jane made a kissing face at Elise's big brother and said, "Likewise."

After they'd run through the ceremony, the minister said, "We're going to move to the reception hall now, where we'll go over the reception entrance cues, the timing of the toasts, and the first dances."

Darkness was falling as they walked from the B&B to the main event hall. Jane paused and looked up at the sky. She wasn't a religious person, but, man, she could use a little divine courage right about now. Her gaze landed on a twinkling star, the first of the night. She closed her eyes, letting the sounds of crickets soothe her.

She didn't make a wish, though, because she was done sitting back and letting things happen. She was done staying out of the way and keeping her head down. Cameron had taught her all that.

She was making her own luck now.

—◌‍—

Cam cursed his brother for giving him such an easy job. Being an usher might demand a lot of attention tomorrow, but in terms of the rehearsal, there wasn't much for the ushers to do except nod when the minister said, "Make sure people are comfortable. Take care on the uneven ground if you're helping anyone with mobility issues."

Which left a lot of time for him to watch Jane.

He tried not to. Well, kind of. In that killer red dress, she was like a beacon in a dark night. Hell, she was like the flashing lights on top of a fire truck. There was no way not to look at her.

And he wasn't the only one.

Kent, predictably, stared openly. He had to be nudged when it was his turn to walk down the aisle, with Wendy. But Elise's brother, too, who had never displayed any overt interest in Jane before, had suddenly gone all Casanova, judging by the way he was teasing Jane as they waited their turn to process down the aisle.

Andy seemed like a stand-up guy. He was easygoing and friendly. He was a high school history teacher and football coach. Smart *and* athletic, he was probably exactly what women meant when they used the phrase, "the full package."

And Cam wanted to fucking punch his lights out. That the dude thought he could *touch* Jane, like it was his right? Cam's fingers flexed of their own volition, but he had to remind himself that there was no way for Jane and Andy to walk down the aisle together without touching.

He also had to remind himself he had no jurisdiction over Jane.

He might be in love with her, but that was not relevant.

It was a huge relief when they left the building to head for the reception hall. He walked behind everyone else, holding back a bit because, for once since he had arrived at the wedding site, he wanted to prolong the time spent outside. The fresh air was a relief after the stifling dining room. Out here, he could look at the trees in the distance, smell the goddamned lavender on the evening breeze, and put things in perspective. The world was big. Big enough to start over. Or at least big enough that he could go somewhere else and make some more mistakes out of sight of all these people. He just needed to get through this wedding.

Jane, who had been walking in the middle of the group, next to Andy, tilted her head back to look at the sky. He followed her gaze. There was only one star visible.

Star light, star bright, first star I see tonight. Wish I may, wish I might, have this wish I wish tonight.

The rhyme popped into his head fully formed, though he hadn't thought about it for years. He wondered if Jane knew that rhyme, too, if she was making a wish. He wondered what she was wishing for.

She hadn't come to a full stop as she looked up, and she stumbled a bit as the path she was on transformed from gravel into pavement. Andy caught her arm and steadied her. Turned his head to her and said something that made her laugh. She looked into his eyes, smiling. She did not look back at the star.

Cam did, though. It was faint against the midnight-blue sky.

For a moment, he was tempted. He even came to a full stop, contemplating the twinkly little motherfucker.

"You coming, bro?" Jay's voice.

"Yep," he said, taking his gaze off the heavens. He had never belonged there anyway.

—Ↄ

"All right, so after the toast, we're done with the formalities until dinner is over," said the DJ, who was sitting behind his setup and talking to the group, the members of which were all seated at the head table in the otherwise-empty reception hall. Cameron was seated at the far end, next to the other usher. He couldn't see Jane, who was close to the other end. But, he reminded himself, there was no reason to be antsy about the fact that she was out of view. She wasn't his.

"We'll give people about twenty minutes to eat after the toasts, but let's be flexible about it," the DJ said, directing his comments to Elise. "I'll take note of when the servers are mostly done clearing the main course, and then we'll start the first dances. Does that sound all right?"

Elise nodded.

"So this is what I've got," he went on. "Ladies and gentlemen, may I have your attention please . . . Then I generally wait a moment until everyone settles down, and that will be your cue to get up. But don't hurry. I'll be cuing the music to you. I can slow it down if need be, so take your time. It will generally take you longer than you think because of the dress."

The opening strains of "Your Song" started pouring from the speakers, and Elise and Jay shared a tender look as they got up from the table and walked to the small dance floor.

"When you're ready, we'll dim the lights and then I'll say, 'Please join me in congratulating Elise and Jay on their first dance as husband and wife.'"

Jay took Elise's hand and pulled her against his chest with a ferocity you didn't generally see from him. Cam knew it was there, underneath the applique of the mild-mannered accountant. Apparently Elise did, too, because she looked at him with what could only be called bedroom eyes. Watching them felt intrusive, like they were witnessing a private, intimate moment. But it was impossible to look away.

The DJ must have shared his sentiment, because he kept the song going. Cam would have thought that they were just running through the cues. But the entire song played out as Jay and Elise swayed under the spotlight, seemingly oblivious to their surroundings.

As the final notes of the song ran out, it was like the bridal couple came to and suddenly remembered that they had an audience. Embarrassed, Elise buried her head against Jay's chest for a moment before she reemerged, smiling sheepishly.

"Elise and Jay wanted to do something a little different for their second dance," said the DJ. "So I'll be making this announcement tomorrow at this point in the program." He looked down at his notes. "In lieu of a lineup of dances with their parents or with the wedding party, Elise and Jay invite all the lovebirds out there to join them for the next dance. Old love, new love; it's all welcome. So if you're under Cupid's spell, grab your beloved and get out here."

"Oh, that's cute," said the minister. "I've never seen that before."

Gia, who was standing next to him, snorted softly. "Well, that leaves everyone here out, except...oh."

He followed her gaze.

There was a goddess walking toward him.

Oh, fuck.

"Oh, fuck," Gia whispered, echoing his thoughts so quickly and perfectly it was like she had heard them.

His first impulse was to agree with her, but he couldn't because everything started happening to his body all at once. All the stereotypical shit: his stomach dropped even as it felt like a herd of mini-elephants was migrating through it; his mouth dried up; his skin prickled with the pressure of a thousand tiny needles; his throat closed.

That last one was why, when Jane reached her hand out toward him and said, "Dance with me?" all he could do was stand there mutely, staring at her.

She was so beautiful. Objectively so: her fair skin contrasted with the burgundy of her dress and her lips. Her hair was piled loosely on her head with strands of it coming down from its updo. And those curves, covered in a second skin of lace. It almost hurt to look at her. But it was more than that. It went deeper. It was the way she looked when he told her about Eric and Haseeb. About Becky. And, bastard that he was, it was the way she looked when she came, surprised and delighted in equal measure. The whimpering sounds she made as she begged him to fuck her. He was pretty sure he was the only one who had ever seen that beauty. Hell, he was also the only person who knew what she looked like hanging off the CN Tower.

But that didn't mean he *should* be the only one to see her like that.

Just because he was the one who'd been around when she came out of her shell didn't mean he was the one for her. That was assigning him too much agency in the equation. She deserved someone who could give her everything. Someone without a Boeing 747 full of baggage. Someone who didn't disappoint everyone he loved. An *actual* angel, not a fallen one.

Someone like Andy, or, eff him, even Kent the Ken Doll. And once he was out of her hair, she'd be free to find that someone.

He was waiting too long to speak. Though her hand was still outstretched, a shadow was starting to pass over her eyes.

He couldn't speak; that was the problem. Not around the massive lump that had formed in his throat. If he'd been able to, he would have said, "See? That shadow is me. That's what I do. I take something bright and beautiful and hopeful, and I dim it as I pass by."

And he couldn't do that to her. No fucking way.

So he did what he had to do: he shook his head.

He wanted to do it gently, to infuse that "no" gesture with all the regret in his heart. So he only shook his head a little—the slightest amount, really.

It was enough.

Tears rushed to the corners of her eyes, and she clamped a hand over her mouth.

He wanted to crush her to him, to soothe away the hurt he had caused. But that would only be self-serving, would only prolong the pain and complicate the untangling. The best thing he could do for her was cut her loose as kindly but decisively as possible.

So he dropped his gaze from her gorgeous face to the ground—where it belonged.

Somebody gasped.

The square pattern in the parquet flooring at his feet blurred.

He swiped his hand over his traitorous eyes, and, keeping his gaze squarely on the floor, he turned and walked out of the room.

Chapter Twenty-Three

*H*e ignored them all. Jay's insistent pounding. His mother's gentle pleas. Even Elise had come by and knocked and yelled at him through the locked door of his room.

Eventually, they gave up. He heard them whispering in the hallway, wondering if he had actually left somehow, though they noted his car was still in the lot.

"If you're in there, I need to talk to you," Jay shouted.

Yeah, that was not happening. No one was going to tell him anything he hadn't already told himself. Nothing that came out of their mouths would shame him more than he already was. He had fancied himself a fallen angel before? He'd had no fucking idea how much farther there was to fall.

"The end."

He read the words aloud because they applied to so much more than just book one in the Clouded Cave series, didn't they?

He set his Kindle down on the bed beside him and closed his eyes.

What a book.

He allowed himself one moment of...*happiness* wasn't the right word. *Pride* maybe? *Gratification*? To think that the person who had written such an amazing book had, for one moment, deluded herself into thinking she wanted him. It was astonishing.

He could see where all her bravery came from, too. It was all right there in her book. In her characters. It was like she was trying out those feelings, playing with different permutations, in her story. As the main character emerged into the alternative world through the cave and her eyes were opened to the injustices of that world, she could have gone right back through to her own world. The universe of the book allowed that—it was a two-way portal.

It did not seem to him a mistake that the woman who had leaped off the CN Tower despite her intense fear—and who confronted her sick father—had also written this book.

He picked up the Kindle again and downloaded book two. Since she was writing for children—on the surface of things—her books weren't long. It had taken him only two hours to read the first one. And he was going to spend the whole goddamned night torturing himself with the rest.

He was halfway through book two when the pounding started again.

"Cameron MacKinnon, open this motherfucking door, or I will break it the hell down!"

Gia.

He almost laughed. The doors in this place were old and the locks so flimsy as to be almost decorative, but the idea of the tiny wisp of a model breaking down his door was incongruously amusing.

She broke the door down.

He bolted to a sitting position. "What the fuck, Gia?"

"That's my line, Cameron!" she shouted, stalking toward the bed and grabbing the tie he still wore and using it to haul him up to a sitting position. Once he was upright, she let go of him, put her hands on her hips, and said, slowly, "What. The. Fuck."

Then she slapped him.

The commotion drew Jay, who was next door.

He walked in, shaking his head. "God, man." The disappointment radiated off him in waves, but Cam was used to that.

"What's going on up here?"

Fuck. His mom. He was used to disappointing her, too, but after their unspoken reconciliation, it was hard to face her.

And bringing up the rear was Elise. The one who'd stuck Jane with him in the first place. The one who hadn't trusted him not to ruin things. The smart one.

"Where's Jane?" he asked through the hands he had buried his head in.

"As if you have any right to know," Gia said, and he nodded because she was right.

"Wendy took her to a motel in town for the night," said Elise with an eerie calm, given how particular she'd been about making sure all things wedding related were perfect. "She didn't want to spend the night here. They just left."

Which explained why Hurricane Gia had descended with such force just then.

Elise, who'd been standing closest to the partially unhinged door, fit it back into place. There was a soft click as it closed, but he heard it like the slamming of a jail cell, sealing his fate.

They all started talking at once. Gia was screaming about how she'd specifically warned him not to hurt Jane. His mother kept saying she thought he had changed, she *hoped* he had changed. Jay was trying to get everyone else to stop talking.

Cam sat there and let them come at him. Let the ocean of recriminations wash over him, but instead of scouring him clean, the current left a pile of algae and sea trash in its wake.

"Do you love her?"

When Elise asked the question, everyone stopped talking. She hadn't raised her voice, so Cam wasn't really sure how he, and everyone else, had even heard her. But the simple, calm question cut through all the agitation in the room, quieting the storm.

"Tell me the truth," Elise said. "Do you love her?"

He looked down at his discarded Kindle. It was in sleep mode, with a picture of the cover of Jane's book on the screen. He reached out to touch it, as if it were a talismanic object that could lend him some of its power.

"Yes."

Once he told the truth—after that little "yes"—he tried to make them see that it didn't actually change anything. He tried to explain to them that it was *because* he loved Jane that he had rejected her. That a quick, singular humiliation was better than the lifetime of disappointment he was otherwise capable of inflicting. When had he ever done right by a woman? He tried to make them understand that he'd gotten it wrong from day one, with Alicia.

"That wasn't your baby," his mother said quietly, drawing an astonished gasp from Jay.

"What? You knew?" Cam demanded, suddenly angry. She had known that all these years? Hot adrenaline coursed through him.

"Her parents came to see me before they left town," she said. "I should have told you, but..."

"But what?" he demanded, trying and failing to wrap his head around this new information.

"You were hurting so much," she said, still speaking softly, like he was a wild animal she was trying not to spook. "You started pushing me away. I was afraid you would see my knowledge as an intrusion on a matter you were trying to keep private. As overstepping." He thought about how often in those years he had accused her of precisely that. Even an innocent question about his day he would twist into an unwelcome invasion of his privacy. "I'm sorry," she said, holding her hands out to him like she wanted to come closer but didn't dare. "I can see now that it was the wrong decision, but at the time I thought I was preserving your dignity. Respecting your privacy. Protecting what was left of our relationship."

So his mother knew the truth about Alicia.

And of course Jay knew the truth about Christie. Which he proceeded to share with everyone. The whole humiliating story about how Cam had come home to find that she'd...moved on.

And it went on from there. Cam felt like he was in a witness box being cross-examined by a hostile prosecutor. Except that was wrong, because everyone in this absurdist courtroom was *defending* him. He was the one insisting on his own guilt. So if he was the prosecutor, who was that guy on the stand everyone was arguing about?

And just like in a courtroom, they were twisting what he said, ferreting out little bits of truth, piecing together the big picture. When his mother asked him a series of direct questions about the circumstances surrounding his discharge from the army, he couldn't lie to her. Whatever else happened, he was done hurting his mother. Their time together yesterday had meant everything to him.

"So what you're saying," said Gia, holding up her hands like they were at an evangelical revival, "is that you let yourself take the fall for this Becky person. The same way you did for your high school girlfriend."

"It's not that simple—"

Jay cut him off. "From where I'm standing, I'm thinking, yes, it is that simple."

How to make them understand that intentions didn't matter? That it all added up to the same outcome? That what people believed about him had become true—or maybe it always had been true. That the distinction didn't matter. A fallen angel was still fallen.

"I owe you an apology," said Jay.

"What? No." Goddamn it. He did not need that. He didn't *want* it.

Then the room exploded again, starting with Jay and Cam arguing over who owed whom an apology, then on to Gia and his mom drawing wild, unfounded conclusions over what they were calling his secret heroism.

"Enough." Cam raised his voice to cut through the din, unleashing some of his accumulated anger at his audience. "The details don't matter. What matters is that I'm no good for—" Fuck. His voice broke. He couldn't even say her name. "For someone like her," he finished on a mortifying whisper.

The room was silent for a long moment. At least that was something. Then his brother spoke. "We've had our troubles over the years, Cam, but I never took you for a coward."

Everything in Cam revolted at the word. It had taken every ounce of strength he had to witness Jane, walking toward him with her heart on her sleeve, prepared to give him everything, and to look at her with a blank face and turn his eyes to the ground. That wasn't cowardice. That was the strongest fucking thing he'd ever done. He wanted to lunge at his brother, to pummel him with his fists. But instead he pulled back sharply on the thin thread of control he still had, and said, "I'll only hurt her. I can't do that. I refuse to let her settle for me."

"You're not afraid of hurting her. You're afraid of getting hurt yourself. I get it. You had a bad run, with Alicia and Christie, but—"

"Christie may have done a shitty thing," Cam said, unable to stop himself from interrupting, "but she saved me. Christie and the army saved me." He huffed a bitter laugh. "For a while, anyway."

Jay scoffed. "Really? Because from where I'm standing, it's looking a lot more like you saved yourself." When Cam didn't respond, Jay threw up his hands. "*Anyway*, as I was saying: You want to be a coward? Slink away with your tail between your legs? Fine. Your prerogative, bro. But at least own up to what it is you're actually afraid of."

The thin thread connecting Cam to his sense of control finally snapped. He moved toward his brother, thinking of nothing but getting Jay to shut that taunting mouth. But Jay, ever the bigger brother, was quicker than Cam. The room exploded again as Jay shoved him, hard.

"Stop," said Elise, holding up a hand. Like before, her quiet certainty cut through the din. Cam realized with a start that she had been utterly silent this whole time, that she hadn't spoken since she'd posed her initial question. A question she repeated now, looking right at him as she spoke. "Do you love her? I don't really give a shit about the past, or intentions, or fears. That's the only question that matters, so I'm going to ask it again. Do. You. Love. Her?"

He was so tired. Tired of fighting. He was a soldier, but
he was a defeated one. He spoke quietly, but the single syllable was a roaring river in his ears. "Yes."

"So what the hell are you still doing here?"

"What am I supposed to do? Run after her and tell her I
made a mistake? That I'm sorry I publicly humiliated her?"
Even as he spoke, though, something heavy and unfamiliar
gathered in his gut. It was like that big shove from his brother
had jarred all the fear out of his body. And this thing he was
left with? He was pretty sure it was hope, though he would
have expected hope to be light like a feather, capable of taking flight, not cumbersome and sick-making. But the weight
of their arguments, as they started to make a twisted kind of
sense, was actually staggering. "Tell her I'm sorry? Those are
just words. That's what I've been trying to tell you all. Intentions don't matter. Words don't matter. Not with me anyway.
My actions have spoken for themselves." It was by his actions he'd been damned. It was because of his actions that he
didn't deserve Jane.

"So don't tell her you're sorry," said Elise calmly.
"Don't *tell* her how you feel. *Show* her."

Show her.

Elise might as well have slapped him. He sucked in a
breath.

Show her.

Could he . . . do that?

"Yes," Gia said, her calm voice all the more potent because she'd spent the last several minutes yelling. "You
think you don't deserve Jane, and God knows I'm inclined
to agree with you. But shouldn't you let her make that decision? You say you love her? Then have some goddamned
respect. Don't assume you know what she wants. So man
the fuck up, Cameron, and show her how you feel."

"How?" He allowed the single syllable to fall from his lips because…Dear God, because he was finally defeated, convicted at his own trial. Either that or he was insane, infected by this hope virus, a fast-acting poison that was attacking all his systems at once.

"I don't know," said Elise. "But it has to be big. I don't think more words are going to work on Jane. She lives with words all day long."

She was right. Jane felt things through her stories—they'd just been talking about that. And what had she been doing tonight but trying to break free? To live her own stories, not just tell them, despite the fact that it was hard for her, terrifying even. That's why she was so brave. Feeling things was hard.

Something he had said to Jane back at the CN Tower floated into his consciousness. He'd said it to her before jumping onto the glass floor, and then a little later she'd said it back to him before jumping off the freaking building.

Sometimes you have to open your eyes and jump.

"I have an idea," he said, looking at Elise. The bridezilla. His future sister-in-law. "But you're not going to like it."

Chapter Twenty-Four

THE WEDDING DAY

*E*lise kept looking at her watch.

Was it weird that Elise was wearing a watch? She was in her dress, which was a stunning strapless thing with a giant, puffy tulle skirt and a veil that hung halfway down her back. She was wearing the understated earrings and bracelet that Jane and the others had helped her pick out after about eleven hundred hours of shopping.

She was also wearing a huge, chunky men's-style watch with a wide, black leather strap. Probably it was Jay's.

But whatever. Elise was running the show here. If there was one thing Jane had learned from her beloved bridezilla, it was that there was always a method to the madness. It was better not to ask questions.

They were obviously keeping Cameron away from her, because she hadn't seen him all day. Part of her was screaming that she shouldn't let them, in the name of preserving some dignity. That she should be above needing to be babied, that they shouldn't have to move mountains on Elise's big day because they were concerned about Jane's tender sensibilities. That she should be able to lay eyes on the man and not collapse on the floor sobbing.

But another part, the part concerned with self-preservation, knew better. Her heart wasn't just broken, it was absolutely shattered.

Cameron had talked about IEDs—improvised explosive devices. It was an apt metaphor. Because what was left after the damage wasn't even recognizable as a heart. And because she'd been the instigator. She'd overseen the destruction of her own heart. She'd pressed the button herself. As much as she wanted to blame him, to be angry at him, she couldn't. He had told her, explicitly, what he wanted—and didn't want. But she, with a degree of hubris sufficient to star in its own Greek tragedy, had thought she could change him. Hadn't she learned from her father and Felix that people didn't change?

Clearly, she would have to see him at the ceremony, and at the reception, but until then, she was happy to minimize her contact with him. She appreciated that the girls seemed to know that without her having to say anything. In fact, she wondered if maybe he'd left, either of his own volition or because Elise or Jay had asked him to. Did she dare hope? She wanted to ask Elise, but she didn't want her friend to think she was suggesting they kick Cameron out of the wedding if they hadn't already. You couldn't ask the bride to eject the groom's brother merely because he'd hurt your feelings.

"Here, sweetie, put some of these in." Gia entered the room the girls were using to get ready and handed Jane some Visine.

"Is it still that bad?" Jane asked, looking around for a mirror. Last night, in the motel she'd escaped to, she'd cried all the tears out of her body, then fallen asleep in Wendy's arms and succumbed to a few fitful hours of sleep. She had awoken to bloodshot eyes with racoon circles underneath them. Gia had done her best with the concealer, but no amount of makeup could disguise the redness of her eyes themselves.

Instead of answering, Gia came over and tapped Jane's forehead, prompting her to tilt her head back.

When she was done, Jane's eyes were watery from the eye drops. The act of wiping them somehow triggered actual tears. Again.

"Why does this keep happening?" she asked as Gia pulled her into a hug.

"I think it's totally normal to cry a lot when you get your heart broken."

"No. Not the crying. Why is it that every time I put myself out there, I get slapped down?"

"That asshole." Wendy joined in the hug. "That asshole," had become Wendy's mantra. It was like she was a nonnative English speaker who knew only those words. Jane had never seen Wendy so angry. It was a little bit gratifying, but she had had to extract a promise that Wendy wouldn't disrupt the wedding by attacking Cameron, or, like, shouting her new mantra at the top of her lungs at an inopportune time.

Elise, who was the only one among them fully dressed and made up, came over and mimed putting her arms around the whole lot of them. "I will totally hug you for real if you want me to," she said, wincing as she looked down at her impeccably groomed self.

Jane laughed and blinked away her tears. "No, don't ruin

yourself. I'm gonna give you the world's biggest tackle-hug after the ceremony, though."

One silver lining of this whole debacle was the reminder that she had the best friends a girl could ask for. Who needed a man when you had this kind of loyalty?

Although perhaps the loyalty of one of them would be tested when she found out about Jane's latest problem. Refreshingly, though, and unlike the whole Cameron disaster, it was a very specific, very tangible problem: as she had feared, her dress wouldn't zip up. Like, at all. It was beyond "who needs to breathe anyway as long as the damn thing zips up" territory.

Everyone besides Elise had been walking around in various states of undress for the past hour or so, so no one had said anything about the gaping back of Jane's dress.

But it was time to face the music now that Gia was back from her eyedrops-sourcing mission. Jane was holding out hope that the model might have some kind of high-fashion ninja skills she could apply to magically make the dress zip up.

"Um, you guys?"

The group hug had broken up, but all eyes swung back to her.

"Two things. Number one: I love you all so much." Jane didn't let the "aww-ing" and "me-tooing" that ensued really take off before plowing on. "Number two: I can't zip up my dress."

She braced herself for Elise's reaction. Just because Jane was a mess didn't mean she expected any mercy on this front. But the bride grinned, looked at her huge watch, and said, "That's okay."

Huh? "No, Elise, I mean it. This dress will not close."

Elise's phone chimed, and she plucked it off the sofa.

"Hey now, let's see what we can do about this," said Gia, speaking to Jane—in a tone that seemed kind of artificially singsongy—but looking at Elise.

Elise's head popped up from her phone. "Right. Yes."

Everyone converged behind Jane.

"I see what you mean," said Gia, trying the zipper, but not with much gusto.

"I'm gonna hold my breath, and you zip," said Jane, even though she knew it was futile. "On three."

Jane counted, held her breath, and sucked in her stomach for all she was worth. Gia tried again, but Jane had the sense that she wasn't putting her everything into it.

"Listen to me," she said, turning to face her friends. "We have to figure this out."

"Eh, it's not a big deal," said Elise, waving a hand.

"Not a big deal?" Jane echoed. Had an alien switched bodies with the bridezilla? "I can't walk down the aisle with my dress hanging open." But then, maybe she could. It would be the perfect completion of her humiliation for Cameron to see her in the un-zip-upable dress. Why not go for broke on the shame front?

She turned to Wendy. Wendy would be the voice of reason. Wendy had never let her down. "Can we at least pin it?"

"Of course," Wendy said. "Let me see what I can do."

Finally, someone who was acting like a normal person. Jane hitched a shuddery breath and lifted her hair so Wendy could get an unobstructed view.

Silence settled over the room as Wendy started pinning. At least until Elise shouted, apropos of nothing, "We need to go outside!"

"What?" Jane and Wendy said in unison.

"Here," Gia said, holding open a robe for Elise. "Put this on so Jay doesn't see you in the dress."

"Ah!" Elise beamed at Gia. "I didn't even think of that—thank you!" Once she was tucked inside the robe, she made for the door, clapping her hands. "Chop, chop, girls."

"Whatever it is, it can wait until I get Jane pinned up," Wendy said testily.

Elise turned and froze, hands on hips. "No, it cannot wait." Ah, there was the familiar drill sergeant bride. "Everyone follow me. Now."

Jane threw a shawl over the gaping back of the dress and did as she was told.

—⌒⌒

"Will someone please explain to me what we're doing out here?" Wendy said as the girls, Jay, and Jay's mom stood in a line in the parking lot outside the B&B. "The wedding is supposed to start in half an hour!"

Jane was curious, too. But she figured all would be revealed sooner or later. Elise obviously had some sort of surprise for them. Maybe she was having personalized thank-you Mason jars delivered. But, hey, she'd take it. Anything to distract her from the smoking ruins of her heartbreak.

Anything except the blue Corvette that came tearing into the parking lot and screeched to a halt in front of them.

"No way," she said, turning to go. To flee, really, opting for the "flight" option presented by the burst of "fight-or-flight" adrenaline the sight of Cam's car had triggered. There was pride, and there was pride. It didn't take a genius to figure out that running away like a coward was better than sinking to her knees and wailing—with the back of her dress unzipped, to boot.

Gia's hand clamped down on Jane's forearm.

What the hell? "Let me go," she whisper-yelled as she tried to twist out of her friend's grip. Her struggle only caused Gia to double down, adding a second hand to Jane's arm and planting her feet as if preparing for a tug-of-war. What happened to the loyal, true friends she'd so recently been snuggling with? Gia's refusal to let her go was a betraying blade, slicing into her chest.

"Hang on," said Gia, even as their struggle for control threatened to turn into an outright tussle. Which is why Jane didn't see what was happening until she heard Wendy gasp. She looked at Wendy, who had one hand clasped over her mouth in horror and the other pointing toward the parking lot.

Correction: her hand wasn't pointing toward the parking lot; it was pointing toward Hercules getting out of a blue Corvette.

"What?" she whispered, barely able to get the word out, which was funny because in her head the question had sounded like a shout.

She swayed toward Gia, thankful suddenly for the bracing contact. But Gia chose that moment to let go and step away, whispering, "You're okay."

She was not okay. What part of this was okay? There was no part of this that was okay. There was no part of this that *made sense*. If she'd felt like Gia had stuck a knife into her chest before, she'd just pulled it out, leaving Jane gasping, a gaping hole in her chest welling with . . . something.

Even though he was instantly recognizable as Hercules, he looked different from the actor who played the character on the show. The clothing was right: leather pants, tattered beige shirt, leather wristbands. He even carried a sword at his waist. But the similarities ended there. Whereas Kevin

Sorbo had long, flowing hair, Cameron still sported the military buzz cut. And of course there were the tattoos. The sleeveless shirt revealed his inked arm, and the angel peeked out from the shirt, which was unbuttoned almost all the way.

There was also the part where he was carrying a shopping bag in one hand.

Jane was pretty sure Hercules didn't shop at Whole Foods.

"See why you don't have to worry about the dress?" said Elise, smiling. "And look at you, you're going to get out of wearing high heels, too, you lucky girl."

"What are you talking about?" she said through an aching throat. Maybe Elise would prove more of an ally than Gia had. But no, there was nothing on Elise's face that Jane could make sense of, that she could grab on to to leverage herself out of this bewildering scenario. Her friend merely smiled like she had a delicious secret and turned back toward the B&B, gesturing for the group to follow her.

Wait. They were going to leave her here with him?

"You asshole!" Wendy shouted, and launched herself at Cameron. Well, at least there was one person left she could rely on. Wendy was small but fierce. As her fists uselessly pummeled Cameron's chest, Jane almost laughed. Would have done so if she weren't battling a powerful wave of confusion and betrayal and fear that was making it hard to stand upright.

Cameron just stood there and took the beating Wendy gave him. Jane had never seen Wendy in such a state. Her best friend was known for her potty mouth, and she reportedly turned into a tigress in the courtroom, but Jane had never actually seen her beat up anyone. Eventually, Jay pulled her off Cameron.

Gia leaned over to whisper in Jane's ear. "You come get me if you need me."

"Wait!" She reached out to grab Gia's arm, desperate, in a reversal of their previous roles, to keep Gia rooted in place. But she was too late. Gia slipped away. They all slipped away. Well, Wendy went loudly and with great reluctance, but the rest of them slipped.

Which left her standing face-to-face with Cameron MacKinnon dressed as Hercules.

"I love you," he said.

That was it. Standing was no longer possible. She sagged back against the retaining wall that bordered the parking lot. He lunged for her, but she held up a hand to stop his progress.

He stopped with his hands in the air, but he didn't step back.

Slowly, she let herself sink down the wall until she was sitting on the ground. Somewhere along the way she'd lost her shawl, too, so the back of the dress flapped in the wind. So much for dignity.

He waited until she'd hit the ground before saying, "I am completely, utterly, fiercely, *surprisingly* in love with you. I know you don't believe in the concept of 'the one.' I wouldn't have thought I did, either, but damned if I don't want, more than anything else in the world, to be yours. Your one and only."

What? Each word was like the little pinprick of an acupuncture needle: surprising and painful, then, suddenly, an instrument of relief. Capable of displacing pain. Of replacing it with something else, something unexpected and warm.

She looked up. He was backlit by the sun, the man dressed as a god.

"It scares me, though," he went on. "*You* scare me."

She saw, suddenly, that he had no experience with things going his way, with things going right.

And even more surprisingly? She also saw, suddenly, that she didn't, either.

A sob escaped.

"Hey, hey, baby. Don't cry." He sat down, arranging himself cross-legged across from her. Reached out a hand as if he were going to touch her face but stopped short, like he didn't have the right. "Kick my ass to the curb, but don't cry over me. I'm not worth it."

She wanted to grab his hand and press it against her face, to complete his aborted gesture, but she didn't dare. She didn't yet trust the hope that was pooling in her chest. "You *are* worth it, though. Don't you see? You *are*."

He smiled, a small, almost wistful smile. "I'm trying. Somehow, I can jump off buildings and be on the front lines of a war, but I don't know how to..." His voice trailed off, and he had to clear his throat. "I don't know how to let someone love me."

She tried to speak, but he didn't let her, just kept talking. "When you walked up to me last night, for that dance, I had a vision of the future. One where I took your hand and followed you out on that dance floor. What happened next? I got to be yours. I got to be the first person to read your books. I got to be your date to Comicon. I got to make you come every day for the rest of my life."

That last item made her cheeks heat, and she tried to look away, embarrassed, but he moved his head so that he remained in her line of sight.

"In that version of the future, I was the lucky bastard who got all that. The lucky bastard who got *you*. I could hardly conceive of it, it was so far out of the realm of my reality.

"But what came next? That was the question. That was the fear. I couldn't—I still can't, really—imagine a future in which I kept getting to *have* all that stuff indefinitely.

And although I was having trouble telling my head from my ass yesterday, I could tell you one thing with absolute certainty, and that was that I couldn't have you and then give you up. It would be worse than the PTSD. Worse than being estranged from my family. I wouldn't survive it, Jane."

Jane swallowed the lump in her throat and reached for his hand. She did what she hadn't been brave enough to do a moment ago, which was to bring it to her cheek. She made the biggest eyes-wide-open jump of all as she leaned into his palm and said, "Then don't give me up. Be my 'one.' Let me love you—because I do."

He rose then, keeping the one hand on her cheek as he used the other to help her to her feet. They stood like that for a long moment, contemplating each other. A smile spread slowly across his face. She had a feeling it was mirroring what was happening on hers.

"I brought you something," he said, breaking with her gaze to retrieve the shopping bag he'd dropped on the pavement.

"My Xena costume?" she said, pulling out the knee-high leather boots. The *flat* knee-high leather boots. "What in the world?"

"I have this thing in my head I call 'goddess mode,'" he said.

Huh? She must have looked as confused as she felt, because he laughed and elaborated.

"Yeah, I've seen you a bunch of times lately sort of out of your element, you know? Dangling off the CN Tower and on roller coasters."

"It *has* been kind of a thrill ride of a week."

"But not just those examples." He lowered his voice and said, "You're also in goddess mode in bed."

Her face heated, suddenly and intensely, like he'd pressed a secret on button.

"And after Comicon," he went on. "When you were dressed as Xena."

"Xena's not a goddess," Jane said, unable to refrain from issuing the correction. "At most, she's a demi-goddess, as there was one episode that hinted that maybe Ares was her real father, but—"

He silenced her with a quick, hard kiss. "You are *such* a sexy little nerd." Then he pulled away and kept right on talking, clearly not done with his speech—his *astonishing* speech. "My point is that you are the bravest, most kick-ass warrior I know. You *do* have a goddess inside you. And I for one think she should come out more often." He nodded at the shopping bag containing her costume. "So I brought your *demi-goddess* costume to help remind you. Plus, this way, you won't have to wear that damned dress that has been stressing you out so much."

He couldn't mean… "Oh my God! Is this what Elise meant about not having to wear high heels?"

"Yeah, Jay bumped Kent. He's ushering now, and you and I are in the main event, my love. My Xena. My goddess."

"No way!" Jane shouted. "There is no way on God's green Earth that Elise is going to go for this."

"She already has," said Cameron, pulling her breastplate out of the bag. "I gotta say, I think Elise is going to make a pretty good sister-in-law. She has a bit of an inner rebel, that one. I'm looking forward to getting to know her better."

Jane laughed. And then she laughed some more. Because it was the only reaction she could summon to the astonishing events of the last few minutes.

Cameron laughed, too, and pulled her close, wrapping

his arms around her. "Hey!" he exclaimed, finding his way to the bare skin of her back given the unzipped nature of her dress. "Easy access...mmmmm." His hands were rough and possessive as they slid immediately down to her waist. "I don't really know what you have against this dress."

She moaned a little but managed to push him away. "Hey," she said, playfully slapping his hand for good measure. "There's one thing wrong here."

He raised his eyebrows. "Is there now?"

"Yeah. If you cared *at all* about accuracy, you wouldn't be dressed as Hercules right now; you'd be dressed as Gabrielle."

He barked a laugh, and just before his lips hit hers, he said, "I love you. But maybe not *that* much."

Chapter Twenty-Five

*F*orty minutes later, Elise and Jay were married. The bride looked stunning in white tulle. Two sets of Pinterest-worthy groomsmen and their bridesmaids followed the happy couple down the aisle, impeccably dressed in tuxedos and mulberry—not plum—dresses.

Last came Xena and Hercules.

Jane was happy. She was so happy, it felt like she was taking up a huge amount of space, which was an altogether unfamiliar feeling. After a lifetime of minimizing her needs, of trying to be quiet and small and good, to suddenly be doing the opposite was…indescribable. It hurt a little, but it was a good kind of hurt, the kind you get when you stretch stiff muscles or when you blink against the blinding sunlight after a long time in the dark.

As the guests crossed the farm, walking from the lavender fields where the ceremony had taken place to the reception hall, Cameron held her hand. What an astonishing thing, to be holding a man's hand. In public. Like it was normal.

What an astonishing thing to be loved.

Cameron snagged two flutes of champagne off the tray of a server standing in the entranceway and handed one to her, winking as he held up his glass in a silent toast.

She choked a little as they entered the reception room. "Oh my God!" she exclaimed. "That's what the teapots were for!"

At the center of each table was an arrangement of gold-spray-painted teapots and vintage teacups, all planted with flowers.

They looked *fabulous*.

"Huh?" he said.

She threw back her head and laughed again. "Never mind," she said.

—⟨⟩

Dinner took forever. The toasts took forever. The freaking couples' dance took forever, though Cam did appreciate the hell out of being included this time.

"Now if all the single women in the room will come to the dance floor," the DJ said, "it's time for the bride to toss her bouquet."

Jane, who had been soft and pliant in his arms during the couples' dance, stiffened. He pulled away long enough to search her face, his protective instincts kicking in.

"I have to get out of here," she whispered. Then she turned and hoofed it toward the door at the back of the reception hall, and, like a fish swimming against the current, she passed dozens of women going the opposite direction.

"What's the matter?" he said, following, grabbing her

hand, and digging his heels in to stop her progress. "What's happened?" He allowed a hint of the panic that was rising in his chest to come through in the question. Had she changed her mind about him?

She turned, her beautiful face painted with a warm smile. "Nothing's wrong. I just don't want to be anywhere in the vicinity when she throws that bouquet." Then the smile became a wry grin. "No offense."

He smiled back. "None taken." Though he had to admit that the idea of marrying Jane someday... well, certain images had taken root in his mind, images of his goddess in a white dress on a roller coaster, to be specific, and he was pretty sure it was going to be impossible to dislodge them. But there was no hurry.

"It's just that I'm done with the whole wedding thing," she said emphatically. "I need a break from the matrimonial scene. I've already, like, confronted a lifetime's worth of emotional baggage. That's enough drama for the day. If I catch that bouquet, it will be like some kind of—oof!"

The bouquet in question *thunked* against the back of Jane's head.

Cameron's arms came around her, searching her scalp to make sure she was okay. Her eyes were wide with shock, but she didn't look injured. Once he was assured that she was well, he had to turn his attention to fighting the wave of laughter that was threatening to engulf him.

"Was that what I think it was?"

He nodded, even as the heat and brightness of a spotlight found them, and let the laughter overtake him.

"Oh, shit," she whispered as the entire hall burst into applause.

⌐◠

Finally, *finally*, the party seemed like it was plateauing. Elise and Jay both seemed slightly buzzed and totally blissed out. Some people were dancing, and others were clustered in small groups, talking and laughing.

He couldn't wait any longer.

He hadn't really left her side all evening, feeling like a kid in a fairy tale, like if he lost sight of his goddess, she'd vanish forever.

But when she got up to go to the bathroom, he made his move: he had a quick word with his brother and then found a quiet corner and whipped out his phone. He might be stupidly, head-over-heels in love, but he was still the same person. And Jane, inexplicably, wanted that person.

Meet me back in the B&B.

The return text came immediately.

Why?

He could almost hear the sexy defiance in the word.

Because I need to fuck you right now. Can't wait anymore.

I'll meet you in your room.

He was about to text back to ask why—he only had a single bed in his room, and hers had a double—when another one from her arrived.

Your room has the condoms.

Ah, yes. She was smart, his Janie. Then, a second later, one more text from her.

Hurry.

⁂

When he came crashing into the B&B lobby a couple minutes later, Jane was already on the bottom landing of the stairs. She paused when she heard him enter, frozen like she'd been caught in the act of doing something bad.

He paused, too, staring at her from across the lobby, his heart in his throat. Jane. His Jane.

She smiled a coy smile, full of wicked intentions, and it was a jolt to his system. He crossed quickly over to her, cursing the chairs and sofas he had to walk around. When he reached her, he slapped her ass. "Move."

Thirty seconds later, he was clawing at her Xena breastplate, desperate to get it off, as they fell into his room. "I used to think these metal tits were sexy as hell," he growled.

"But not anymore?" she panted as she turned, showing him the ties at the sides that fastened the front and back of the armor together.

He started working the knots loose. "No. Now I want it on the floor."

Finally, he got her hardware off, and she helped him with clothing underneath it, then bent to remove her boots.

When she stood back up she was finally, gloriously naked. And she was . . .

"Mine," he said.

"Yes," she answered immediately, sliding her hands inside the scrap of fabric that passed for a shirt on his costume, and sliding it off his shoulders. Her hands on his skin were like brands. He'd claimed her just now as his, but the truth was she *owned* him.

He shoved out of his pants and underwear and fell to his knees in front of her, wrapping his arms around her waist and burying his nose between her legs. "Mine," he said again, not caring that he sounded like a goddamned caveman.

She yanked him to his feet, grabbed his dick, and said, "Mine."

"Yes," he agreed on a groan, his surrender as easy and absolute as the desire that overtook him. "Yours."

As if to demonstrate her claim, she bit him on the shoulder. But then, as if to demonstrate *his* claim, she wound her arms around his neck and hitched herself up, wrapping her legs around him.

He carried her over to the dresser, nodded at the toiletries bag on top of it, and said, "Condom." She giggled and grabbed one. When they reached the bed, he laid back on it, pulling her on top of him so she was straddling him.

She tore open the condom, and because she somehow knew he was about to object, she said, "Fast now; slow later."

He grinned. The concept of "later." The idea that there would be more. Endless opportunities to love this woman. "Yeah," he groaned as she unrolled the condom onto him and kneeled up over him. Floating his hand up between her legs, he found her clit with two fingers. She rolled her hips against his hand, still on her knees, still hovering over him. "Come on, baby, ride me," he said.

And she did.

─౨─

"Oh my God!" Jane sat bolt upright when she was awakened by the sound of someone coming into her room.

No, into Cameron's room. She was in Cameron's room.

"Oh my God," she said again—but this time it was tinged with disbelief—when her sleep-addled brain caught up to the enormity of what had happened. She was in *Cameron's* room. He *loved* her. She was pretty sure he was her *boyfriend*.

And Elise's stupid bouquet was lying on the top of his dresser.

She didn't have time to analyze the weird mixture of exhilaration and fear that bouquet inspired—it was like riding a roller coaster, somehow—because Cameron was shedding his clothes. He must have gotten dressed and gone out for some reason. She stopped wondering what that reason might be when he pulled off his T-shirt, causing predictable things to happen between her legs. Would she ever get tired of looking at that muscular, inked chest? Once he was naked, he prowled toward her looking like he wanted to eat her for breakfast.

Breakfast. As hard as it was to tear her eyes from him, she looked around. Sunlight was streaming through a crack in the curtains.

"Oh my God!" she cried one final time, but this time the dominant emotion was panic. "What time is it? We have to go to the breakfast!"

He landed on the bed as she tried to get up. Grabbing her, he pulled her onto his body so she was lying on top of him, but his arms banded around her, rendering her immobile. He was hard between her legs. "We missed the breakfast. It's eleven."

"Oh, no!" she wailed, even as her hips, almost against her will, rocked against his.

"That's what happens when you stay up all night fucking," he said, grabbing her ass with both hands and grinding himself against the wetness between her legs. "Awww, fuck, you feel good."

She moaned, suffused with happiness so strong it was

like she was high. She didn't want to go to breakfast. She didn't want to do the right, expected, responsible thing.

"If you want to go downstairs, though, let's do it," said Cameron, stilling his movements but not letting go of her. "Though I ran into Jay and Elise, and they don't expect us to make an appearance anytime soon. I told them we were doing two very important things up here."

Her face heated, and she swatted his shoulder. "You did not." It wasn't like everyone didn't know what was happening, but it was hard to shed a lifetime of inhibition.

"I did indeed. Number one, you need to help me look at a course catalog. That's included in your babysitting services, right?"

She grinned. "So you *are* going back to school?"

"Yep. There's a program at the University of Toronto that caters to non-traditional students who are older."

"Are you sure there's no way to make things right with the army? Did you have a lawyer at your trial? I'm sure Wendy would—"

He shook his head. "The army was about growing up, getting myself out of the rut I was in. It played its role. I'm thinking night school. Part-time—I don't know if I have it in me to be a full-time student. Jay is going to hook me up with this foundation that does networking and career counseling for former military. I figure I can get a job and take a few classes at a time, get my feet wet."

She was so proud of him she could bust.

"And Elise has gotten this crackpot idea that I should move into Jay's condo. They were going to sell it, but now she's talking investment property. She wants to renovate it." He rolled his eyes.

Jane laughed. "She *is* going to need another project now that the wedding is over."

He smiled. "I think it will be great, actually. Mind you, I plan on wearing out my welcome at your house, but I don't want to crowd you."

A flash of uncertainty flared in his beautiful blue eyes. Jane squeezed him as tightly as she could with her arms and legs and whispered, "Crowd me, crowd me."

He twisted them so she was flat on her back and kissed her deeply, working his tongue against the inside of her mouth until her belly had gone molten. Then he stopped suddenly and pulled his whole body away from her. She cried out, reaching her arms up to try to hold him, but he was already off the bed.

"I forgot," he said, moving to where a bag rested on the floor by the door. "I said we were doing two important things up here. The course catalog was only the first item on this morning's agenda."

"Yeah," she said, "and I'm pretty sure you just rudely interrupted the second."

He shot her a wicked grin as he opened the bag and removed a Styrofoam container. "Nope. The second thing is French fries."

"What?"

"I promised you French fries the morning after the wedding, did I not? I went back to that diner and got a large order, extra grease."

He opened the container. They weren't just fries. On top of the golden potatoes lay a pair of poached eggs generously slathered with hollandaise sauce.

"And eggs Benedict," he said, winking.

Tears rushed into her eyes. There was nothing he could give her—no jewels, no flowers, no expensive gift—that would be more perfect than this. She sat up and held her arms out to him, and he came, setting the food on the bed between them. He dipped a fry into the hollandaise and fed it to her.

"Oh my God," she groaned, falling back on her highly unoriginal refrain, which had apparently become the catchphrase of the morning. "These are so good."

"Eat up," he said. "You need to keep your strength up."

"And why is that?"

"Because I counted wrong."

She furrowed her brow. "What do you mean?"

He stood. She looked up at him, her strong, beautiful, naked man, the man who somehow knew exactly what she needed, even when she didn't.

"You were right," he said again, looking her up and down like *she* was the box of French fries. "We actually have one more really, really important thing to do." He walked over to the dresser where the condoms were.

Her whole body started tingling, but she made a feeble protest anyway. "I really should go and make sure everything is okay. I can't abandon Elise." He stalked toward her, and when he arrived, he took the box of fries from her and set it aside. "I'm a bridesmaid," she added. "I'm supposed to be, like...doing important things. Important jobs." But then, she had a wild, radical thought. What if she stopped? What if she let her adult friends take care of themselves?

It was a strange, but not unpleasant notion. One she could get used to, actually.

"You *are* doing an important job," he said.

She raised an eyebrow at him.

"You're babysitting the groom's brother."

About the Author

Jenny Holiday is a *USA Today* bestselling author who started writing at age nine when her awesome fourth-grade teacher gave her a notebook and told her to start writing some stories. That first batch featured mass murderers on the loose, alien invasions, and hauntings. (Looking back, she's amazed no one sent her to a shrink.) She's been writing ever since. After a detour to get a PhD in geography, she worked as a professional writer, producing everything from speeches to magazine articles. Later, her tastes having evolved from alien invasions to happily-ever-afters, she tried her hand at romance. She lives in London, Ontario, with her family.

Learn more at:
    Jennyholiday.com
    Twitter @jennyholi
    Facebook.com/jennyholidaybooks
    Newsletter: jennyholiday.com/newsletter/

**Don't miss the next book in the
Bridesmaids Behaving Badly series!**

Wendy Liu would be delighted to be the
maid of honor in her best friend's
wedding...if only it didn't mean spending
a week with Jane's brother, the boy who
once broke her heart.

Noah Denning is determined to make his
little sister's wedding festivities
memorable. The only problem? It seems
her maid of honor is trying to outdo him at
every turn.

When passions—and pranks—collide
during joint bachelor and bachelorette
parties in Sin City, Wendy and Noah
quickly find that not everything that
happens in Vegas stays in Vegas...

Look for *It Takes Two*,
coming in summer 2018.

A preview follows.

Chapter One

*T*he phone rang.

Wendy jumped, cursing herself for forgetting to turn it off before her meeting. Her client, one Mr. Frederick Brecht, jumped too, his solemn tale of woe interrupted by the highly unprofessional "Who Let the Dogs Out" ringtone that Wendy's best friend Jane had set for herself on Wendy's phone.

"My apologies." Wendy fumbled to silence the phone and sneaked a glance at the time. It was late Friday afternoon, and Mr. Brecht was...thorough.

She eyed the now silent but still ringing phone. Historically, her heart had always done a happy little bleat when she saw the name *Jane Denning* on her call display. Wendy and Jane had been friends since the first day of fifth grade. Wendy still thanked her lucky stars that Jane had marched up to her in the cafeteria that first day and said, "Sit with me." Jane had made Wendy's first day at a new school

better. Just like she'd made every day since better. Because
Jane was all the things a best friend should be: a good lis-
tener, a straight talker, and a hell of a lot of fun. That phrase,
"like a sister?" It wasn't enough. Sometimes, Wendy felt
like there had been a little Freaky-Friday-style organ exchange, and her heart had somehow ended up inside Jane's
body.

Lately, though, her best friend was *also* one other thing:
a bride-to-be. To be fair—and fairness was Wendy's stock
in trade—Wendy couldn't accuse Jane of being a bridezilla.
She wasn't making her bridesmaids do any bullshit crafts
or anything. They all, Jane included, still had bridesmaid
PTSD from their friend Elise's wedding last summer. And
Jane had instructed them to wear the black dress of their
choice to the wedding. So in a letter-of-the-law sense, a person couldn't accuse Jane of being a bridezilla.

But...spirit of the law. Even though Jane wasn't obsessed with the perfect wedding, she was sort of fixated
on the idea that she *wasn't* obsessed. She was constantly
talking about how her wedding, which would be held at an
amusement park she and her fiancé loved, was going to be
"low-key."

It turned out that being "low-key" actually required a
shit-ton of mental energy.

The phone's display continued to show Jane calling. Mr.
Brecht pulled out a diagram of his apartment on which he'd
marked—and annotated—every instance of rodent infesta-
tion that had occurred over his five-year battle with his
landlord.

Wendy looked at the clock again.

She weighed her options, then mouthed a prayer of
forgiveness. Because right up there with fairness, Wendy
valued honesty.

"I'm so sorry, Mr. Brecht; I have to take this."

She braced herself and answered the call.

"Wendy! I thought you were never going to pick up!"

"Good afternoon, Ms. Denning," Wendy said in her best professional voice. "Could you hold for a moment, please?"

Jane giggled. "Of course, counselor."

"I'm so sorry, Mr. Brecht. Something has come up with another client." Wendy made a show of looking at her watch, though she already knew it was 4:58 pm. "And given that the day is almost over, might I suggest that we pick this up next week?" She stood, ushering him out as she spoke. "We're all ready to go for your appearance before the board."

Wendy felt guilty about shuffling Mr. Brecht off—what he needed more than a lawyer was someone to listen to him—but not bad enough to endure another hour of rats when it was 4:58 p.m. on a Friday and her best friend was on the phone. She was going to get Mr. Brecht's eviction overturned. She was good at her job—no, she was *great* at her job—and the fact that a rat had appeared under his sink at precisely 7:43 a.m. last Tuesday would have no bearing on the outcome of his hearing.

Once he was dispatched, she slammed her door behind her and sank into her office sofa, letting that lovely Friday feeling overtake her. "Hi!" she said, hoping that she was going to get Friend Jane and not Bride Jane.

"I need you to send me your bio."

Damn.

"My bio?" Wendy tried to ask the question in a way that masked her real question, which was: *What the hell are you talking about?*

"For the website?"

Wendy did a lot of pro bono defense work—witness Mr.

Brecht and his rats—but she was also an associate at one of Toronto's most prestigious criminal law firms. In that capacity, she had a bio on the firm's website—an *impressive* bio if she did say so herself. But she was pretty sure Jane didn't care that Wendy was a top-notch criminal litigator with special expertise in the Extradition Act.

"Your bio for the *wedding* website?" Jane asked.

What Wendy said in response was, "Riiiight." What she meant was, *damn it all to hell.* The wedding website was part of Jane's "everything about this wedding is super fun and low-key" philosophy. She thought if she had a website with all the pertinent details, it would ease logistical challenges for the guests. Not sure about parking? Check the website! Want to see some funny pictures of the bridal couple that demonstrate how fun and low-key they are in a way that looks effortless and un-curated but is actually the result of several hours with a professional photographer? Check the website!

Wendy hadn't realized, apparently, that the wedding website was also supposed to include bios of the wedding party.

"And you're coming to the website photo shoot tomorrow morning, right? That's why I'm nagging you about the bio. I want to give the bios to the photographer in advance so she can get to know the members of the wedding party a little before she shoots you."

Whoa. Bios, and, apparently, *portraits*.

Wendy wanted to ask if there was any way the photographer could *actually* shoot her. Because at this point, a quick and painless death would probably be less excruciating than what Jane was suggesting. Wendy could not imagine anything worse than spending a beautiful spring morning hanging around taking wedding party pictures.

"I was going to get some bagels and cream cheese for people to snack on while they wait their turn with the photographer," Jane went on, "but do you think I should have something more solidly brunchy catered in? I'm not good at this stuff like Elise was. Will people expect, like, eggy things?"

Stifling a sigh, Wendy hoisted herself off the sofa and went to her computer to check her calendar for anything that looked remotely like "photo shoot/brunch/eggy things" listed for tomorrow. She was guilty of maybe not totally paying one hundred per cent attention to everything wedding related. But in her defense (pun intended), she was pretty sure she had taken note of all the major events that required her presence, if only because she was determined not to *appear* to be the disgruntled bridesmaid she actually *was*.

She found an entry that said "Ten am—Jane's." Vague enough that it could have meant anything, including, she supposed, "photo shoot/brunch/eggy things."

Wendy wanted to ask if she could skip it—she was training for a marathon and had been planning a long run tomorrow. Could she send a selfie or her law firm portrait and be done with it?

But no. Of course not. She needed to up her game here. Yes, she wasn't into all this wedding bullshit. But her bigger issue was that in her heart of hearts, she was wasn't into the wedding itself. She was, selfishly, sad that Jane was getting married. She had nothing against Cameron, Jane's fiancé. Well, nothing that would stand up in court. He had started out as kind of a jerk, but anyone with a brain could see how happy he'd made Jane.

It was just that it had always been Wendy and Jane against the world. The Lost Girls, they used call to themselves. The Dead Dad's Club. They were a duo.

And now they were going to be...not that.

But that train had left the station, so Wendy put on her court face, even though Jane couldn't see her. Wendy's court face was like a poker face, but a lot more badass. "Sorry the bio is late. I'll send it within the hour. And, no, I don't think people will expect eggy things. Why don't I bring the bagels?"

"You don't need to bring anything except the questionnaire."

"The questionnaire is different from the bio?" Wendy asked.

Her question was met with silence. There were messages encoded in that silence, though, messages that only two-plus decades of best-friendship could interpret. Wendy had failed Jane. She wasn't quite sure how, yet, but the disappointment in Jane's silence was unmistakable.

"Right, yes, the questionnaire," she lied, typing "questionnaire + Jane" into the search field in her email and coming up with a message from two weeks ago about how each member of the wedding party was supposed to answer a few "fun, low-key" questions. The answers would be posted next to their bios on the wedding website. The bio that Wendy had forgotten all about.

Wendy sharpened her court face. "Of course the questionnaire and bio are totally different things. I'm sorry; I just got confused for a moment. It's been a really long week."

Mollified, Jane made a sympathetic clucking noise. "When is your next trip?"

Wendy sighed. She could feel herself getting itchy. The wanderlust was strong with her, and it hadn't been indulged for a long time. "Nothing until the big one."

"Wow," Jane said. "That's, like, four months away. Have you ever stayed put for that long?"

It was a fair question. She probably hadn't, as an adult anyway. Starting in the fall, Wendy was taking a six-month sabbatical and traveling around the world.

She. Could. Not. Wait.

But it also meant that she had a shit-ton of work to get done before she hit the road. "I have to be in court starting next week, and I think it will be a long trial. Plus I have this side thing I'm doing that's going before the Landlord and Tenant Board on Wednesday, so I'm already going to have to clone myself somehow. So, alas, no trips for me until the big one."

"Landlord and Tenant Board?" Jane echoed with a skeptical tone—the Landlord and Tenant Board was not Wendy's usual scene, and Jane knew it. Wendy was a high-powered defense lawyer, but she frequently volunteered her services in other, less glamorous contexts. "Who's your latest downtrodden?"

"My hairdresser's uncle. His apartment is infested with rats."

Jane cracked up. "You're a superhero, you know? Getting white-collar criminals off by day, de-rat-ifying the city by night."

Wendy's friends found her pro bono work amusingly incongruous. Their friend Elise had even suggested that she did it to balance out the karmic scales. But that wasn't it at all. Wendy believed that everyone—*everyone*—had the right to a rigorous defense. And, sure, she did her pro bono work because it wasn't fair that rich people could afford better defense than poor people. But the essential act of advocating for someone—defending them—was the same no matter the circumstances. Still, she'd long since stopped trying to make her friends see that logic when they launched into their speeches about how "cute" it was that she made two hundred grand a year and still signed up for volunteer shifts at Legal Aid clinics.

"Dang, I love you." Jane's voice had gone all moony, almost like she was talking about her fiancé rather than Wendy.

"I love you, too," Wendy said. It was the truth. It was why she was so torn up about this wedding. Inexplicably, her eyes filled with tears.

Which was mortifying. Wendy was not a crier.

But Jane had basically saved her life back when they were kids, extending her friendship when everything in Wendy's young life had gone to shit.

"You know who else I love?" Jane said, sniffing. The impulse to cry must have been contagious.

"Who?"

"My brother."

You and me both.

Okay, that wasn't true. Not anymore, anyway. Not since she was fifteen. Still, adrenaline surged through Wendy, as it did every time Noah Denning's name was mentioned.

"I wish he could come to the photo shoot," Jane said.

Right, so Wendy had to correct a previous thought. It turned out she *could* imagine something worse than spending a beautiful spring morning hanging around taking wedding party pictures: spending a beautiful spring morning hanging around taking wedding party pictures *with Jane's brother*.

"But of course he's coming to the wedding itself, and that's what matters," Jane said, sniffles transformed into glee. "The whole week leading up to it!"

Noah Denning: one more huge-ass reason Wendy was not looking forward to Jane's wedding.

Usually, when Noah came to visit, Wendy managed to

be off on one of her trips. When she couldn't avoid seeing him—he was her best friend's brother after all, and she had practically lived at the Dennings' house when she was a kid—she had to armor herself so extensively that it was exhausting. And that was just for short encounters—a dinner, a brunch, church with Wendy's aunt Mary, where Jane and Noah often insisted on accompanying her.

A freaking week, though?

How was she going to survive?

"Well, Jane said, "I'll let you get back to your rats, Wendy Defendy."

Wendy Defendy had to take a couple deep breaths to get her shit together.

"Okay," she said once she had succeeded. "I should get a bit more done before I knock off for the night." She picked up Mr. Brecht's file.

Yep, Wendy defended people. It was just what she did.

Too bad she didn't know how to defend her heart.

Chapter Two

Oh my God, you totally saved the day," Jane whisper-yelled when Wendy arrived for the photo shoot the next morning bearing not just bagels but several bottles of Prosecco and a gallon of fresh-squeezed orange juice. "Everyone is standing around waiting for the photographer to finish setting up her equipment, and I *knew* I should have done more with catering."

"Nah." Wendy flashed Jane a smile. "We'll just get 'em drunk. Much more efficient."

Elise approached and gave Wendy a quick hug before relieving her of her bags.

"Is Gia here?" Wendy asked, looking around for the fourth member of their close-knit group.

"She's a Calvin Klein shoot in Rio," Elise said.

"But she sent a picture!" Jane pulled out her phone. "She asked me for specs on how these shots were going to be done, and she had *Steven Meisel* create one of her in the same vein. Like, in an off moment during the shoot. Can you imagine?"

"I really can't." Wendy took the phone to better see the photo Jane had called up and refraining from asking the obvious question: *Who is Steven Meisel?* And also from wondering why she hadn't thought to fake an international high-fashion photo shoot this morning. That was probably the only thing that would have gotten her off the hook today.

"Hi, Wendy." Jane's fiancé Cameron approached.

Wendy tried not to stiffen as he leaned down to peck her cheek. Cameron was such a *guy*. He was a former soldier with all the tattoos and muscles that stereotypically went with the gig. Now he was working construction. He was also in university part-time, though, which Wendy had to grudgingly respect.

It just seemed like such a weird match. Jane was serious and accomplished. Cameron drifted through the world getting by on looks and charm.

But really, all of that was neither here nor there. The only admissible fact was that Cameron made Jane happy. He treated her like a queen.

Wendy sighed as Cameron placed his hand on Jane's butt and Jane shot him a big, besotted smile.

She needed to try to muster some genuine enthusiasm for this wedding. She couldn't keep half-assing everything and forgetting shit or she was going to hurt Jane.

"Wendy, why don't you go first with the photographer, being the maid of honor and all?" Jane said, turning away from her betrothed and letting her gaze travel up and down Wendy's body. Wendy tried not to squirm—she'd done as instructed and shown up in jeans and a white top, but Jane's silent appraisal still managed to make her feel like she'd made a mistake.

"What?" Wendy looked down at her white silk tunic. "Too dressy?" She probably should have just gone with a straight up T-shirt. But the only actual T-shirts she owned were from the races she'd run, so she'd resorted to the only white top in her wardrobe, which was something she generally wore under her work suits.

"It's fine," said Jane in a tone that suggested that it was not, in fact, fine.

"If you have a spare shirt, I can change." Wendy knew Jane would try to pretend not to be too invested in the photo shoot, but she suspected her friend had a backup shirt or two stashed somewhere in the house.

"Well, I do have a couple."

Bingo.

"Which I just got in case anyone spills orange juice or something on their shirt."

Wendy refrained from pointing out that since she had surprised Jane with the orange juice, her logic was flawed. "Give me one. It'll look better—more in tune with everyone else."

Jane tilted her head. "You sure?" But she was already pulling a shirt out of an Old Navy bag sitting on the kitchen counter. "Elise is in the bathroom, I think. You can go change in my bedroom."

Wendy glanced around. Everyone else had gone outside—Jane's house was tiny, and it looked like the actual picture taking was happening in the backyard. "Nah, I'll just change quickly here. Shield me." She whipped off the offending garment. Darn it. The new shirt was inside out. "What size is this?" she asked as Jane turned around and put her arms out in an "airplane" stance in an attempt to provide privacy to Wendy's presto-chango.

"Small. But if it's too big we can pin—oh my

Gaaaawd!" As Jane shrieked, not only did the airplane arms crash, but she ran away, leaving Wendy exposed, struggling to turn the new shirt right-side out. Wendy jammed her arms into the sleeves and lifted the shirt over her head, but it was still twisted so she got sort of stuck.

"Noah!" Jane yelled. "I can't believe you came!"

Danger! Danger! Wendy's body screamed, reacting in such a clichéd way, she may as well have been a cartoon. She could feel her jaw drop, her eyes widen. All she needed was for her cartoon-heart to literally hammer its way out of her chest.

He wasn't supposed to be here. Not yet. Jane had *just* said he wasn't coming until the week of the wedding.

She peeked over the edge of the shirt. There he was, tall and handsome and freaking *perfect*, framed in the doorway of Jane's kitchen like it was no big deal.

She was not prepared for this. She had no armor. Hell, she didn't even have a goddamned shirt on.

"Janie," Noah said, his voice the same warm baritone it had always been.

There was a pause in which Wendy considered whether she could somehow run away. Her arms were caught in the T-shirt high above her head, so maybe he wouldn't recognize her.

But no. Because then he said, "Hey, Wendy."

Wendy had no protection against Noah Denning. She might as well have just handed him her renegade heart to him and said, *Here's my heart. Break it. Again.*

Fall in Love with Forever Romance

USA TODAY BESTSELLING AUTHOR

DEBBIE MASON

Driftwood Cove

"Heartfelt and delightful!" —RAEANNE THAYNE,
New York Times bestselling author

DRIFTWOOD COVE
By Debbie Mason

FBI agent Michael Gallagher never dreamed that his latest investigation would bring him back to his hometown of Harmony Harbor. Or that one of his best leads would be the woman he once loved. Shay Angel is tougher than anyone he knows, but she still needs his help. Even if it means facing the past they can't forgive...or a love they can't forget.

Fall in Love with Forever Romance

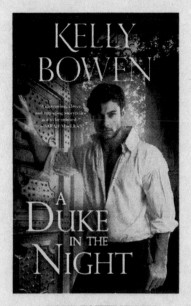

A DUKE IN THE NIGHT
By Kelly Bowen

Headmistress Clara Hayward is a master of deception. She's fooled the ton into thinking she's simply running a prestigious finishing school. In reality, she offers an education far superior to what society deems proper for young ladies. If only her skills could save her family's import business. She has a plan that might succeed, as long as a certain duke doesn't get in the way...

Fall in Love with Forever Romance

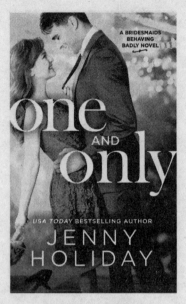

ONE AND ONLY
By Jenny Holiday

In this laugh-out-loud romantic comedy, *USA Today* bestselling author Jenny Holiday proves that when opposites attract, sparks fly. Bridesmaid Jane Denning will do anything to escape her bridezilla friend—even if it means babysitting the groom's troublemaker brother before the wedding. Cameron MacKinnon is ready to let loose, but first he'll have to sweet-talk responsible Jane into taking a walk on the wild side. Turns out, riling her up is the best time he's had in years. But will fun and games turn into something real?

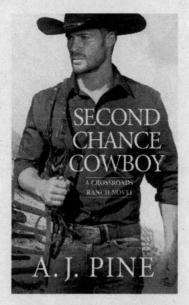

SECOND CHANCE COWBOY
By A. J. Pine

Once a cowboy, always a cowboy in A.J. Pine's first Crossroads Ranch novel! After ten years away, Jack Everett is finally back home. The ranch he can handle—Jack might be a lawyer, but he still remembers how to work with his hands. But turning around the failing vineyard he's also inherited? That requires working with the one woman he never expected to see again.